THE EMPRESS' PALACE

TIKL THE SECOND OF NEHEL

JOSEPH KOPEL

CONTENTS

DEKEN KARSAKER

T he coronation of Empress Nehel marked the restoration of the balance, but the *Deken Karsaker* exposed its fragility. The Jyistereerk's emergence as an unprecedented empire on Sankaris presented a constant reminder of the latent danger posed by the solid Korba Dominion, expecting to disrupt the delicate equilibrium at any moment.

Kong Rim's betrayal and the Gathering's death led to a transformation in Berrem, shifting it from a lordship to an imperial regime. The Empress had ultimate power in the realm, despite the Guild's oversight of Berremen affairs. She ended the deceitful treaty between Berrem, Fenn, and the Breken Nation. Her action dramatically put an end to the Giefo Treaty and marked a vital step towards eradicating slavery in the Mines of Tiunnff. Nevertheless, secretive entities were still conducting trade, and the city state of Siennt differed with the prohibition.

The preservation of Berrem's integrity was of utmost importance, given that Korbas and Korbeens had affected a significant portion of its population.

The Giefo Treaty's end divided the Breken Nation into two factions. To please the Korbas, the conservatives traded the giefo in secrecy. In contrast, many people adhered to the Empress's principles, resulting in an exodus towards the Isle of Garterrem where a flourishing Breken colony has taken root.

Queen Shiann of Fenn and her court backed the trade altogether with the Breken conservatives, while the Kiffenn Rebellion plotted to abolish the last kingdom on Sankaris.

An unfathomable curse involved the continent of Tyza following the *Assault at the Estos Grasslands*. The imposing Korbas dominated the skies, while ferocious giant squids ruled the seas, creating a menacing barrier that prevented travel in any direction.

Devastation and despair consumed Casak.

Isolation affected the Casakans, and Kasnasgans found themselves trapped in a land that did not belong to them for four years.

Head Missar, however, could communicate with the palace in the Ri—through the mystical orbs. Archmage Selee served as his direct contact.

Even the world of magic was not an exception, as it remained highly dependent on Salter. The *Frelee Dee* prophecy foretold a tragedy that was expected to unfold, bringing the annihilation of the Citadel and its entire realm. Nothing would save Salter, not even the *Deken Karsaker* or the Empress.

A tikl had passed.

The balance did not reach equilibrium.

The *Deken Karsaker* remained unreclaimed.

I

KORBEEN SLAYER

Four years ago, Empress Nehel's coronation marked the establishment of the Jyistereerk.

The *Deken Karsaker* had not yet gained control, as the Korbas continued to resist the imperial forces and taint the land. Thus, a war without war.

The current was the *Tikl the Second of Nehel*.

The sound of the doors being kicked open by the hooded man echoed through the tavern, halting the music and conversation, and plunging the room into a tense stillness. As a storm raged in the background, all eyes remained fixed on him.

Droplets of water fell on the wooden floor from his soaked black cloak. The mysterious male began walking across the tables. He seemed to search for something, or someone, with a rough brow.

The commensals from different races and genders assumed he was heading to the counter to order a drink, but he roamed around the tavern, disrupting the waitresses' work as they balanced brew mugs on their trays. In the end, they saw him come to a halt at a particular table tucked away in a corner.

He stood at that exact spot, the sound of a cane hitting the floor reverberated, causing him to turn his gaze towards its holder—an elder with a disfigured face that revealed the effects of his corrupted soul. "So long time, and so far, yet, you have persisted in the search, Master," accompanied by a nod and a menacing grin, he spoke in a voice that seemed to echo from the depths of a cavern.

Alessandro Eskar, Pillar of the Jyistereerk, lowered his hood and fixed him with a suspicious gaze. "I would keep searching for you until the last corners of Sankaris, Lord Rim," a hoarse voice emerged from him as he replied, his words were with distrust. "Ever since our last meeting in the Dri, I have been determined to make amends for my failure with the treaty, as I promised the Divine Empress."

Kong Rim's eerie grin vanished as he scrutinized Alessandro, examining every part of him. "You have grown into a mature man," the old man pointed at him with his cane, emphasizing each word. "I could not help but notice how much more determined and confident you have become since our time in the villa, in stark contrast to your insecure past."

"Do not speak about me," he warned, "as I request your presence. The Divine Empress will ensure justice is served!"

Some commensals left the tavern in fear as they heard the Master's firm and authoritarian voice, feeling a chilling tension.

"The only justice in this land is Ardek Korba! Lord of the Netherworld!" His grin appeared again, but more malevolent than before. "I must warn that the death of me will cause the utter ruin of your niece's existence!"

Rim's eyes turned fiery red as he shifted into a menacing black dragon, prepared to launch an attack on Alessandro, while the witnesses shrieked in terror. Determined to end him, the grotesque Korbeen jumped from his chair.

With a quick and accurate reaction, Alessandro executed his special maneuver, unsheathing his greatsword from his back and delivering a fatal blow to the diabolical creature beneath its neck, where its tainted heart was located. As the monster crashed onto the wooden floor, the entire room shook with the force of its impact.

The witnesses observed the incident with widened eyes, their jaws dropped in disbelief.

Lord Kong Rim, the last surviving member of the Gathering, had breathed his last. And with him, the last remnants of a rule that had outlived the downfall of the monarchies disappeared.

Once Alessandro confirmed the lifelessness of the lord's body in his Korbeen form, he retrieved his greatsword. Gripping the hilt, adorned with the Akareen star, a symbol of both the Empress and the Jyistereerk, he carefully wiped the blood from the blade using a piece of leather he had tucked away in his pocket.

His mature, dark eyes scanned the crowd, exposing his face adorned with an airy black beard that oozed his masculinity. He returned his weapon to its sheath on his back and addressed everyone. "Lord Rim died long ago when he became in this spawn," he turned to the taverner. "Do you have a rope?"

The taverner nodded, signaling his helper, a young boy, to fetch one.

In a rush, the lad made his way outside to the stables in the rear. With a swift search, he located a lengthy rope that he could bring back inside.

With a thankful smile, Alessandro carefully took the thread from him and knelt down to secure it around the motionless body of the Korbeen.

The people observed him with curiosity and awe.

"I apologize for any distress I may have caused," he stood up. He threw a bag of coins onto the counter, the weight of them causing a thud. "Will it make up for the unfortunate event?"

"Aye, Master. . .,"

"I shall leave now."

Alessandro, with the help of the rope, pulled the body across the floor, leaving behind a streak of blood, which shocked the diners and employees, until he left.

The storm subsided, the dark clouds gradually dispersed, revealing the icy white moon of No Sak and signaling the onset of a frigid night.

Alessandro exited the tavern. He felt a wave of relief wash over him from the crisp, cold air outside. He looked around and recognized the familiar town of Doimet, but noticed that most of the surrounding buildings were dimly lit, casting an eerie darkness over the area. Alessandro knew that since the events prior to Nehel's coronation, such as the *Feast of the Dragoness*, *Assault at the Estos Grasslands*, or the hordes from the Dri, Berrem had transformed into an unrecognizable place in just four years, evoking fear and uncertainty in every town or village.

The consequences of the *Deken Karsaker*.

The Empress' arrival had initially sparked hope and joy, but now it only brought a feeling of doubt and unease.

To exacerbate the situation, suspicions arose that a significant portion of Berrem's population had fallen victim to the Korbas or Korbeens, causing the Imperial Guard, former vagrants, to spring into action, actively taking part in the fight against them. At the border with Trunke, where the infected red mantises were gaining control, most of them were engaged in the south, trying to contain the spread.

Alessandro, along with Marissa Taskar, stood as the Pillar and engaged in various battles against the dragons. However, little luck seemed to side with him as he only encountered Korbeens and not the larger Korbas. Despite this, he proved successful in defeating them and earned the title of *Korbeen Slayer*.

The Korbeen of Lord Kong Rim was his bigger prize.

Apprehensive to advance on his long journey back east to the Ri, he tied his rope to the saddle of his red stallion named Breeze and mounted up.

In a quick gallop through the night, he pulled the lifeless Korbeen's body, guided only by the pale moonlight, as he made his way towards the outskirts of the Black Forest, determined to reach The Lake by dawn.

An abrupt, mild dizziness overcame him and his mind grew hazy. However, the moment passed, and he felt fine again. He assumed his condition was because of his continued period without meals.

Next, he reached under his sleeve and pulled out a white handkerchief, infused with Lady Fabehel's rose-scented cologne. Whenever he brought it close to his nose, a rush of memories flooded back from when she had given it to him in the Jarrdine Villa, before Nehel's ascension.

Four years, one tikl, a tiny drop of time, yet long.

Is time also an illogical aspect of magic?

On a scorching afternoon, the members of the Imperial Guard watched from the towering ancient walls surrounding the palace as Alessandro rode down the main street of the Ri on his red stallion, dragging the decrepit body of a black demon. The stunned crowd in the bustling street market paused their activities to witness the extraordinary scene. As guards caught sight of him, the resounding blast of trumpets echoed.

Alessandro was still far away, but the sight of the towering gates was unmistakable.

Constructed centuries ago, the gates required the strength and effort to open them with a team of twelve men. The massive beam loomed behind, requiring the help of horses to be pulled to the right. Only then could the dozen guards grasp the handles connected to the sturdy wood and slowly opened it, creating a narrow passage for the rider to enter.

Once opened, the Pillar Alessandro, renowned as the Empress's second-in-command, made his way into the interior.

With a final push, the gates were closed, and the beam slid back into position, securing the area.

At the interior court, several men approached with lances and swords and pierced the still Korbeen body on the ground.

Alessandro dismounted and untied the lifeless body, unaffected by the men's callous actions. "When you are done, throw that scourge in the pit!"

The guards listened and took the cadaver.

Archmage Selee had constructed an endless pit, a bottomless abyss where the bodies of slain demons and dragons could be discarded, erasing any trace of their existence from the earth. It was a marvelously magical yet utterly terrifying.

As Alessandro turned, he recognized the immense and ancient palace, which emitted a chilling and foreboding aura. Though unattractive, the palace proved to be a convenient location for conducting Jyistereerk affairs, as it served as the capital of Ri.

Exhausted from two sleepless nights, he let out a tired sigh and veered towards his left. He made his way through the fountain garden, passing under small arches, until he reached a second court, smaller than the previous one.

He paused and observed a familiar scene that played out every day. Knight Marissa and her squire, Juni, engaged in a lively sword and shield combat in front of a group of twenty young pupils wishing to be knights, who eagerly watched and imitated their moves with their wooden weapons.

Alessandro crossed his arms, deep in thought, and touched his chin. Four years ago, Ser Marissa became the First Knight amidst controversy, but the Empress saw something in her and appointed her as her personal knight. Also considered the other Pillar. With the Empress' blessing, the third most powerful in the Jyistereerk planned to establish a distinguished order of knights.

He was uncertain about the specific role the knights would play in the Jyistereerk. The Imperial Guard had undergone a complete transformation, integrating vagrants and sentinels to form a unified force. Under the joint leadership of Keleana and Kekten, their efficiency in combating the Korbas improved significantly. Alessandro was concerned that the future knights would join them.

He directed his gaze towards the small stone monolith near the wall, its presence a constant reminder of the devastating loss suffered by Peken, the first victim claimed by the *Deken Karsaker*. He remembered Nehel's persistent refusal to give the title of Second Knight upon Juni, despite being fully trained for knighthood. Knowing how strongly his niece had grown attached to Juni, Alessandro understood that her hesitation was driven by the fear of losing him, just as she had with the elf Peken.

Marissa had hoped that her squire, Juni, would achieve knighthood, as she wanted her youngster to follow her steps. She had been very patient with Nehel.

Marissa was engaged in her mock combat, and she caught sight of Alessandro. Relieved, she realized he had returned unharmed from his hunt for Lord Rim and greeted him with a nod and a smile.

He replied, but with a serious semblance.

Alessandro left them to their training and continued on his way. The sounds of their sweat faded behind him.

At the moment Alessandro stepped into the palace, the heavy presence of dust particles that filled the air immediately bothered him. The workers, diligently laboring on the walls and constructing a dome, added to the bustling atmosphere in the grand hall, which was illuminated by the sun's rays filtering through a hole in the ceiling. To the right, she spotted an elegant staircase crafted from gleaming marble and guarded by a group of sentinels. He covered his eyes to observe the spacious yet powdery place, noticing the whiteness everywhere.

A mere four years ago, this hall was a haunting sight, with its gloomy darkness and muddy grounds. Thieves had ransacked parts of the palace, leaving behind a trail of emptiness and destruction that erased any trace of the bygone monarchies.

Alessandro quickened his pace to escape the dust with coughs. He entered a smaller hall, recently remodeled in a minimalist style, with clean white walls and no embellishments. He intended to arrive at the double doors, which stood as the entrance to the Empress' chambers.

Fabehel exited at the exact moment she discovered his arrival, relieving her of her worries. With a gentle tap on the star of arrows engraved on the armrest of her magical wheelchair, a gift from Nehel and masterfully crafted by the skilled Jumeni, she left the chamber. Her fingers delicately grazed the length of her red braid, accentuating her flushed cheeks and the hint of a smile, all while she wore in her flowing purple dress.

Alessandro greeted her with a gentle kiss on the lips, feeling the concern as he held her hands. "Is there something wrong?"

"It is Nehel, she had these mood changes," pointing to the left. She nodded. "Instead of meeting the Breken delegates awaiting there, all she does is lie on the bed, crying."

"Let me have a word with her."

With determination, Alessandro pushed the door, eager to enter, but Fabehel seized his hand, preventing him from going any further.

"I would be careful if I were you, Alessandro," she warned with expressive eyes. "She is no longer a girl, but a woman. It happened this early morning. I had a long conversation with her."

His nod brought a complex blend of understanding, surprise, and a hint of expectation. Nervously, he took a deep breath before stepping into the chamber. His heart pounded as he locked eyes with the guards stationed by the doors, who saluted him.

As he closed the door behind, Alessandro sighed and allowed himself to be back to the familiar place he knew so well. The chamber displayed a unique multicultural decor, meticulously showcasing treasures that represented realms like Molke and Berrem. Warm afternoon sunlight bathed the balcony, illuminating the room.

His gaze shifted to the right, where he spotted his niece in white clothing on a generously sized circular bed. It was Nehel who lay there, holding a large cushion close. Her face remained hidden as only her head, buried under splendid black curly hair, peeked out. Alessandro could not tell if she was in a deep sleep or completely motionless.

Alessandro took his first steps forward and removed his sheathed greatsword from his back. He then settled it on one of the four chairs positioned around a small table. As he did, he could not help but notice the circular checkered Molkan game called Falte resting on the table, adorned with white and black stones. He believed that Nehel, knowing her well, had spent most of the night immersed in playing it. He also discovered she was not alone, but Juni accompanied her. It was during these informal meetings that they cherished their role as close friends and confidants.

Besides the Falte, he discovered a small pouch containing some pears and Nehel's favorite knife. Recognizing the absence of pear trees in the vicinity, he knew Juni had gone to the market to get the fruit as usual in him.

With each step he took, Alessandro could not help but smile at the sight of Nehel's scattered leather and wool clothes on the floor. He avoided the pieces of bread and the metallic cup she used for drinking water, pondering whether the Court of Maids would attend to the cleaning. His primary aim was to swing open the glass doors leading to the balcony, inviting in a refreshing breeze and the delicious fragrance of the nearby gardens. The sound of his footsteps startled the pigeons on the balusters, causing them to scatter in all directions.

"I knew you would come, uncle," Nehel murmured as her body remained motionless on the bed. "I can feel it, a sensation running down my spine that you have slain him after years of quest."

"Aye, Nehel. The tainted body is now disposed in the pit."

Despite feeling tired, she mustered the energy to sit on her bed. Her youthful face exposed signs of exhaustion, her bright hazel eyes revealed a clear lack of sleep. She adjusted her long, black hair and flashed a small smile at her uncle.

Alessandro replied with uneasiness, "Fabehel informed me earlier."

Nehel's smile vanished, and her eyes widened in surprise, but she still nodded. Standing barefoot on the ground, she exited towards the balcony and placed both hands on the rail. Gasping, she gazed at the interior gardens, surrounded by the palace's ominous presence. "I knew it had to happen someday to become a woman."

"I believe you are going through the same things as many girls your age," Alessandro said with understanding. "You are not the ten-year-old I met before, but a grown-up of fourteen."

"Aye," she turned around to see her uncle. "Have you forgotten my stance? I am an Empress." Her lips trembled as her eyes wetted. "The one who holds the responsibility to safeguard the balance from the forces of darkness."

"What does it have to do with yourself?"

"Do not you comprehend?" she sighed and rolled her eyes up as she leaned against the stone rail. "Almost every night they whisper to me. . ."

"Who they?"

"They! The monarchs! It is so hard to sleep in this awful palace that truly does not represent me or the Jyistereerk!" Exasperation accompanied her words. "They always remind me of my responsibility as a monarch!"

"I still do not comprehend."

"As an Empress, I must ensure the continuation of the Jyistereerk's bloodline!" she replied with despair.

A gentle gust swept across the balcony, rustling the leaves in the nearby gardens. Nehel had to exert herself to calm the gentle breeze before escalating into a strong gale.

Alessandro seemed to understand her as he touched his chin, adopting his usual posture of deep thought, studying her anguish. He could not help but recall Fabehel's cautionary words before entering the chamber, understanding the perilous emotional dynamics that came with encountering an Empress during her transition from girlhood to womanhood.

Her development as a demigoddess remained a mystery, with many unanswered questions.

"Please try to control yourself," he advised. "You still have time to consider your future lineage."

Nehel took a deep breath, closed her eyes, and nodded at him when she opened them. "Aye, you are right, uncle."

"We will discuss it later with Archmage Selee's help, but for now, prepare to meet the Breken delegates."

With another smile, she nodded and walked towards her large mirror.

Alessandro watched her combing her hair while meditating. Aware of her emotional outburst, he conceded she was correct and expected that, in due time, she would need to produce an heir, a child, in order to preserve the Jyistereerk, similar to how the old monarchs had done. With the fragility of the *Deken Karsaker*, especially in a world with uncertainties, himself as Nehel's only blood relative and Marissa as the next in the line after him, the importance of a strong imperial bloodline became clear.

Despite the accomplishments within a tikl, the Jyistereerk's existence remained precarious and vulnerable to collapse and disappear. Brutality accompanied the Korbas, but it was Ardek who personified their erratic and deceitful nature, capable of bringing chaos on Sankaris.

Two members of the Imperial Guard granted entrance to the audience room to the Empress, with Alessandro following closely behind. A crowd of people, who had been eagerly waiting for a long time, greeted their arrival.

As the Herald, Dessidere, stood at the front and tapped the scepter against the ground three times, the sound echoed throughout the room. "All salute to the Empress Nehel of the Jyistereerk!"

Fabehel shifted her eyes toward Nehel with an intense gaze. Her conversation with the visitors came to a halt.

As the guests spotted the Empress, they immediately lowered themselves in a respectful bow, as their eyes fixed on her flowing white robes.

Nehel ascended the steps to the platform with haste, settling onto a large wooden throne crafted by local artisans. Two plush armchairs flanked it. Her footsteps lacked their usual grace as she eagerly gave steps to end the audience as soon as possible. She was not in the mood, but her duty required her to comply with her job.

Marissa leaned in and whispered her usual advice to Juni about how to guard from a corner, and took her seat at the Empress' right. Alessandro got his place in the other armchair.

Juni, clad in a worn yet polished armor, kept his hand on the hilt of his sheathed sword. His eyes watched vigilantly towards the surrounding crowd, ensuring the safety of the Empress.

Selee, dressed in azure clothes, stood beside the aspirant to knight. The Archmage had his grip tight on the Sorcerer's Staff accompanied by Akhimeni, the Overseer of the Court of Maids, beside him in a flowing silver gown.

From a hidden spot in the darkness, Corr observed everything with a feline glow in his green eyes.

Nehel discreetly signaled the Herald with a subtle gesture, expressing her readiness.

Dessidere, attired in gray, acknowledged with a nod and proceeded towards his tribune. Positioned in the opposite corner from Juni's, he struck the surface with a gavel to capture everyone's attention. Next, he unfurled a blank papyrus, weighed it down with paperweights, and moistened his long feather pen using the inkwell. He then clamored for everyone. "In the Twenty-Third day of the Seventh Month in the First Year of the *Tikl the Second of Nehel*! At the Audience Room of the Imperial Palace in the Ri! I officially start an audience between the Divine Empress and representatives of the Breken Nation!"

"Please accept my apologies for being late to the audience. I had to deal with an unforeseen inconvenience," Nehel addressed everyone, her eyes browsed the room before she gestured towards the visitors. "Please, come to the front so I can see you well."

Three men and a woman, with their massive height, noticeable bellies, and minimal waki furs, moved through the crowd. The foul stench emitting from them caused people to wrinkle their noses in disgust. To them, axes were not just weapons—they were extensions of their bodies, inseparable and essential to their culture—. Standing before the platform, Juni clarified they could not approach any closer, leaving several steps of distance between them and Nehel.

Despite her fatigue, the Empress tried her best to present a smile. "Welcome to the palace," she said with a kind gesture. "It is my understanding that, after countless attempts, you are extending the offer of the Breken Nation to join to the Jyistereerk."

With a step forward, the eldest man of the four bowed in a show of respect before uttering a word. "Divine Empress, every Brek longs to become part of the Jyistereerk and devote themselves to your service."

"From what I remember, the Breken Nation is not a unified entity. Instead, it comprises many tribes, each with their own independent governance. How is it possible that every single one of you wants to join the Jyistereerk?"

"Indeed, Divine Empress. This is the general sentiment from everyone."

Alessandro leaned forward in his seat, his brow furrowed in deep thought, before intervening. "May we know your name and position in your realm?"

"Senaten, Master. Chief of the Trasken Tribe."

"Are the ones with you also chiefs?"

"Aye, Master."

"And how many tribes are with you in the intention of joining the Jyistereerk?"

The Breken Senaten hesitated, a gleam of uncertainty in their eyes, as he debated whether to respond to his inquiry. The intensity in Alessandro's dark eyes prompted him to speak. "Only the four of us."

As murmurs emerged from the audience room, Alessandro shook his head in disbelief and covered his eyes. Then, he turned his attention to the Breken, addressing to his group. "May I speak with the truth?"

"Please, Master."

"Since our Divine Empress's coronation a tikl ago, countless requests have flooded in from your realm and your allies, urging us to join our empire," he replied, tapping his armchair. "We want to clarify that we are not invaders, and we will not impose our beliefs on anyone who does not wish to engage with us." He sighed and made a pause before continuing with his declaration. "You can not join the Jyistereerk as it requires the unanimous consent of the people, which you do not have. Instead, you have in your realm forty tribes constantly divided and always at war, seeking advantages from the giefo prompting your own people to abandon your land. Half of you have sided with the Korbas, and in doing so, you are endangering yourselves!"

The room was so quiet that the silence felt like it would never end.

None of the four Breks dared to speak. They revealed faces of deception and sadness.

Nehel evidenced composure and serenity with a light smile and warmth from her hazel eyes. "I do not conquer or expand by taking away their wills. I am sorry that you had traveled far without getting nothing," said with a sweet voice. "But my arms are open. If you and your people decide to emigrate in search of a better life than the one you have, you may join to your people at the Isle of Garterrem."

"We sympathize with your attention, Divine Empress," Senaten nodded. "We have achieved nothing, but seeing you in person was a great privilege."

With reverence, the four Brekens exchanged solemn nods with the Empress and silently exited the room.

Except one. The female Breken broke away from her group and startled Fabehel as she approached.

From her chair, Fabehel covered her nose in discretion, attempting to shield herself from the woman's pungent odor, all the while wearing a nervous expression. "Is there anything I can help you?"

Juni took his first cautious steps, feeling the sword with his fingers.

Apprehension invaded Marissa as she considered leaving her seat to look over Fabehel. But Nehel stopped her, assuring all was well.

The massive figure of a tall, strong Breken woman, never seen without her axe, would instill nervousness in others. "Are you the one who is constantly in pursuit of your own kind?"

"The Arankans in exile? Aye, I am always seeking for them. Why do you ask?"

"I heard the Fennens at a tavern talking about an Arankan settlement at Fenn."

Then the Breken female joined her companions, leaving the room.

Corr observed the last interaction between Fabehel and the Breken, from his hiding spot. He did not have any reaction, as he seemed to know something.

2

THE TRENCH

C aptain Diesso of Kokork, once a lancer in the thirty-fourth squadron and a veteran of the infamous
Assault at the Estos Grasslands, traversed the deep trench
along the main street with haste.

In the ongoing struggle for control, the Port of Sostolk
became a fierce battleground between the Allied Forces
and the relentless Korbas, who refused to abandon their
plans to conquer Casak and rule over the entire continent
of Tyza. What was once a bustling and vivid harbor with
quaint buildings where the ships could depart to Katalk or

Ryza, it became in a dejected collection of ruins, becoming in a desolate place worse than a cemetery.

The smell of powder loaded Diesso's nostrils, confirming his suspicions as he pressed on through the deserted trench. However, his movement halted when stumbled upon a group of Casakan men in deep concentration as they strategized in preparing holes carved into the eastern wall.

Diesso's distinctive uniform in black and green immediately caught the soldiers' attention. On his left chest, they noticed two pins—the golden Akareen star symbolizing the loyalty to the Empress, and the Casakan silver orchid with its twelve delicate petals. With utmost respect, they paused their labors to salute him.

"Where is the watchman?"

"There, captain," one man pointed.

Diesso looked and saw a partially destroyed building, which used to be a church. On top of the remaining tower, a soldier stood, monitoring the sea and the elvish troops stationed near the harbor, facing the sea. "Please, keep going! They are near!" The captain said.

They heard him out and carried on with getting the orifices ready.

On the opposite side of the church, Commandant Kartak and his hundreds observed the sea, waiting for something. He twitched his eyebrow as he covered his yellowish eyes with his hand to observe better under the scorching sun.

The First Official Partak also examined the sea.

"Commandant, how can you be sure they are coming?"

"They are, brother. I have learned to recognize my intuition when they come closer."

"Regardless of intuition, we cannot avoid fighting them!" complained with annoyance. "We have been trapped here for four years, unable to return to our home in Kasnasga," he replied with frustration. "How many more lives must we lose?"

"Our loyalty now lies with the Divine Empress. Don't overlook the fact that Casakans and us are standing shoulder to shoulder, fighting together for the cause of the *Deken Karsaker.*"

"What is the use of the reclamation when the air is still heavy with the stench of corruption?"

"Silence!" With a raised hand and a clenched fist, Kartak signaled his men to be prepared.

As the elves brandished their scimitars, one of them shifted his attention to the defaced church by raising his blade and swaying it.

With a quick nod, the watchman in the tower raised the twelve petals orchid flag, alerting those in the trench to be on high alert.

"Light them!" Captain Diesso echoed to his men.

The soldiers quickly inserted long strings into the openings, allowing them to extend outside, as a group of four rushed to ignite torches from a nearby bonfire at the trench's end.

Both the captain and Kartak understood the importance of executing the planned defense with precision. Any deviation in timing, even by a mere second, would jeopardize the entire operation—a lesson learned from the *Assault at the Estos Grasslands.*

The commandant, burdened by the weight of authority, meticulously oversaw the execution of each defense in order to ensure accuracy.

The wait was brief, but the time longer.

The Casakan soldiers stood frozen, their eyes widened with anticipation as sweat flowed down their faces.

They could sense death. If their defense fell apart, their chances of survival would be slim.

Like statues made of amber, the elves stood in anticipation, as their eyes fixed on the horizon.

Still with the fist in the air, Kartak watched the line that divided the sea from the sky.

The commandant awaited.

And waited again.

The sight that greeted Kartak was breathtaking—a vast flock of dragons in their daunting forms casting shadows against the horizon as they flew—. Showing no reaction, he continued to expect the creatures as they made their way halfway to Sostolk.

The dragons moved with lightning speed, their wings beat in a blur.

Kartak opened his hand.

Spotting the elf's sign, the watchman sprang to his feet and waved both hands to signal the others in the trench.

The men carrying torches moved closer to ignite the strings, while sparks of fire spread towards the openings.

The soldiers shifted to the opposite side of the trench, finding shelter against the wall as they crouched beneath the sturdy iron shields.

"If these demons obliterated a kingdom. I still do not understand why they have not taken the same action against Casak." Partak's voice was barely a whisper as he spoke to his commandant.

"Brother, this is beyond my comprehension. Despite the circumstances, Archmage Missar believes that there is an unseen force preventing them. Even with the blockage against us, they can not repeat another Gesha."

As the Korbas approached the harbor, their sharp claws gleamed and their screeches echoed. Once again, the horde of black dragons descended upon Sostolk.

The sea trembled with rumbles, and sudden cannon-ball blasts erupted from under the harbor, decimating the creatures in an instant. Only a handful of survivors retired, as they had no choice but to retreat.

Afterward, a peculiar rain fell on the surface, not of water, but of pieces from the exploded dragons.

The elves sighed with relief and holstered their scimitars, while the Casakans from the trench uncovered their heads and lowered their shields.

Captain Diesso observed the black rain falling from the clear sky. A small piece landed on his hand that allowed him to study it, noticing the dragons had not blood nor flesh, but as simple pieces of black paper instead. Yet, these creatures could so cause great harm.

Following the victorious encounter at Sostolk, Kartak dismounted his white horse, and a servant took it to the stables. He reached the Vykar Palace in Estolk.

He felt the morning air transition from brisk to warm, later turning cold, serving as a reminder of the persisting effects of the Gesha in the tropical realm of Casak.

While observing the building from the gardens, memories of Orssandro flooded his mind, with images of his tragic downfall by the Korbas. Despite being Kartak's obstinate enemy, he could not help but acknowledge that it was not entirely his fault when he witnessed his peculiar madness.

A madness caused by a tainted blood. Orssandro had been a Head for many years with the corruption coursing through his veins.

The touch of the Korbas on him persisted , though the details of when and where remained a mystery.

"Welcome again, commandant," Archmage Missar, Head of Casak, greeted him. He wore his usual brown robe, but underneath, he donned elegant, dark clothes with a simple pin of the Akareen star on his left chest. He had recently exited from the palace.

"Shall we go to meet the *Ykarte*, Sir Head?"

"Aye."

Missar turned his gaze towards the clear skies, his arms gracefully moved through the air as he conjured intricate swirls with his hands. The twitch of Kartak's raised eye-brow revealed his amazement at the archmage's magical abilities. To their astonishment, a small cloud materialized at their feet. "Shall we mount it?"

The elf nodded.

To the surprise of the surrounding sentinels watching the gardens and the gates, both men stepped onto the cloud and floated.

The cloud first rose high up, then glided towards the blue sky.

As Kartak and Missar took in the Casakan panoramic from the heights, wonder washed over them. The clouds, moving in a horizontal trajectory, weaved through thick clusters of clouds, creating a mesmerizing spectacle. From great altitudes, they could appreciate the intricate details of the realm that most people in Sankaris never noticed.

They had flown before.

"I received information about the news from Sostolk. I am relieved that we could repel those demons," With anticipation in their eyes, Missar looked upwards, hoping to glimpse their awaited destination.

"Yet, the creatures persist and continue to come back," a slight shrug escaped Kartak's shoulders. "Without a doubt, my brother Partak is right. For some mysterious reason, the Korbas have not started another Gesha over Casak, as if there is an unseen force preventing them from doing so."

"That is why I have summoned you. To seek answers with the *Ykarte*." He requested to look up and pointed towards the sky.

"Aye. Our piece of Kasnasga. We arrived on Kao Island four years ago."

The men on the cloud appeared on the beaches, rising from beneath the sea of air to hover over the island, then slid into the island, revealing a completely different scenery from Casak, far below amidst the clusters of clouds. The island's golden grasses and bronze leaves, along with ponds and lakes, still amazed the Head. However, it was familiar to Kartak.

"No one could have imagined that you arrived on a floating island," Missar chuckled. "You completely puzzled Orssandro, unable to figure out."

Commandant Kartak remained silent in response to his remarks.

As the cloud moved across the land, they witnessed Casakan children and youths enjoying their freedom in various elvish towns run by the sisterhood. Saved from Orssandro's madness on that tense night prior to the Assault at the Estos Grasslands.

Kartak, as the leader of the elves on Tyza, visually examined the encircling mountains and verified that his positioned soldiers were maintaining a constant lookout to protect against any assault. Overseer Akartaki and her sisters ensured that a stealthy mystical field shielded Kao Island to ward off the Korbas.

Kartak and Missar observed the cloud slowing down as they came closer to the golden city of Kaope. Instead of going into the shiny town, they continued towards a valley on the outskirts, where a solitary golden long house stood on a hill, encircled by mountains.

Upon reaching a specific distance from the house, soldiers came forward to greet the commandant.

With a simple gesture, the archmage made the cloud dissipate and acknowledged their presence with a nod.

Missar found it both marvelous and perplexing to step on a land that stretched far above his own, even at great heights. Few were aware of the immense magical abilities held by the Kasnasgans, but only Archmage Yasstro could truly comprehend the essence of elvish mysticism.

Descendants from the Tannes, the ones who left after Kasana's decapitation, the elves from Kasnasga were the most advanced culture in all Sankaris. Apparently.

As Kartak and Missar approached the house's exterior veranda, four elvish soldiers accompanied them. The veranda itself was a sight to behold, adorned with vibrant vegetation. Two standing sisters, dressed in shimmering silver gowns, with bare feet, held a bowl of fresh fruit and a glass jar filled with sparkling, crystal-clear water. As the sisters made their way, the two visitors trailed behind them until they reached a soft and inviting bench behind a round table, where a recognized figure sat.

A girl with round, thick glasses played a mesmerizing tune on her panpipe. As her delicate ebony fingers glided over the instrument, a captivating melody emerged, leaving all listeners in awe.

She was not human. Though she went by the name of *Carlissa*, this was not the true one, but a specter conjured from the memories of the deceased. Yasstro's incredible magic had disguised the *Ykarte* as an average girl, concealing her true identity.

Her music came to a halt as she immediately sensed Missar's presence and his unmistakable purpose. "How can I be of help?"

The question perplexed the archmage and could not identify her because of her coldness, but then he remembered she was not the same Carlissa Bistror he had known, but an extraordinary mystical artifact with a living essence. "Our realm is constantly under attack by the Korbas, as they send wave after wave to occupy it. Another Gesha had not happened yet."

The Ykarte stared at him in silence, not moving, then carried on playing her panpipe again.

The commandant twitched his eyebrow.

Head Missar patiently waited as she played her instrument, listening to the flawless melody. His gaze followed her as she acknowledged her maroon dress and glasses, recognizing that they were not ordinary clothing but integral parts of her being. She seemed uncanny. A living weapon turned human, indifferent to notions of good or evil. That is why with Kasana decapitation, the *Ykarte* summoned both the Nehel and the Korbas.

The sisters stood patiently on the veranda, watching as the soldiers retreated to their posts without entering.

Finally, she stopped her music and glanced over at Kartak and Missar. "I am both dark and light," said, almost mumbling. "This is a consecrated land to the Empress ever since her ascension."

"What is the meaning of it?" Kartak inquired, dumbfounded.

"When the realms are touched by light, darkness loses all power," she assured. "Because of her ascension, I seek life, but if Ardek ever comes to me, I will seek death," and she returned to play her panpipe.

"Do you think the Korbas have become weak?" the commandant murmured to Missar.

"I do not. There is a greater reason I despise," the arch-mage concluded.

3

THE FENNENS

The eldest Fennen, who wore scarlet velvet clothes and had a white coat, greeted the Empress in the audience room. Following his example, two young felines, one with a black fur and green garments, and the other with a gray pelage and a maroon dress, also bowed.

The Empress, dressed in delicate white robes, smiled and nodded as she inquired. "May I have the pleasure of knowing your name?"

Alessandro studied the Fennens with a skeptical expression. His hand rested on his chin while Marissa tapped her armchair.

Fabehel's hands clenched with concern. Despite being far from sight, Corr's persisting figure in the darkness caught her attention. She had to maneuver her wheelchair around to search for the feline amidst the crowd in the venue, hoping he would join his kind in the audience. However, much to her dismay, he opted to remain hidden, sparking suspicions.

Positioned outside the platform's steps, the aged Fennen watched the Empress. By his side stood the aspirant to knight Juni. In this moment, Fennen broke the silence and spoke. "As the special emissary, my name is Orr, and I am joined by Barr and Dienn on this important mission."

Nehel's smile transformed into a stern expression, conveying her authority as she addressed him.

"With the Breken Senaten and his people? I am aware."

Orr fell in silence of surprise, his clear blue eyes widened with vertical pupils dilating.

"Merely observing you, one cannot elude the truth of your hidden misdeeds," she replied with unconformity. "There are lives far more significant than the giefo!"

"There were spies lurking in that tavern." Ser Marissa stated,

With a pensive expression, Alessandro rose from his chair and approached the steps, his piercing dark eyes locked onto the Fennen. "Tell me, sir. Do you intend to reestablish the Giefo Trade with only Fenn and Brek?"

Alessandro's authoritative and dominant presence silenced Orr, leaving him trembling and only able to nod in nervous agreement.

An acute voice made its presence. "May I speak in his name, Master?" The female Dienn pleaded.

"You may, lass."

"In order to strengthen both the Kingdom of Fenn and the Breken Nation, we openly acknowledge our intention to restore trade between our realms. This is essential for our intended pact against the Korbas and their allies, as we must rely on ourselves without the aid of the Jyistereerk."

"Why a meeting at a tavern in a far-off place like the Ri?" Alessandro questioned with curiosity. "Why did not you consider meeting at a location that is closer to both of your places?"

"It was Chief Senaten's suggestion, Master," Dienn responded. "He already had plans to meet with the Divine Empress and suggested that we convene in this burgh to negotiate and revive the giefo trade."

"Despite this, we remain unconvinced. . ."

"Wait, uncle!" Nehel interrupted from her throne. "I can sense them and they speak with the truth. I feel fear and despair in both realms."

"What do you suggest, Divine Empress?" Alessandro inquired, extending his hands with unconformity. "The Jyistereerk, unfortunately, is not yet prepared and sufficiently fortified to extend the *Deken Karsaker* into the other realms of the Karekall."

Nehel closed her hazel eyes, placing her hand on her forehead, and shook before tapping her throne. "I did not suggest none of your assumptions!"

"I cannot accept a queen who had endorsed slavery for such an extended period!"

"Uncle. . ."

"Do not you recall my brother? Your father? His suffering. . .?"

"Uncle! Silence!" she ordered, irritated.

With a profound and strange quietness, Alessandro stared at his niece.

In the audience room, all eyes witnessed at the intense confrontation between the Empress and her uncle, creating a distinct sense of suspense. Faint murmurs rose.

"My apologies, Divine Empress," Alessandro bowed with respect. "I realize now that it was a mistake to express my sudden emotions."

"Please, disregard," Nehel replied with calm and sighs. "The fate of the Arankans mentioned by the Breken is what matters most at this moment." She inquired to Dienn.

Orr regained his composure and spoke with confidence, "According to the belief, there is an Arankan settlement near Siennt, situated north of Finnerr on the other side of the lake."

"Did you hear about it, Lady Fabehel?" Nehel pointed.

Despite everyone searching with their eyes, Fabehel was nowhere to be found in the room.

And with that, Corr had also departed, leaving a void in their midst. Alessandro noticed it.

Corr stepped into the inner gardens of the palace, sensing a multitude of aromas from various plants and flowers. He never liked the vegetation found in the north. His powerful sense of smell caused him to despise rainy places in the northern forest, where wet trees tried to hide the sweet scent of flowers, and made him long for the delightful fragrance of colorful flowers in tropical rainforests.

It was a natural trait in the Fennens to detect particular flowers when touched or moved by a hand. Corr detected the scent of roses and instantly recognized the path to find Fabehel, whom she had summoned before. Amongst the bushes, he interned until he reached a small garden adorned with flowers. It was there that he spotted her in a wheelchair, gathering red roses with her back towards him.

At a significant range, the feline eagerly awaited.

Fabehel placed roses on her lap, covered by her purple dress, and cut a third one using her small knife. She expressed him her gratitude for responding to her request for a private meeting, placing her right hand on the armchair to manipulate the engraved star of arrows and turn around. She gave an edged look to Corr. "A tikl had gone by since our initial meeting at Archmage Yasstro's funeral," she sighed." And as time passed, a unique bond formed between us. So, why do you refuse to show yourself in the most important audiences related to Fenn? Do you have something you conceal?"

Corr noticed her silence as he gave a peculiar glare of profound green eye and vertical pupils. He studied her raised eyebrow, signaling her expectation for an answer. Meanwhile, he crossed his arms, revealing his robust, black striped orange-furred hands emerging from his expensive brown clothes. Finally, in his deep voice, he admitted. "Milady, I have secrets I must keep hidden, as they may upset you."

She shook her head. "Even though your actions were out of affection for Master Alessandro, I know you have hidden truths from him. So, try me and go ahead."

"I distrust of Queen Shiann, and the Brekens. They were strong supporters of the giefo trade, as they almost made a deal with the Korbas."

"Is that the secret?" She replied in disbelief.

"Lord Kong made a secret treaty with the queen and Senaten. It was much later, during my time with the Guild, that I uncovered his tainted nature. He then proposed the idea of using the Arankan settlement as a chance to gain slaves for the Mines of Tiunnff."

Fabehel clenched her hands against the armchairs and widened her hazel eyes. "You never told me it when I sought for help!"

"My apologies, milady. My affection for Master Alessandro did not allow me to reveal it."

"You have only vaguely mentioned Arankans in Fenn, providing no specific details."

"Indeed, I did not deceive. No one knows for certain where the Arankans truly dwell. Only rumors and beliefs of a hidden Arankan settlement between the bordering city of Siennt and Gasderfinn," he nodded. "Whatever those Fennens say are merely assumptions. In truth, nobody, not even the queen and her followers or the rebels from the Kiffenn Rebellion, can identify their exact whereabouts."

Fabehel slammed her armchair in a mixture of helplessness and anger, glaring at him with moist eyes. "I must go!"

"I forbid you!" Alessandro's sudden appearance startled her. In his search, he had eavesdropped on their exchange. "You shall not go to perilous places!"

Nehel had trailed behind him, but she experienced dizziness, paleness, and nausea, causing Corr and Alessandro to assist her and guide her to a stone bench near the small rosarium. Fabehel approached with the wheelchair.

"Are you all right?" Fabehel inquired, concerned. " Is it. . .?"

"No. . ." she widened her eyes and glanced at everyone with trembling lips. "It is filled with darkness. . ."

"What do you mean?" the red-haired girl touched her shivering hand, concerned. "What darkness?!"

"Aye, I feel darkness but unable to explain," the Empress responded with fear. "I sensed in those Fennens and now with you!"

"Are you referring to tainted blood? Corruption?" Alessandro asked.

"It is not tainted blood nor Korbeen." Nehel smelled a rose from Fabehel's lap, hoping to ease herself. "There is darkness in Fenn."

"With reason I must go!" Fabehel insisted.

"I will not let you go!" Alessandro replied, annoyed, and turned to Nehel. "Please, I beg you send someone else but Fabehel!"

"I require your approval to leave for Fenn. I must help my people!"

"How she will go in a wheelchair?" Alessandro pointed at her.

"You imbecile!"

Corr silently expressed his disapproval by shaking his head.

"Silence, both of you!" Nehel screamed, determined to end the argument and closed her eyes to take a deep breath. With her usual authority, she then observed the three. "We heard the Fennen and the Brekens. They had come to me because they are always afraid, not to request help. But to beg for help!"

"But I did not see any petition from Orr and his companions."

"Because they also fear me, uncle. Do you recall I had to end with the giefo trade? Do not you know they are the emissaries from a queen who supported that trade, including slavery?" she sighed. "The queen and the Breken chiefs have the desire of my blessing that will protect them from the Korbas!"

"The Jyistereerk is still not strong enough to help them." Alessandro confirmed.

"Actually, they want to be part of the *Deken Karsaker*, but for that, Fenn and Brek must have their issues resolved first. As the queen battles the Kiffenns to preserve Sankaris' final monarchy, the Brekens find themselves divided. Both realms are experiencing civil wars caused by a mutual enemy."

"The Korbas," Corr spoke with a nod. "You truly have absolute knowledge and wisdom, Divine Empress."

"Please, let me go. I will put things in order and investigate about the Arankans," Alessandro suggested.

"I beg you to take me into consideration, Nehel," Fabehel insisted. "I can use my experience to represent you in these realms."

In silence, Nehel took in the presence of her uncle, who had been a father figure to her for the past four years, and Lady Fabehel, her support in her mother's absence. She could not decide. Her hazel eyes oscillated between both of them. In the end, she stood up, frustrated. "Tonight I will ponder, and I will communicate my choice tomorrow morning." She sighed in frustration and she left the gardens, only wishing to be locked in her private chamber.

Corr also departed.

Alessandro and Fabehel exchanged uneasy glances, unable to find the right words to say.

"My apologies. I let my emotions out," he said in a soft voice.

"These strange outbursts you had in the audience and with me." Her words contained her usual sharpness. "Will have serious repercussions. Do not allow resentments to sway your emotions. Are you unwell?"

"I give you the reason. . ."

"Save your tongue and hear me!" interrupted bothered. "Despite my lack of feet, I am determined to search for my people, and serve the Jyistereerk! I, as your cherished one, urge you to acknowledge my freedom and my aspirations."

"Believe me, I intend only to protect you."

"Do not protect and do not belittle me!" she demanded, agitated. "You know very well my potentials!" Turning around in her wheelchair, she left the gardens behind her.

Nehel closed her door behind and closed her eyes, as she embraced the peacefulness of the moment. As an Empress, she despised her stance and loathed these premonitions that lacked clarity.

As her hazel eyes opened, she glanced around her chamber. Everything appeared cleaner and more orderly than before. As usual, she knew the maids had completed their regular cleaning duties. The Court of Maid served Nehel, the jewel, which included housekeeping duties.

She observed the Falte on her circular table, containing stones in a pouch neatly placed beside it and secured with a small cord. She then proceeded to a nearby vanity, where she poured water from a jar into a copper cup and sought sips.

Nehel, feeling relieved from her drink, examined herself in the large mirror with white clothes. As she gazed into her own eyes, a flood of thoughts raced through her mind, realizing her youthful appearance. "What had occurred to you, Lakia?" she muttered to herself. "Where is that little girl who traveled everywhere as the Promise? Who am I?" her voice snapped.

Through the mirror, Nehel cast a downward gaze and discovered her hand holding a cup of water. As her eyes followed the curve of her finger, they landed on the Akareen ring, an emblem of her authority as Empress. Made from giefo, the ring was a creation gifted to her by the Berremen blacksmiths, known by their extraordinary craftsmanship along the Trunk-Fenn border.

In a sudden outburst of frustration, she hurled the cup, its contents splattering against the mirror, while she snatched the ring off her finger and flung it too. The glass remained unshattered.

A powerful gust of wind threw the balcony's doors open, causing her to take a startled step back. Realizing the consequences of her actions and recalling Archmage Selee's teachings, she took deep breaths to regain control.

The wind halted.

Nehel turned around, sensing a presence, to find Juni standing before the doors.

She observed him. That scrawny boy she met a tikl ago, in troubadour clothes, had grown into a strong mature tall man of sixteen years old. His striking presence captivated her, as she admitted her attraction to him in silence. He adorned his bright armor with an engraved Akareen star on the left chest, showcasing his unique style and adaptation.

The Empress rushed to embrace him, seeking solace in his arms.

With understanding, Juni nodded and responded by wrapping his metallic arms around her. He knew it was not the first time since she had been experiencing these episodes for over a year now, and they typically occurred when she was under stress. "Corr was kind enough to share with me about your encounter at the gardens." He spoke with a mature male voice that differentiated from the one he had as a boy four years ago.

Juni allowed herself enough time to release her conflicted emotions.

In the end, a silent Nehel glared at him with wet eyes and a soaked face. "I thank you by being my sincere and close friend," she offered a slight smile. "You are my strength and comfort."

He expressed his agreement with a serious, yet warm, nod. "How about a match using the Falte, missy?"

Noticing the vivid colors of the sunset pulling away from him, she replied, "Not tonight. I must lie in the bed to spend the night deciding who is going in a missive to Fenn," she sighed in despair but tranquil, gesturing the eyebrows . " I wish. . . "

"Say nothing more," he replied, as a beam adorned his face. He reached into his waist pouch and pulled out her favorite fruit, a pear, delicately placing it in her hands.

She nodded as an appreciation.

"I shall go now. Have a good night." He announced as he exited the chamber, closing the door after.

As the early morning sun's rays filtered into the room, Empress Nehel's hazel eyes quivered open, catching sight of the maids pulling the curtains aside to reveal the glass doors and windows. The moment she sat on the bed, knew she had reached a decision and immediately requested Alessandro and Fabehel.

Unable to sleep, she spent most of the night deep in thought, pondering her decision, as she barely grasped a bit of sleep.

One maid nodded and left the chamber. "Right away, Divine Empress".

Nehel's bare feet contacted the chilly floor as she took cautious steps towards the balcony doors, clad only in her nightgown. To her surprise, a group of doves had perched themselves on the railing, but the birds flying away from let her down.

In the past, she had the gift of bonding and communicating with animals, but as she aged, she lost that ability.

The Empress, when she turned around, discovered not only Alessandro and Fabehel, but also Corr and Marissa. She perceived in them expectation and uneasiness.

Nehel approached the group near the entrance of the chamber, but before reaching them, she paused by the round table where the Falte was. She eyed the stones inside the pouch and muttered words without averting her gaze.

With a determined stare from her hazel eyes, she spoke, "I ask for your respect, as I have reached a resolution. Please bear with me." She sighed with anguish in her insides. "Uncle, I know you from the inside and outside, and although your motives are honorable, you occasionally let resentment blind you."

"What is the meaning of it?" Alessandro asked as his heart pounded fast.

"Please, forgive me," she said as her eyes shifted to the red-haired girl, who had a tense expression on her face and clasped her hands together, resting her elbows on the arms of the wheelchair. "Fabehel, you have gained experience from a young age, possess excellent intercultural skills, and have a strong passion for your work. Therefore, I appoint you as Ambassador to handle Fern and Brek on my behalf, granting you full autonomy. Your primary goal is to locate the Arankan settlement and move its inhabitants to the Jyistereerk." she sighed. "You have my blessings and absolute confidence."

With a blend of relief and trepidation, Fabehel nodded subtly.

From behind, Marissa could see the disappointment in Alessandro's eyes as he shook his head, disapproving of his niece's choice. Knowing him well, she was certain of his shattered heart not only because he could not go, but also because of the painful separation from his beloved.

The Empress called out to the feline. "Corr, please, accompany Lady Fabehel in her endeavors and keep her safe. Be her Guardian."

Alessandro disagreed with Nehel and withdrew from the chamber, unintentionally shoving Marissa, leaving her startled.

"I am sorry, uncle," she whispered, as she watched him walking into the halls in haste.

4

SECOND KNIGHT

Dessidere looked tense upon entering the forge. He did not want to be there, not because he disliked it, but because he never been close to a maid before.

Despite being twenty-eight years old, his insecurity and shyness prevented him from having any female company. Every time he had to meet Jumeni, the Artifice who owned the forge, he would start sweating and shaking.

When he first met her four years ago, she was a chubby girl, always engrossed in her crafts, and he did not pay her much attention. However, as they spent more time together, he witnessed Jumeni's incredible transformation into an eighteen-year-old girl. Her fascinating silence and sharp personality created a charm that attracted Dessidere.

He approached her, swallowing his saliva, feeling the intense heat of the forge, mesmerized by Jumeni's presence with her leather apron, black smudges on her face, and long black pigtail. He watched as she repeatedly swung her mallet and used her firm arm to strike a glowing, round piece of metal she held with long tongs.

Without warning, Jumeni halted and spun around, staring at Dessidere with a penetrating glare. Her despise for interruptions was clear as she waited for his response.

He blushed and his voice trembled as he stammered through his reply. "Divine Empress. . . had sent me. . . for the knight's sword."

Upon hearing him, the girl's gaze shifted downward, revealing a tinge of sorrow. Despite this, she agreed in silence by nodding. She set aside her tools on the anvil and approached a large table, concealed under a cloth she later uncovered, which displayed a myriad of weapons and artifacts that she had produced. She searched through the jumble until her eyes landed on a perfectly crafted sword. An Akareen star adorned it, nestled between the pommel and the blade. She used the reflection of the flames from the furnace and lifted it up, marveled at its intricate details, examined it.

With a gentle kiss on the sword, she entrusted it to Dessidere. Next, she gestured towards the staircase that led up to the palace.

He bowed in agreement and left in a hurry.

Nehel had worn her leather clothes and boots, ready for the long trip to Torret Post. A crisis had emerged that required her immediate presence.

Through one of the six large windows, her hazel eyes scanned the surroundings as Nehel stood inside the Imperial Hall, with crossed arms. She gazed at the great burgh of the Ri, a sight she had seen countless times before. From a distance, she admired the wisps of smoke rising from the chimneys, the graceful flight of doves above the towers, and the buoyant hustle and bustle of the people in the streets.

With sorrow, she also noticed the somber mood as long lines of youngsters awaited their turn to enlist for the upcoming battle.

Her eyes wandered to the hall, a large and lavish room that seemed to belong to the bygone era of monarchs. Following the coronation, she and her people explored the rustic, almost decrepit, and chilling palace. Nehel saw potential in this windowless and dark place, once loaded with excessive and chaotic parties by kings and queens. She envisioned it as a perfect venue for meetings.

Over the course of the next four years, skilled local contractors and craftsmen meticulously restored the hall. They installed beautiful glass windows, covered the walls with smooth plaster and a fresh coat of white paint, and hung large chandeliers from the ceiling. They also added a round table with twelve chairs reserved for the members of the Guild.

Nehel turned to her left. Her long black braid swayed as she admired the colossal painting that Carretem's artists had gifted to her. It hung on the gigantic wall, framed in shimmering gold. The portrait depicted the forever ten years old Empress, her delicate fingers clutched the rod as she sat upon the ancient stone throne.

The painting aimed to capture the extraordinary coronation.

While observing the piece of art, Nehel could not help but feel the weight of the Jyistereerk and the struggles she faced in her transition into adulthood. The memories of her time as Lakia, the Promise, flooded back to her once more, reminding her of the days spent in Molke and the remarkable journey that led to her crowning.

Her relationship with her uncle broke when she made the tough choice to send Fabehel to Fenn. She missed the moments they had shared over the past four years, which had created a special bond between them, and it distressed her. In recent encounters, Alessandro's behavior towards her became increasingly formal and arrogant, becoming in someone she could not recognize. However, to her surprise, he showed his support for her decision to aid the vagrants and sentinels in their fight against the red mantises from Trunke, the mantid realm that had invaded Torret Post and Southern Berrem.

Alessandro was the first to receive the unsettling news from a pigeon that had flown all the way from the south.

Despite her years of ruling as an Empress, making countless decisions and dealing with many audiences, facing these mantises under her name was her first actual test as a monarch. She had to step up and lead her soldiers through the crisis, whether she wanted to. Her first encounter during the *Deken Karsaker* she had started a tikl ago.

Besides the strained condition with Alessandro and the unfolding crisis, Nehel faced the insistence from both Pillars to name Juni as a knight. They wanted him to lead Marissa's aspirants and fight the mantises. Along with sending Fabehel to Fenn, she experienced the bitter reality of prioritizing her duty as a monarch over personal attachments, appointing her best friend as the Second Knight of the Jyistereerk.

Selee had outlined the rules she needed to adhere to in order to fulfill her role as a proper monarch.

She admitted herself with a profound fear of losing Juni in battle. Since his choice into the knighthood, Nehel had postponed many times his appointment because of her whim tenderness and the bind she had to him. Archmage Selee urged her that the duty as an Empress came first than the friendship.

The sound of the doors opening made Nehel startle.

Ser Marissa, the First Knight, entered the room with Juni, the aspirant, behind.

His striking presence caught the Empress's attention as she observed him in his newly polished armor, a masterpiece crafted by his talented sister Jumeni.

With a firm halt, the two armored individuals saluted as the sound of metal crashing against their chests echoed through the air.

Not much time passed since their entrance when Dessidere stormed into the hall. His hurried movements and anxious expression signaled his urgency to offer the sword he had received at the forge to the Empress.

With a silent nod, Nehel acknowledged the Herald and grabbed the weapon. She confirmed the immaculate job of her Artifice by studying the perfection of the blade. She held back tears and recalled the steps to name a knight glaring at Juni, following Selee's teachings according to the ways of the old monarchs. "Juni of Sarrem. Are you willing to dedicate yourself to serve and defend the Jyistereerk?" With her voice barely holding together, she asked.

Juni made a firm nod and clashed his arms against his body. "Aye, Divine Empress!"

Marissa and Dessidere were there to witness the scene.

"Please, kneel and bow to me," Nehel commanded, watching how Juni followed her instructions with utmost obedience. She could see him in a position of complete submission, unlike anything she had ever witnessed before. With gentle care, she raised the blade and brushed Juni's shoulders. "With thy sword I name you Second Knight of the Jyistereerk!"

Rising slowly, Juni's appreciation was clear as he accepted the blade from the Empress, picking it with both hands.

"I wish you the utmost health and welfare in all your endeavors, Ser Juni!" she said with her voice tinged in sadness as she looked at him with her hazel eyes. "I have given upon you the title of knight because of your remarkable patience, dedication, and devotion. However, I can not give my blessing to this sword because I do not approve of it."

"Divine Empress, I appreciate your words." Juni's remarks were formal and lacked his usual familiarity, as if he expected her response. He sheathed his new sword and gave a farewell salute, turned, and departed from the hall.

Marissa and Dessidere exchanged concerned looks.

"Please leave me alone," Nehel mandated with a fragile voice.

Both agreed to her request and departed, closing the gates behind them.

Falling to her knees, the Empress sobbed, turning into cries.

Only she knew the reason for her opposition to Juni's naming into a knight.

5
IMPERIAL LINE

As the Imperial Line of thousands departed from Carretem, it moved southwards, drawing closer to The Highlands. It had been a week since it departed from the Ri, and was for another one, heading towards Torret Post. The ones at the caravan could not help but wonder what it would be like to encounter the swarms of red mantises that infested the area. In order to diverge from the regions of Dri and Arrasem, infested of Korbeens, they had bypassed the direct path across The Banks and The Plains.

Green mantises, the Artensens, or the *Flying Divine Vessel* could have ensured a fast arrival for them. Yet, Archmage Selee refused these transportation options, citing the irresistible temptation they presented to the Korbas, as Alessandro had repeatedly emphasized. So, Selee suggested the old ways—by horse.

Orr and his comrades, Barr and Dienn, as well as the Brekens, had already embarked on their journey, purposefully avoiding the mantid-dominated lands of Trunke.

Despite the maids' preparations of a carriage for the Empress, she opted to ride a borrowed brown horse. Ser Marissa patiently taught Nehel how to mount both equines and mantises, and as time went on, Nehel developed a newfound joy in handling horses. The Empress had honed her riding abilities.

Fabehel rode her amber mare alongside Corr on his golden stallion, Thunder. Both of them were accompanying Nehel on either side. They had to delay their trip to Fenn because of the events at Torret Post. They recommended everyone to travel as a group before parting ways to their destinations.

Orr and his comrades, Barr and Dienn, as well as the Brekens, had already embarked on their journey avoiding the mantid-dominated land of Trunke.

Fabehel turned her head back and glanced at Alessandro riding Breeze. He rode alongside Marissa and her chestnut horse, Twist.

She noticed Fabehel's reaction and turned to stare at the road, noticing Alessandro's indifference. "Several days have gone by since you distanced yourself from Nehel and

Fabehel. How much longer are you going to continue behaving like this?"

Marissa continued forward and her gaze directed to the front, revealing a stone road that a group of sentinels had already marked.

At first, her remark seemed to fall on deaf ears, as he showed no reaction. Instead, he observed the last scarce trees as they entered the brisk ascending valleys of The Highlands, where the scent of fresh grass saturated the air. "I do not remember ever being here before."

"Aye, you were!" Marissa responded with irritation. "You can not evade my question, so do not even try!"

"How would you feel?" he replied with certain resentment. "Having surrendered my soul to the Jyistereerk, I now find myself separated from the most important affairs!"

"Damn you, Alessandro!" she jabbed, outraged. "I find your arrogant attitude repulsive! I can not believe this person is the same Alessandro I was engaged to! Are you not aware that your actions are causing harm to both your niece and your beloved?!"

As he stared at her, his expression turned severe. "Whatever!" With determination, he dismissed the comment and urged Breeze to gallop faster, eager to join the crowd of sentinels.

Nehel sensed in his uncle feelings of acrimony and seclusion. A mysterious emotion washed over her, leaving her puzzled and unable to comprehend it. She was concerned when she perceived the chaos in his resentment.

Through her essence, she listened to his conversation with Marissa and felt anguish in her heart. She held back tears, took control of the horse's reins, and turned around to survey the long line of the caravan. Occasionally, the Empress would ride a horse to inspect her Imperial Guard.

While trotting along the line, Nehel confirmed that Selee and Akhimeni were behind Marissa. There were also some maids on horses escorting an empty carriage. Following them were hundreds of Imperial Guard members and thousands of well-prepared young fighters who had joined to combat the vicious mantises.

As the riding Empress passed by, everyone bowed.

Upon arriving at the last part of the caravan, the sight of Juni leading a group of aspiring knights driving their horses mesmerized her. With some hesitation, she resolved to join him, guiding her horse closer to his. As they rode together, she noticed his focus on the road ahead, as if he were oblivious to her presence. "Tell me Juni. Are you all right?" She pleaded while her heart was pounding.

"Respectfully," he requested with a light bow, never losing sight of the road ahead and the caravan, "I must ask you to address me as Ser Juni, Divine Empress."

"Why do you speak and act in such a formal manner?" she asked with despair. "What I have done to you? Is it because of my constant refusals to make you a knight?" Overwhelmed by a whirlwind of conflicting emotions, she tightened her grip on the reins and urged her horse to gallop faster, breaking away from the group. She headed towards the hills, craving solitude.

The sudden disappearance of the Empress caught Ser Juni's attention, causing him to bring the caravan to a halt. He shouted, and the entire group started visually scanning their surroundings in search of her. However, the Second Knight requested to wait, volunteering to search for her himself. He even stopped Marissa, who was eager to find her.

Ser Juni got off his black stallion when he discovered Nehel sitting on a rock near an unusual dark cave. She had tied her brown horse to a dead, small tree. He questioned her choice to be there, but found her sobbing with her face hidden in her hands.

"Please go away!" Nehel requested, still covering the face. "Take your damn horse and go back to the line!"

Ignoring her demand, he stood beside her with his arms crossed. "I apologize, missy. I was merely following Archmage Selee's instructions." A sigh escaped him. "He suggested that if I am to be a knight, I should address the empress with the utmost respect."

With disbelief, Nehel lifted her dampened face and confronted him, bothered. "I can not believe you would do this to me! Our friendship is based on trust, so formalities should not matter!"

"I. . . am at a loss for words. . .," he sputtered.

Nehel impulsively climbed the rock, placed her hands on his metal shoulder pads, and sealed her lips with his. In that instant, the Empress experienced tranquility and regained her composure, as the kiss restored Nehel to her true self, causing tears of joy to flow instead of sorrow.

Juni embraced her, unable to resist her. Ever since Nehel vanished in Carretem four years ago, he has yearned to have her by his side, always. And that kiss brought a presumed wholeness to his being.

"Wait!" Without warning, Nehel pushed him away.

At first, Juni could not understand the sudden change in her behavior.

From the depths of the cave, piercing screeches reverberated, causing them both to look at it with widened eyes.

Nehel felt the ground tremble as a massive, wingless dragon emerged and its feet stomped with each step, approaching her.

Surprise took her, leaving her vulnerable and immobilized in the face of the threatening creature, powerless.

The black Korba let out a fierce roar with a deadly determination.

Juni drew his sword, ready to protect her, but a frenzied scream caught his attention. He spun around to see Alessandro, wielding his greatsword with both hands, not to face the dragon but intending to assassinate the Empress. The Second Knight stepped in to protect Nehel from the mad slayer.

Blades clashed into a fiery combat.

Juni, a novice, faced the formidable strength of an experienced swordsman. However, his impenetrable defense kept Alessandro at a distance, unable to comprehend the strange motive to execute his own niece.

Nehel felt terror from both sides. Paralyzed, she was helpless to react or even comprehend the gravity of the situation.

Alessandro, unrecognizable, threw Juni to the ground, disarming him. He then pointed his greatsword against Juni's throat as his dark eyes held an unnatural hatred.

The dragon leaped towards the Empress, ready to kill.

Out of nowhere, a powerful unseen energy slammed the Korba against the cave, triggering a cascade of rocks from above that buried it alive, while bone-chilling screeches echoed.

In a surprising turn of events, Alessandro lost consciousness and fell to the ground, freeing Juni from the menace of death.

Nehel's hazel eyes widened in amazement as she turned and saw Archmage Selee in the distance standing with his extended arms and hands in the air and a grave expression on his face, revealing that he was the one who had used his magic to crush the monster. Concerned, she ran to check on her uncle, crouching beside him.

Juni carefully rose to his feet, taking a moment to survey his surroundings, trembling as he retrieved his sword from the ground.

As Selee watched from behind, Nehel removed Alessandro's black glove and touched his hand, comprehending the reason for his sudden madness. "Lord Kong Rim cast a corrupting spell on him before dying. Fortunately, he did not finish it, so I can save my uncle." She used her abilities and cleansed his insides.

"It explains everything." Selee nodded with understanding. "From now on, I believe we must resort to drastic measures."

Juni sheathed his sword with relief, yet breathing fast as sweats ran through his face.

"It is not him who I am concerned about, archmage. But me!" she said, agitated, while still keeping her uncle's hand. "I should have done something. Instead, I just stood there like a defenseless sheep."

"Nehel. . ." Alessandro's mouth emitted a soft murmur, barely audible.

The Empress turned. She caught sight of her his eyes, which were quite open, revealing his exhaustion. She rubbed his cheek with empathy and understanding. "It is alright, uncle. I have cleansed your soul of its minor perversions. Please, rest."

"Why did you not react? You could, at the very least, put yourself in a field." Selee mentioned as disapproval was in the tone of his voice as his shadow covered her.

"I do not know, Archmage," Nehel saw at him with hesitation.

"You should be more careful, Master," Selee reprimanded Alessandro, shaking his head. "Being a Korbeen Slayer is not a simple task and you do risk being tainted. As a Pillar, it is prudent to restrict your involvement to the Empress' affairs."

With profound, dark eyes seated on the ground, Alessandro glared at the archmage. His mouth savored sips from a steaming bowl of ox stew with potatoes and carrots along with pinches of rices he placed in his mouth. He was replenishing his depleted energy from earlier in the day. "Someone has to do the job."

Nehel sat beside her uncle while savoring her stew.

Fabehel, leaning against a rock next to him, cut a piece of cheese and placed it on a slice of bread. "Every time you are away hunting Korbeens, my heart sinks!" She nodded with composure in her face to her beloved. "I understand how upsetting it is for you to know that I have to go to Fenn. But when you go far, I experience the same feeling."

Marissa and Juni caught Alessandro's attention as they stood watch nearby, as their voices blended with chatter across the bonfire alongside Corr. His eyes lifted to see the night sky to notice the dual presence of the moons of the white No Sak and the brown-green No Nunn, on a clear starry night accompanied by a shining coming from the invisible No Kra in a manifestation rarely seen, only the red No Ta was absent.

Alessandro placed the bowl on the ground and drank some water from a canteen. "Though I am back to my senses, I am still not in favor of you leaving for Fenn. I believe in the success of your mission. I apologize for my actions, even though I can not take all the blame."

She kept her silence with a nod.

Akhimeni and her maids prepared a savory stew and shared it with the Guild, as well as the Imperial Guard, recruits, and those aspiring to become knights. The Court of Maids had also arranged a tent for the Empress, but she insisted on staying by the bonfire instead.

Despite her position as an Empress, Nehel despised the extravagant luxuries. Feeling uneasy with the particular attention, she believed that those who served her were more deserving than herself.

"I feel it is my duty to give you the proper training to restore your courage when facing Korbas, Divine Empress," Selee nodded with a light smile. "Relying on others for defense is not fair, as you should be able to fight for yourself."

Nehel observed him with no reaction. "You have done enough to teach me how to control my emotions."

"Aye, but it is essential for you to have a thorough sorceress training. I believe that this is the particular path to reclaim your courage."

"And I believe you should return to the Ri," Alessandro suggested, addressing to his niece. "Even though the battle requires you, we can not risk your life."

"I refuse to do so! I am needed there!"

"I apologize, but I agree with Master Alessandro," Selee insisted. "If you can not provide a suitable defense. How can you fight these mantises?"

"Ser Juni and the Court of Maids will escort the Divine Empress back to her palace," Alessandro mandated. "She shall await for us!"

With a frustrated sigh, Nehel stood up and walked away from the bonfire.

6

YKARTE'S SONG

In the early morning, two female elves from the Sisterhood of the Comforting Wind rushed out of the house and alerted the sentinels guarding outside, prompting a collective search.

As the search proved fruitless, one sister blew the horn so its resounding sound could reach long distances to Kaope City.

Soon, a group of soldiers and sisters on their white horses came galloping to join the search.

The *Ykarte* had inexplicably disappeared from her chamber.

Commandant Kartak, who had stayed on Kao Island after meeting with Head Missar, was the last one to arrive. His eyebrow twitched as he began his desperate search for her. Instead of despair, he felt intense trepidation.

His fear arose from the possibility of a malevolent being, such as a Korba, a Korbeen, or maybe even a corrupted soul, had betrayed and kidnapped her for purposes more ominous than the Gesha itself.

In an impulse, the Commandant yanked the reins and ordered his horse to gallop alongside the island, racing across hills, small towns, lakes, and rivers, until he reached the air beaches. From an immense altitude, his wide, yellow eyes scanned the clouds and settled on the greenish landscapes of Casak.

The weight of failure fell on Kartak as he realized he had been unsuccessful in protecting the *Ykarte*. He believed his poor job had sealed the fate of Sankaris because of his negligence, and he felt remorse for it.

Startled by cries, eighteen-year-old Vasso became curious about the origin of the noise. Despite being in his sleeping gown, he reached for his scimitar, a gift from his arrival in Kao four years ago. It sat on a chair next to his folded elvish clothes. As he stepped up from his small cot, his dark eyes fixated on the open door.

Stunned, he met a giant gryphon outside his small house. Its eagle head signaled him to mount its lion's body. Unsure if it was a mystical creature or a shapeshifter, but when he glanced into the creature's eyes, he immediately noticed that they were dark and unlike the clear ones seen in the birds. And they filled him with tenderness, instilling a sense of trust. Vasso's intuition told him that there was something unfolding, so agreed to its request. "Aye. . . Give me a moment to get dressed."

The gryphon's nod seemed almost human.

Vasso hurried inside and changed into a simple elvish uniform, exclusive to young Casakans on Kao. As he slipped on his mocassins, he almost fell down on his way back out.

The youngster noticed the gryphon's persistent wait.

He brought a small ladder with him to mount on it, as it was too big. Once on the creature, he grasped its thick fur.

The gryphon flapped its wings and soared, making its way across the island towards the air beaches.

After a moment of scare, Vasso noticed the sentinels and sisters on the land, as if he and the creature were invisible.

With surprising speed, the enigmatic creature descended, prompting the youngster to cry out in fear, worried about a potential fall, yet somehow maintained a firm grip. As he rode on a gryphon for the first time, the joy of flying and the breathtaking sight of the clouds beneath the morning sun struck him. With a bird's-eye view from a great altitude, he could appreciate the vastness of Casak.

During Orssandro's mobilization in the past, when he and the children arrived on the island, the darkness of the night obscured their flight to their new home, Kao.

Vasso's heart leapt as he recognized his family's estate.

But unlike the vibrant greenish homestead he remembered before his forced recruitment into the Casakan Army at fourteen, the sorghum plantation now appeared lackluster, with patches of dryness and burnt areas. He guessed the Korbas had also left their mark on his home.

He glimpsed his childhood home and his heart sank at the sight of its partially destroyed house, fearing the worst.

As the gryphon feet touched the ground, Vasso darted across the damaged plantation, hoping to find his family.

As she stepped out of the house, a dark-skinned mature woman extended her hands towards her only son, who had been away for so long.

"Mama!" Vasso exclaimed, rushing to embrace her.

The sound of cries and soft words of consolation filled the air, catching the attention of two girls. They also ran towards their mother and brother, hugging them.

Vasso looked around. "Papa?"

With sorrow, one of his siblings gestured towards a nearby spot where a tombstone stood.

In sadness, he comprehended his father's tragic fate.

Out of nowhere, an immaculate song emerged from the plantation, interrupting the emotional moment.

Vasso could hear the enchanting song growing louder, leading him to the precise center of the plantation where he hoped to encounter the gryphon. Instead, he found the *Ykarte* in Carlissa's aspect, with her thick round glasses perched on her nose and a maroon dress as she sang verses in Salteran, a language he could not comprehend.

The flawless harmony of her beautiful voice amazed him.

He came to a halt, captivated by the remarkable performance, and waited for her to stop. Afterward, she stood still, resembling a statue as her gaze locked upwards, captivated by the sky. "Was the gryphon you?"

"You said so," she acknowledged, without changing her position.

"Why did you bring me here?" he asked with a voice of confusion and curiosity.

She lowered her head. The *Ykarte* stared at Vasso with eyes so deep and chilling that he reached for his scimitar. "The time had arrived for you to be reunited with your kin."

He suspected something about her. He removed his hand from the scimitar, "I appreciate your intentions." There was a reason as he sensed her need for something. "What do you seek in exchange?"

"Assist me reunite to my kin," she said with a cold semblance, pointing to the north. "I must give a home."

"Home? Who?"

"Nehel Jyistereerk Mudihufaser."

Vasso stood there, speechless and wide-eyed, uncertain of how to respond.

"We shall go to Aranka, and give her a home," the *Ykarte* asseverated.

"How can you give to the Divine Empress a home in a barren land?"

"I am the home!" she insisted. "Do not doubt and follow my lead."

Puzzled, he scratched his head and glanced several times at his house, unsure. "I have hardly had time with my family, and now you are saying we need to separate again!"

"The Nehel awaits!"

He shook his head and observed to the ground, pensive. "Fine, whoever you are! I am doing it for the Divine Empress. Once I am finished, I hope to go back to my mother and sisters."

The *Ykarte* responded with a nod.

Vasso had no choice but to part ways with the elvish scimitar that he had received as a welcoming gift from Overseer Akartaki in Kao a tikl ago. He had to consider priorities.

The reunion with his family was far from pleasant. Apart from his father's unfortunate death during a dragon attack on their home, his mother and sisters had to resort to desperate measures for survival.

The persistent Korba incursions prevented the plantation from thriving and had killed the livestock, causing poverty for his rejoined family. His mother and sisters had to work at a tavern in order to sustain themselves and buy groceries. Adding to their already precarious situation, his oldest sister was pregnant.

Vasso was insistent about them discontinuing their work, especially after dark. He made them a promise—if they stopped their labors, he would support them unconditionally.

The elves crafted the elvish scimitars from a rare and durable precious metal, surpassing the strength of the giefo itself, and reserved only for themselves. It was rare for a common man to possess such a weapon, but the blacksmiths desired it, and they offered significant amounts of gold coins. For that reason, Vasso searched for one of the two surviving forges in the neighboring small town of Porkork, and he received fifty coins from the sale. This amount was enough for his family to live well for half of a tikl, even with ten coins for himself.

In addition, he traded his elvish attire for a simple set of leather garments and a couple of silver coins.

After being away for four years, Vasso noticed Casak was no longer the same. A lot had changed. He found himself surrounded by devastation and anguish everywhere he looked. The once prosperous land was now plagued by misery, poverty, and constant menace from the Korbas—the *Deken Karsaker* only intensified the desolation.

The intention of returning to Kao, a paradise floating above the chaotic Casak, consumed his every thought.

With the Moon of Life, No Nunn, reaching its zenith on that frigid night, Vasso bid farewell to his mother and sisters, uncertain of when or if he would ever can see them again. And reunite with the *Ykarte* just outside the estate.

Despite the melody of her chant echoing across the plantation, he kept her hidden from his family. Being discreet was his goal, as he didn't want to burden his mother any further.

When Vasso found the *Ykarte*, he noticed her gaze fixed on the lone moon in the sky, just as she often did. He gently set down his small bag, secured to a stick, and placed his iron sword, acquired from the blacksmith as part of the transaction, beside it. With his hands on his hips, let out a skeptical sigh. "Before we depart. What shall I call you? *Ykarte*? I also learned that your name is Carlissa."

Through her thick glasses, she turned her frightening gaze and spoke with coldness. "Address me as Carlissa. We shall be discreet in our path to the north."

Vasso chuckled. "Your song sure was discreet!" His smile vanished as soon as he comprehended her words. "Wait! Do you mean walk all the way north?"

"You said so."

"You were a gryphon! Why could not you change back?"

Once again, Carlissa gazed at the moon. "Taking you out of Kao was already daring. Whether we fly north again or travel on horseback, they will sense my presence and come to find me. If I can not locate Divine Empress in time, I will align myself with the darkness."

"Very well!" Carrying his bag and weapon, he approached her, bringing her full attention to stare at him. "Let us begin with haste."

Despite lacking the luminescence of No Sak, the Moon of Life guided the travelers towards Porkork, where they planned to continue their journey to Berkork. The travel, particularly at night, would be dangerous as bandits, or even worse, Korbas, could show up, but Vasso was prepared.

At least he believed was ready, having received proper training in the art of war, but had never faced an outlaw.

As soon as the dawn arrived, a flock of flying crows materialized, announcing the slow approach of an ominous figure in dark attire atop his emaciated gray steed, who halted in a clearing amidst the marshes. Even though the cowl hindered his view, he could still identify the dilapidated shack that the skeletal palm trees encircled.

When he saw someone emerging from the shack, he could not help but expose a sinister grin. He felt an eerie presence that sent shivers down his spine, and he enjoyed the sensation.

As he approached the visitor, the face of Orssandro Vykar came into view. His voice escaped his lips, reverberating through the air like echoes. "You have summoned me, Carrasso, so to speak."

The warlock dismounted his horse and made a reverence, amused. "Why you have taken the form of Orssandro, Lord Ardek?"

"Speak now! Could you please explain the reason for summoning me?"

"The Empress has reached her coming of age, and the *Ykarte* intends to meet her," he assured.

Hiding his hands beneath the sleeves of his long dark robes, Ardek acknowledged with the shapeshifted face of Orssandro and understood his remark. "She is hard to break. I have to recognize."

"Yet, I think we can break her," Carrasso grinned. "By her soul!"

In an act of intimidation, Ardek changed the color of his eyes to a piercing red, giving him a menacing stare. "What does your Aquelarre suggests? A Gesha again? An assault? I truly doubt that repeating them will shatter her spirit!"

"You have come to me for help, and we will grant it because you are our chosen Lord of the Netherworld who shall rule Sankaris."

"Quit buttering me and start talking! How do you plan to snap the Empress' spirit?"

The warlock nodded, still grinning. "Do not go straight to the Empress. But to her beloved ones!"

7

THE PLEA

The maids' convoy arrived at the outskirts of the Black Forest with the imperial carriage.

Carretem was nearby, but Juni deemed it vital for the Empress' safety to traverse the woods and evade people. Despite being in safe areas, the Second Knight wanted to avoid Korbeen encounters. The Pillars instructed him to accompany Nehel back to the palace. Master Alessandro cautioned Juni about the consequences of not completing the task—losing his knighthood.

It was fortunate that no one witnessed their first kiss in The Highlands.

Juni was uncertain whether it was a strange twist of fate or mere coincidence, as a Korba appeared afterwards. Almost identical to what had happened between Master Alessandro and Lady Fabehel prior to the *Feast of the Dragoness*.

In his life, the Second Knight kissed no one before, but still felt Nehel's touch as he rode Arthus, his black stallion.

Questions overwhelmed his mind as he tried to make sense of everything.

He never expected the troubadour's son to meet the Promise, who delivered a message from his deceased father. In the beginning, he saw her as a dark sorceress. No one could have predicted that Juni would become emotionally entangled with an Empress, in particular after their brief journey to Carretem.

Nehel vanished into Carretem after foreseeing the massacre at Ambassador Square. She then reappeared at the jousting event, where Marshal Keleana of Estherleon defeated Marissa.

No one knew her location during her disappearance.

Despite Juni's repeated inquiries, he received no answer about her whereabouts. He could not help but think about her absence, as he glanced at the carriage carrying the Empress, driven by the Court of Maids' Overseer.

While inside the carriage, Nehel felt bothered by the persistent shaking from the iron and wood wheels colliding with the rough road across the forest. But her biggest concern was not being able to join the crisis at Carret Post.

Nehel planned to persuade Juni to allow her to battle the red mantises, but the constant vigilance from the maids hindered her attempts to approach him.

Akhimeni would not listen to her, and maids with her would only follow her lead.

Realizing that a simple request would not be sufficient, the Empress had to plead.

Many lives would depend on that plea.

At the sunset, the Second Knight deemed it necessary to halt their journey and establish a camp in a clearing close by. The maids wasted no time in gathering wood and igniting a bonfire. As the only armed escort, Juni felt no fear of the night, knowing the maids had their own magic to protect the Empress from any lurking Korba or Korbeen in the Black Forest.

He sat beside Nehel, enjoying his bowl of lamb stew, yet never let his guard down. Four years ago, the infestation was not widespread. Unfortunately, the late Lord Kong Rim allowed the infiltration of Korbeens into the Dri and converted the once bustling and charming Arrasem into a hellish burgh.

To everyone's surprise, the outbreak in the Black Forest or in the north, where the Ri and Sarrem were located, had not reached, yet. However, the discovery of some vague incursions poses a threat to other areas, which is why Juni was always alert.

"If I may suggest, Divine Empress, it would be wise to rest inside the carriage," Akhimeni offered, accompanied by two aides, while the rest of the maids were at a distance by the carriage and their horses, where they started another bonfire. "The night is getting late and the No Sak moon suggest a cold weather."

With a nod, Nehel patted Juni's metallic shoulder. "I appreciate it, but I much prefer to stay here outside beside my knight and friend."

"I must recall that Master Alessandro had mandated. . ."

"I do not care what he said! I am the Empress among us!" she interrupted, bothered, imposing. "All of you go back! I only need my damn waki furs!"

Startled by the abrupt character, Akhimeni and her maids nodded their heads and left.

As Nehel turned, Juni's stunned gaze met her, unable to grasp her sudden and striking attitude.

"My apologies, Juni. I was just pretending," she was gentle and whispered. "I feel bad for my maids, but I had to make a plea to you."

"What is wrong, missy?"

She took both of his hands and appealed. "Take me to Torret Post. Many lives will be impacted by my absence."

"I can not! I shall not disobey Master's orders. Besides, he and Archmage Selee were right about you. How will you defend yourself now, when you could not do so earlier?"

"I know it! It was unexpected because you and I were. . . "

"We kissed, missy. Perhaps we should not have done it. . .," he shook his head. "I am uneasy and believe that it is wrong because I feel like I am taking advantage of you."

"Do not you recall I am the one who kissed you?" Her hands remained clasped with his as she guided them to rest on her chest. "At that moment, I had a great deal of disappointment. My emotions were in conflict, yet I longed to feel your lips. What kind of reaction were you expecting from me regarding the Korba?"

"I wish to believe, missy. But I swore to defend and serve the Jyistereerk. Do not you recall?"

"You said so! Serve and defend the Jyistereerk!" she pressed his hands. "So, help me in getting there!"

Without saying a word, unsure, Juni noticed some maids watched him and Nehel from afar. "If I take you there, it will take longer to reach our destination," he murmured with discretion.

"We can take Brisel!" she replied whispering.

With a gentle gesture, he pulled his hands back and shrugged, trying to comprehend. "But Brisel is no longer with us! Do you not recall how he vanished within weeks after we arrived at the palace four years ago?"

"Aye, I sure remember it, but believe me. Brisel has always been an attentive watcher, ready whenever I summon him."

"Uh? How?"

"He is smarter than you think," she nodded. "For years ago, he came to me and spoke."

"Spoke?" he scratched his head. "Does he talk?"

"He does, but not in the way you think. I can see his mind, and he does with mine," Nehel sighed with a light smile. "He told me he needed to disappear and leave Ser Marissa, as he no longer needed her, but promised to be at my service." In a sudden gesture, she took his hands again and stared at him with hopeful hazel eyes. "What do you say? Aye?"

The Second Knight groaned, letting go of the air from his lungs. "I have earned my knighthood, and I will sacrifice it all for you. So, aye, I will take you, but not without a word of warning. If I ever see you in danger, I will do whatever it takes to rescue and bring you to the Ri."

This time, she drew a big smile. "I appreciate it!"

"Are you going to summon Brisel?"

"I have already taken care of it. He will be here as soon as the sun rises in the morning."

"Missy, missy!" Juni kept pushing Nehel to wake her up. "The morning is almost here!" He whispered, remaining cautious of the maids.

As Nehel's bright hazel eyes fluttered open, she stared into her knight's face. With a nod of acknowledgement, she noted the fading darkness and morning.

Hand in hand, Juni and Nehel ventured into the Black Forest as they made their way toward the destination Nehel had spoken of earlier. They started off discreetly and silently, but the urgency of the situation soon had them sprinting away from the maids.

Juni's heart raced as he abruptly halted, shielding the Empress, startled by the sudden appearance of a sword tip materialized in front of his face.

The elder Akhimeni's voice rang out with mistrust and disappointment as she yelled, "A traitor attempting to kidnap the Jewel deserves death!"

The Second Knight, trembling and surprised, raised both hands without resistance. "I am simply carrying out the mandates given by the highest authority in the Jyistereerk."

"Master Alessandro made it clear—we must take the Divine Empress to the Ri!" The Overseer of the Court of Maids shouted in anger. "I know about your deep friendship, and I received advice that it might compromise your commitment to duty!"

"Please withdraw your weapon and hear me out!" Nehel abandoned her place on Juni's back, stepping forward to reveal herself. "I am the one who convinced him to take me to Torret Post. Even if he did not agree with them, he had no choice but to follow my orders."

Akhimeni's eyes burned with indignation as she nodded and lowered her blade. "He should know his duty, Divine Empress! And as for you, Master Alessandro has said that. . ."

"The heck with my damn uncle's order! Can not you see lives rely on me in the fight against the mantises?"

The maid let out a sigh of disagreement, rolling her blue eyes upward. "My responsibility is to oversee a court that has pledged unwavering loyalty and obedience to Nehel, our esteemed Jewel. Do we have a choice?"

A sudden hissing sound caught everyone's attention, causing them to turn.

As the morning sun bathed the forest in golden hues, casting intricate patterns of light and shadow. Brisel appeared for the first time in four years, stepping out from behind a tree.

Akhimeni and Juni fell in awe as they gaze at the green mantis, a sight they had not seen in a long time.

As Brisel approached the Empress, his amusing round black eyes studied her. He bowed, realizing that she had blossomed into a grown girl, yet she her scent was the same.

Nehel responded with a smile and a pat on his head.

"Why is he here?" Akhimeni asked with annoyance. "Did you summon him?"

"Aye, I did," Nehel responded with joy. "He will take us there. He will now transport me wherever I need to go."

"Very well! Should Master inquire, I will inform him you left while we were sleeping. But please, come back alive!" she shook her head, then placed her index finger against Juni's metallic chest. "And you, young man, watch over her with your life!"

"I will, madam," he gave his word.

In silence, Akhimeni hastened her departure, dragging the sword with her.

With excitement and a smile, Nehel locked her hazel eyes with Juni and touched the metallic pads on his shoulders. Rising onto her tiptoes, she planted a quick kiss on his lips, catching him off guard. "This is my way of thanking you for always being there for me!"

Then, Juni, who had learned how to mount mantises from Ser Marissa, climbed onto the back of Brisel, even though his head lacked reins, which made it somewhat challenging to steer him. Offering his hand, he pulled Nehel to sit behind him.

Despite his metallic armor, Nehel, who expressed her readiness to depart, warmly embraced Ser Juni.

Brisel sprinted at an extraordinary speed, disappearing into the forest as he headed towards the south, transporting two in his back.

8

WAR PRELUDE

Alessandro stood with his fists on his waist, gazing at the open gates that enticed him to come in, Seled Post. "Once, Lady Fabehel left a farewell letter for me here, and I foresee another farewell coming my way, likely for the similar reasons. She is leaving not just as an Ambassador but also to find her people."

Corr listened and nodded, but his expression remained unchanged. "It is as if your story is repeating all over again."

"Aye, my friend," said as he turned to see the feline with assertion. "I would rather see her leave than stay with me, even if it brings sadness."

"May I know the reason, Master?"

"Nehel made me a confession shortly after turning eleven," he sighed in disappointment. "She employed her abilities to manipulate the fates of both Marissa and myself, all to ensure her encounter with Dessidere and to amend my relationship with Fabehel. Ser Juni never approved of it, and she experienced remorse."

His green eyes with vertical pupils widened. "The power of the Divine Empress is undeniable."

"While she may be a demigoddess, she is still a human who can make mistakes like anyone else," Alessandro said with a nod. "That is the reason I do not agree with Fabehel's commission."

"Regardless of your liking, we ought to respect the Divine Empress's wisdom and decisions. Being her uncle does not entitle you to contradict her," Corr assumed a strict posture as he crossed his arms. "Were you conscious while under Kong Rim's mystical cast?"

"Aye, Corr. I recall the feeling of my soul being consumed as I was becoming into a mad monster," he replied while shrugging. "The weight of guilt persists on me, even though I know I am not to blame for hurting my niece and my beloved." He gave a rare smile, reserved only for those closest to him, and rested his hands on the feline's shoulders. "Please, take care of Lady Fabehel with all your soul, and bring her back to me unharmed."

A pinto horse galloped between the troops outside Seled Post, causing a disruption as it interrupted their conversation. Admiral Kekten, showing his stained armor uniform, had arrived from the front lines at Torret Post. "Master! I bring with ya a missive from Marshal Keleana!" He handed over a rolled papyrus.

Alessandro unwrapped the message and inspected its contents. "Torret Post is currently under siege, with our soldiers behind the palisade trapped inside," He told Corr with a sigh and then turned his attention to Kekten, on horseback. "How were you able to make your escape?"

"Indeed, I was fortunate to escape through an underground passage reserved for our residents," his reply came with a tired tone and scratches on his face. "But, indeed, ya do not have an idea how difficult is to evade these monsters!"

"How about the flying ones? How many mantises are attempting to enter? Hundreds?"

"We could to bring down the flying ones, but, indeed, ya do not have an idea as they are for thousands!"

"Considering our current situation," Corr said with doubt. "Do you think we stand a chance against them? What if they infect the troops, which is worse?"

"Selee has proven that an insect can not infect a human, Corr. That is a significant advantage." Alessandro placed his hand on his chin. "There are two ways to be tainted—flesh to flesh and blood to blood, or by a Korba—." He then turned again to Kekten with a concerned gaze. "Let us discuss it later in our meeting. Get indoors and treat yourself to a meal and some rest."

He bowed, then rode his on horse into the garrison.

To ensure the map stayed in place, Ser Marissa used the weight of wine bottles, positioning them on the corners of the map. She held another bottle with a lightened wax candle and carefully examined it with clear focus.

The texture of the paper was palpable under her dark index finger as it followed the ink, mapping out Torret Post's surroundings and strategizing ways to defeat the mantises. Fear was on her, her lips trembled. As First Knight, she faced her biggest test yet—commanding and planning a battle she had never done before.

Despite her initial refusal, Alessandro insisted her to take the lead in the battle, citing her extensive military education from the Academy. Archmage Selee's entrance interrupted her concentration, sensing the strain in her. "Ser, how are you coping with it?"

"I do not know how to handle this infuriating thing!" Her response came with both annoyance and frustration. "This is the first time I have to deal with a genuine situation, not just hypothetical scenarios for students! And it scares me! Especially red mantises!"

With a smile of comprehension, Selee closed the distance and sat down. Pouring a glass of wine from a bottle, he held the cup out to her. "Have a drink and feel yourself at ease!"

Marissa complied with his request, giving sips of her drink and stared at the Archmage, studying his face. "Are you someone who never stops to smile, even when we face dire moments? Do you have any concern about the challenges we are dealing with?"

The Archmage's face turned serious and sighed. "In the *Frelee Dee*, I witnessed glimpses of our potential futures. Even though I am aware of our unfortunate destinies, I can not help but marvel at the beauty of life itself, especially in my advanced years, awaiting the end of my immortality." He placed both hands on the table to give one more smile. "Knowing that Salter's collapse is inevitable, I can only choose to smile."

"I thought only Archmage Yasstro smiled like that, but seeing you, I now believe that all archmages have a fondness for smiles," she beamed as she gave more sips of her wine.

Selee stood up from his seat as his eyes narrowed as he fixed a piercing glare on the door. "Here they come."

Alessandro came in, guiding Fabehel's wheelchair, accompanied by Corr and Admiral Kekten.

Marissa got up and invited everyone to come closer to the table where the map was.

"What is your plan with this? What precautions should we take when entering Torret Post?" Alessandro inquired.

"We shall confront the mantises and open a way to enter, and fight from inside," she shrugged. "But I do not know how to win it."

"Many will die, and I do not wish it," Alessandro responded, touching his chin, pensive, and addressed to Selee. "Archmage, could we rely on your mystical abilities?"

"Even with my expertise, I doubt I can succeed against such overwhelming numbers, Master." He shook his head. "The most I can do is create an invisible shield, but I can not promise it will keep us safe."

"Are you all idiots?!" Fabehel exclaimed as she intervened from her wheelchair. "Supposedly, you are going to lighten the load for our soldiers, and defy these insects! You are not going inside for vacations!"

Startled, everyone glanced at themselves in response to her harsh words.

"What do you recommend, Lady Fabehel?" Selee asked.

"May I speak?" Kekten requested.

"Granted," Alessandro replied.

"As ya see, indeed, from the times before the Promise, when we were only vagrants, we have fought these vicious insects. The mantises are fast and terrifying, they do not have any disregard for any life."

"Aye, you are right, Admiral," Marissa confirmed. "I still have nightmares from that red mantis I encountered a tikl ago."

"Indeed, all ya have to consider mantises are not only one kind, but there are varieties. And if we did not enter to the heart of Trunk is because of the colossal swarm of, perhaps, hundreds of thousands." He shook his head. "For years after the Gesha, when the Gathering hired us, we tried to prevent them into entering Berrem, yet we have failed."

"What are you trying to say?" she inquired.

"The mantises are Korbeens, are highly treacherous and use all their lethal abilities to eliminate every one of us. They tried it for long." Kekten sighed. "Indeed, Divine Empress' coronation only intensified their craving for bloodshed. It does not matter how much ya try, many will die."

"We have five thousands ready to fight. Will this number suffice?" Master Alessandro informed. "Despite the dangers of traveling near infested lands, we came all the way from the Ri."

The Admiral swallowed his saliva and shook. "When Ser Marissa found us a tikl ago, indeed, we were a little more than a thousand and it was then enough. With the establishment of the Jyistereerk, we received an additional two thousand members from the new Imperial Guard, which helped us withstand their attacks. However, this sudden attack and siege has resulted in the death of over eight hundred people in just three weeks despite our resistance." His blue eyes widened while describing, as a trepidation invaded him. "They have gone insane!"

Before anyone uttered a word, a heavy silence overflowed the room.

"The only option is to either try or face death," Marissa murmured. "What is the point of coming up with strategies when their magnitude renders us insignificant?"

On the court of Seled Post, Alessandro walked in circles under the pale glow of the bleached moon of No Sak, enveloped by the chilly night air, with concern and pensiveness.

He had been this way for so long, right after the meeting.

On his way to the dining chamber, Archmage Selee caught sight of him and altered his course in order to engage him. "Are you still plagued by thoughts of tomorrow's uncertainties?"

"This, and Fabehel's departure," he replied after a sigh. "I am also curious about Nehel's safe arrival."

Selee nodded in comprehension, yet instead of smiling as he often would, he revealed a serious expression. "Did we make the correct decision in sending the Divine Empress home?"

"I think so, but I'm uncertain," he said with a hesitant nod. "What is your reason for not summoning the Artensens? It is strange they disappeared after Nehel's coronation."

The thunderous sound of a dark bay horse echoing through the court distracted them, and they turned their attention to a mysterious gray hooded rider. As soon as the equine stopped, Jumeni uncovered her head, startling them.

With careful precision, she dismounted and unloaded the long package covered by a dirty and rough cloth. She crouched down, placing it on the floor.

Consumed by curiosity, Selee mirrored Alessandro's actions by kneeling and together they opened the cloth, exposing a peculiar artifact constructed from wood and metal, hard to identify.

"What is the purpose of this?" Alessandro asked, perplexed.

Jumeni launched a severe gaze at them and took the artifact. Vertically positioning it, she inserted a small iron ball through the muzzle and retrieved a pouch of powder from her waist to fill it. Then she directed her device towards a barrel on the opposite side of the court.

The moment she pulled the trigger, a resounding blast erupted from the artifact, jolting her body as she fought against its formidable force. And instantly, it punctured a hole in the barrel, causing a steady stream of water to pour out.

When Jumeni turned around, she saw both men with expressions of impact and fear etched across their faces. She smiled and nodded, sure of herself.

Alarmed and with drawn blades, sentinels and other soldiers approached, but Alessandro quickly raised his hand to signal that everything was under control. They returned to their positions.

"What kind of magic is it?!" Selee exclaimed, still in awe.

Fascinated yet calm, Alessandro took the artifact from Jumeni's hands and examined its intricate details. "In their letters, the engineers mentioned it repeatedly, emphasizing its importance through vivid descriptions and even providing schematics." He smiled with excitement. "They call it *musket*, but no one could make it, not even a prototype. However, here Jumeni possessed the skills to craft one."

"Master, it seems like you are quite familiar with it."

"Aye, Archmage. This compact weapon is actually a miniaturized version of the cannons found in Casak, engineered for convenient portability."

"Now I understand why you were adamant about receiving a pinch of that powder!" Selee smiled at the girl.

"While it serves as a great aid, it will prove futile for tomorrow's confrontation," with the musket still in his hands, Alessandro said. "We need many of them, but we do not have enough time to manufacture them." He turned to see the Archmage. "From where did you get the powder?"

"I bought it from a merchant at the Ri who had a small bottle of Casakan powder."

"That is the other part. Our powder supply is insufficient. And importing from Casak is impossible because of the damned Korba blockade!"

9

THE MEDALLION

Through a large mirror, Fabehel stared at her own reflection. She brushed her long, graceful dark red hair, which was free of knots, to prepare for braiding it later after a bath she took.

She was preparing to spend her last night in Berrem, unsure when would be her return to the Ri after her journey to Fenn.

Fabehel felt relief as she looked at her reflection, finding comfort in the softness of her silk white nightgown, a temporary escape from her usual clothes. She combed her hair with a brush made of wood and bones.

Her gaze turned to her wheelchair, and she could not help but notice how her lingerie inadvertently exposed her limbs. She often longed for natural feet like everyone else, which is why she secretly enjoyed stealing glances at women's feet whenever she could. Despite her best efforts, she could not shake the feeling of tender jealousy that arose when she saw those women.

Despite her condition, she found contentment in herself and felt even blessed to have Alessandro as her partner.

When she looked to the left, a small table with a dagger beside of an Arankan novel book *The Grand Conspiracy* caught her attention, waiting to be concealed under her dress next day. Although she had stopped using the weapon when she arrived at the palace, she now considered wielding it once more to ensure her safety on the dangerous journey ahead.

As she placed her fingers on the wheelchair's engraved star of arrows, she turned around to take in the chamber's sight. Positioned in the center was a round table featuring a bowl of fresh fruits and a tray holding a jar of water, while a spacious bed in the corner lured from the nearby balcony. No longer reserved solely for high-ranking individuals, the room became the Empress' temporary accommodation before embarking on her voyage to Arrasem for her coronation in the Ri.

A sudden chill overcame her body as she remembered Nehel, who was then twelve years old, sharing her experience. In this very chamber, Ardek Korba appeared one night as a woman, attempting to persuade the Empress to join him. Although she never met the Lord of the Netherworld, she heard dreadful things about him. Everyone agreed that his mere presence inspired fear.

She wheeled herself onto the balcony to feel the coolness of the night and find solace, her gaze fixed on No Sak, unsure if it would hinder her chances of having a peaceful night.

Upon hearing the door creak, she spun around, assuming it was someone lacking the courage to knock before entering, especially since she was in her nightgown.

Alessandro entered, perceiving a noticeable jolt within her. "My apologies, Fabehel. I did not intend to startle," he said while closing the entrance behind. "I had to see you before your journey, even if it was just for one last moment."

"Are you here to discuss Torret Post until my patience goes down the drain?!" she asked, bothered. "I am feeling fatigued and fed up with it!"

"I did not come here to discuss any of this. I simply have a request... To spend a few moments with you before we part ways for a while."

"Alright," she replied with a nod, then pointed to the balcony. "What caused that loud noise while I was bathing earlier?"

"Jumeni introduced us to a new weapon, the musket, but unfortunately we could not use it as she had hoped."

Fabehel acknowledged with a nod. "Please have a seat and savor one of these delicious fruits. Regrettably, I do not have any wine, but you can have water instead."

With a light smile, he glanced at her and placed his black cape on the chair's backrest. Seated, he carefully examined a vivid red apple that he had grabbed. "How does a garrison like this get fresh fruits?" he asked before taking a delightful bite.

With a combination of weariness and lack of interest, she yawned before filling her cup with water. "You should hurry. I am getting tired."

"You know?" he said, while toying with his fruit. "During my troops' inspection, I came across merchants observing us, and one of them was a gypsy in a wagon displaying a table full of items that were not valuable, but still caught the eye." As he seized her expression of confusion, he took something out of his pocket. "Please, give me your hands."

Unable to resist curiosity, Fabehel complied and displayed both palms.

Alessandro placed it in her hands and discovered it.

Attached to a small chain, the iron medallion revealed a beautifully engraved orchid figure, much to her surprise.

"Take this memento in your travels. Just looking at this old medal from Kokork brought back recollections from my realm," he sighed with tender dark eyes. "I do not know how it ended up with a gypsy in Ryza, but I assumed it happened before the blockade, perhaps even before Nehel."

Gasping in surprise, Fabehel examined the ornament. Alessandro, known for his reserved nature, awed her by giving her a gift for the first time in four years—a gesture she would always treasure. "It means a lot," her lips quivered with emotion, trying to smile. "Tin is the only one who has given a meaningful gift, that dagger on the small table."

"The handkerchief you gave me at the Jarrdine Villa is a cherished possession. Its delicate aroma of roses brings your essence to life in my mind." His smile was a rare occurrence, but he nodded with one. "I do not know if I will make it through tomorrow's battle, but I wanted to give you a piece of me to keep it near your heart, as you have done with me."

Fabehel's eyes twinkled, yet she held her tears. "I have never seen that side of you before!"

Alessandro stood up from his seat and draped his black cape over his shoulders, and he approached to kiss her lips gently. "Fabehel, I love you. Take care and get a good night's sleep." As he was about to go, he felt a grab on his hand.

"Please. . . Do not go!" she pleaded. "It would be meaningful if you could hang this memento in me."

He consented to her appeal and went behind her, lifted her red hair to place the medallion around her neck and clasped it with care.

"I must confess something," she said as he placed her hair back. "We have shared countless kisses, bidding each other farewell frequently. We have weathered our fair share of fights and expressed genuine concern for one another. However, we keep our distance. We have different sleeping quarters and you do not go on dates with me. I questioned your love for me and believed you were only being protective, out of concern because of. . . my condition."

He kneeled down next to her, gazing at her face, and held both of her hands. "Do not misunderstand me. I have always loved you, but I did not want you to have the wrong impression of me. I crave your being, not your appearance."

Their eyes engaged, and Fabehel sensed pouring her heart out to him. "Although you may exhibit stubbornness and occasional outbursts, not to mention the unfortunate curse you had, my impression of you has never been negative. I acknowledge your gentle qualities, and I admire the way you treat everyone with respect." A sigh escaped from her lips, exposing her slight anxiety and the fluttering sensation in her stomach. "I heard from Corr about how you freed him from the dungeons of Sarak and how you sought a medic to heal him. Your deed captivated me!"

"I. . . do not know what to say. . .," he shrugged.

Releasing her own hands, she took hold of his, bringing them closer to her. "Can you please spend the night with me? I long to give myself to you, so that we can forever remember the moment we shared once we part ways."

"Are you certain about your decision for me to lie next to you?"

Her confident smile and nod expressed her certainty. "I need you to guide me through it, as I do not know what to do."

Alessandro lowered his head and chuckled softly.

"What is the matter?" Confused, Fabehel's smile disappeared.

He looked at her. "I would not know, since I'm in a similar condition."

"How? The Academy's students have shared countless spicy stories with me!"

"Aye, you are right. But not me," he chuckled a bit. "Back then, Marissa and I made a promise to save ourselves till marriage."

With trembling hands, her smile returned, feeling a combination of excitement and apprehension. She replied with shining eyes. "It makes this moment unique." And extended her arms. "Go on, take me."

Despite her harsh character, Alessandro caught the girl's sweet and lovely side. Agreeing to her request, he removed his cape and gently lifted her out of the wheelchair.

As they embraced one another tight, their eyes met together in a strong connection, and they sealed their lips in a passionate kiss that ignited a desire that had been absent for quite some time, overflowing with vulnerability and intimacy.

Both headed to the bed to consummate their love.

Alessandro's eyes opened as the sun's first rays streamed in through the balcony. Recognized he was in the chamber and glanced at his surroundings.

He closed his eyes and could still feel the intensity of the emotional moment he shared with Fabehel, as if it had just happened.

He turned, hoping to find his beloved on his right, and got ready to greet her with a good morning. To his surprise, there was no one beside her on the bed. Except for the lone rose resting on the pillow.

He recalled her words after they had consummated. A whisper. "I will be gone." And more words murmured in his ear. "I love you."

Seated on the bed, his eyes landed on the disarray of clothes on the floor. He scratched his head, deep in thought as a strange sensation of heartache washed over him, a longing for her he could not explain.

They had experienced separation before, even for months, while he was hunting Korbeens, and he never felt that way. Was this the result of their first experience?

The sound of horses galloping outside reached his ears, reminding him it was the day to go into battle. He rushed to get dressed, grabbed the rose, and slipped it into his pocket, feeling its soft petals against his fingertips.

By chance, a knock echoed through the room, and the door creaked open.

"Are you ready?" Marissa appeared. "Our soldiers await for you."

"Aye," he replied, straightening his disheveled clothes. Without uttering another word, he exited the chamber, leaving the First Knight standing alone.

Marissa's eyes scanned the room, taking in the bed's sight with its disheveled sheets and stains on the white fabric. Understanding the situation, she bite her lip until it bled.

"I am happy for you, Alessandro," she murmured to herself. "But your first night should have been with me!" concluded with resentment and sorrow in her heart as she could not yet accept to let her feelings go even after one tikl.

She left the chamber and slammed the door.

With a firm grip on the reins, Corr directed the amber and golden horses, pulling the cart. He wore his usual fancy clothes and sat beside Fabehel. In her total silence, he noticed the weight of sadness reflected on her face.

Under her hood, Fabehel's fingertips continuously brushed against the unfamiliar medallion.

His heightened olfactory abilities as a feline allowed him to discern a distinction in her scent from the previous night. He nodded, realizing that she had her first encounter, just as Corr also detected Alessandro's scent.

"Is everything alright, milady?"

When Fabehel looked at him, tears filled her eyes, and she could not hold back her sobs. "I crave him! I had to leave before his awakening as a farewell causes me anguish!"

IO

THE DESOLATION

The gelid moon of No Sak illuminated the land-scape, casting an ethereal glow altogether with the brown-green No Nunn. In the darkness, their light revealed an abandoned road that had once been a vital artery for merchants, bustling with the energy of constant trade.

Vasso chose this path that would protect Carlissa, the *Ykarte*. Her resolute decision to head north to the desert in Aranka was absolute and final. Her determination to meet the Divine Empress never faltered, even when he could not fathom a way to make it happen. And sometimes, she would break the silence with her enchanting melody.

Assisted by the moon's gentle glow, he took in his surroundings. The old road, scarred and worn, connected a barren, charred grassland to a decimated jungle, revealing a fierce battle that had taken place just half a tikl ago between the dragons and the Kasnasgos on the outskirts of the burgh of Berkork. This was the path that Vasso and Carlissa intended to traverse, heading towards the heart of the ravaged population.

While in Kao, Vasso heard news from Overseer Akartaki about the impact of Korbas and Korbeens in Berrem. Also about the red mantises in the Trunke Territory on the continent of Ryza. However, no realm had been as severely affected as Casak itself.

When Vasso was just fourteen, the repressive rule of Lord Orssandro Vykar forced him to leave his home in Casak, to fight a war he never wanted. Thankfully, the elvish sisterhood took Vasso and the other children away to the floating island of Kao.

Surrounded by other children in paradise, the unseen suffering happened just below him.

Now, he had the chance to witness the desolation firsthand as he gazed upon the ravaged scene.

He turned his head to check if Carlissa was still behind him and continued onward.

He heard a sudden screech that startled and made him draw his sword. The sound of flapping wings caught his attention, and he turned to see a flock of birds scattering in fear from the ravaged palm trees.

When he turned back again, he realized Carlissa had vanished without a trace. In a dilemma, Vasso debated whether to confront a hidden danger or search for her.

Vasso had to hide in a bush. The screeching grew louder and closer, loading the air with an unsettling cacophony.

But he could not stop thinking about Carlissa, yet he made a bet with himself that she would be safe and postponed his search for her until he felt secure from whatever it was.

He regretted taking this abandoned road. The people back at Porkork warned him not to choose this path, whispering about the lurking Korbeens and the occasional presence of dragons.

However, he could not remain hidden there. He had to make his way to the burgh.

Filled with courage and determination, he gathered his belongings, drew his sword from its sheath, and continued his journey along the road. His heart pounded and his cold sweat mingled with persistence.

As he approached, the first buildings came into view as their inner lights flickered from the glow of castor oil lamps.

He halted. Behind him, he could feel a presence that sent chills down his bone.

He turned.

The sight of a large black dragon with its piercing red eyes staring shuddered him.

Paralyzed.

He stood there, feeling lost and unsure of his next move. Should he flee or fight it?

He chose the first option and sprinted as fast as possible, even though the slippery mud made him difficult to hasten. With no hesitation, the dragon chased after him with murderous intent.

When Vasso reached the limits of the burgh, dozens of local sentinels on horseback galloped towards the dragon with their lances raised. They fought the creature with all their strength, pushing it away.

The dragon's wings drooped as it waded back to the jungle, as its disappointment was clear.

The local sentries held Vasso for interrogation but eventually released him once they became convinced he was not a Korbeen.

Late at night, as he exited from the barracks, the gelid moon of No Sak greeted him while No Nunn had disappeared. The desolation and destruction that had befallen Berkork was obvious, once a bustling and vibrant burgh. The place had once been renowned for its Academy, where students like the Pillars Alessandro Eskar and

Marissa Taskar, along with other children of influential figures, studied.

They gave him a reprimand for venturing down the infested road and cautioned him to stay at the inn until morning.

Nearby, he stumbled upon a dilapidated inn. However, all he desired was to spend his time at the tavern, indulging in a drink—even though he had never tasted brew or wine before.

As he entered, an even greater sense of desolation embraced him. The chairs and tables, in their dilapidated state, had undergone many repairs. Despite being clean, the interior of the space was in a state of utter decay, with the windows sealed using wooden planks. Signs of a prosperous past were visible in the tavern.

To his surprise, Carlissa had occupied a seat at a table. She was by herself, motionless, with no food or drink, and showing no response to his presence.

The taverner approached the youngster. "Do you know that maid?"

"Aye, sir. Why?"

"Earlier, she arrived and asked to sit and wait for you, but she refused to purchase any food or drink, despite my insistence."

"I will get for myself. What do you have?"

"Rooten fish and stale wine."

"Is there something of quality that you can offer?" he sighed, wishing to have something in his stomach. "I will pay for it."

"Only rotten fish and stale wine, lad. As you may realize, we are enduring difficult times."

Vasso shrugged his shoulders and reluctantly accepted the taverner's offer. Taking a seat beside her, he launched her a disapproving look. "Disappearing right when I needed help the most while facing a dragon!"

Through her round, thick glasses, Carlissa turned her face to look at him. "Why? To risk the Empress' home? Priorities are to be chosen. Otherwise, I would turn myself to the darkness."

The realization hit him hard—she would abandon him, even let him die, just to achieve her purpose.

The taverner placed a rusted and metallic plate in front of Vasso, with fish that looked far from appetizing. The cup of wine that accompanied it emitted a putrid smell.

The youngster refused to touch the meal, paid for it, and redirected his attention towards Carlissa. "Why did you select me if your intention was to mistreat me?"

"I have chosen you because your innocence and purity shield me from darkness," she concluded.

II

RED MOON

As the sun descended, a palpable sense of uncertainty hung in the air. As thousands made their way southwest from Seled Post, their hurried movements created a chaotic symphony. Every soldier, every aspiring knight, and every official revealed tension on their faces. Their fates were unknown, and as they inhaled the fresh morning air, some could not help but wonder if it would be their last breath.

In complete silence, save for the persistent beat of hooves, the two Pillars at the front advanced on their horses, Breeze and Twist, with Kekten and Selee following behind.

When Ser Marissa turned to her left, she caught sight of Alessandro placing a handkerchief under his nose to detect the scent of roses from Fabehel's perfume. As she witnessed, a wave of envy surged through her, but she composed herself and spoke. "You sent Nehel with Ser Juni and the maids. Fabehel departed with Corr. Except for Dessidere and Marshal Keleana. Is that the Guild we hope for?"

With a serious expression, Alessandro replied with his eyes fixed on her. "You know, Nehel is not ready for the imminent battle. The risk of losing an Empress is something we can not afford to take," he sighed. "Fabehel has left to accomplish her task, but she will return shortly."

Marissa observed his quivering lips as he spoke his beloved's name, realizing that beneath his calm exterior, their separation tormented him. She set aside her own selfish emotions and embraced empathy for him. "I am aware of the last night. How are you feeling?"

His gaze shifted forward while driving Breeze. Silent.

The First Knight felt compassion for him, yet also longed to comprehend his circumstances. Her feelings for him remained intact as she continued to harbor both affection and concern. Since they first met at four years old, their bond was unbreakable, making it impossible for her to change her affections, especially after the Gesha.

"Halt!" Alessandro shouted as he drew his greatsword from his back, wary.

With a single gesture, he signaled the others to un-sheathe their blades. Their murmurs of fear resounded through the crowd.

"Quiet!" Alessandro's voice rang out with strict author-ity. The movement of the leaves from the bushes under the trees caught his attention, and he listened, hoping to hear the distinct sound of a mantis. Contrary to what he had heard from witnesses and Kekten's assurance, there was no flapping or hissing. However, the vibrant vegetation hinted at the presence of something else.

The tense silence fell over the group as they grasped their weapons, their eyes fixed on the approaching figure.

A bunch of armed men and women on horseback ap-peared from the left, their gazes fixed in surprise as they encountered the Imperial Line. The group comprised roughly fifty people from various regions of Aranka. Their attire, a mix of everyday clothing, reflected their connec-tion to the sea.

Alessandro studied their leader, a blond man with long hair and piercing blue eyes. He could not help but notice the leader's strong, muscular arms. "State your name and explain why you are here!"

As he held his horse, the man bowed his head with deep respect. "Captain Kanden at your service, Master! And all these behind me are my crew from *The Wandering*, a merchant ship stationed in Sarrem. Because of the Beyond Sea blockade, we had no choice but to remain there." He paused, then continued. "We heard about the emergency at Torret Post, and we rushed to assist the Divine Empress in her *Deken Karsaker*."

"Do you understand the immense risks at play in this confrontation?" the Pillar asked, gesturing to his people to holster their weapons, ensuring that no immediate danger threatened. "You still have time to reconsider and go back home."

"What home, Master? Aranka is gone, and the once accessible Beyond Sea is now unreachable. We are outsiders in a foreign land, forced to accept the most undesirable occupations in order to subsist. No matter the forthcoming sacrifices, it is a mutual choice."

"Very well," he said, nodding in agreement. "Captain, please stand beside me and join us in this battle. We welcome those who seek to reclaim our world and honor the Divine Empress."

Kanden thanked the gesture and ordered his people to blend into the line, intending to follow the Pillars behind. However, Marissa asked him to stand by her side with kindness.

All resumed their course.

Marissa examined him in awe, captivated by his unique appearance of clear brown hairs. Based on her geographic lessons in the Academy, she recalled that people with blond hair and blue eyes were typically from Mid Aranka, while those with red hair were from the north and the ones with black hair, like the vanished monarchs, were from the south.

"We will place an encampment near but safe from these monsters, Captain," Alessandro revealed the plans. "Since the mantises rest during the dark hours, our plan is to reach the post at night. But we must proceed in complete silence, as even the slightest sound can alert them to our presence. With just one small creak, they become alert, putting our lives at risk."

The night arrived, and it felt like more than just a coincidence. The red moon, a symbol of fire and blood, cast an eerie glow. Its dim, opaque color and modest size made it ineffective at providing illumination in the dark.

The advantage of the darkness was that it allowed the Imperial Line to move covertly towards their destination. However, it also posed a risk as the mantids blended into the night, making them difficult to spot.

Alessandro kept his promise, and they had an encampment to rest in until nightfall. According to the plans from the Pillars, the caravan would traverse the vast clearing that lay between them and Torret Post.

Peering through the spyglass from the encampment, Kekten shook his head as he observed their destination hidden behind the bushes. "Indeed, the palisades received damaged. It is in worse condition than when I left."

"You mentioned your escape through an underground passage," Alessandro pointed out, while observing the post at a distance with his mere eyes. "Will we be able to go through together?"

"Indeed, the guards closed the passage after my exit, Master. A mantis could also enter that way."

"Dammit!" Alessandro muttered in frustration as he snatched the spyglass and examined the post. Kekten confirmed the post's damage, clear in its silhouette. However, the lack of light during the night hindered his ability to assess the level of destruction. However, his eyes caught sight of glowing spots, hinting at the presence of bonfires and torches within. "If the night was silent and the mantises sleeping. Why did all you not escape to safety?"

"Do you know that if they abandon Torret Post, we lose Berrem?!" Marissa shouted, annoyed, shoving him by the shoulder. "Are you damn dull?!"

"Aye, you are right. . .," he replied to her assertion with a startling look. "I have exhausted my mind with fruitless solutions, you daft!."

"I am also damn tired!" she answered, angered.

"Calm down, lads!" Selee advised to both Pillars. "It is crucial to maintain composure and stay vigilant."

"Aye, Archmage. My apologies," Alessandro nodded.

"Even if we are not confident in its outcome," Selee advised. "We should still adhere to the plan. The best advice I can give you is to begin right away."

The weight of his words hung heavy in the air, causing a collective surge of heartbeats and a sickening feeling in their stomachs.

With crossed arms and leaning on the tree, Captain Kanden observed them in calm and serenity.

"Ser Marissa, as a Pillar and overseer of the military branch of the Jyistereerk, the last word is yours." Alessandro spoke.

She hesitated at first, but nodded. "Let us begin!"

In response to her order, thousands prepared and followed the instructions mentioned earlier by the Pillars. They regrouped, taking extra caution to avoid mounting horses and instead pulled them by the reins, walking slowly to prevent any noise. With trepidation, they navigated through the darkness, avoiding light and potential obstacles.

Although they could reach the post in an instant, the Pillars believed it was wiser to arrive safely, even if it required an entire night. At steady and slow steps, they went.

Little by little, the line pushed through the thicket of trees and steadily advanced across the clearing. The dim light from No Ta only hushed visible silhouettes in the surroundings.

Alessandro and Marissa guided their horses in a relaxed stroll, with Captain Kanden and Selee trailing behind.

With Admiral Kekten in the lead, the line followed his expert guidance, trusting him to navigate them to their destination.

It was a slow, muted rhythm. Their calm masked the fear that coursed through their veins.

Though unseen, everyone felt the mantises, creating an eerie atmosphere.

It took them a while, but they finally approached the nearest palisade.

Kekten used a special small lighter to signal his people guarding the post.

The gates slowly creaked open, providing a much-needed respite for the Imperial Line.

Out of nowhere, a sneeze broke the silence, startling everyone.

All heads turned in panic.

A sudden cacophony of terrifying hisses and screeches loaded the air.

Marissa's eyes grew wide with fear, and her scream pierced. "Go inside!"

In a rush, they mounted their horses and the sound of hooves thundered as they galloped towards Torret Post.

As they exited from inside the palisades, the archers knelt and aimed their arrows towards the darkness, creating an intimidating barrier for those entering amidst the chaos.

The sound of thousands of flapping wings grew louder, instilling fear in the Imperials.

As Alessandro and Marissa dismounted at the gates, urged everyone to enter quickly.

Archmage Selee gestured with his hands, summoning an unseen barrier to protect most of the group, acknowledging his limited magical capabilities, unable to protect everyone.

From the rear of the caravan, piercing cries of death reached their ears. Everyone realized the mantises had unleashed their murderous instincts.

"Keep running!" As Alessandro drew his greatsword, he cried orders to his soldiers.

As Marissa unsheathed her blade, her face trembled with a mix of determination and fear.

The last horses that entered had a haunting presence as they dragged the lifeless bodies of fallen soldiers slain by the creatures.

Selee rushed inside as the Pillars loomed behind him.

As the archers entered, the gates closed.

A chorus of voices called out, ordering everyone to put out their bonfires and torches.

The darkness was almost complete, with only the moon cast a faint scarlet glow.

Silence settled once more, as the mantises ceased their movements, blending back into their surroundings.

"A sneeze!" Alessandro's furious shout resounded through his people. "A damn sneeze killed my soldiers! I will hang that wrecked fool!"

The crowd behind the gate watched in stunned silence as the Pillar scolded without control. A clear mixture of fear and surprise showed on their faces. Meanwhile, a group of sentinels wrapped the bodies of the deceased, about two dozen offering silent prayers before placing them in a pile.

The locals from Torret Post, all members of the Imperial Guard, held torches as they stood as witnesses.

"Stop it!" Marissa shoved him away by the chest. "I am certain it was unintentional!"

Captain Kanden embraced him, trying to halt his bold advance and whispered in his ear. "Calm down, Master! It is not worth and let us look ahead instead."

With a look of struggle on his face, Alessandro pushed him away, abandoning his original intention and agreeing to his advice. He stared deeply into his blue eyes. "I find it interesting that despite our recent introduction, you treat me as if we have known each other for a while. Why is it?"

"Being a thirty-five-years-old captain with broad experience, I had encountered individuals from all walks of life, specially in *The Wandering*. I treat all of them as brothers."

"Can you please put an end to that foolishness?!" Marshal Keleana made her way among her people and intervened, bothered. "And let us discuss the mantises that the threat persists!"

Keleana's almond eyes, displaying signs of profound tiredness, inexplicably gravitated towards Kanden, as faint scratches marked her olive skin. Despite her forty-four years old, her face bore the deep lines and wrinkles of someone who had spent years battling against the mantises during the last tikl.

"Marshal, please elaborate," he requested, with Marissa and Kanden both eager to hear the reply.

"I need all women and men to be watchful, as these creatures are no longer dormant. They await the first ray of sunlight in the morning," she nodded. "Master, Ser Marissa, Archmage, please accompany me to my quarters."

As Marissa followed her, she came upon a place that felt familiar and unknown. Memories of the post flooded her mind, reminding her of the unfortunate incident with *The*

Seneschal. However, the place was still under construction, with timber trunks being installed to create palisades. Until now, she had not had the chance to return to the place, but she noticed it was overcrowded and had an older appearance. She learned from Nehel and Alessandro that they had dispatched reinforcements to the post to counter the ongoing mantid incursions. Yet, the number of troops was still not enough to contain them.

They walked alongside the Marshal towards a single-story wooden building at the center, passing by quarters and barracks, until they reached her personal chamber.

Keleana carefully arranged the candles on the table next to the map, moving aside the Arankan volume named *The Grand Conspiracy* aside. As she scanned the group, she could not help but notice someone missing. "Where is the Divine Empress? I had the understanding she would be with you."

"While passing by The Highlands, an incident occurred involving a Korba, and we determined that sending her back was the safest choice," Alessandro replied.

With a nod, the Marshal started pointing out key locations on the map. "The mantises had stayed at the center of Trunke for quite some time, where a nest was located. Our scout braved the mantid realm and made it to its very core. Upon his return, he shared unsettling news." She gasped, unsure of their reaction. "They are cannibals, but they feed themselves from the green mantises."

"What does it have to do with the current crisis?"

"Unlike us or the Korbas, they do not get territorial gains as possessions. They plan to venture deeper into

Berrem in search of these domesticated mantises. They already killed and exterminated the wild ones in Trunke." She shook her head. "But they want to go over us because we are standing in their way."

"These red mantises were not only vicious and tainted, but their evilness seemed unlimited." Archmage Selee explained. "We shall eliminate these mantises at all costs."

"They are starving because there are no more green mantises left. Therefore, they are building up all the atrocities."

"What shall we do, Marshal?" Alessandro asked.

"The same advice I had given to all my fighters, Master," she shrugged. "Kill them by cutting their heads. This is the only way. We are only a bunch against many, and pray to the goddesses for our lives."

A silence reigned over the group.

"I must have a word with my soldiers," Alessandro responded and walked outside, trailed by Selee.

Marissa was the only one who stayed, and with a quick glance, she noticed a sword hanging on the wall. "I notice you still possess that weapon you once wielded against me."

"It is a memento from that jousting," Keleana replied with a head gesture. "The intensity of our fight is still fresh in my mind. I had a second chance to earn my place in The Guild and serve the Divine Empress thanks to that combat."

"Since Nehel's coronation, our tasks and the distance between us prevented us from getting to know each other well." Marissa affirmed. "Do you continue to hold a grudge against me?"

They exchanged stares, silence, no replies.

Keleana approached and planted a swift and affectionate kiss on her lips.

Marissa felt shaken.

"What do you think?" Keleana asked with a tender look. And she left behind the place, leaving her alone in the confusion.

Marissa left the chamber and immediately began searching for her pupils. During her visual inspection, she discovered Branni, a fifteen-year-old girl hoping to become an Empress' knight, sitting under a small wooden shed. She had placed her sword on the muddy ground and did not mind, as she appeared to be crying with her face hidden in her arms against the legs.

Ser Marissa came across her a year ago when she was examining the reinstated Carret Post. Branni begged her to join her group of aspirants and noticed her slender physique, which seemed unsuitable for a knight and incapable of wielding a heavy weapon like a greatsword. But Ser Marissa found her insistence bothersome, so she agreed to accept her on the condition of a rigorous training.

Her body had gained strength, making her one of the most prominent disciples after one year.

"What had occurred?" Marissa asked, approaching her.

"I killed them!" Showing a wet face with tears and sweat, Branni replied between uncontrollable sobs. "I could not stop myself from sneezing, and killed them!"

For a moment, the First Knight was startled and unsure of how to handle her sudden feelings. She was unsure whether to scold or comfort her. However, she concluded that her guilt was enough. "It was unforeseen, my dear. No one can control a sneeze even in the crucial moments."

"I. . . I. . ." she shook her head with trembling lips, unable to speak. "I killed them!"

Marissa's blood boiled as she shoved Branni's chest with the blade from the ground. "Stop damn little girl crying, you fool! This is the way of the battle whether you like! Your fault or not! So stand up and fight as a damn brave knight you want to be and not like a dull one!"

Stunned, the girl stared at Marissa, stopped all sobs, and stood to run and join her comrades later.

Marissa made a personal commitment to never disclose the person behind the sneeze as she observed her leaving.

With a crate as his seat, Alessandro used his teeth to pull at a piece of dry meat. While observing the Torret Post, he noticed the soldiers and guards displaying clear signs of anxiety, whether they were on duty or gathered around the bonfires.

Everyone expected the sunrise. However, everyone dreaded it.

The first rays of sunlight might be the last sight they ever see in their lives.

Alessandro observed from afar Captain Kanden's natural leadership as he treated his group like his siblings. Losing everything with the Gesha, it was understandable that they would act like a family. Comparing himself to Kanden, the crew and their leader impressed him and questioned himself about his role as a Pillar.

Selee appeared, offering him a canteen of water and a light smile. "Are you envious of the captain?" The Archmage, being a wise old man, picked up on his curiosity and could predict his thoughts. No magic was necessary to use.

"Not envious, but eager to learn from him," he replied after swallowing water. "I question if being a Pillar is sufficient for my role. I drove Nehel off and searched for the one who sneezed, even it was unintentional."

The Archmage sat beside him and spoke with tenderness. "Not two men are the same. And it is natural to be a human." He sighed. "Even though four years have gone by, you still have more to learn."

"I am a Pillar because Nehel chose me."

"No, it was because you earned this title!" he nodded with a smile.

Alessandro made an agreement gesture at the time he placed a fresh red rose under his nose.

Selee noticed the flower and understood with surprise. According to Arankan customs, when a maiden gives a rose to her suitor after their first night together, it signified an unspoken intention to spend her life with him. As a Casakan, he thought Alessandro was unaware and remained quiet about it. His blue eyes shifted towards the night sky, where he spotted a streak of red and blue, which signaled the sun's arrival. "It is said that the stillness comes before the tempest. That stillness is ending as the creatures are about to come."

The Archmage's statement was accurate. Using banners, Keleana and Kekten, along with some of their men, signaled everyone.

Every soldier, vagrant, guard, aspiring knight, and volunteer assumed their positions with fear written across their faces.

The much-dreaded and expected battle was just about to start.

The watcher's gaze remained fixed on the dense forest leading to Trunke as the sunrise appeared in the middle of a light haze, while sweat drops streamed down his skin. With his lance in hand, he stood on the last level behind the wooden palisade. His breath emitted white smoke at a quick pace.

The tranquility of the morning concealed an imminent death.

Everyone knew it.

The moment the red moon No Ta vanished, a feeling of fear and doubt spread among the thousands inside the Torret Post.

Keleana's small almond eyes observed the watcher, expectant, from the ground. She awaited with apprehension for any sign from the adversaries. But all she could see was him waving a small white flag as a hint that no sight from the red mantises was clear.

"What da ya think is happening?" Kekten, behind her, whispered in dread.

"It is strange," she replied. "It is a usual occurrence for mantises to be present at the break of dawn, especially if they were awakened in the night, but they are not here this time."

Alessandro, Kanden and Selee were near and heard her.

Marissa was in a remote location, taking care of her pupils and urging them to be courageous. Apart from Ser Juni, the older student had been training for three years and the rest of her group were under sixteen. The inexperienced youngsters were not ready to be part of a battle, and this was their first test.

Marshal Keleana once again signaled to the watcher, and by sudden, a strange gust of chilly wind materialized. All she got back from him was another waving of the white flag.

Ignoring the watcher's shrug, Marshal Keleana persisted until he ascended a small ladder and employed a spyglass for improved observation.

"Did you really encounter these monsters?" Alessandro questioned, unsure. "As per your summoning letter, you had to face them every single day."

"Every day, we had to face them," she responded, glancing at her watcher and shielding her eyes with her hand. "It is odd that they are not attacking us this morning."

The watcher, finding nothing, shook and tossed the spyglass to the floor. He faced the other direction and gestured with his arms to note that there was nothing.

Out of nowhere and in a daunting manner, a flying Korba materialized from behind the palisade and viciously tore off the watcher's head with its snout. From a higher altitude, the headless body plunged and hit the ground.

The other guards announced a flock of Korbas and red mantises flying over the forest against Torret Post.

Keleana and Kekten wasted no time in joining the guards to protect the palisades and await their arrival from above.

When his soldiers and volunteers rushed to help the guards, Alessandro unsheathed his greatsword.

Selee used hand gestures to create an invisible field over the post, uncertain of its ability to withstand the imminent incursion.

Ser Marissa and her pupils sprinted toward the gates, drew their blades, and prepared to protect them.

Out of nowhere, a chaotic and noisy chorus of hisses and screeches enveloped the area, attempting to gain entry. Despite their best efforts, the army of vicious creatures could not breach the magic field despite their unending insistence, allowing the defenders to gain some much-needed time.

The horses inside cried in panic.

The guards and vagrants strategically positioned five ballistas behind Marissa's pupils, aiming their massive arrows at the gates to defend against the creatures, especially the dragons.

Before the field was created, the same Korba who killed the watcher infiltrated Torret Post and fought off a dozen guards stabbing it with their lances. The dragon took two lives, but ultimately met its own demise when a lance pierced its heart.

Without delay, an immense number of mantises completely covered the palisades, creating a scene of utter depravation. Meanwhile, groups of Korbas mercilessly circled above.

"We will not endure!" Kanden exclaimed while grabbing his blade, observing his chaotic surrounding. "Does it make sense to fight against a large group when we are only a few?"

"We are seven thousand against a sea of monsters!" Faced with the situation, Alessandro screamed and wielded his blade, feeling overwhelmed. "I did not foresee the darned Korbas and these scoundrels to join forces!"

While the magic field weakened, Selee remained resilient and resisted the dragons' persistence, though he was on his knees.

Branni questioned Ser Marissa about their chances of survival as they witnessed their comrades and the gates being destroyed by the mantises' attacks.

"I believe the only thing we can do is to pray to the goddesses!" As she spoke, her dark skin glistened with sweat.

The gates crumbled under the aggressive hissing and pushing. As they fell, the red mantises entered and began a murderous rampage, leaving a trail of destruction as they slaughtered anything in their way as lifeless bodies collapsed to the ground.

The soldiers shot the ballistas, but even the arrows killed many were not enough to stop the advancement.

The magical field disappeared, and Selee fell unconscious. The Korbas began their relentless attack.

Surrounded by chaos, Alessandro and Kanden stood side by side, readying their blades, bracing themselves for the swift and ferocious wave of mantises about to crash against them.

Leading her group of pupils, Marissa prepared herself for the oncoming threat. With her sword hard gripped in her hand, she closed her eyes, bracing for the inevitable clash with the charging mantises and dragons awaiting her death.

Without warning, a fierce tempest descended upon them, causing the palisades to be whisked skyward and unsecured items to be plucked from the ground, leaving Torret Post uncovered. As a dust storm suddenly appeared, it nearly blinded everyone, causing them to shift their focus from self-defense to prevent themselves from being swept away by the raging wind.

It was nearly impossible to see. But Alessandro, with one hand over his eyes and clutching a root from the ground, dropping his blade. He could watch how a massive multitude of creatures rapidly disintegrated and merged into dust, meeting a swift demise.

The screeches and hisses ceased, leaving only the sound of the wind.

The sudden tempest quickly subsided, causing the large timber woods near the palisades to cascade down like rain in a remote, unpopulated clearing between forests, ensuring everyone's safety.

Peace came back, and the monsters were gone. Dead. Without a trace of them.

A multitude of frightened horses galloped and vanished into the forest on the Berrem side.

Covered in white dust like everyone else, Alessandro stood up in a mix of surprise and dread, locking eyes with Kanden and Marissa.

Exhausted and in need of rest, Selee crumbled onto the ground, yearning for a moment to catch his breath.

Shaken by the sight, Keleana observed the ruins of Torret Post, feeling a sense of profound loss after investing years of effort into its construction. As she turned around, she noticed Kekten on the ground, unconscious, but nodded to reassure herself that he was alright.

Everybody was aware of who had caused the tempest, and despite the quick and devastating destruction, there was a sense of relief and gratitude that she had arrived just in time to prevent a major tragedy, even though losing many lives had already occurred.

Every gaze converged in a single direction.

Empress Nehel, as a small but formidable figure, stood on a hill with her arms raised and breath coming fast, after defeating the countless invaders that had threatened to wipe out Torret Post.

Behind her, Ser Juni dropped to his knees in awe with his eyes widening in astonishment.

It earned the name of *The Battle of the Tempest*, and people never forgot it thereafter. A pivotal moment in the young Jyistereerk's history, a stage of the *Deken Karsaker*.

12

TEMPEST POST

A s Nehel leaned against a tree, seated on the grass, taking a refreshing sip from her canteen, she could not help but notice the curious gazes of some of the Guild members and other onlookers, who had gathered around her. Her hazel eyes met the gaze of each person, and she could see the surprise and fear reflected on her.

To shelter her from the internal cold that came along with her fatigue after the incident, a guard had placed a warm waki fur on her.

Exhausted and leaning on a stick for support, Selee spoke with a tired nod. "How did you unleash all your power, Divine Empress?"

"It was you, Archmage," she replied, showing a semblance of surprising serenity. "You always taught me to control myself, to avoid consequences that come with them."

"How? I do not quite understand yet."

With a sigh and a shake of her head, she took another sip from her canteen and carried on. "Each time I had to restrain it, my strength grew stronger. I remembered you, but this time chose not to listen to your words and I unleashed all my strength to stop them."

"Are you implying that your strength is not something you can intentionally trigger?" Alessandro placed his hand on his chin and inquired with a messy appearance.

"You have said so, uncle," she sighed and shrugged. "When back in The Highlands we encountered with that Korba from the cave, I could not confront it because I restrained myself, with hesitation."

"There is plenty left to uncover about your mystical state, Divine Empress," Archmage Selee assured.

Nehel presented a quick smile and started scanning the surrounding crowd. "I believe there is someone from the seas that came with his crew to defend the Jyistereerk. Can he reveal himself so that I can finally meet him?"

From the crowd, emerging, the blond man knelt before the Empress, plunging his blade into the ground. "I, Captain Kanden, along with my crew from *The Wandering*, pledge our service to you, Divine Empress."

She smiled. "Stand up and hold my hand, please."

Kanden astonished everyone by obeying and holding her hand with the utmost respect. Her request even surprised him.

"I have waited for you since long, Captain," she declared with a kind nod but with a brief stare at Keleana. "Join my Guild and bring your crew to my Jyistereerk."

"It is an honor!" he could not hide his excitement, with an emotional smile.

The crowd witnessed in awe. Some gave murmurs of disapproval to a stranger's invitation to the Guild, but ultimately, they restrained themselves and agreed to the Empress' petition.

Amidst the wreckage near the destroyed Torret Post, Marissa affectionately touched her forehead to Brisel's. It had been years since she had smiled so much. She could not stop petting him.

Brisel replied her with tender hisses.

Ser Juni noticed them seated on a fallen trunk, showing signs of fatigue and contemplating removing his armor for some relief. He found it difficult to process what he had witnessed in the rapid battle.

After seeing his discomfort, Marissa turned to him and asked. "Juni, what is the matter with you? Despite your usual confidence, you seem unsettled, as if you have seen a ghost."

"It is. . . Nehel, Ser Marissa," he stammered. "I mean, I have seen her using her abilities, but I. . . never in the way she manifested."

"What she did was impressive. I can not deny it," she sighed and sat beside him, touching his arm as a solace, reading his struggling face. "Are you conflicted?"

"I might agree," he looked towards the sky with wet eyes, not knowing if to cry or not. "I had the feeling that being a knight was an honorable and heroic pursuit. Even she did not approve of my naming. Yet, I was unaware of the burden that it carries."

"I believe Nehel disapproved of your naming because of the burden. You are her closest friend. She is trying to protect you."

"Aye, Ser Marissa. She is trying to protect me, but not because of the burden," shrugging, he lapsed into silence. "I must make a confession."

Marissa grew concerned about his coming revelation.

"I have kissed her. . . well. . ., she kissed me. . ., I am not sure. . .," once more he stammered.

"May I have a word with Juni?"

Much to their surprise, Nehel was standing right in front of both knights, interrupting their conversation.

"Sure, I will leave the two of you alone," Marissa responded with a serious nod, and startled not because of her presence but of Juni's declaration. She mounted Brisel, gasped with nostalgia, and rode with him towards the ruins of Torret Post.

Juni had at first the impression that she was upset or angry. But besides her obvious fatigue, he noticed in her a serene expression on her face, as if she had released herself from a weight.

Nehel presented herself in her characteristic leather attire she always used for travels or in her spare time, highlighting her slim figure, with the waki fur at her back. "Juni, I can sense your confusion. What is causing it? Or do you find yourself afraid of me once more?"

The Second Knight stood up and gave an answer. "May I speak casually, missy?"

"Aye, go ahead."

"Even though I have shared a kiss with you, I do not know what is my stance. What are you?"

She lowered her gaze and looked at the ground, before raising her eyes to glance at him with affectionate hazel eyes. "Before you I am simply Lakia," she exhaled with a nod. "I wish for a moment you forget I am an Empress that possesses special abilities."

"Alright. So?"

"All I am is a girl who desires your affection and presence because of that unique closeness."

With widened eyes and hands on his waist, Juni was at a loss for words. He had to take some gasps and some instant to find the right words. "Then forget about me being a knight for a moment and let us delve into my sentiments. Are you aware of my struggles to love you?"

Nehel smiled in a way she rarely does, allowing her waki fur to fall to the ground. "You just admitted your love for me, even though you are torn!"

"I truly love you, missy!" Emerging tears filled his eyes as he exclaimed. "But what I saw earlier conflicts me. . . I am only a humble troubadour's son wishing to love a mighty divinity!"

Serenely, she approached him and gazed into his eyes, maintaining her smile. She held onto both of his hands and gave a confirming nod. "Are you aware of the meaning behind my name? Lakia?"

"I suppose it is some kind of Molkan name that means *The Unfortunate*," he answered, shrugging.

"Aye, it is Molkan. But it has a deep meaning other than being unfortunate," she sighed. "Mother Venka had lost her childhood friend, her child within, and her husband. All she desired was to regain the lost love. While she sought the favor of many goddesses, it was Lakia, the cursed Goddess of Love, whom she prayed to the most."

"You received her name."

"Mother Venka taught me a prayer to express gratitude, as I was her miracle," she shut her eyes in a state of devotion. "*Lakia Terk del Terk uka Lakia del Terk arjk Amn. Del Lakia amin dishu ash. Del Lakia yert Tray berk Semke.*"

"Can you tell me the significance of the prayer, missy?"

Nehel opened and showed her expressive hazel eyes with tenderness. "Give us that love as a priceless treasure that can not be bought or bartered. Love that does not know distinctions. Thy love that blesses and offers itself as an invaluable gift for the soul despite the misfortunes."

They said nothing else, but their lips moved closer.

Juni's eyes shifted when he spotted one of Marissa's pupils approaching, and he nodded as a permission to speak just as Nehel turned around.

"Divine Empress, Ser Juni," he said with reverence. "Master Alessandro has instructed me to let you know we should be prepared for the ceremony."

Even *The Battle of the Tempest* was short-lived. Under the efforts of Marshal Keleana and the brave men and women who fought against the ruthless mantises, the situation only grew worse since the Jyistereerk's foundation. This prompted cities, especially Ri, to start a widespread mobilization in response, involving the Guild and the Empress herself.

With no exceptions or distinctions, everyone cooperated and worked swiftly to ensure it was ready before dusk. Given the need to honor and offer a proper farewell to the fallen, the funerals had to be arranged without delay.

The toll of four years had claimed the lives of eight hundred, but it was this one night that would add two hundred more to the list of the mourned.

Previously, the Imperial Guard, but still called vagrants despite the fusion with the Berremen sentinels, had reserved a clearing inside the Torret Post, especially to burn the bodies during funeral ceremonies. It was not possible now.

The surviving seven thousand gathered wood from the timber trunks, creating piles across the clearing. They worked together, even the Guild members, also arranging the bodies.

Following his usual protocol, Admiral Kekten, accompanied by a group of men, identified the corpses, hoping to notify to their families if they had. In the meantime, a scribe etched their names on a papyrus scroll.

Not too far from the forest, a bustling group of cooks and women, some from the nearby Seled Post, prepared food and distributed it to everyone. Nehel and Juni, setting aside their roles, joined to help feed the very people who had fought for the Jyistereerk.

Branni and the other pupils had searched all day for the horses that had escaped and sought refuge in the forest. Eventually, they rounded up most of them and corral them in a temporary enclosure they had constructed.

Just before dusk, Archmage Selee made a final revision while walking alongside the funerary piles. Alessandro and Marissa followed behind, approaching Nehel, who was enjoying a meal next to Juni. "It is time, Divine Empress. We must start the ceremony."

Seated on a trunk, she widened her eyes in surprise, suspended her spoon of stew in mid-air over the bowl of stew. "What shall I do now, Archmage?"

He smiled, acknowledging her unfamiliarity with the various protocols she still had to familiarize herself with. "In the begone times, it was customary for the monarchs to not only lead their men into battles but also to conduct funerary ceremonies, offering words of encouragement."

She gasped, then exhaled, passing the bowl to Juni, startling him. "Very well. Let us start."

Selee led the way as the Empress stood up and walked, Alessandro and Marissa followed her. It took them a while to traverse the vast expanse until they were within proximity of the piles.

Nehel examined both the piles themselves and the lifeless bodies that lay upon them. She could not help but listen to the whispers of the fallen, as many of them struggled to accept their departure from life, remaining in a state of limbo as they made their way to the underworld. As she grappled with the presence of death, her sadness became clear to Juni, who only he understood her intimately. The Empress attempted to mask her emotions and projected an aura of tranquility as she addressed the expectant crowd.

Keleana sensed an unusual presence as she approached Kanden, but that did not deter her from requesting his crew's help in preparing the torches and igniting the piles when the time was right.

The Captain nodded, feeling a strong connection with the Marshal that he could not quite grasp, and everyone immediately complied with her request.

The guards listened to Selee's advice and used the remnants of the woods to construct a platform in the gap between the ruins of Torret Post and the funerary piles.

As all eyes looked on, the Empress stepped onto the platform with a smile that seemed not to be authentic. When she glanced at the crowd, she felt uneasy about delivering the speech, especially since the brief battle actually did not meet her expectations and left much to be desired.

Once she got to the Torret Post, she encountered multiple deficiencies in the defense, which forced her to unleash her power with the sole intention of preventing further deaths.

She intended to put a reprimand on the Guild. Despite this, she had initially planned to delay until she could organize a special meeting in the Ri.

Selee's insistence on a speech compelled her to change her mind and speak her thoughts right away.

With a nod, Nehel closed her eyes and carefully selected her words. Opening her eyes, she addressed everyone, especially the Guild members, before her. "My beloved, whilst we mourn and honor the thousand, two hundred among these piles, who died defending the Jyistereerk. I feel obligated to share my thoughts on this battle." With a hint of uneasiness, she let out a sigh and proceeded. "You were unpredictable, ill-prepared, and reckless!"

In response to her remarks, the crowd murmured in surprise. Contrary to their hopes, the Empress used harsh language instead of offering words of encouragement.

With authority, she demanded silence and cast intense gazes at a few people in the front. "Master Alessandro! Why thou have doubted me and sent me back to the Ri?"

Alessandro hesitated and stammered, stunned. "It was in the best of your welfare. . ."

In anger, she interrupted. "Am I not your Empress who possesses higher authority in whom you place your trust?!" The crowd trembled in newfound and unexpected agitation.

"Aye. . ." startled he made a reverence.

"Ser Marissa! Did not you study military tactics at the Academy?"

"Aye, Divine Empress," ashamed, she replied with a nod.

"Your ignorance and lack of preparation caused the loss of many lives!" She then averted her eye to someone else. "Archmage Selee! Where are our Artensens that could have helped us greatly?"

"Beneath the palace in the Ri, they keep a close watch on the bottomless pit to prevent any demons from emerging," he responded with a nervous smile.

"Is that necessary to keep all of them beneath?!" As her anger grew, a gust of wind appeared, almost daunting everyone. But a touch on Nehel's hand made her turn, only to find Juni gazing at her with affection and shaking his head, which she interpreted instantly. Turning around again, she let out a breath to ease herself and then spoke with a sense of calm and melancholy. "My apologies. I did not mean to startle all of you, just to speak with the truth. A tikl ago, I began the *Deken Karsaker* to reclaim our world from those who do not deserve it, because Sankaris does not belong to them! But if we keep failing as we did last night, they will overcome us!"

In the end, the crowd comprehended and nodded, in calm, to her remarks.

The Guild members, Keleana inclusive, kneeled and offered apologies one after another. Nehel acknowledged and insisted them to stand up again.

"We can redo nothing now," she exhaled. "Our duty is to pay tribute to the fallen and grant them my blessing as they depart for the underworld." She signaled Captain Kanden and his crew to ignite the piles. "This battle was only the very beginning, the worse is not even near, as they still await us to fight against them face to face, and they expect us to lose in our reclamation. So, to honor them, my proposal is to erect a monolith in the center of these ruins and rename this location *Tempest Post*." She concluded, inclining her head.

The volunteers sang farewell in Molkan verses, which they had memorized, as a dedication to the Empress' Elvish home.

Their song overwhelmed Nehel, resulting in tears streaming down her face. It was not due to grieving, but a fatal premonition she could not yet understand.

13

ARANKAN DESERT

Departing from Kokork, Carlissa and Vasso soon found themselves in Stronghold Setok, where they noticed the first signs of the desert's scarcity leaving behind the abundant Casakan vegetation. The stories they had heard about the north painted an arid picture, not a kingdom, all because of the Gesha.

A warden with a lance stood at the gates of the stronghold, waiting for them as he had already seen them approaching from a distance. "Please state the reason for your arrival," he studied them once they halted. Their attire caught his attention, as it seemed oddly mismatched for a journey. Unaware that it was part of her body, he noticed Carlissa's purple dress before spotting Vasso's cheap attire.

"We have the intention of crossing over to the north, into Aranka," Vasso replied with a nod.

With chuckles, the warden expressed disbelief. "Are you aware that this is not a game? Turn around and go back to your mummy!"

Outraged, Vasso made a move to unsheathe his sword, only to be stopped by Carlissa's touch.

"Do nothing!" she suggested.

Vasso accepted her request and looked back at the warden, only to discover a lance pointed at his face.

"We will confine both of you in our cells! Let us see if you are not Korbas!" at the time that some of his comrades joined him, he said with aggressive suspicion.

The sentinels tossed Vasso, leaving him battered and bloodied. Later, they locked the metallic door.

Carlissa looked at him through her thick, round glasses, but she did not react to his wretched condition. Seated on the floor, she remained completely motionless, showing no sign of empathy towards him.

Despite the excruciating pain, Vasso uttered a frail murmur. His body refused to cooperate, yet he got the will to raise his mangled face and meet her gaze with swollen and bruised eyes. "Even after all I have done for you, do you even care about me?"

"What should I be mindful of when I shall remain unbiased?"

"I can not believe you!" He attempted to fetch a water bucket on his own, realizing she would not offer help, thus dragging the best he could and taking sips from his inflamed hand, spoke to her. "Do you know the Divine Empress is on our side?!"

"The Nehel awaits us, aye. But should he be the first to arrive, I will dedicate myself to serving the lord."

"That is damn childish!" Took a seat beside Carlissa with pain and effort, and he spoke with a cutting edge to his words. "Do you even have any conscience?"

"What is conscience when all you do not have?"

"Good point!" he agreed with a gasp, using the sleeve of his grimy shirt to wipe away the blood from his face, as his breathing grew more pronounced.

The cell reverberated with the sound of the door opening.

Vasso widened the eyes with concern. "They are coming for you!"

To his surprise, Overseer Akartaki rushed to Vasso's side and retrieved special ointments from her waist pouch. She acted as an elder sister, helping her injured little brother. The elvish girl and he had formed a unique and strong bond the last years.

Behind them, Commandant Kartak twitched his eyebrow as Captain Diesso watched.

"I was expecting for you," Carlissa said with utter indifference.

"Was your purpose of him being brought here solely to endure torture?" Kartak said to her, with a certain annoyance.

Vasso's condition improved thanks to the elvish maid's healing touch, as the pain decreased and the swelling went down. The Kasnasgans surpassed Tyza and Ryza in advancement, thanks to their renowned abilities in blending magic and medicine.

The kid noticed the concerned gesture on the Overseer's face. She had been looking after him and other children for about four years.

"I will issue a stern reprimand and strip these fools of their ranks!" Diesso appeared to be upset, as his voice seemed to be filled with anger.

Kartak touched the Captain's shoulder. "Does it justify the reprimand? By sticking to blaming and punishing, we will only exacerbate the discord. That is the goal the Korbas have in mind for us." The Commandant redirected his yellowish eyes to Carlissa and posed a question. "Why do you want to go to barren lands?"

"The Nehel will meet there as the moons align to create her forever home."

Her reply left everyone speechless. Except one.

"I have no clue what her intentions are, but she keeps mentioning about a home for the Divine Empress," Vasso clarified.

"Is she going to build a home?" Overseer Akartaki suggested.

"She brought up about the moons's alignment," Diesso clarified with a thinking posture. "Before our Assembly meeting, I overheard some mages and the Head discussing an extraordinary astronomical event."

Kartak twitched his eyebrow and nodded. "We have to summon Head Missar."

Archmage Missar tore the military regional map from the large wooden table, causing a loud ripping sound. Instead, he had unrolled another, a large one, showcasing the vastness of the world of Sankaris.

When they saw the chart, revealing the places they never knew existed, everyone reacted with wide-eyed wonder. Besides Tyza and Ryza, the map uncovered a new continent to the west that was inhabited by Kasnasga, Zyza, and an unfamiliar territory known as Xyza, the island continent.

"I notice that there is an island further east from Katalk," In a muted tone, Diesso whispered into the ear of a healed Vasso discreetly pointing.

"While in Kao, I heard Bick is the home of the Tinklens," Vasso answered with a clear voice. "The gnomes."

"Indeed, lad!" Archmage Missar placed bottles and stones on the corners of the map, then glanced at everyone noticing Carlissa's absence. "This updated map is a special copy, meticulously drawn under the guidance of the *Frelee*

Dee in Salter, only tailored for the mystical beings to behold."

"So, do you believe where the Divine Empress' home will be?" Kartak asked.

"There will be a rare astronomical event that occurs only once every five hundred tikls. And every time that happens, it is a sure sign that something significant is about to happen."

"Kasana decapitation happened during the moons's alignment," Kartak confirmed.

"And Berrem lost the monarchies too," Diesso stated.

"Aye," Missar nodded. "When Kasana died, the shadow of the four moons eclipsing the sun fell on Molke and traveled south to Berrem."

"Two major events on the same date," the Commandant affirmed. "At that same time, our ancestors, the Tannes, emigrated to Kasnasga."

"Do you have any idea about the specific area where the shadow will land, Sir Head?" Overseer Akartaki asked.

"We will see." While exploring the chamber of the stronghold, Missar's eyes fell upon a sextant arranged on a set of shelves. He reached out, took hold of the instrument, and carefully placed it on the map. With a wave of his hand, he summoned a small booklet that gracefully soared from his pouch on a bench, gliding across the chamber until it landed in his palm.

"Why the Head placed a sextant on a map?" Vasso whispered. "Should not he be aiming it towards the horizon outside?"

"He should," Captain Diesso responded. "But being him an Archmage, who knows!"

"Silence!" With an irritated tone, Missar commanded. He levitated the sextant and directed it towards the window, where the radiant midday sunlight streamed through. His left hand moved, aligning the flying instrument to let a glow of solar light illuminate the map, a magical occurrence. As he held the book in his other hand, it flipped open by itself to the exact page he had been searching for. It revealed a crafted drawing of the stars and moons. The Archmage murmured words from his lips no one could understand.

A narrow beam of solar light pinpointed a specific location on the map.

Missar smiled and nodded. He carefully set down the sextant and then tapped his index finger on the chart.

"Right there!"

Everyone gathered around the table, and they fixated their eyes on the location.

"East Aranka, where the Kingdom's Citadel once stood," the Archmage confirmed.

Vasso left the chamber and searched everywhere until he finally found Carlissa. She was staring stagnant and fixedly at the horizon in the northeast, outside the stronghold, while dumbfounded sentinels watched her. Days had passed since that moment he met her as a gryphon, and he had become familiar with her customs. However, he still struggled to comprehend her, but something in his logic revealed itself.

"You are building her a home. Am I right?"

"I am building myself a home for her to bestow," Carlissa replied, devoid of reaction. "However, in the lord's event's arrival being first, it shall be his residence."

"It makes sense now, now that the Head revealed the moons' alignment," he nodded with a sigh. Why did not you tell me that earlier?

"Was it necessary to tell?"

Vasso scratched his head and returned to the stronghold, leaving her in the same position. As soon as he walked in, Missar, who had incidentally heard both of them from afar, startled him with his mere presence. Surprised with a gasp, he made a nod as a sign of respect.

"My apologies, Sir Head!"

"No need to apologize, lad," the Archmage replied in a hushed tone. "I overheard you even it was not my intention."

"Sometimes I do not get her!" Vasso said with some despair in his voice. "She is indifferent and does not care about our feelings! Yet, I keep following her as a lapdog!"

Missar shook his head and emitted a light smile. "You are mistaken. The *Ykarte*, or Carlissa as you call her, is not a person. She is a magical entity, a living weapon, also a gate. Although you can include her as one of us, always remember she is not human and needs to be treated with utmost care."

"Why did she choose me? Is there no one else more worthy than me?"

"I encountered this and other mysteries with no answers. However, I believe that as time passes, she will gradually unveil everything."

Vasso assumed a thoughtful position and spoke. "I have a strong feeling that something will occur."

A sumptuous carriage greeted the gates of the Setok Stronghold, pulled by four majestic horses, which came to a halt. Once the vigilant sentinel noticed its presence, he approached and conversed with the chauffeur seated in the upper seat of the vehicle.

"Why and where do you hail from?!" the guard asked with distrust and stern.

"Two important ladies from Estolk were adamant in coming."

As the officer opened the door, he immediately recognized the two faces of the ladies.

"Is there any damn problem preventing us from passing?!" Lady Tasarissa asked, annoyed as Alyssa Taskar attempted to avoid any further upset by touching her shoulder.

14

EAGLE'S TOWER

They had to cross the boundaries separating the Trunke Territory and the Cayderr Mountains, passing through a tight space that marked the last fragment of Berrem to the south before reaching Fenn. As Corr was guiding the cart with two horses, he was cautious to avoid any red mantises while securing his companion during the journey.

Next to the feline, her Escort, Fabehel had been a witness to the breathtaking transformation from the dense and expansive pine forest of the Black Forest to the refreshing landscapes of The Highlands with its winding valleys, and finally to the emergence of a tropical forest that signaled the imminent arrival to the lively jungle of Fenn. While traveling to these unfamiliar places, she had a sense of awe. However, she constantly reminded herself that she was not there as a sightseer, but as an Ambassador with the mission to resolve a pending situation with the giefo trade and uncover the rumored Arankan settlement within the feline kingdom.

Her fingers still rubbed the smooth surface of her orchid medallion hanging from her neck. Even though several days had gone by since she was last with Alessandro, she could not shake the memory of that night. She could not help but worry about the battle's outcome and the safety of her beloved. The yearning to be in his arms consumed her, clouded by the fear of losing him on the battleground.

Yet, she had to restrain herself from giving in to her impulses. At that moment, the assignment that the Empress had entrusted her with was of utmost importance. She had faith that their paths would cross again, allowing her to see him after her duty was done.

Her hazel eyes noticed a group of infants playing hide and seek by the side of the stone road, far on a clearing among trees, but what attracted her curiosity more was the mixture between Berremens and Fennens. "Where are we, Corr? I see children from both kinds playing and laughing together. Fenn already?"

"It is not Fenn nor Berrem, milady," he replied with his usual deep voice. "We are approaching Siennt, right on the border."

"Why someone built a city on the line and why I see people of two kinds? It is out of my comprehension."

With a fixed gaze and a moment of silence stretching on, Corr continued to drive the horses as she waited for an answer. "Have you learned about that treaty?"

"The Giefo Treaty? I have read it was an agreement between Berrem, the Breken Nation and Fenn, that ultimately benefited the Berremen realm. The same one the Divine Empress intended to end."

"The treaty permitted the creation of a border settlement to foster collaboration between blacksmiths from Berrem and Fenn in crafting giefo weapons," he replied. "It grew into an important city with its own government and laws." His green eyes glanced at Fabehel. "They even permit mixed marriages, but these couples cannot conceive offsprings because Berremens and Fennens are two different breeds."

"How do they reproduce and ensure the population's growth?"

"There are also couples of a single breed, milady," Corr replied with a nod. "It is also customary to form families by adopting orphans from either Berrem or Fenn."

Without thinking, Fabehel took a deep breath, detecting the delightful aroma of the jungle. The warm and humid weather, though annoying, reminded her of the years she spent in Sarak, growing up alongside her beloved but deceased Tin. Just like the place she was in, the island of Katalk had a similar environment.

The cart came to an abrupt stop as Corr tugged on the reins, commanding the horses to halt. A small crowd of locals who had gathered on the road obstructed their path.

The sudden occurrence startled Fabehel, and she noticed curiosity and distrust on their faces.

With caution, a pair of guards, a Berremen and a Fennen of gray fur, pointing their mirrored swords of giefo to the visitors. They had appeared from somewhere near as they noticed the people.

"Share the nature of your visit!" the feline soldier demanded. "What is the reason for an Arankan woman in our domain?"

"I assure our destination is Fenn. . . "

"But why a damn Fennen as you accompany an Arankan?" the guard interrupted. "No Arankan has come this way in the past three tikls!"

In a wise move, Fabehel raised both hands as a gesture of peace to prevent further conflict. "Please, let me have the word."

"Go ahead, woman!"

"As an Ambassador, I am accompanied by my Escort, who protects me during my travels in the name of the Divine Empress before Brek and Fenn," she sighed with concern. "I aim to find my people, the Arankans in Fenn, and address the giefo trade before the leaders."

"The Empress' mandate to end that trade left us no choice but to seek other ways to sustain ourselves!" Someone spoke with a male voice.

Corr and Fabehel searched the crowd, hoping to identify the origin of his words.

As the people cleared a path, a bald, mature man with small eyes rode on his brown horse towards the guards, who walked away to give him his turn to speak.

"The giefo was not only the reason for Siennt's existence, but also the very foundation on which it stood. Why should I allow passage to the Empress' emissary, considering all the harm she has caused?" the man nodded in distrust but calm.

"May I know who you are?" Fabehel asked.

"I am Lord Doni, master and ruler of our independent city of Siennt. I am not king, but freely chosen by my people!"

"It is my pleasure, lord," she lowered her head as a salute. "Let me introduce myself as Lady Fabehel of the Red Tides, and accompanying me is Corr of Finnerr. But believe me, lord. The Divine Empress did not know it would affect your city."

"Please forgive me, milady," he strangely shifted to a friendly behavior. He got off his horse and walked to her, took her hand, and spoke kindly. "Little did I know you were the very sister of Princess Natahel. Please allow me to aid you in stepping down from your cart, and I will be your companion as I present you to the city."

Startled, she could not respond or even speak.

Slightly offended, Corr clarified that Lady Fabehel could not walk.

Lord Doni's eyes widened in surprise when he noticed she did not have feet under her skirt. "My apologies again!"

It took quite a while to reach the outskirts of Siennt, but Lord Doni, positioned in the middle of the seat, commanded Corr to halt the horses. Behind, the guards and the crowd followed.

Corr was familiar with it, but Fabehel was completely awestruck by what she saw.

In the foothills of the Cayderr Range, a scenic location emerged at the start of the mountainous region that embraced half of the Kingdom of Fenn. Siennt resembled a town more than a city, smaller than Carretem. Between the quaint houses with vibrant flower-filled balconies, black smokes rose from the forges of blacksmiths, most of which were wooden two-story buildings.

But, for some odd reason, the streets were devoid of people. Corr and Fabehel assumed all the locals were the ones behind, but they could not comprehend how a small group of dozens could occupy a city with hundreds of buildings.

However, at the heart of the area, rather than a plaza or downtown, arose a towering structure with a sculpture of a giant black eagle perched at its top.

The Eagle's Tower intrigued Fabehel. "Why did Siennt choose to place a statue of an eagle at the peak of a tower?"

A sigh escaped Lord Doni as his expression turned serious and tense. "That is not a statue. That is a real eagle!"

"How?"

"Majestic brown eagles once soared this area, flying from across southern Salter, milady," Corr explained.

"But that is a black eagle!" She exclaimed.

"Aye," Doni nodded. "The tower provided food for eagles, but unfortunately, a specific one encountered a Korba and got infected. As a result, it landed there and became strangely paralyzed, like a statue. It has been there since four tikls ago with no change until . . . its red eyes opened last night, then closed again in an instant."

"It is a Korbeen in the middle of your city!"

"You said so," Lord Doni replied with another nod. "Despite this, we have a hunch that its eyes were a sign of the previous battle that took place in Torret Post. Yet, the manifestation was terrifying."

Startled, Corr's curiosity took hold of him. "Do you have any news?"

"Aye, a messenger from our city traveling north sent us a pigeon from near The Empress' Pass and sent me a pigeon. The Imperial Guard had to resist a fierce siege during the night, sort of, but ultimately the Empress annihilated the red mantises in the territory."

Corr responded with understanding. "While we were near the outskirts of Trunke, I could smell the scents of few red mantises. They had fear."

Fabehel clasped the orchid medallion and bowed her head in silent prayer to the goddesses. "Nehel. . .," she whispered to herself. "Did Master Alessandro survive the battle?"

"From what I understand, milady. Despite the confrontation resulting in thousands of casualties, the Guild remained unaffected, as rumors suggest."

While many locals stayed indoors out of fear, Fabehel opted to have the balcony on the inn's second floor opened. Seated on her wheelchair, her intention was to examine the surroundings, concentrating on the tower during her reflection.

Dozens of patrols guarded the towering structure since the eagle's manifestation.

Upon reaching her chamber earlier this noon, Corr informed her that during the city's settlement, giant brown eagles would swoop down and snatch people, particularly young children, to feed on. The locals built a tower at the center to feed the birds with livestock. This would ensure everyone's safety.

But now she was alone. Corr visited Lord Doni to set up a meeting with locals, to assess the state of Siennt and find solutions to the struggling economy.

As an Ambassador granted powers by Empress Nehel, Fabehel contemplated mandates that would bring benefits to all.

A sudden noise jolted Fabehel out of her deep thoughts, causing her to turn around in her wheelchair. She discreetly slid her hand beneath her dress skirt, ready to unsheathe the dagger strapped to her leg. A female feline with dark gray fur and spots emerged from a dark corner of her chamber, cautiously approaching with outstretched hands as a gesture of peace.

"Why are you here?!" Fabehel's voice grew with sternness.

The feline observed her with her blue eyes and a nod. "Milady, please forgive me for coming to you this way. I come in peace, with no ill intentions, only seeking a conversation."

As Fabehel kept a wary hand on the dagger admitting fear, studied the feline's intricate hunter attire, trying to guess her intentions. "Who are you?"

"I am Aeienn of Aorr, and I command the Kiffenns," she responded.

"You are not exactly well-regarded by my Escort Corr," Fabehel said, tilting her head to the left. "He has a profound distrust of both you and the monarchy. Still, I am curious to hear your side of the story."

The feline nodded and grabbed a chair from the nearby bed, taking a seat, and spoke. "Lord Kong's alliance with Queen Shiann and the Breken Senaten sparked the rebellion. Following that, our monarchy started slavery, starting with the capture of the poorest and later expanding to include other groups such as the Arankans and Casakans."

"So, the Giefo Treaty triggered your rebellion, right?"

"Aye, milady. As I come from an impoverished house, they took my spouse and my eldest to the Mines of Tiunnff. I and others who have experienced the same have vowed to dethrone the queen and establish a realm of autonomy and self-governance."

"Are you aware that it did not just affect the Fennens, but also impacted outsiders?"

"Faced with the struggle to survive, a few vagrants disregarded their commitment to King Vihen and, seduced by gold, turned to slave hunting in Ryza and Tyza. Their purpose was to catch criminals, fugitives, or prisoners who ended up being enslaved."

"I am well informed about it, Aeienn. Perhaps you could tell me about the Arankan settlement I seek for."

Standing up, the leader of the Kiffenns let out a sigh and placed her hands on her waist. "We think we know where the settlement is, but there is no assurance, and we promise to inform you once our search is complete, all because we wish to believe in the Divine Empress. We will find you." She handed Fabehel a small paper from one of her pockets. "This contains a name."

"What name?" she asked, surprised.

"The name of the vagrant who agreed to sell Cassandro Eskar as a slave for gold." Aeienn nodded before exiting through the door of the chamber.

Fabehel opened the paper, and her hazel eyes widened in horror as she saw the name written inside.

Corr and Lord Doni had arrived at the base of the tower, surrounded by a multitude of guards, in the open air, where the city's ruler stood with outstretched arms.

"Do you see my men?" he said with discomfort. "They are indifferent to whether they identify as Berremen or Fennen, as long as they remain loyal citizens of Siennt. They are not traditional soldiers, but reservists who lead normal lives, with families and jobs to attend to. The only thing we seek is a life with happiness and harmony."

"Aye, I could agree with you. However, I cannot condone the methods you employ in dealing with the giefo, a metal that carries a heavy toll of lives." Corr let out a sigh, shaking his head in disappointment. "Cassandro Eskar, the father of the Divine Empress, and myself, were slaves."

Lord Doni got startled by his response. "I truly did not know. Please accept my sincere apologies for my lack of knowledge."

"I was only a child when they came for me, and I had to work in the mines for years. I could not reunite with my family anymore."

"It must be hard on you. . ."

A piercing screech interrupted their conversation, causing both of them to witness the guards fleeing in fear. Their gazes turned upwards, and they witnessed the eagle's frightening wingspan as it soared away, flapping towards Salter.

"You are free now, after enduring those long tikls with the eagle," Corr asseverated in awe.

"However, I have a strong sense that something unfortunate is about to occur." Lord Doni shielded his eyes

while watching the massive bird take flight away with a
strange grin.

15

LAST KANNESTE

That day, the Citadel of Salter was alive with the energy of merchants engaging in lively commerce and locals flocking to the bustling annual market. The eternal night and the unchanging pleasant climate were characteristic of both the city and the mystical realm of Salter, and people enjoyed them.

However, in relation to other seasons, the abundance of people declined noticeably. The warning from a tikl ago about the predicted destruction by the *Frelee Dee* resulted in a mass exodus towards Berrem, Fenn, and even Brek.

Despite the urgency, there were those who had no alternative and remained, hoping for a new promised land within the Jyistereerk.

From every corner of Sankaris, orphaned children since birth grew up under the care of the maids, never knowing the warmth of sunlight, only the eternal presence of the night sky. These children awaited their chance to be received by the Empress in her Jyistereerk. As with the Salterans, they too had dreams of a promised land. They did not depart.

"For only five golds, you can buy dark sand from the Korba Dominion!" a merchant promoted his pile on a table as offended onlookers stared at him.

"You have no shame!" a woman stopped and yelled. "How dare you to sell the ground from the demons?!"

"I have risked my life to bring it to all you customers!" the merchant, upset, responded. "This sand is as valuable as the giefo!"

The woman glared at him with resentment and disagreement as people joined to back her. "Selling this damned sand is like selling the very grounds of the Netherworld!"

With a sudden burst of aggression, a man from the crowd hurled the table with the sand to the ground. A crowd of curious pedestrians gathered around the incident. "Keep risking your life just to meet your end and descend into the Netherworld, you despicable creature!"

Without warning, the merchant unsheathed his dagger, revealing his determination to confront the man.

An unexpected light from the sky caught everyone's attention, causing them to gaze upward.

The eternal night was fading, making room for daylight to emerge for the first time in all of Salter's existence.

It meant something portentous.

The mystical field that had shielded Salter for thousands of tikls vanished.

With anticipation, multitude's gaze wandered, fixating on the spectacular, yet sinister, Karekall, which gleamed under the sun's rays, beyond the shimmering silver towers.

From behind the mountains and the Cayderr Range, ominous flocks of Korbas and Korbeens, infected flying creatures including giant eagles, soared toward the Citadel. The darkness had returned, but it was not the familiar cloak of night. Instead, it was a menacing swarm of hellish hordes that flooded the day.

The sharp sound of their screeches echoed, instilling fear in the crowd, who frantically fled, searching for any hiding place they could find.

The creatures did not take victims with their own claws as they did in the past. The gigantic dragons, using their immense power, mercilessly crashed the silver towers onto the people, causing striking devastation and lost lives.

As the buildings collapsed, the flames from the chimneys danced in synchrony with their destruction and spread with dramatic acceleration. Fires quickly consumed buildings and houses, creating a hellish sight for the Citadel.

The city, once loaded with beauty, now stood as a haunting collection of blazing ruins in a matter of moments.

Most of the flocks were still continuing northward.

But amidst the destruction, the tallest silver tower stood tall, untouched. It was on purpose.

The most colossal black dragon landed at the top of the tallest.

Ardek Korba.

The sound of his mighty roar reverberated, a chilling reminder to all who had survived of his presence.

He expanded his Dominion to Salter, and he made sure the survivors were well aware.

The Lord of the Netherworld observed with pleasure the sea of fire engulfing the Citadel.

Ardek Korba landed near the conquered Citadel and searched his surroundings. In his dragon form, he stomped forward with frustration and addressed his companion, a black dragon slightly smaller than him.

"Where is the *Frelee Dee*?" he said in deep voice.

"It should be here, Lord Ardek," he responded. "This is the right place."

Ardek lifted his gaze towards the clear sky, before shifting his attention to a humble landscape of grass and trees.

"Never mind, Parek. We have taken the realm of Salter for us, and we are closer to our objective now."

"Berrem, Lord?"

As he turned, his red eyes locked onto his. "The Empress and her servants. My pawns are going to break her."

Sorcerer Uskam's limping had worsened. On the worse days, he crawled on the ground to accomplish his errands. His body had become noticeably frail, weakened by illness, and he had lost his left eye to a severe infection.

Four years had passed since he bid farewell to Nehel.

He had constructed a small hut situated just beyond the outskirts of Akiaba, where he could find solace, away from that plague and madness prevailing in the city.

Perched on a rock, he struggled to chew the rancid meat he had with him, his teeth long gone and his appetite nonexistent. As he had done for what felt like an eternity, he awaited death.

The sorcerer knew that hundreds of people still grappled to survive, remnants of the once thriving and glorious Kanneste Clan, doomed by Kasana.

As slight tremors rumbled beneath his feet, Uskam turned towards the Karekall. With his one remaining yellowish eye, he nodded somberly, with a mix of assertion and melancholy.

He knew the outcome.

It was time.

"You are the last of the Kannestes, Lakia," he murmured and hoped the wind could take his words to reach her ears.

A herd of fast black demons overran the Karekall with thunderous footsteps. To his right, large flocks of flying creatures glided above as their wings flapped with sinister presence. Both had their eyes fixed on Akiaba, ready to strike.

The pinkish grass seemed to come alive as a gentle breeze swept through, causing it to sway and dance. Uskam could not help but smile as he remembered the teachings he gave to Lakia while living near Venka's hut.

The sight of the herd and flocks going against Akiaba burned into Uskam's single eye.

The monsters disregarded the life. Without pity, showed no discrimination in their victims—children, women, men, even those who were ill.

They showed no interest in infecting them. Their sole goal was to massacre them.

To exterminate the Kannestes.

Uskam knew his life was approaching to his end. He stood up with effort and awaited to show dignity to his tribe.

A flying dragon from Akiaba spotted the sorcerer and hastily launched itself towards him, propelled by its imposing quickness.

The Sorcerer from the Elvish Clan of the Kannestes closed his eyes and extended his arms, trying to stand himself, awaiting his tragic fate.

With no mercy, it slaughtered him.

Nehel's eyes snapped open, and she took in a sharp breath, gasping for air as she convulsed awake.

She heard the whisper of Sorcerer Uskam carried by the wind. He used his last ounce of magical energy to bring his words to her.

Death had arrived at Molke, and she realized it.

With trembling hands she opened the curtains of her tent where the Second Knight, Juni, stood outside mounting guard. "Something had occurred!"

Her sudden and unexpected remark caught him off guard, and he turned, noticing her face glistening with sweat and streamed with tears. "Are you all right, missy?"

"Where is Brisel?!" she frantically asked. "I must go to Molke!"

Ser Juni, paying attention to her abrupt reaction, figured out that something had taken place. He was at first unsure how to respond to her question, but, with a hesitant tone, he spoke. "He is. . . by the woods, I think. . . Camouflaged as always."

Nehel's lack of gratitude towards him was surprising. It was as if she had transformed into a different person. She shoved him aside, creating a clear path for herself to start her rush.

She paid no attention to the people engaged in the reconstruction of the Tempest Post, even those who bowed to her as she kept sprinting with all her might. She pressed on without stopping until she emerged into a peaceful clearing at the edge. Gasping for air, she let out a pleading yell. "Brisel!"

In a matter of moments, the mantis appeared at a slow pace and came to a halt before the Empress. His round, black eyes noticed her profound distress, sensing her inner turmoil. As a sign of respect, he lowered his front legs to the ground and his antennas descended in a gesture of consent.

Nehel mounted the mantis and whispered.

Brisel wasted no time and set off with the Empress on his back, speeding northwards.

With her eyes closed, she called her magic, letting the breeze to pick up and hasten their route. With a streak of wind pushing him, the mantis sped up, determined to reach its destination before sunset, cutting the travel time from three days to a fraction.

Eager to reach Molke, her birthplace, Nehel hugged Brisel's neck tightly.

What she saw was not the familiar Molke she grew up in. Instead, it was a darker and more ominous place.

Brisel reduced his speed and maneuvered the Empress through the remains of the city of Akiaba.

The sight of the massacred bodies left her eyes wide with horror and disgust as the stench of blood permeated the air. She understood the Korbas were not only killers, but they also took pleasure in toying with their victims.

These demons had no regard for anyone.

No Molkan had survived the cruel attack.

They ensured the extermination of everyone.

The Empress turned her head to the left, her gaze fixated on the valley, and pinpointed the precise origin of the faint whisper. Regardless of the bloodied or polluted grounds, she dismounted the mantis and felt the crunch of debris beneath her feet as she raced towards Uskam. And she dashed without stopping.

When she reached her destination, she found only small fragments of what was left of Uskam scattered on the ground. The tall pinkish grass, splattered with red, barely concealed the remnants, making him almost unrecognizable. The Korbas, knowing exactly who he was, showed no mercy as they ruthlessly finished him, despite his harmless and fragile state as an elderly person. Even though he had lost his sorceress abilities, the creatures saw him as an enemy and dispatched him.

Overwhelmed and unable to speak, she dropped to her knees, her eyes widened with moisture, unsure of how to proceed.

The piercing wound in the depths of her heart was impossible for her to ignore.

The Korbas successfully shattered her spirits by slaughtering her people, who had once thrived and lived with her as if they were of her own.

At a slow pace, Brisel approached a silent and para-lyzed Nehel.

Her reaction was one of pure astonishment as she turned and discovered the mantis standing beside her, his neck and head lowered at her level. Crushed with a despair, she embraced him, and sobbed.

First Venka, then Peken, and now Uskam, along with an entire nation.

A clan eradicated forever.

She still could hear the screams of the dead.

Nehel had become the last Kanneste.

It was a slow and arduous journey despite their hurried rhythm, but after six days, they finally arrived in Molke.

Alessandro stopped his red stallion named Breeze. His heart sank as he surveyed the aftermath of the city's massacre.

Ser Marissa, standing behind, could not help but experience a deep sense of hopelessness. The Archmage Selee, beside her, could only cover his eyes in discom-fort.

Both Kanden and Keleana, just like everyone else in the squad, could not hide their distress.

As soon as the Second Knight arrived with the group, he broke away in a search of Nehel, concerned.

"They are truly monsters from the Netherworld!" Alessandro exclaimed, disturbed. "They had not even a damn regard for any life!"

"I knew they were merciless creatures. . ." Selee responded with a shaking voice, not daring to see yet. "But I never imagined they could do something like this!"

"Where is Nehel?" Alessandro looked around for his niece. Soon he spotted the direction where Juni went and hurried Breeze to go after him, followed by his squad.

The sound of hooves reverberated through the valley as the group galloped across the pinkish long grass, taking in a heart-wrenching sight as they stopped.

Juni stood beside his black stallion, still, as he watched Nehel on her knees, as her gaze fixated towards the exact west. Despite the splattered blood on the surrounding grass, she showed no sign of paying attention to it.

Alessandro dismounted and walked with a slow pace, and stopped behind the immovable Empress. "Are you all right?"

A momentary silence followed, with no response given for quite some time.

The rest of the group also dismounted, but they awaited by the Second Knight's site.

"When I arrived here, the dead filled my head with screaming pleas. I could not stand it." Nehel spoke, still immobile but composed. "I was with so much grief and pain that I wished vengeance!" She stood up and looked at her uncle with her deep hazel eyes, already tired from many tears and with a serious semblance. "But a soothing melody reached my ears, bringing me peace and reassurance that the Kannestes had finally found solace in the Gakia after a long time of burden and struggles."

"Who sang to you?" Selee asked, suspecting something, showing a profound sadness.

"The *Ykarte*, Archmage," she nodded. "It is calling me, urging to build a new home for the Jyistereerk in Aranka as the moons' alignment approaches."

"But how you will go to Aranka when there is a robust barrier in the Beyond Sea with Korbas and giant squids?" Alessandro asked, hard to believe.

"No matter what it takes, I will risk myself to navigate the sea even if I go alone."

16

THE GUILD

In its heyday, the port of Sarrem bustled with commerce, serving as a vital link between Berrem and the Kingdom of Aranka, in particular prior to the Gesha. It quite combined maritime activities, industrial enterprises, and commercial trades.

This location offered a perfect fusion of the best features from both continents, Ryza and Tyza. The west at the east.

A suitable geographical location.

Besides, it offered a pathway to the almost unknown elvish realm of Molke. However, only a handful of brave explorers and hunters ventured into that treacherous land to secure the prized waki meats and furs.

Unfortunately, the port declined during delicate times thanks to the Gesha, compelled to alter its maritime route from Aranka to the island of Katalk in Casak, resulting in significant changes to commerce and industry.

The blockage imposed by the Korbas and giant squids exacerbated the neglect of the port, along with the recent events at Tempest Post, Salter and Molke, all coinciding with the *Deken Karsaker*. Misery and despair existed now.

Sarrem was living in a time of war, though the conflict was far away. The anxiety in the air was obvious.

All the Imperial Guard had arrived at the port from the Ri by orders of the Empress. Upon learning about her arrival along with the Guild, the locals, most deprived of their basic needs, had a glimmer of hope.

The people of Sarrem also stood in awe as the Artensens, majestic silver sentinels, made their way out of the underground of the palace. The presence of these magnificent mystical beings brought a drop of joy to the bewildered residents, providing a brief escape from their hardships. Only some few Artensens stayed in the Ri to watch the infamous endless pit.

The sight of Nehel, attired in leather clothes, riding a brown horse, drew the gaze of everyone in the streets of the port. Surrounding her were the Second Knight, Juni, and the entire Court of Maids, all dressed in white and led by Akhimeni. With a fatigued expression and a focused stare, she paid no attention to the locals.

The people were in awe to see the Empress in person, even if only for a moment, but they understood her sad condition upon hearing the news of the tragedies in Salter and Molke. Around Berrem, the public consensus was that Nehel and the Guild were losing the *Deken Karsaker*, and it would not be long before Sankaris succumbed to the fires of the Netherworld.

The Guild had transformed the once ballroom into a meeting space.

The atmosphere in the chamber on the second floor of the hostel near the harbor was heavy with disappointment as Selee spoke and turned his back to his fellow members while he stared out the window, lost in thought.

Among them all, Alessandro was the most surprised. "Are you sure do you want to leave us, Archmage?"

"Aye, Master," he replied as he turned around with a face lacking his characteristic smile. "Once the Divine Vessel is ready, I intend to depart to Salter."

"When we need you the most in these delicate times, that is when you decide to leave," Ser Marissa spoke with disillusion. "I did not expect it from you."

"In fact, no one of us expected it," Alessandro added. "You were well aware of the fall of Salter since a tikl ago. Why that sudden change of mind?"

"Did you expect the Korbas to behave like that? I believe no one," Selee gasped. "What we saw in Molke take my words."

Keleana and Dessidere only witnessed the conversation with a serious semblance.

"I still do not comprehend your reason when Salter is no more."

"I do not expect to do so. . ."

"You should respect his choice!" Everyone turned their heads at the sound of an authoritative voice and saw Nehel, who had just entered the chamber as Ser Juni opened the door for her. With a compassionate look, she approached Selee and reached out to hold his hands. "It is burning inside. Am I right?"

The Archmage nodded as his blue eyes wetted. "Aye, Divine Empress. Since the fall of Salter, my immortality is now a heavy burden I wish to lift from me." His voice shook with a serious regret. "I have taken the lives of innocents, just like those demons did, and now I comprehend the nature of my punishment."

"And you have vindicated for enough time." Nehel assured. "You may go to Salter now and not worry about the vessel. We will find a solution to cross the Beyond Sea."

Selee assented in a mixture of appreciation and relief, with no words, and before the sights of everyone, he made a quick kneel and left the chamber.

While gazing at the door he had just walked out of, Nehel addressed a perplexed Guild. "I had to let him go. He became ill with profound anguish, and his soul is giving up his body."

Alessandro adopted his usual pensive posture and nodded, perplexed. "Did he die along with Salter?"

"Perhaps, uncle, perhaps he is departing to the Gakia," she affirmed. "He deserves it."

"I thought he would continue assisting us with the Jyistereerk, but now I regret scolding him." Ser Marissa said while her tears ran across her cheeks. "It seems like the Guild will always miss something. The departure of Peken and Selee, along with Lady Fabehel and Corr being absent, has disrupted the strength once more. Is being a Pillar worth witnessing countless sacrifices?"

"I have chosen you as a Pillar altogether with my uncle, Ser Marissa." Nehel said with confidence despite her tired face. "The Guild's intention is also to never stay the same for the welfare of the Jyistereerk."

"Do you ever know who will replace the ones who departed?" Alessandro asked. "We are shrinking in size."

"Do not let us to deviate from our purpose in the meeting and let us focus on our route to Tyza." She suggested, and everyone agreed.

The hostel servants had taken the time to prepare a round table with twelve chairs. Alessandro found himself at the Empress's side, taking a seat to her right, while Marissa settled into the chair on the left. Standing opposite the Herald, Dessidere, Keleana, and Akhimeni were the only ones left from the original Guild that had founded just a tikl ago.

The meeting left them with a sense of incompleteness. Nehel sensed the uneasiness among the members, and called out to the Second Knight, who stood watch at the door. "Ser Juni, please gather Jumeni and Captain Kanden to join us in the Guild. This invitation extends to you as well."

Juni, surprised, nodded and left the chamber.

"What will be their new roles once they join us?" Alessandro asked, puzzled.

"Jumeni is no longer a girl but a mature woman and her role as the Artifice will be crucial for the Jyistereerk." When Nehel fixed her hazel eyes on Keleana, a suspicion washed over her, though she could not quite grasp why. "Captain Kanden's leadership will ensure our dominance over the vast waters of Sankaris."

Ser Marissa sighed, closing her eyes. "May I inquire about something, Nehel?"

"Aye, you can," she replied with a light but sad smile.

"Are you a clairvoyant who can see into the future and know the destiny of every one of us?"

"Not at all, Ser Marissa. I am not omniscient," she shook her head. "I could not expect that the Korbas would actually eradicate the entire Kanneste population." Her voice almost broke. "When I see you, I can feel the weight of your destinies, and I am aware of secrets. However, there is a shadow that obscures me, preventing me from seeing with absolute clarity."

"The more I hear from you, more maturity I notice in you." Alessandro said with a nod.

As the servants arrived with the beverages on their trays, Jumeni and Kanden coincidentally entered the room with Juni.

Almost everyone accepted their wines. Jumeni and Akhimeni requested mugs of rice milk. Nehel, however, stood out as the sole exception, accepting a humble cup of water.

When the Artifice took a seat beside, either by accident or on purpose, Dessidere blushed as he shook himself.

Nehel signaled the Herald to begin.

Dessidere acknowledged her request and prepared his papyrus on the table. He got his feather pen, struggling to find his inkwell. Luckily, Jumeni had placed it within his reach, as their eyes locked in a silent sympathy. With his hands still trembling, he averted his gaze and immediately started his work by writing the first words. "In the Thirty-Fourth day of the Fifth Month in the First Year of the *Tikl the Second of Nehel,* I officially begin this meeting." He let out a sigh and took a moment to complete his writing. "Before me, as the Herald, I have the Divine Empress Nehel of the Jyistereerk, the Pillars Master Alessandro Eskar and Ser Marissa Taskar, Marshal Keleana of Estherleon of the Imperial Guard, Overseer Akhimeni of the Court of Maids, Second Knight Ser Juni of Sarrem, Artifice Jumeni of Sarrem, and Captain Kanden of *The Wandering.* Absentees are Corr of Finnerr, and Lady Fabehel of the Red Tides."

"Please, Herald," Nehel addressed him with a nod. "Include Archmage Missar and Commandant Kartak."

Her request startled everyone, leaving them speechless. Dessidere hesitated, weighing whether to include them in the papyrus.

"Once in Aranka," she assured. "They will join us and complete the definitive Guild."

"Was not it the definitive Guild?" Alessandro asked, scratching his head.

Nehel turned to see her uncle with a deep stare through her tired eyes. "As I reach of age, I realize that the original Guild had its role, but now it is irrelevant, even though a handful of members continue to stay. It helped to establish the Jyistereerk and maintain the delicate balance on Sankaris, but we need new people to preserve the *Deken Karsaker.*" She sighed. "Do not you recall that I just mentioned that it should not be always the same?"

"Are you still stuck in your foolish old habits of asking childish questions?" Ser Marissa reprimanded him with a fierce look.

With no more replies, Dessidere agreed to include the two absent members and wrote their names. "Not present, I also include Commandant Kartak of Kasnasga, and Archmage Missar, Head of Casak."

The Empress placed both hands on the round table, closing her eyes with a long gasp, as if entering a trance or engaging in a silent prayer, leaving everyone curious about her inner thoughts. After a while, she opened her hazel eyes and took sight of everyone. "As we enter a period of pain and suffering for Sankaris, it is a necessary but undesirable step to continue with the *Deken Karsaker* I started a tikl ago."

"Are you referring to the most recent conflict and tragedies the world has endured?" Alessandro asked.

With a sad nod, she admitted, "It is, in fact, my fault."

The Guild murmured, as they tried to guess the reason behind her guilt.

"Murmurs and surprises fix nothing," she continued, silencing the members. "A group from an influential Aquelarre had suggested breaking my spirits, weakening our resolve, and trying to sow division among us. Their loyalty already pledged to the demons as they consider Ardek Korba as their supreme and only leader." She paused with a sigh. "The Korbas planned to wait, but they were not pleased with their loss in the *Battle of the Tempest*, so my intervention sped up their plans. If only I had not intervened, the Molkans would still be alive." She gasped as her voice tinged with regret. "To make matters worse, I allowed Archmage Selee to depart just when we need him most for the vessel, and now I'm filled with uncertainty about our chances of crossing the perilous sea towards Aranka."

"May I have word, Divine Empress?" Overseer Akhimeni spoke.

"Aye, you can."

"Looking back, I now understand that I made the correct decision to disobey Master Alessandro and allowing you to join the battle because of your persistent plea. Aye, I had the constant worry that you might meet an untimely end and it consumed my every thought, wondering if I did the correct decision." She nodded with a smile rarely seen in her. "Along with the entire Court of Maids, I pledged my allegiance to the Divine Empress, even though Master Alessandro and Archmage Selee had harsh words and choices after the encounter against the Korba from the cave. I could feel the fire inside you, and I knew that your strength would eventually be unleashed. Your participation in the battle saved this Guild from destruction and prevented *Deken Karsaker* from being cut short prematurely. And as you overcame, I have faith you will do the same with our next journey."

"I agree with her, Nehel," Ser Marissa said.

"As I do," Juni also spoke.

"I have to admit we were wrong about you," Alessandro said, acknowledging his mistake in sending her away to the Ri. "But if you wish to point the recent massacres in Molke and Salter, it was the Korbas and the Aquelarre group you mentioned that are responsible."

"Besides, I believe we all comprehend why you came to Sankaris, a demigoddess among us," Keleana also took part in the responses. "Without your existence, we would be powerless against the tough Korbas."

"I appreciate all you," she nodded, taking a sip of water, showing her obvious fatigue.

Noticing her exhaustion, Alessandro made a suggestion. "It would be wise to pause the meeting until the following morning, giving the Divine Empress a chance to rest well."

Nehel could not decide whether to listen to her uncle's advice or continue. But in the end, she agreed with him and signaled the Herald.

"The Guild's meeting is adjourned until the first rays of sunlight to reconvene tomorrow." Dessidere concluded.

17

THE TINKLEN

Since the tragedy at Molke, Nehel found it impossible to drift off to sleep. Even while lying in bed, her eyes remained open, fixated on the darkness above. The cold, white light of the moon from No Sak seeped through the window, casting a glow that allowed her to observe the complex details of the wooden ceiling. As she lay there, invisible images of the bodies from the Akiaba massacre continued to haunt her thoughts.

Afraid to close her eyes, she dreaded her nightmares would come to life. She longed for Ser Juni's presence throughout the night, yearning for even a hint of solace, but she deemed it inappropriate to be alone with him in her chamber after dark.

They were not kids anymore.

She also knew it would not be proper for him to be alone with her in the night, given his new role as a knight.

Her mind shifted from the haunting thoughts, now consumed with meditating on Juni and the possibilities of their future together. She had a strong, intuitive feeling that he was the one she would spend the rest of her life with.

Nehel knew that eventually they would end up together, but the ambivalence of what would happen next loomed over her clairvoyant abilities. All she could perceive was darkness, yet a sense of suspicion crept into her consciousness.

A disturbing sound and an unsettling feeling of someone's presence interrupted her thoughts, making her jump and sit on the bed, afraid that a Korba had entered the chamber.

From the darkness, a tiny bare figure of evidently large, round black eyes on his enormous head appeared with its pale skin standing out. It did not resemble any mystical or ordinary animal, but a small creature.

She recognized it immediately and learned of a race that was known only to a few, as taught by the late Sorcerer Uskam.

A Tinklen. Or a gnome, as the people would call it.

No one knew its origins. Opinions varied on the Tinklens, with some considering them to be magical entities and others categorizing them as a special breed of animal.

Archmage Selee confided in her that in Salter, only a few Tinklens lived within the Citadel. The nature of their functions remained a mystery.

With a match, Nehel promptly lit a candle and repositioned its holder to get a better look at the creature. She wore a warmth smile, signaling her intention to make it feel welcomed as she noticed the hesitance to get closer.

"Do not be afraid and talk to me, little," she said with courtesy. "Why had you come?"

An acute voice emerged from the Tinklen and spoke with paused words. "I am Pi-U, Leader of the nation of Bick and the Tinklens. I apologize for my sudden arrival, Divine Empress, but I must bring an urgent matter to your attention."

Nehel made a small nod of agreement and descended from the bed. She walked over to a corner of the chamber where a chair was and pulled it closer. With measured steps, she approached Pi-U and settled herself into the seat. "Please, go ahead. I'm all ears."

"Considering our otherworldly nature, we held the belief that it was best to not interfere in the matters of Sankaris. But news of the catastrophes reached us, demanding our attention and we shall not ignore them."

The Empress studied the small creature with curiosity, noting the paused accent in his words as she agreed with him. "Before we get to the matter, I wish to know about you. And why you remained hidden all that time?" She offered the Tinklen a seat.

But the strange creature named Pi-U did not react nor moved from his place. He stood in the same place, but kept talking. "In ancient times, long forgotten by our memories, our ancestors arrived in this world and created a civilization on the island of Bick, named after our homeland. They made a solemn vow to remain hidden and unseen by the people of Sankaris. . ."

"I apologize for the interruption, Pi-U, but. . . What was the actual reason your ancestors left their homeland?" She could not avoid her apprehension and asked. However, the Tinklen remained silent, but Nehel sensed the answer inside his mind, and her face instantly transformed into a serious one. "It was Ardek Korba. Am I right?"

"You have said so, Divine Empress." With a somber and fearful tone but still paused in his words, the Tinklen replied. "Despite our all acknowledgement we have gathered, we cannot explain the enigmatic nature of the Korbas, and we believe they are eternal. They are beings who traverse from one world to another, leaving destruction and carnage, infecting countless many others to transport them elsewhere."

Nehel's surprise became clear when the true nature of the Korbas was revealed. "I had an intuition that they were venturing from world to world, but. . . Are not they from the Netherworld?"

"All the locals on Sankaris have long believed this myth to be true." Pi-U assured without a hint of emotion on his face. "Contrary to your belief that the Netherworld is in the deeps of the world, they actually originate from an unapproachable domain where only malevolence thrives. They have already obliterated countless worlds before reaching Sankaris."

The Empress lowered her hazel eyes, deep in thought, as she fell into a contemplative silence. "Listening to your words, I now cannot grasp the true essence of my existence as a demigoddess and what is my stance. Still, my purpose for being here is unmistakable."

"I have reached to you because you are one of a kind, as the other worlds were not fortunate as Sankaris is in having you accurately during the Korba intrusion," the Tinklen said. "No emperor or empress existed in the worlds that perished, leaving them defenseless. Until every living being, from the largest mammals to the most imperceptible microorganisms, is extinguished, they will persist in their destructive rampage, decimating this world."

Nehel quickly observed Pi-U speechless, realizing the gravity of the situation. "What do you wish from me?"

"Let us be part of the *Deken Karsaker*. Our advanced transportation system is at your service, ready to guide you across the Beyond Sea, as you must be present when the moons' alignment occurs."

The Empress nodded in awe with an open mouth.

"In the Thirty-Fifth day of the Fifth Month in the First Year of the *Tikl the Second of Nehel,* I officially reconvene this halted meeting the evening before," Dessidere declared, restarting the Guild's session.

Those who were present the previous day were in the hostel's ballroom. The strain and concern of the current situation in Sankaris kept some people awake at night, as their constant yawning was a clear sign of their sleeplessness.

The Empress, too, could not suppress a yawn. With all eyes on her, she leaned forward, placing her hands on the smooth surface of the wooden round table, releasing a sigh before finally breaking the silence. "My dears, I have important revelations to make that might improve the state of *Deken Karsaker.*"

"What is it?" Marissa asked, startled.

"During the night, a Tinklen appeared before me, sharing crucial information that you need to be aware of." Everyone murmured in surprise. But with a single gesture, she silenced them. "Pi-U, the Leader of his realm, hails from a celestial world that no longer exists. His descendants sought refuge here, aiming to establish a new home. Contrary to our belief, they are not gnomes."

"I have read about them at the Academy, but I never imagined that they could come from the heavens!" Alessandro exclaimed.

"I wondered how he slipped past my guard unnoticed." Juni said, amazed.

"And so the Korbas too!" she added.

The last revelation shook everyone, causing a few to rise from their seats.

"Aye, they are not from the Netherworld as we believed, but from an unreachable place where the evilness exists and their nature is to seek annihilation in every world until life is no more."

Silence.

"Why Sankaris?" Alessandro said, unsure of his question.

"They are like locusts. Once they finish with a crop, they move on to the next one at random," she sighed, still feeling her exhaustion. "The Korbas ended up in Sankaris not by choice, but because it was the next option once they had finished their previous destination's resources."

"But they are not locusts!" Alessandro clarified, still hard to believe. "They are creatures with mind and consciousness!"

"Yet, they emanate an unmistakable aura of pure malevolence."

"If they are also from the heavens. How they could figure out the weakest points of Sankaris? How they know to put us under our knees?"

"Aye, they almost defeat us back at Tempest Post with their red mantises," Keleana pointed out. "The devastation spared no one—Salter, Molke—and do not forget the Gesha."

"I shall mention the infection's reach in various areas of Berrem," Ser Marissa stated.

"With that revelation, a question lingers," Alessandro said, as his fingers grazed his chin. "Who sent you?"

"During our discussion, Pi-U and I agreed we cannot explain it. Why Sankaris?" Nehel replied with a nod.

"Perhaps you are a blessing in disguise," Marissa said with assurance.

"Let us not stray from the matter that holds our utmost concern and concentrate," the Empress advised. "Pi-U had come to us to share some of their machinery as they agreed to join us in the *Deken Karsaker*."

"What kind of machinery?" Alessandro asked and took a sip of his wine, as he leaned back in the chair, feeling its soft cushion against his back.

"The good news, uncle," her eyes flickered towards someone in particular. "And the same goes for you, Jumeni, that the Tinklens possess the abilities to manufacture a significant number of muskets, identical to the schematics left by the engineers."

A smile spread across the silent girl's face.

"Is that all, Nehel?" Alessandro inquired while toying with his cup, suspecting she had something else to say.

"Rather than utilizing the Divine Vessel to reach Aranka, they offered us with an array of their unique transportations, ensuring that anybody could travel," the Empress assured, stunning everyone. "They even know how to pass through the blockage on the Beyond Sea," she concluded.

18

THE QUEEN

Lady Fabehel could not believe her eyes as she looked out at the city of Siennt in the morning light. It had been days since she arrived, but the presence and the late absence of a giant black eagle on the tower still felt unreal.

Sat in her usual wheelchair, she had two papers in one hand.

A note had the vagrant's name of who sold Alessandro's brother. She had kept this name hidden, not yet sharing it with anyone, and was unsure if she should reveal it or keep it to herself.

During sunrise, a ruby pigeon delivered a message from Alessandro, adding to the other paper she held. She hoped for kind and sweet words from him to ease her heart, but he spoke with the detachment of a news messenger rather than her intimate partner. The medallion felt warm against her touch, a tangible reminder of the night they spent together, feeding her belief that deep down, he truly cared for her. She knew it because she could feel him.

She took the choice to continue on her path by suppressing her feelings, committed to the mission gave upon her by the Empress. She could not afford to indulge in missing her partner or showing her emotions, not after the ravaging events in Molke and Salter.

As she heard the approaching steps, Fabehel swiftly concealed the papers inside her pocket and spun around, manipulating the magical arrows in her wheelchair's armrest. Wary and afraid, she felt the touch of her hidden dagger under her purple dress, always ready to defend herself. The sight of Corr entering her chamber brought her instant relief, causing her to let out a sigh.

"We are ready, milady." The feline assured.

Fabehel responded with a nod and moved her wheelchair out, followed by her Escort.

Upon exiting the inn, she was surprised to see a luxurious carriage with Corr's and her amber and golden horses, along with two brown ones, instead of the simple cart she had arrived in from Seled Post. A feline chauffeur welcomed her as he opened the door.

"I thought it would be best if you delivered a memorable presentation before the queen upon arriving in Finnerr," Lord Doni said with a light smile. "I believe you should go with all the comfort of an Ambassador of the Divine Empress."

With a nod of gratitude, Lady Fabehel requested Corr's help to lift her from the wheelchair and settle her into the carriage seats. Despite her familiarity with a life of luxury, she could not help but feel uneasy in the opulent insides. Much to her surprise, Corr entered later, followed by Lord Doni, as the door closed behind them.

"May I inquire about your motives for joining us on this journey?" she asked Doni as her voice had a tone of distrust.

"Please do not misunderstand me, milady. I have the responsibility of looking after Sienntin the current crisis. With the eagle gone and the unfortunate fates of Molke and Salter, we might be at the end of the world."

Her eyes glared with indignation at Corr, who remained unsurprised. "Did you know about it?"

"I believe his reasons were valid, as he intends to look for a solution alongside Fenn and the Brekens. So, aye, I must apologize for granting him permission without informing you first." The feline replied.

"At first," Lord Doni clarified, "Corr adamantly refused to allow me to come with you. Please, do not blame him."

"Why did not you come to me first to find a solution and speak on your behalf to the queen?"

"For what purpose? Just like how the Divine Empress ended the Giefo Trade?" With a voice full of suspicion and authority, the lord spoke. "As you have informed me, she is busy with her interests with Aranka during the alignment of the moons, abandoning us defenseless against the malevolent demons."

"That is why I am here!" she yelled in anger. "As Ambassador, the Divine Empress entrusted me to make the right choices in her name!"

"Do you really think an Arankan with no feet could do something like that?" In a mock tone, he responded.

"Do not dare to disrespect Lady Fabehel!" As Corr growled, he readied his claws.

With speed, Lord Doni drew a dagger from his belt and pressed it against the feline's neck, just below its chin. "Try to harm me and I swear all Siennt will come to give both of you death!"

"What is the meaning of it?! You scoundrel!" Fabehel shouted while looking at her Escort paralyzed by the dagger.

"Word reached Queen Shiann about your presence and your intention to seek an audience with her," he replied with a silent nod, as his grip on the blade against Corr's neck kept tightening. "In a promise to bring you to her, she offered me giefo to work with, so it will ensure monetary resources for my homeland."

Fabehel signaled Corr to behave, and she watched how Lord Doni withdrew his dagger and returned it to its sheath. "Let us do your way, then! Take us to the queen!" She replied defiantly.

The lord's sinister grin spread across his face as he nodded, satisfied with his accomplished wish. He then rapped his knuckles against the ceiling of the carriage, signaling to the chauffeur that it was time to leave.

As the vehicle started moving, the three passengers could immediately sense the motion.

"Anyway, the queen is expecting us." Despite Fabehel's fierce glaze, Lord Doni remained unfazed by her words.

The silence among the three passengers grew more pronounced as their eyes remained fixed on the dense jungles of Fenn while the carriage traveled south. Fabehel distrusted a certain lord and felt disappointed by Corr's decision without consulting her. The feline was constantly watchful of Doni. And the lord appeared satisfied with his purpose.

Fabehel noticed Corr's relief as he inhaled deeply, finally catching the familiar aroma of his homeland that he had talked about for years, expressing his disgust for the humid and rainy scent from the north. Curiosity compelled her to look through the window to her right, eager to observe the unfamiliar surroundings and get to know Fenn, the last kingdom on Sankaris.

While passing by a small, impoverished town of un-known name, Fabehel could not help but notice Fennen vehicles and machinery she had only read about. Despite not having horses, the felines invented and constructed steam-powered engines to transport themselves, bypassing the scarcity of horses in the kingdom, although their speed was inferior to that of equines. The Fennen were skilled not only in constructing ground-based vehicles but also in crafting steam-powered vessels that were used as ferries by inhabitants of other realms.

The contrast between Berrem and Fenn was stark, de-spite their proximity.

As everyone on board was startled, the carriage halted in the middle of the jungle, confusing everyone.

Filled with fear, the chauffeur flung the door open in a split second and spoke with everyone. "I plead with all of you to step off right now."

The passengers could not help but notice the dozen sentinels standing behind them, dressed in dark orange uniforms adorned with the engraved royal symbol of a feline face in yellow on their vests. Their small crossbows remained aimed at them.

Corr carried Fabehel in his arms, and both made their way outside.

Lord Doni exclaimed, feeling insulted. "Do you not all know who I am?!"

"We all know who you are!" A raspy female voice an-swered.

Catching everyone's attention, an aged female feline with white fur and striking green eyes walked towards them. Dressed in elegant dark red velvet clothes, she moved slowly, relying on a stick for support.

Doni bowed as a sign of respect. "My apologies, your majesty! As requested, I bring you your prisoners."

"Prisoners? My only request is for them to be brought to me unharmed and secure!" she clarified with indignation. "It was your idea to bring the giefo you had been wishing for!"

"I thought. . ."

"No! You do not think you fool! Your insanity knows no bounds, as you have even dared to disrespect the Divine Empress by imprisoning her emissaries!"

With a subtle nod towards the closest sentinel, in silence, she instructed him to carry out her previous orders.

In response, the sentry pulled the trigger of his crossbow.

With a fatal arrow lodged in his head, Lord Doni's body collapsed to a sudden end to his life.

Terrified and surprised, Corr and Fabehel stared at the elderly female as they tried to decipher the motive behind his death.

"He was a wicked man who would sell his own children for his benefit, with a reputation so fearsome that even the mention of his name sent shivers down the spines of everyone in his city. But his people remained silent, refusing to speak for what they felt like an eternity," as she replied, she poked the lifeless body with her stick. "Siennt fell into misery not because of the ending of the Giefo Trade, but because of his depravity."

"And you must be Queen Shiann," Lady Fabehel guessed, still held by Corr's arms.

"Aye, and it is a great honor that the Divine Empress listened to my envoys and sent someone to me to speak on her behalf, especially with a fellow Fennen like your Escort," she said with satisfaction and admiration. "Shall we step into the carriage and attend to our matters as we travel towards Finnerr?"

"Orr described everything what had happened in the Ri before the Divine Empress, including the meeting they had with Chief Senaten," observing through the window of a moving carriage, the queen remarked. "While I did not desire the fates for Molke and Salter, I urge you to grasp the gravity of the situation and consider reestablishing the trade, even if it is limited to Brek and Fenn, for our collective defense."

"Even if you intend to continue the slavery in the mines?" Corr replied with resentment. "Have you forgotten your deal with Lord Kong?"

Fabehel hushed her Escort to not speak in the conversation, using only a quick, wordless reprimand.

"I am just as guilty as Lord Kong, my dear," the queen replied with a stare deviating from the window. "I was younger... and naïve. Being the sole royal heir, I enjoyed a life of luxury as the spoiled princess. However, everything changed when my father passed away, and I made choices I believed were for the greater good. Now, I must bear the weight of my decisions, knowing that the outcome of the last kingdom hangs in the balance."

"Do you believe that continuing with the trade and exploiting the mines will rectify the errors you have made?" Fabehel asseverated with harsh words. "I do not care if you are a remorseful monarch. What matters is acknowledging the damage inflicted on countless families!"

"I do not want to choose sides, but the Kiffenn Rebellion is merely a result of your actions," Corr stated.

Queen Shiann remained silent. Her gaze drifted outside the carriage window as it rolled along. It took her a while before she found her words. "It was unfortunate that, as the last monarch with no heirs, I find myself on the brink of departing this world. My impending death leaves behind a legacy that everyone wishes to erase from memory."

"What is the meaning of it?" Fabehel inquired, confused.

The monarch's green eyes bore into her soul. "I have known you since so long, milady. Being Princess Natahel's sister, although not by blood, I am familiar with your type and character. I have heard plenty about your skill at the Arankan Quarter in Sarak. You, my dear, are a remarkable woman who should be in my place when I leave!"

Fabehel's eyes widened in astonishment as she let out a gasp. "What do you mean?"

"You are my chosen successor, and my greatest desire is for you to become a queen and correct the mistakes I made. Following that, the decision of Fenn's fate lies in your hands."

As Corr witnessed the conversation, he was at a loss for words as his astonishment was clear on his face.

"Could not you have picked someone who is more fit? A Fennen?"

With a brief chuckle, the queen replied. "The Divine Empress, being the ultimate monarch, surpasses us. The Fennens, regardless of their loyalties, will accept her as their Empress. As her Ambassador, you would play a crucial role in restoring the peace and prosperity that the kingdom once enjoyed."

"Even after hearing your motives, I am not the one who can determine the fate of Fenn!" she replied, annoyed. "I suggest you meet Aeienn and together determine what is best for your realm!"

"How do you know Aeienn?!" Corr inquired, perplexed.

"One night, she paid me a visit and shared her story," then turned to the monarch. "And she also told me about your alliance with Lord Kong and the Chief Senaten, whose collaboration ignited the rebellion."

Queen Shiann retrieved a delicate handkerchief from beneath her sleeve and gently wiped her face. "May we continue this conversation at the palace?" As she requested, her breathing grew fast and labored. "We may possess feline traits, but we share many human-like aspects."

The queen ignored the two passengers and peered outside, clearly anxious about reaching her destination.

Fabehel, wise as she was, examined every subtle movement from the queen, interpreting the motives behind her behavior, and it left her feeling uneasy.

Finnerr, the capital of the Kingdom of Fenn, stood as a sprawling metropolis of stone structures and elevated towers, in the middle of a dense wilderness, surpassing even the likes of Ri, Carretem, and Estolk in size, yet distinct and singular in its own way. It was something that Fabehel noticed as soon as she arrived.

As she had learned earlier, the transportation in the realm relied mostly on steam engines, so the only horses she saw were the four pulling the carriage. The palace had a multitude of splendid vehicles reserved for the queen and her people, while the ones for the common people in the burgh were a mix of cheap iron and wood. The versatility of steam-based transportation, which could replace horses for many purposes, amazed Fabehel.

She found carriages that transported entire families, as also others that carried heavy loads, like wood or charcoal. She had read and learned from others that the Fennen were known for their ingenious inventions, which also included precision time-measuring pieces.

Despite their advancements, the Fennens preserved their traditional way of life, maintaining the same architectural style in their structures and embracing simplicity in their clothing and daily routines.

Regardless, Fabehel held onto the belief that the Jyistereerk would find their inventions valuable.

After returning to his hometown, she also noticed Corr's indifference towards everything. It was understandable why he had such a hardened attitude, considering he was born and lived in this city for only a few short years before being forced into slavery in the Mines of Tiunnff.

As Fabehel exited the carriage at the palace, she felt struck by the familiar but smaller scale of the surroundings, reminding her of the estate where she and Princess Natahel grew up in Byarte, yet lacking the grandeur of King Vihen's faded palace in Aranka. However, the exuberant vegetation under the tropical climate intensified the contrast.

As Corr settled Fabehel into her wheelchair, the queen apologized, feeling unwell. But she assured them of a future audience to continue their conversation. Both watched as the monarch departed, accompanied by two servants.

Dienn approached them, catching them off guard, and made a respectful bow. "Welcome to the Royal Palace of Finnerr," she said. Her voice was kind but her poise apparently peculiar, as if she were a completely different person from the one who had spoken to the Empress at Ri. "Please, follow me."

"Thanks," Fabehel noticed something in her. "Where are the emissaries, Orr and Barr, if I may know?"

Before she could give an answer, the feline of gray fur and purple eyes fixed her gaze on them. "Under the queen's instructions, they must be in the Breken Nation to hold treaty discussions."

She no longer spoke, instead turned and requested to be followed once more.

As Corr pushed Fabehel's wheelchair towards the interior of the palace, he leaned in and whispered in her ear. "She is in fear. I smell it."

In a soft mutter, she inquired. "Why?"

"Something is going on with the queen. I do not trust her."

After getting her much-needed rest and cleansing herself, Fabehel could not resist the temptation to take a peek through the window. What she found there filled her with excitement—a vast rosarium stretching out before her. Her amazement grew as she saw vibrant roses flourishing in the tropical environment of Fenn. She had no idea that the Fennens had cleverly adapted techniques to enable cold-climate plants to thrive in warmer regions.

She requested permission from one servant to visit the gardens, which were not just filled with flowers but also housed an extensive collection of botanical wonders. The servants at the palace generously granted her entrance and even assisted her with the wheelchair.

Following a guided tour of the gardens, Fabehel sought solitude to contemplate her position as an Ambassador, the queen's unexpected choice of her as a successor, and the growing doubts surrounding the monarch. The memory of Corr claiming to detect the scent of fear in Dienn, the diplomatic emissary known for her open-mindedness in the Ri, lingered in her mind. She could not help but wonder why Dienn seemed oddly reserved, as if she was hiding something.

She basked in the gentle warmth of the sun caressing her face, enjoying the enticing scent of roses that compelled her to close her eyes and savor the moment. Suddenly, a rustling sound broke the tranquility of the moment, causing her to spin around with a mixture of surprise and caution. With her hand concealed under the skirt, she wielded her dagger and threw with precision at the ground near the hidden intruder among the nearby bushes.

"Please, milady! It is me, Aeienn!" The feline of dark gray fur and a spotted pattern emerged with her hands raised.

"Could you share with me the reason for your arrival in this way?" Fabehel inquired with distrust.

The leader of the Kiffenn exited, taking measured steps. She picked up the dagger, studying it with a mixture of admiration and curiosity as her eyes widened with a mesmerized gaze. "Arankan made as I recognize it."

"It. . . was a gift from my mentor," she replied with a knot in her throat. "Tin had been by my side since I was five and stayed with me until just a tikl ago. Unfortunately, he died during the *Siege of Sarak*."

Aeienn nodded as a sign of sympathy and returned the dagger to her. "Keeping my presence in the palace hidden, I come to you with news of the Arankan settlement, as I promised."

"What news do you bring me?" she inquired while observing the curious male attire of the Fennen female.

At first, she was at a loss for words, but eventually, she found the empathy within her to respond. "I am sorry, milady. We found the settlement, but with only remains of dead Arankans. We found all of them scattered over the place."

"We are not sure how it happened," Aeienn said with somber gesture. "The locals from a nearby town saw how the queen's army stormed in, to enslave all the settlers."

A tearful Fabehel observed the place with horror and consternation. The charred remnants of wooden buildings lay hidden beneath a thick layer of vegetation were a testament. As she looked down, she noticed the Arankan artifacts, partially buried but still distinguishable. Amongst the ruins, she could discern the bones of settlers, a corroboration of the atrocities committed.

Not even the children could escape the horrors of the massacre.

Corr stood behind the wheelchair, silently observing his surroundings with arms crossed. "If they came to enslave all of them. Why is everyone dead?"

"I am told that a confrontation unfolded as the Arankans resisted. Faced with an inevitable loss against the guards, they chose the unthinkable: sacrificing their children to avoid a life of slavery."

"This is our way," Fabehel mentioned. Her voice had grief and bitterness. "In the bygone era of Aranka, when a burgh was under siege and the defeat seemed inevitable, the locals resorted to sacrifice their own children, hoping to spare them from falling into the hands of the invaders."

"The queen is guilty of this atrocity," Corr said with tense silence through his particular voice.

"I will make her pay for it!" Fabehel muttered through clenched teeth. She tightly gripped the medallion, causing pain, almost making her trembling hand to bleed. "But it has to be in my ways!"

19
THE SIBLINGS

Keleana of Estherleon sat on the chair, absently sipping her wine from a metallic cup, before an empty round table, the very spot where the Guild had convened, while her small almond eyes remained focused ahead as her mind had a whirlwind of thoughts.

Her entire life, she had believed in countless things, but the Empress' revelation about the Korbas and the Tinklens altered her perception of Sankaris forever. The Korbas had always been associated with the underworld in her mind, just like the Korbeens she had combated, as the intimidating red mantises. She was still trying to wrap her head around the fact that the Korbas, beings from another world, were the invaders of this world.

Whether it was the Netherworld or the outer world, still, they were the invaders.

Out of nowhere, a door swung open and slammed shut, causing her heart to race. With urgency, Captain Kanden barged into the ballroom, his blue eyes immediately found on the table crowded with wine bottles. He grabbed a full bottle and used his teeth to pop off the cork, spitting it out.

Keleana observed him with a disliking frown and raised eyebrows.

After taking a large sip from his wine, the Captain approached the window and paused, pointing it with his half-empty bottle. "From this spot I can see *The Wandering*, our beloved home, sits still, to never sail the seas again." He sighed with a mix of deception and anger. "I have heard that those damned Tinklens have vessels that are much better than that!"

As Keleana rolled her eyes up, a strange feeling of connection to him surfaced. "Why did you become a seaman, then?" She placed her head on both hands, which were supported by her elbows on the table.

Kanden finally gave a stare to her after hearing the question, as he was about to give another sip. "Growing up on the beach, I cherished waking up at the sight of the sea every morning."

"Instead of buying a forever moving boat, you could have invested in a house by the beach!" She said with sarcasm.

"Well, at least with the forever moving boat, I will never have to bother the damned neighbors!" Offended, he rebutted and took another sip from his bottle. Taking a seat on a chair, he positioned himself next to the Marshal. "When I lost my mother during my childhood, my father brought me to a burgh to live with my uncle. Ever since then, I developed a deep resentment towards him as I was away from the beach and I made a vow to become a seaman to be always in the sea."

Keleana became intrigued, and her curiosity piqued. "Please, tell me your story."

The Captain sighed and replied. "My mother found my father, a man of mysterious origins, on the beach, injured and with no recollection of his past. Over time, he healed his wounds, but his memory remained absent. Yet, he eloped with my mother and had me." He exhaled. "What is your story, Marshal? I heard you were a fine paladin."

"I was, Captain. But I rather not to talk about it," Keleana requested with a light smile as she tried to avoid a reply. "Please share the names of your parents with me. Comprehending your story would be easier for me if I knew their names."

Kanden noticed her evasive attitude, but he overlooked it for now. "Mother's name was Liliehel of Tharyte, from the Arankan west coast," he sighed and gave a sip from his bottle. "But mother called my father Polehen, meaning *Forgetful*. As I mentioned earlier, he could remember nothing, not even his own name."

"Did Polehen ever remembered his true name?" she asked, while holding her cup and leaning on the chair's back, loosened. "Your story seems more interesting than the ones from troubadours."

"I do not think so. Despite his best efforts, he could recall nothing from his past." Kanden raised his index finger. "However, he treasured a memento, important to him. He knew it, but the memory eluded him."

"What memento?"

Kanden nodded, setting his bottle down on the table. He reached into his pocket and pulled out a small leather bag. Inside, he found a well-loved bracelet woven with threads of different colors. Its letters were partially erased by passaging time. "It had some unreadable name, but my father guessed it, and hence, I carry that name."

When Keleana saw the bracelet, it immediately shook her, causing to throw the cup to the ground and spill the wine. "Where did you get it?!"

Kanden could not explain her sudden and strange reaction. "Despite feeling resentful, I reluctantly accepted this gift from my father and held on to it. I regretted not to throw it." He noticed how she paled and shivered. "What is wrong?"

"This!" she exclaimed, pointing to the bracelet with a trembling finger. "I was eight when I made it for my father!"

"Eh?" the Captain was a loss for words.

Keleana nervously stood from her seat and paced back and forth until she abruptly halted, gasping for breath as she struggled to speak. But in the end, she explained. "Your father and my father are the same person!"

Kanden observed the bracelet, throwing it onto the table with a startled expression, and stood up to give her an astonishing gaze. "Are you telling me you are my eldest sister?!"

"Aye," she nodded with a trembling nod. "Our father was Kaiden of Estherleon."

"That mage?!"

She affirmed.

He wasted no time in finishing the wine from his bottle to unwind.

Nehel was behind the door, hidden, as she had listened to them.

Ser Juni approached, and she gestured him to remain silent with a firm hand.

"What are you doing, missy?" he asked with perplexity and disapproval as he observed her actions, crossing his hands and shook his head.

"Quiet, Juni!" she hissed. "Marshal Keleana and Captain Kanden are siblings."

Puzzled, the Second Knight observed the door. "How is it possible that they have crossed paths?"

And a smile emerged from her. "I used my abilities to bring them together."

"Again?!" he groaned in disapproval. "Did not we agree you would not use your powers to interfere with the destinies of others?"

20

THE NAVIGATOR

The Empress, attired in her iconic white tunic and holding her golden rod, let out a sigh as a gentle breeze caressed her face. She was on a wooden box positioned in a mostly empty harbor from vessels. Behind her, a large crowd stood in tense silence, but the two Pillars and Ser Juni were the ones nearest to her.

The wait felt endless.

The day was misty, with brilliant white lights reflecting off the clouds. A hazy mist shrouded the horizon, masking the view of the sea.

As a skillful sailor he used to be, Captain Kanden shielded his blue eyes from the silvery glare and try to observe the evasive boundary, as the crew of *The Wandering* joined him.

Marshal Keleana and her soldiers from the Imperial Guard maintained control over the crowd of thousands, mostly Sarrem's locals and outsiders. However, she could not help stop the constant glances at Kanden, as her eyes drifted from the event multiple times. She felt uneasy, unable to comprehend the existence of a sibling she never knew about. "Focus on the Divine Empress and the Tinklens!" she reminded herself to keep a close watch on the Tinklens, as they were unfamiliar and a threat to Nehel, as she believed.

"Nehel, are you certain they will arrive?" Alessandro asked his niece, noticing her fixated gaze towards an invisible horizon, but she remained unresponsive.

"Aye, uncle," she responded. Her hands tightened around the rod as concern sneaked into her thoughts about the Tinklen named Pi-U, unsure if he would make his promise. "Let us wait a little more."

"I highly distrust they would make an appearance. I truly doubt it." Ser Marissa spoke her mind.

"Do not be skeptical and wait!"

Alessandro and Marissa glanced at each other to shrug their shoulders.

With a stare at the mist, Nehel's insides churned with begging, hoping that it was not just an illusion, a lie. As she recalled that night, she could still sense his aura, which made her believe in the truthfulness of his words and revelations. She knew it.

Dessidere and Jumeni stood nearby, observing the scene rather than participating. However, he was visibly nervous. His hands trembled as she noticed. The girl wanted to console him and gently took his hand. Her touch calmed him. He stared at her, startled at first, but eventually nodded in appreciation.

The Empress could not conceal her anguish, as the obvious rhythmic tapping of her sandaled foot against the wooden box revealed.

Alessandro's heart sank as he noticed it, and he thought of taking his niece inside the inn, preparing himself for what he expected to be a disheartening disappointment to her. As he took the first step closer to Nehel, a sudden rumble emanated from beneath his feet.

The vibrations permeated through everyone, causing a mutual sense of fear.

Nehel could not contain her excitement and a smile drew across her face, knowing they were on their way.

Keleana commanded the Imperial Guard to stand firm and get ready as she unsheathed her sword as a cautious measure.

The roar grew louder, and the vibrations intensified.

The Empress' hazel eyes watched as a colossal vessel emerged from the mist, accompanied by sudden flashes of lightning against the sea. Rather than sailing, hovered above the waters. Slowly, it made its way closer, leaving everyone in a state of stunned silence.

"By the goddesses!" Kanden exclaimed in astonishment. "It is ten times larger than *The Wandering*!"

Unlike most ships, the Tinklen vessel did not have a wooden structure. Instead, it had a metallic gleam, like an unusual material, and was white in hue, but not silver. It resembled a fish, but its design appeared unintentional.

A gradual decrease in vibrations accompanied the vessel's descent onto the water, until finally, it reached the harbor in complete silence.

Impressed and excited, Nehel observed how it stopped just before her. Its surface was devoid of any visible openings or orifices as she could not find any.

A stillness fell over the crowd, creating an air of anticipation. Fear and curiosity mingled within them.

Just in front of the Empress, a door materialized from the surface of the vessel. With its opening, a new orifice appeared, transforming into a ramp that joined the harbor's wooden floor.

The small creature named Pi-U appeared, causing a collective gasp from the members of the Guild, the guards, and the crowd.

"Welcome to Sarrem, little one," Nehel said with a smile.

Soon after, another identical creature followed him from the vessel. After a bow to the Empress, the Tinklens stepped into the harbor.

Marissa, stunned, leaned towards Alessandro and whispered. "Can you believe it? They are tiny and naked!"

"Archmage Yasstro and Selee both taught me that these creatures are genderless and unfamiliar with wearing clothing." He responded in the same way. "However, despite their size and nakedness, they might be our greatest allies we needed."

The smiling Empress descended from the wooden box and made a curious gesture about the second Tinklen.

"Allow me to introduce Ti-K, my aide and the first in line to take charge should anything happen to me, Divine Empress." Pi-U said in paused words. "And it is an honor to announce that unanimously all Bick favors the *Deken Karsaker*."

"It is I who should feel honored! Your assistance is invaluable, and I am grateful."

Pi-U nodded and, together with Ti-K, gestured towards the entrance of the massive vessel. "Please, step aboard *The Navigator*, our transportation system designed to serve the Jyistereerk."

Nehel agreed to the invitation and urged everyone, including most of the Imperial Guard, to join her inside.

The Tinklens had enlarged the vessel's entrance. Most wondered if the small creatures possessed some kind of magic, even though it was a manifestation of their technology. The entrance was wide enough for horses, some mantises including Brisel, carriages, and even large loads of chests filled with stuff and gold coins.

The Jyistereerk's belongings, previously housed at the Palace in the Ri, were being transported to Sarrem, intending to transfer everything to Aranka.

The Empress followed the way on horseback behind Pi-U and Ti-K, who were on foot leading across of a crystal overpass that did not touch any surface. The intricate machinery that surrounded them, along with the diligent works of hundreds of Tinklens, covered most of the interior, leaving no area exposed. And the interior of the vessel was unbelievably vast, appearing to be larger than its exterior dimensions.

Overwhelmed and filled with a mix of excitement and fear, Nehel called Ser Juni with a hand-waving, who came to her side. Seeking solace, she tangled her fingers with his, finding a sense of security in his touch, and he acknowledged her uneasiness.

Riding on her horse Twist, Ser Marissa could not help but exclaim, "This is truly impressive!" A gasp of awe escaped her lips.

While Alessandro heard her words, his dark eyes remained fixed on his niece's intimate interaction with Ser Juni, carefully retrieving a handkerchief beneath his sleeve. As he sensed the memento in his fingers, his heart raced with concerns and desires, realizing the painful distance that would separate him even more from Fabehel, longing for the touch of her fingers. He was about to embark on a journey to the other side of the world.

The Imperial Caravan, comprising the Guild, Imperial Guard, some of the First Knight's pupils, and the Court of Maids, including the crew of *The Wandering*, paraded in complete awe as they beheld an unprecedented marvel, realizing that The Navigator had a stunning otherworldly nature. They could not identify if it was a ship or a moving castle, not even the experienced Captain Kanden.

In the end, the Tinklens made the entrance even larger, allowing the tall, slender, silvering Artensens with their lances to pass through. Instead of taking the bridge, they descended through a ramp, leading them into an area of *The Navigator's* belly, where the void sentinels would pause and await. The perfect formation of the void but mystical sentinels was a testament to their disciplined nature as they rested on their feet.

Pi-U and Ti-K arrived at the end of the overpass. They suggested halt and turned to the Empress with the Guild, requesting to accompany them. Meanwhile, everyone else had to descend to other rooms.

They had to dismount their equines as they entered to another section, discovering it was the Commanding Chamber where two dozens of Tinklens were in charge of the navigation controls. The Pillars, the Second Knight, the Herald, the Artifice, the Marshal, the Overseer of the Court of Maids, the Captain, and the Empress stood in awe, marveling at the enormous window that revealed a view of the sea and Sarrem's port.

Pi-U approached Nehel and with a bow, spoke. "This vessel is yours, Divine Empress. At the service of the Jyistereerk."

Their offering took her aback, unsure of how to respond.

Alessandro noticed his niece's discomfort and walked over to her. "May I have a word with you, Nehel?"

"You can say whatever you need to say here," with a serious face she said, as if she could already expect his response.

As he looked at the Tinklens and the rest of the Guild, he felt a dryness in his throat, realizing they were all waiting for him to say something. In the end, he locked his eyes with her. "Despite the risks, our plan was to embark on the Flying Divine Vessel and sail across the sea, accompanied by Archmage Selee. Unfortunately, we lost both him, and the damn vessel which now sits outside Sarrem." Gasping for breath, he pushed himself to continue. "I find this colossal vessel and the Tinklens' unveiling as too much of a coincidence."

While the Tinklens remained indifferent, the witnesses gasped in anticipation, waiting for the Empress's reaction. Except for that one time when Alessandro was under the spell from Lord Kong Rim, there were moments when he and Nehel had differing opinions on the Jyistereerk's affairs.

The Empress lowered her head, closed her eyes, and focused on taking deep, calming breaths. She turned her gaze towards him, searching for the right words to bring her reply. "Aye, uncle. It is too much of a coincidence, but we do not have another choice." To calm herself, she let out a quick gasp. "Even with the Divine Vessel and the help of the Court of Maids, I doubt our chances of survival against the Korbas and squids."

Alessandro touched his chin and nodded in agreement as his dark eyes fixated on his niece and a whirlwind of thoughts raced through his mind. "We could not risk bringing an end to the Jyistereerk, and now I understand why." He then turned to Pi-U. "Tell me, Tinklen. How did you know about our predicament?"

There was a moment of silence from the Tinklen, but then he revealed a surprising confession. "Since the beginning, we have maintained constant communication with Archmage Selee and Salter. Four years ago, when we discovered the existence of the Divine Empress, our intention was to reveal ourselves and offer our help in the construction of the Jyistereerk. However, Archmage Selee's strict orders prevented us from reaching out to you, instructing us to wait for the opportune time with patience." Pi-U paused for a moment and continued. Archmage Selee announced his departure and instructed us to support the Divine Empress.

"Let me understand what you have said, Tinklen," Alessandro said. "Did he demand your aid with the Divine Empress after his departure from the Guild?"

"Indeed, Master Alessandro."

"I thought of Selee as an honorable man devoted to the Jyistereerk," he stated to Nehel. "But now I realize he had secrets we did not know."

"I am sure he had reasons to keep secrets from us!" she replied, then talked to Pi-U. "What we shall do now?"

Discreetly, Akhimeni approached to Ser Marissa and whispered with a quiver voice. "I just remembered the Sorcerer's Staff. What had the Archmage done with it?"

Marissa looked at her with widened eyes.

"Since the vessel is now under your ownership, I recommend stepping inside to take control," At that moment, Pi-U revealed a circular platform right in front of the massive window as the two dozen Tinklens halted their labor, eagerly awaiting the Empress.

Nehel hesitated as she observed the platform. "Do I have to drive this vessel?"

"Your voice alone will command, I assure you." Pi-U answered.

With her hazel eyes fixated, the Empress examined the white platform before placing her foot on it. As she looked out the window, she noticed the desolate harbor, with only a crowd of locals and the ominous sea stretching out before her, as the mist opened to reveal an early sunset that exposed the red moon, No Kra, in the sky. As she spoke, her eyes formed tears, even though she remained still. "Sadness is taking over me as I know the fatal fate of Berrem."

"What do you mean, Nehel?" Alessandro asked with surprise.

"After we leave," she said as her voice broke, "Berrem will succumb to the Korbas, and the entire region from Molke to Salter will be under the Dominion's control."

Everyone, except for the unresponsive Tinklens, fell into a heavy silence as a wave of sorrow washed over them. Their sudden startle made them realize the importance of establishing a safe and permanent sanctuary for the Jyistereerk, away from any potential threats.

"So, you're suggesting that all the work we've put into fighting these demons has been fruitless?" Ser Marissa asked, concerned.

"What about Tempest Post, Divine Empress? And our people there?" Marshal Keleana's surprise was impossible to mask.

"Are we going to abandon those you have sent to Fenn?" As Alessandro inquired, he anxiously tightened the handkerchief in his hand, feeling his heart race longing to reunite with Fabehel.

The Wandering was always on Captain Kanden's mind, the feel of the wheel in his hands and the familiar scent of tar and rope that made him his home. He could not fathom the idea of never seeing her again.

The Empress kept looking out the window, and she let out a melodious voice. "Only the time will respond to your inquiries and concerns." She extended her arm, directing their attention to the left, where the sea sparkled in the distance. "My littles, this is the exact way we must go, as the *Ykarte* is guiding me with her song."

With Ti-K's supervision, the Tinklens carried out to prepare the vessel for departure.

"I must warn that difficulties lie ahead as we transverse the Beyond Sea." Pi-U explained to the Guild. "Please, hold yourselves while we travel."

Stunned and scared, they watched as the Tinklens manipulated various controls in the Commanding Chamber, causing a subtle vibration to ripple beneath their feet.

Nehel watched through the window as the vessel lifted off from the sea. Her hazel eyes widened with excitement, and a smile spread across her face. However, a hint of fear crept in, causing her to reach out and grasp Ser Juni's hand once more for comfort.

The Navigator maintained a low altitude, barely clearing the water, and adjusted its course according to the Empress's sign.

Beside the harbor, a crowd of hundreds of locals, flanked by the remaining Imperial Guard and Sarrem's sentinels, stood in complete awe as they witnessed the breathtaking appearance of the otherworldly vessel. Nowhere else had they encountered something so unique and unfamiliar.

Alessandro, in awe, strained his eyes to glimpse the crowd as he clenched the handkerchief, watching the vessel where he was going into the open sea with his dark gaze. As he recently learned the truth, his heart shattered as he came to understand the fate of these people.

"Divine Empress, I would advise you to hold on to this guardrail for safety," Pi-U suggested.

Nehel noticed the handrail in front of her and motioned for Ser Juni to join her on the platform, seeking comfort in their shared grip for what was to come.

Citing safety concerns, some Tinklens urged the Guild to stay against the wall.

Ti-K spoke in an unfamiliar dialect as he issued orders to his people behind the panels.

The vibration intensified, causing the horses outside the chamber to neigh in fear.

The air shifted, creating a subtle pressure against the water beneath the vessel.

With a sudden burst of speed, *The Navigator* raced across the sea, leaving a brief trail and creating a splash that caught the attention of the crowd.

The otherworldly white vessel resembling a fish glided over the Beyond Sea as it made its way towards Aranka.

Nehel and Juni tightly gripped the guardrail, feeling the ship suddenly lurch as *The Navigator* swiftly traveled. However, to their surprise, the vessel settled into a strange stillness, as if it had come to a complete halt. As it raced at unimaginable speeds, everyone witnessed the sky transforming from sunset to morning approached as it approached the continent of Tyza.

As expected, a flock of black dragons swooped down from the sky, their wings created a thunderous roar. Meanwhile, giant tentacles of squids emerged from the sea, trying to reach out for *The Navigator*.

In no time at all, it left the creatures behind.

"We just have witnessed a revolution in our ways to sail!" Captain Kanden said, impressed, as the tears fell from his clear eyes, in a mixture of commotion and nostalgia.

Keleana discovered her youngest brother, distraught, and gently grasped his arm with both hands, offering him comfort in his moment of emotional vulnerability.

It took some time, but the vessel distanced itself from the creatures.

There it was.

Aranka.

The once land of monarchs. Nehel's ancestors.

The Gesha had banished the kingdom, leaving it forgotten.

A realm barren like a wasteland.

The true home of the Jyistereerk.

As the gate swung open and a ramp touched the beach's sands, Nehel, gripping her rod, inhaled the salty aroma of the sea and the pungent scent of the arid air tinged with death.

The place was not desolate. Instead, a small crowd had gathered, awaiting her arrival.

Casakans and Kasnasgos.

Archmage Missar approached the Empress, his face devoid of emotion but with his voice brimming with excitement. "In the name of Casak and as a Head, I welcome you to Aranka, Divine Empress. Four years were a burden of time that did not let us to see you in person." He stood. "We were expecting you since the message sent by Archmage Selee communicating you were on board of a Tinklen vessel."

Nehel made a slight nod in awe. "Selee? How?"

"Through the sphere."

Behind the Pillars appeared, causing murmurs of surprise among the crowd, especially Casakans.

Lady Tasarissa, with Alyssa Taskar close behind, rushed towards her daughter Marissa, as tears streamed down their faces as they embraced in a long-awaited hug. She noticed Alessandro standing beside her, and reached out to touch his right cheek with tenderness, offering a nod as a sign of affection and understanding regarding the end of his engagement with her daughter.

While Alyssa cautioned against disrespecting the Empress, Nehel's reassuring gesture suggested that it was of little consequence to her.

Accompanied by the First Official Partak and Overseer Akartaki, Commandant Kartak approached the Empress, bowing with the utmost respect. "As representatives from Kasnasga, we pledge our unwavering devotion and loyalty to the Divine Empress and the Jyistereerk, just as we have done in your absence!"

Nehel's hazel eyes examined the elves with their golden skin, yellow eyes, and pointed ears, reminding her of the Molkans. She fought back the urge to cry, responding with a trembling voice. "You, Kasnasgos, are my brothers and sisters since you come from the same place I was born and raised. Descendants of the Tannes, but from one origin alongside the Kannestes." She sighed, creating a brief silence. "Not as your Empress, but as the last Sorceress of the Clan of the Kannestes, I tell you."

Please, believe us, Divine Empress. We also carry immense pain because our brothers and sisters have departed for the Gakia, disrupting their cycle of life. Kartak replied with sadness. "In both Kao and Kasnasga, I have declared a period of mourning."

"Let us not to deviate from our purpose and tell me where the Ykarte is."

"She is here!" a youthful voice emerged from among the group.

The crowd split in half, forming an aisle guarded by unwavering Casakan sentinels and Kasnasgos soldiers with their hands resting on their scimitars in a gesture of reverence.

As Vasso appeared, the young man crossed the aisle and approached, saluting with a respectful bow. "She is right behind me, Divine Empress."

In a maroon dress and wearing thick round glasses, a skinny young black woman made her way towards Nehel, lingering until she finally stopped, resembling a motionless statue.

As they exchanged stares, causing an eerie silence to descend upon the crowd.

"Tell me. Who you are?"

"I am the living weapon turned human, the gate I was once, and the home for the Jyistereerk."

"Are you the gate that brought those demons?" Nehel asked, sensing her. "Why did you let them to come?"

As most of the Guild had exited from the vessel, they witnessed the unusual exchange of words unfolding before them.

The Ykarte remained indifferent, showing no emotion whatsoever. "Kasana had achieved such harmony over

Sankaris that in me I became a gateway to other worlds. By doing so, she could bring harmony with each one."

"The balance. . ." Nehel murmured with a nod.

"Aye. Empress," the Ykarte replied with no gesture. "The thirst for vengeance consumed Kasana, drawing on all the malice to this world. The Korbas."

"Tell me. Do I share a common place of origin with them?" Afraid of the response, she asked with hesitation.

"To some extent, indeed."

21
THE MOONS

The cloudless sky let Nehel to observe the four moons, even the cloaked No Kra, inching closer to the blazing sun as its rays bathed the desert. She had to walk across the barren land by foot, with no food or water, not mattering how exhausted she was. The hot ground scorched the soles of her bare feet, causing a searing sensation, but she endured and kept going.

It was the *Ykarte* mandate to begin the ceremony that way once the moons started on their path to align. She had ordered the Empress to take these necessary steps.

The Empress had her face glistening with perspiration, feeling her wavy hair and white tunic were moist as she pressed on. Her tired tendons were with fatigue, but never lost sight of *Ykarte*, who moved ahead with flawless steps and with no effort.

Behind her, a lengthy and multifaceted procession of the Imperial Line, including Casakans, Kasnasgos, and even Tinklens, trailed in her footsteps, some on foot and others on horseback. Among them, sentinels brought the gold and belongings from the Ri in Berrem in carts and green mantises, which were transported in *The Navigator*.

Captain Diesso sat on his moving horse, observing a subtle melancholy in Vasso, his newfound companion since their encounter at Stronghold Setok. Seeking to ease the silence between them, he extended a canteen filled with refreshing water. "Are you all right, friend?"

"It is Carlissa, Captain," Vasso sighed, feeling a wave of relief wash over him as the cool water eased its way down his throat, cleaning the sweat from his forehead.

Diesso observed carefully to the youth and understood. "Have you fallen in love with her?"

Vasso widened his eyes, immobile, allowing only the flow of his horse.

With a chuckle, the captain redirected his attention to the front as his eyes witnessed the enduring *Ykarte* followed by a drained Empress. "Do not you recall what Archmage Missar had said?"

"What?"

"She is not human!"

"I heard him!" he shook his head. "I have not fallen in love with Carlissa, but there is a growing fondness that has caught me by surprise."

"Mmm," he nodded with a smile. "You have surely spent a long time together to reach this place."

While riding his red stallion named Breeze, Alessandro watched his niece from behind, feeling helpless as she stumbled from exhaustion. The *Ykarte* sternly forbade anyone from assisting her, emphasizing the significance of the ceremony.

Alessandro took his handkerchief and delicately held it under his nose, hoping to catch a scent of Fabehel's perfume. It reminded him of the night they spent together before parting ways at Seled Post. However, he could smell nothing except for the dry odor of the Arankan desert, where the sand dunes were not made of sand but remnants of the Gesha.

He recalled the *Ykarte*'s instructions.

"Empress, please do not touch me until I say so!" Fixing her gaze through the round glasses, the *Ykarte* requested to Nehel and then turned towards Kartak, who was in the small group. "Commandant, I require a tiny fragment of Kasnasga," she asked.

The elf's eyebrow twitched and rolled his yellowish eyes, lost in thought. He nodded in agreement and reached into his pocket to extract a small crystal vial filled with soil. "This memento is from Kao Island, still considered part of Kasnasga, even though it floats over Casak." He placed it on her open palm.

The *Ykarte* turned to see the Pi-U. "I require a piece of your machinery."

The Tinklen handed her a tiny, delicate piece that belonged to *The Navigator*.

"Archmage, I need yours as well," she said, pointing at Missar.

In response, he offered her with a special piece of jewelry—a mystical object adorned with the emblem of the Akareen, an eight-pointed star.

Fatigued and under the scorching sun, she followed the *Ykarte*, thinking back to her words about her origin.

"While the Korbas and the Tinklens share your common origin, you took on a distinct form—that of the Nehel." The *Ykarte* revealed.

"I was born here, in this world, yet you tell me I am not from here!" She implored, as her voice had confusion and frustration. "Tell me what I am! I know you have the answer!"

"Yet, you chose it as your regnal name," the *Ykarte* assured.

"I know you have the meaning of it!"

The mystical being, whom some referred to her as Carlissa, remained silent but assumed her usual cold and rigid posture. But in the end she revealed. "*Nirkjet, Elakert, Heerkret, Etkert, Laartet.* The Jewel!"

As these five words reached Nehel's ears, everything fell into place for her. Only she could understand them.

With the first meeting between the Empress and the *Ykarte* unfolding, Alessandro's curiosity got the better of him, prompting him to approach Archmage Missar for more details. "What do these words signify? Are these even Arankan?"

"These are words from a long-forgotten ancient Salteran language, Master," he replied in a hushed whisper. "Only the Empress and a select few in Sankaris possess the knowledge to assimilate them. I can not comprehend how they merged with the nuances of the Arankan language."

Alessandro was well-acquainted with Missar, as he had been a student of Yasstro before he set off for Salter. He never spoke to him, but saw him during his study sessions. He always sat in the corner, engrossed in an open book resting on a small table. Beside him, a metallic mug of water sat untouched, used solely for his magical practice.

After becoming a mage, Missar found himself involved with the Casakan government, taking on the responsibility of overseeing the Great Sanctuary in Estolk and eventually earning a seat in the Assembly. First, with Lady Larissa Eskar as Head, later with Lord Orssandro. It was a regular occurrence for Alessandro to see him in his house, engaged in deep conversations with his mother about state affairs.

Although Alessandro was glad to see the archmage, he could not help but miss Selee and the late-night conversations they had, often accompanied by glasses of wine, while in the Ri.

Just as Alessandro was on the path to becoming a mage, Orssandro stepped in and thwarted Yasstro's purposes.

Ser Marissa rode Twist alongside her mother.

Lady Tasarissa had borrowed a horse from the Imperial Guard to accompany her daughter. Yet she did not stop turning to look at the long line formed by people of various races from Sankaris—Casakans, Arankans, Berremens, and those of mixed races, as well as elves and Tinklens—. Despite the losses on the continent of Ryza, she noticed the Jyistereerk was growing larger and stronger. She could not contain her pride as her daughter had the position of Pillar, the third highest rank, just below the Empress and Alessandro. During the rumors that followed the months of the Promise, she realized the Jyistereerk was merely a young girl's idea. Since then, an entire mystical empire had risen to transform Sankaris.

Without pausing, looked at Dessidere walking alongside a stunning Berremen woman, later discovering her to be Jumeni, Ser Juni's sister, and the Empress' Artifice. And she was glad that the Herald had someone as a company, as his presence reminded her of the bond she had and her late husband with him. When they noticed him begging outside their residence with frequency, they took him in. Later, they learned he was alone, with no parents to care for him.

Marissa had found in him the brother she never had.

Alyssa covered her eyes to steal a glimpse of the sun and marveled at the moons near aligned in the clear blue sky. She then turned to Lady Tasarissa, who rode opposite Ser Marissa, and inquired. "Do we ever arrive at our destination on time?"

Marissa who replied to her mother and not to her aunt. "Once you are with Nehel, always expect surprises." She gave a shrug of her shoulders and let out a sigh. "According to the plan, I should be happily married to Alessandro, possibly expecting a child and working as a teacher at the Academy. Instead, I am here as a knight, committed to serving an Empress."

"What the hell does it have to do with the question?!" Tasarissa exclaimed, as her eyebrows furrowed in annoyance. "This is what she did not ask!"

Reprimanded by her mother, Marissa could not help but roll her eyes and release a frustrated breath. "My point in here is. . . we might expect to arrive at our destination, or we might not. With the Empress, there is nothing certain."

"I understand you, girl," Alyssa assured with a nod and a smile.

"Me as well, daughter," Tasarissa's voice held a tone of regret as she scrutinized her from head to toe. "I apologize for my sudden outburst, as there was no valid reason for my reprimand. Your choice to disregard your uncle's instructions and take the right path makes me proud. Now I can see your maturity just looking at your armor, replacing the fancy and inviting dresses you used to wear."

"Mother!" She protested with embarrassment.

From the front, Alessandro's voice resounded, calling her name. "Marissa! Look!"

The Imperial Line came to a halt on the outskirts of the ruins, quickly answering Alyssa's question. Monoliths of pale yellow rose from the sand, blending seamlessly with the ground.

Alessandro's mind flooded with memories of his lessons at the Academy, vividly recalling the descriptions of the Kingdom of Aranka from countless books. He had a mix of awe and sorrow as he laid eyes on the capital, the Citadel of Aranka. It was once a thriving monarchy, rivaling the likes of Berrem or Fenn in their prime. The surprise was so overwhelming that he could not even close his mouth.

A rush of sensations that brought tears streaming down her cheeks overwhelmed Nehel. She felt a strong sense of joy as she entered what she considered her ancestor's home, despite its tragic history. The persisting existence of fear and the echoes of eternal shrieks only deepened her connection to the ones who died.

After noticing his niece in discomfort, Alessandro dismounted Breeze, intending to approach her.

Ser Juni followed his example.

"Stay away from the Empress!" The *Ykarte* mandated with displeasure. "If you even touch her, I will embrace the darkness!"

"Listen to her and halt!" Nehel commanded as she extended her hand.

Just steps away from her, both men froze in surprise with uncertainty.

"You shall listen to the *Ykarte* if you want to keep going with the *Deken Karsaker*."

"Indeed," the mystical black woman agreed serenely. "All of you, stay put right here while the Empress and I enter the Citadel."

The rocky moon of No Kra aligned with the sun, but its diminutive size made it barely noticeable, causing only a slight stir among those in the Imperial Line yet anxious, particularly Archmage Missar, who had dedicated much of his research to studying such celestial occurrences.

As Vasso dismounted, he took measured steps towards the *Ykarte*, pausing at a distance. "Carlissa, will I see you again?"

Witnessing him, Ser Juni felt his heart shatter as he realized Nehel would leave indefinitely, uncertain of when she would return.

The *Ykarte* ignored Vasso and addressed Nehel instead. "Let us go, Empress. We shall reach that place promptly and with no delays."

As No Sak covered most of the sun, the sky partially darkened, and No Kra came into perfect alignment. It would not be much longer before the other two joined.

It was day and night. The Citadel's ruins had faded into mere silhouettes, remnants of a bygone era that had ended with the Gesha.

In extreme fatigue, Nehel yelled, "How much longer do we have to keep going?!" She felt bothered and desperate to stop.

The *Ykarte* remained silent and continued walking towards the destination.

The Empress sighed in frustration as her footsteps continued to follow her. She lifted her face and noticed that the red moon, No Ta, had joined the other two, creating a celestial spectacle with the sun. Soon, No Nunn would join them as well. The partial darkness provided a welcome respite from the blistering heat and parched lips caused by the absence of water.

"We have arrived, Empress," the *Ykarte* stopped.

Nehel's eyes widened as they took in the sight of a colossal circular ruin surrounded by monoliths. A familiar yet unknown and terrifying sensation.

She knew it.

The home of her ancestors.

The place where the monarchs once ruled over the Kingdom of Aranka.

The *Ykarte* spoke with a cold semblance. "Here a palace perched atop a mountain, encircled by the Citadel, offering a view of the vast Beyond Sea, existed." With a momentary pause, her index finger rose higher. "The Korbas used this place as an epicenter for their Gesha."

Nehel could not believe a mountain existed in this precise place. The landscape stretched out before her, completely flat except for the small dunes and scattered ruins.

As the last moon, No Nunn, touched the sun's tangent, nearing the impending darkness, the *Ykarte* offered both hands to the Empress. "Once the four moons align with the sun, my identity as Carlissa will cease to exist. Instead, I will become your home. The mere act of touching me will forever bind me to you and your descendants and I will pledge my allegiance to the Jyistereerk."

In a bit of mistrust, Nehel inspected the *Ykarte*'s hands before locking eyes with her. "Tell me. Why did you choose me over the Korbas?"

"I have not chosen you, Empress," she clarified. "My song was for both you and the Lord of Darkness. But only you listened to my call while he was in invaded by evilness."

Full of understanding, she nodded and grasped her hands.

No Nunn completed the alignment.

Total eclipse.

22

ARANKA YKARTE

As the full darkness engulfed, panic and stupor emerged. Some riders maintained control of their horses and mantises, but many others struggled as the animals spooked and fled in terror.

With the fear of a possible Korba encounter, Alessandro drew his greatsword and prepared for battle alongside Commandant Kartak, who wielded a scimitar, and Ser Juni, who brandished a sword gifted by his Empress. Marshal Keleana and her guards, as many sentinels, were quick to emulate their actions.

Captain Kanden and his crew from *The Wandering* dropped to the ground. Archmage Missar stood tall, prepared to defend them with extended hands.

However, it was strange that the mystical Artensens stood still when they should react to any aggression.

Ser Marissa's instincts kicked in, and she quickly located a shield to protect her mother and aunt. With her sword unsheathed, she stood ready for any threat. Brisel only ran around them.

The ground trembled, as if an earthquake had erupted, and the entire land shook uncontrollably as the moons moved away from the sun that even the Tinklens struggled to maintain their balance.

Invaded by panic, Dessidere fell to his knees and lost it. Jumeni, the tough and silent girl, exposed her compassion by consoling him, revealing her bravery in the face of the events unfolding around them.

As the first rays of light appeared, they cast a golden glow over the land. From the ruins of the Citadel, a majestic mountain rose, and atop of it, a mysterious construction took shape, constructing itself at a gentle pace. As the tremors subsided, everyone could witness the mesmerizing spectacle unfolding before their eyes, yet remained cautious of any probable danger.

The building, which was lightly taking the shape of a majestic palace, appeared to be bathed in the same radiant tone as the sun. From beneath it, a lush carpet of vegetation emerged, transitioning from grass to plants, then to bushes, and finally transforming into towering pine trees. In this remarkable process, they were rebuilding the forest that had long been lost with the Gesha. The scent of death, once prevalent and dry, dissipated, making way for the fragrant aroma of life.

As the sun emerged once more in its complete splendor, and the moons disappeared into the vastness of the blue sky, a sense of awe overwhelmed everyone as they beheld the magnificent sight that lay before their astonished gazes.

The Empress' Palace.

Throughout his ascent towards the mysterious and emerged palace, concerned, Alessandro's determination to locate his niece only grew stronger. He brought with him Ser Marissa and Ser Juni, as well as Commandant Kartak and Archmage Missar. By his stubborn insistence, Vasso also came along.

They rode their horses uphill, navigating through the thick forest without an obvious path, dodging trees, bushes, and even rocks along the way. Alessandro pondered for a moment that constructing a road should be among the initial tasks if the Jyistereerk were to establish this place as a permanent home.

As Ser Marissa turned, a dense wood appeared like to greet her, stretching all the way to the coast, where moments ago there had been nothing but barren land. Reality and dream seemed to meld together, leaving her in a constant state of disbelief.

"What was the *Ykarte*, Archmage?" Kartak twitched his eyebrow, in awe, appreciating his surroundings.

"I thought I had answers, but all I have now are more questions, Commandant." Archmage Missar replied as his gaze locked ahead and scoured the towering pine trees for the palace as they stood tall and vibrant, untouched by time, giving no hint of decay or aging. His keen eye picked up on the elusive glimmer that seemed to emanate from every aspect of nature—the birds, rodents, bunnies, plants, and pines. "I have a strong feeling deep in my gut that this forest harbors mystical forces."

"Are you saying the *Ykarte* made it?"

"Or the Divine Empress herself!"

With curiosity, Vasso absorbed every word of their conversation.

After a long time ascending on their horses, Alessandro could spot some aspects of the massive palace between the trees noticing the proximity, and addressed to Ser Marissa and Ser Juni as they were his companions. "It gives the impression that it has sprouted from the mountain, rather than being built."

"That palace gleams like gold, but it is not gold, Master," Juni added.

"The color of the sun," Marissa affirmed. "Archmage Selee once explained to me that Salter possessed the silver from the night. I reckon if it is the same thing."

"Let us search for an entrance."

The riders maneuvered their horses around the mighty trees until they finally reached the colossal walls and rode alongside them. It did not take long for them to locate it.

The group halted, awestruck by the immense beauty and magnitude of the majestic golden gates. The precise engraving of the eight pointed Akareen star on these gates left them speechless.

"Now what?" Alessandro said, as he touched his chin in incredulity. "Do we push it? I am unsure if we are supposed to use a key, as there does not seem to be any visible opening."

"Or we call someone from inside," Vasso suggested. "Perhaps there is someone in there, like Trasso, when he held the title of Guardian of Sarak."

Startled, everyone looked at the youngster with disapproving frowns, which made him feel uncomfortable.

"Why do you have to bring him up?!" Ser Marissa scolded him.

"Why? What is wrong?" Vasso asked with innocence.

With a strict tone, she requested, "Please refrain from mentioning his name again! Leave him in the tomb!"

"His degraded actions and agonizing demise rendered him unworthy of his given name, lad," Archmage Missar clarified, shifting his gaze back to the gates to study them. "The divinity's element shall open the *Ykarte* gates." He recited from his memory.

"What is it, Archmage?" Kartak inquired, dumbfounded.

"The volume that Lord Orssandro had in his possession, the one that matched the color of this palace, contained these lines. To open them, I believe we must harness the Divine Empress' element."

"The wind," Ser Marissa affirmed, receiving a nod in return.

Still in disbelief, Alessandro's gaze bore into Missar. "So, do we have to blow at the gates?"

"I will bring the wind to open them," with a smile that barely reached his eyes, the Archmage replied. "However, as my expertise lies in water, I am uncertain if I possess the ability to summon the wind without it."

"If our tutor Yasstro could impart his knowledge to me, the world of magic might be within my grasp. Regrettably, it rests in your hands, determining whether we will ever know the Empress' well-being." Alessandro asserted.

Missar agreed and dismounted from his horse. He then asked Vasso to take care of his horse. He solicited everyone to give him some space and step back a bit. Standing in front of the gates, he took a moment to cover his head with the hood of his cloak, closed his eyes, and shook his hands in preparation. He opened his eyes once more and raised his arms, gesturing his hands, using all his strength to summon a gentle gust of air. He struggled with it, as he had never practiced this before. Gradually, the wind grew stronger, transforming into a powerful force that caused the new trees to bend.

The gates were successfully opened.

"Shall we enter?" Missar said, with a tone of satisfaction and a hint of pride.

The six riders entered through the gates as their horses moved in a low gallop down an aisle. The structure caught their attention with its dazzling golden hues. Wary and uncertain, they ventured into the enigmatic place as their eyes scanned the surroundings for any signs of danger.

With the greatsword gifted by his niece in his hand, Alessandro could feel the weight of the feathered weapon as he took the reins of Breeze with his other hand.

Ser Marissa, Ser Juni, and Commandant Kartak emulated the Master's actions with their weapons.

They all rode in silence. All had expressions of amazement, apprehension, and caution without uttering a single word.

As they made their way down the aisle exiting from under the bridge that sheltered the gates under, they came across a court beside. This was a vibrant and colorful vast garden, overflowing with many bright flowers.

Alessandro's dark eyes discovered a sprawling patch of vibrant red roses, reminding him of his beloved. His heart sank as he realized they were a painful reminder of their distance. He broke silence with a half murmur. "Without a doubt, this garden will delight Lady Fabehel."

Everyone heard him, but no one replied.

As they continued towards the entrance of the structure, Vasso, who was at the back of the group, could not help but notice the strange transformation of some of the red roses into an icy black. Thoughts raced through his mind, questioning whether this was a prophetic warning or a symbolic message, but his attention remained fixated on the Empress, particularly on Carlissa.

As Ser Marissa looked up, she marveled at the enormous towers that sparkled in the sunlight, emerging from the fortress-like walls surrounding the palace.

They came to other gates, similar to the previous ones, adorned with the Akareen emblem. They were still large, although slightly smaller than the ones they had seen outside. Alessandro suggested dismounting the horses and to enter the building, wondering if the wind would once again be necessary to open it.

With ease, Ser Juni pushed the doors open using his hands.

What they discovered was that the aisle still continued inside through a vast room, with enough space on the sides to accommodate hundreds of people. Once inside, the six walked warily as their footsteps echoed in the space.

But as they approached, they discovered the end of the aisle a circular golden throne.

Nehel, naked, was seated on the throne.

Ser Juni reacted by removing his cloak and dashed to her, to wrap it around her, even though her nakedness did not bother her.

While gazing at the ones in front of her, she had a serene expression on her face, with Juni by her side, covered with the cloak.

"Are you all right, Nehel?" Alessandro, with a concerned expression, asked while watching from below the steps of the throne.

"I am right, uncle," she replied with a light smile. "The *Ykarte* had breathed new life into me, and now I no longer feel drained."

Archmage Missar inquired about the whereabouts of the *Ykarte*, examining the area with his eyes for any sign of her presence.

"This place is now the *Ykarte*!" Nehel asserted. "Transformed into a palace, she harbors the Sword of Kasana beneath her, biding its time until the proper moment arrives."

With a disheartened sigh, Vasso distanced himself from the group to explore the surroundings. Behind the throne, he caught a wall adorned with one more Akareen. He cautiously made his way to the other side. His curiosity urged him forward, only to be greeted by an open chamber with no visible means of entry or exit. In the center, there was a round table adorned with yet another eight-pointed star on its surface. Many seats reserved for the members of the Guild surrounded it.

"She asked me about my dream home. As I designed it in my mind, I took her hands," Nehel continued retelling her experience. "With darkness, it felt as I had descended into a deep sleep, only to emerge in this throne, with nothing on me but revitalized, and all the answers she has given me."

"Let me fetch you some clothes from my saddlebag on Twist, Nehel," Ser Marissa made her way back through the aisle to the outside.

"Let us explore the palace," Alessandro suggested Missar and Kartak. "Juni, I need you to keep a close watch on her."

"I will be with her, Master," Juni said as Nehel gently clasped his hand.

While exploring, the three men encountered upon Vasso on the other side of the wall behind the throne. He had a fixated look on it with tears streaming down his cheeks, prompting them to approach and inquire about the reason.

"Carlissa was human!" with a cracked voice, he pointed to the wall.

Archmage Missar discovered the wall adorned thousands of sophisticated hieroglyphics, each depicting a different chapter of the *Ykarte's* rich history. At the end of the story, right before transforming into a palace, it revealed the tale of how she discovered Vasso as a gryphon on Kao and developed an unexplainable fondness for the young companion she had selected for her quest. Placing his hands on his shoulders, he showed empathy. "Stay strong, lad. Even not the same. Now you are within her and you can feel her presence."

"Let us continue our exploration, Archmage," Kartak's suggestion came as he noticed the Akareen star's constant presence, even in the most discreet crevices and crannies, alongside intriguing hieroglyphics and Salteran words. However, the palace only had the aureate color.

Alessandro's gaze fell upon the round table. The polished surface of the table gleamed, reflecting the bright room as sunlight streamed in through tall, nearly transparent windows. Approaching the tallest chair, he felt the cool, metallic surface beneath his fingertips, and nodded. "From now and then, Empresses and Emperors will claim this chair as their seat."

"Look there, Master," Missar pointed.

Their eyes focused ahead, revealing two exits positioned on each side, two sets of curved stairs leading to a first floor, and a ramp in the middle that led down to the underground.

"Out of everything, it is the Sword of Kasana that I am most intrigued by." As Kartak spoke, his eyebrow twitched.

Still cautious, the four men tightened their grip on their weapons, prepared to use them if needed as they approached the ramp.

Strangely, the further they went down, the brighter it became, defying their expectations of descending into darkness. The sight of a heavily locked golden gate initially aroused their curiosity, but as they shifted their gaze, they realized the ramp continued to another chamber, even brighter and more inviting.

At the heart of the room, positioned precisely beneath the throne through the ceiling, an enchanted sword gleamed against the floor, encircled by a band of ancient Salteran words.

As the four men approached the sword with mouths open in astonishment as they admired the mystical weapon that once belonged to Kasana. And it was the same sword that had sealed her fate with a decapitation, bringing both Nehel and the Korbas.

Alessandro narrowed his eyes, attempting to make out the engraved words on the ground. "Archmage. Can you read them?"

"*The Mudihufaser can only draw this Enchanted Sword in his ultimate battle.*" Missar translated. "*Anyone else who dares to draw it will die.*"

"You can turn around now, Juni," Marissa suggested.

The Second Knight found Nehel wearing borrowed leather clothes that she had to adjust as they were slightly big for her. "Missy, what plans do you have in store?"

Not paying heed to him, she directed her words to Marissa. "I appreciate it. These garments will keep me covered for a while."

"I always have them with me when I am tired of this armor," she replied with a sigh, sliding her sheathed sword back onto her waist. "Occasionally, I long to freshen up and feel at ease during my travels."

"Find the others," Nehel suggested. "They are underground."

Ser Marissa nodded, turned and walked away.

Nehel took the cloak that was left on the throne and affectionately fastened it around Juni's neck. Later, she gazed into his eyes and planted a soft kiss on his lips while caressing his cheek. "I apologize for causing you concern, but I appreciate your determined care for me."

"I have accepted to love a girl who is an Empress, missy," he replied with a gesture. "I should always expect surprises from you."

With her hazel eyes deeply locked with his, she caught him off guard and made a request. "Then, as a girl who cherishes you, I implore you to join me in matrimony." A sigh escaped her lips, revealing her obvious nervousness. "Ever since that unfortunate encounter in the forest during our younger years, I have been aware of the emotions you have harbored for me. It is my feeling that compels me to offer this proposal to you."

Ser Juni's eyes widened in disbelief as he struggled to find the right words to respond to her petition. He trembled, unable to form a coherent answer. As he looked at her face, he took a deep breath and centered himself before finding his voice. "Missy, I must inquire if you are absolutely certain about it. After all, I am only a troubadour turned knight."

"I would still wish to marry you, even if you were a beggar on the streets!" She gasped, rolling her eyes, eager for his reply. "I think we discussed that matter at Tempest Post."

A heartfelt expression on her face accompanied his nod, revealing her genuine intentions. It was clear from the start that their paths converged, united by a strange fate, and he knew that his life without her would feel meaningless. "Aye, missy. I accept your offer, because ever since I called you *a sorceress who speaks with the dead*, I knew our bond was undeniable and unbreakable."

Nehel chuckled and nodded, bringing back memories of their first encounter, which had been under adverse circumstances. "Please, Juni, keep our engagement a secret for the time being." With a gentle pull, she persuaded him to come along. "Come, let us explore the palace."

23
THE VAGRANT

With urgency, Corr spurred his gold stallion, Thunder, to race across the Cayderr Range, veering off course from the Trunke Territory and heading towards the newly named Tempest Post, a testament to the fierce and brief battle that had taken place just weeks ago. He left Finnerr in a hurry, willing to take the risk of leaving Lady Fabehel with a mad queen because he had no alternative.

Danger loomed over the Empress as her life faced a grave threat. And it came not from the Korbas or any of her enemies, but from deep within the Jyistereerk.

He had solid grounds to trust the reliability of the sources. Dienn, Queen Shiann, and the name written in a small paper given by Aeienn of Aorr.

At first, Corr had refused to leave Fabehel alone. He could not bear the thought of her being by herself, in particular after discovering the abandoned and lifeless Arankan settlement, which had left her saddened. Despite his reluctance, she urged him to leave and protect the Empress.

As the feline's eyes landed on the Holy Mountains, he could not help but notice the ominous darkness that hung over them in the sky. That darkness was not the result of looming clouds or an approaching thunderstorm, but an anticipation of the imminent Korba invasion.

From the moment he caught the overpowering scent of fear, blood, and death lingering in the air, eclipsing all other smells, including the dampness of the wet grass beneath his stallion's feet, he knew that the continent of Ryza was doomed.

Through the pigeons from Alessandro, Corr discovered that the Empress and the Guild had left the ancient palace in Ri and made their way to Sarrem, intending to reach Aranka. Since then, no more pigeons. Despite the threatening creatures that had disrupted all maritime routes, neither he nor Fabehel knew if they had successfully crossed the Beyond Sea or reached Tyza.

When the feline had arrived, he found a completely reconstructed Tempest Post. As he brought Thunder to a halt, he noticed the imposing pile of rocks right before the towering, reinforced new palisades. While in Siennt, he received news of a Torret Post that the Empress's strength had destroyed, leaving no trace behind to defeat the red mantises.

If only he had been alongside Master Alessandro, he could have engaged in the battle.

The pile of rocks was a monument that paid tribute to the fallen who lost their lives in the *Battle of the Tempest*.

The sentinels, perched high on the gates, spotted the Fennen rider and blared their horns, signaling his permission to enter. After ensuring that the entrance was clear, Corr commanded Thunder to gallop inside.

Despite the completion of the palisades surrounding the post, the reconstruction inside was still underway as members of the Imperial Guard still worked on it.

Corr recognized Branni, the First Knight's pupil, as she walked by with a shovel resting on her shoulder. She was among the group of individuals who had remained at Tempest Post while Ser Marissa ventured north to Molke. For the time being, they were under the command of the Admiral. "Hey lass!" His deep voice caused her to jump in surprise. "Please call your companions and lead me to Admiral Kekten!"

With a nod, Branni dropped the shovel and beckoned the group of twenty aspirants to knighthood. They guided him towards a small building.

The feline dismounted and weaved through the group of pupils until a familiar short figure emerged.

"I did not expect ya, Corr!" Kekten's eyes widened in surprise. "What are ya doing here?"

The feline's green eyes shifted towards Branni and her group. "Please, arrest him."

Lady Fabehel dipped her feather pen into the inkwell. Her heart had uneasiness as she wrote her seventh papyrus to her beloved Alessandro. Lost in deep thought, she glanced at the wall in front of her. She could not understand why they had positioned the desk on this side of her chamber, but her curiosity shifted to the clock, a Fennen invention, with its two pointers pointing to different numbers.

Thanks to that artifact, there were moments when time felt stretched and slow, making her contemplate its destruction.

It has been nearly a week since the rumored departure from Sarrem to Aranka, and since then, there has been an uncanny silence surrounding the Empress and her people, particularly Alessandro. She did not know if they were alive and safe on the continent of Tyza, or if they had perished in the Beyond Sea along with most of the Jyistereerk.

The feeling of being abandoned and forgotten fell over her. The strongest fear that consumed her was the solitude she experienced when she found herself far away from Alessandro. As she caressed her medallion, she felt stranded by her own beloved, especially after she had given herself to him that night.

But the solitude became even deeper after she had bid farewell to her Escort Corr, leaving her alone to protect the Empress and the Jyistereerk. If they were still alive.

Besides her, she held a small paper given by Aeienn, with a name written on it.

Kekten.

The events that drove Fabehel to convince Corr to depart to Tempest Post came back to her mind.

Upon inspecting the abandoned Arankan settlement, Corr aided Fabehel, who could not propel her wheelchair, to a secluded area where Aeienn proposed they have a brief yet crucial discussion.

As Lady Fabehel tried to collect herself after the unsettling scene, both felines kept a watchful eye on her. Corr offered her a canteen with water, allowing her to quench her thirst and find some comfort.

With her hazel eyes locked onto the leader of the Kiffenn Rebellion, she spoke smoothly, yet her voice carried a tinge of grief. "For the time being, let us not dwell on the settlement. Instead, please inform me about your knowledge regarding this paper."

"What paper, milady?" Corr asked, bewildered.

From her pocket, she pulled out the small paper and showed him the name.

In astonishment, the feline's green eyes widened.

"Do not make the mistake of assuming Queen Shiann is idle within the confines of her palace." Aeienn nodded and sighed. "With eyes and spies spread throughout Sankaris, she possesses an understanding of everything spanning back countless years."

"It explains why she knows about me," Fabehel agreed. "But you have not responded to my inquiry."

"It is Dienn," she replied. "Besides being an emissary, she takes on the responsibility of an archivist, collecting and organizing all the information provided by the spies. She documents every detail in thick volumes, destined for a special library nestled within the palace. But also she works for our Kiffenn Rebellion."

"It explains why I smelled fear when she met you, milady," Corr asseverated.

"We shall speak with Dienn," Fabehel said.

Fabehel guided her wheelchair with the mystical arrows engraved on the armchair and entered the library. Corr escorted her, closing the door behind.

The visitors were awestruck by the sight of towering wooden bookcases stretching towards the lofty ceilings. They realized that millions of papyrus scrolls documented Sankaris extensive history inside the spacious shelves.

Despite the clear lights streaming in through the large windows, it was a challenge to locate the archivist hidden among a labyrinth of bookcases. While searching, Fabehel observed everything had been well classified with numbers and names in Fennist characters. Despite her limited familiarity with the Fennen language, she had gained some basic understanding through Tin's lessons.

As she looked around, her eyes landed on a shelf loaded with ancient papyrus, each holding information on Aranka's primitive era.

Finally, they arrived at the center of the vast library where Dienn was.

They found the archivist engrossed in writing at her cluttered desk, surrounded by stacks of blank papyruses. She sat on a long stool doing her work, illuminated by the natural light pouring in from outside. When she turned around, she saw both visitors waiting for her. "Aeienn told you already."

"Aye, lass. She told us," Fabehel replied with a nod.

With a silent expression in her purple eyes, the feline placed her pen in the inkwell. Stepping her feet on the ground, she approached them, extending her hands to point her place. "When my father passed away, I took on the responsibility of being the Royal Archivist, a role that has been passed down through generations and will be carried on by my descendants. The ancient monarchs issued a royal mandate to ensure that Fenn would never be isolated from everyone by recording every happening in our world."

"Why were you afraid?" Corr asked with curiosity.

"What do you think, sir?!" Dienn replied, exasperated. "How would you feel caught in the middle of serving the queen and fighting for your people?"

"We came for another reason, lass," Fabehel said, soothing to her. "Are you familiar with the vagrant Kekten?"

"I am familiar, aye," she showed disdain in her reply. "And for some unknown reason, Queen Shiann possesses the papyruses containing all the information about that Kekten."

"What do you mean?"

"She is already expecting your arrival in her private chambers."

Corr and Fabehel's path to meet the queen took them from the library to the farthest reaches of the Royal Palace in Finnerr. Along the way, attentive guards who knew the complex building guided them. These sentinels proved invaluable, even offering their help in lifting the wheelchair on various sets of stairs that along the extensive building. The complexities of the palace's interior amazed the Ambassador and even made a comment to Corr about it. "This is like a game of snakes and ladders!" It reminded her of the popular Arankan board game the children used to play, bringing back memories of her childhood with Princess Natahel.

As they went along, the soft glow of the outside lights bathed some paths, while others held an impenetrable darkness resembling a penumbra. Corr made a reference about them. "I have heard strange gossips about this palace, but now I can see it with my own eyes."

As they reached the end of their course, they were hopeful of discovering a fancy and inviting place, but their expectations dashed when they came across a door that looked more like the entrance to a miserable dungeon cell watched by two guards.

Upon opening the entrance, they discovered a series of interconnected chambers, each adorned with exquisite decorations. There was no shortage of opulence, and at the center of a long table sat Queen Shiann, inundated by various papyruses and a jar emitting a delightful fruity scent, surrounded by some mugs. Fabehel remembered that Fennens, being of their kind, could not indulge in the taste of wine.

The place gave Fabehel a weird feeling, as if something was about to happen. She remained silent about it.

The old monarch, with her white fur peeking out from beneath a white silk gown, nodded and motioned for them to join her at the table. "I knew that you would have a conversation about that Kekten."

"Do you dwell here, queen?" As she approached with her wheelchair, Fabehel inquired with a curious look on her face.

With her raspy voice, she responded to her, "My dear, death is closing in on me."

"Your fate, whether it be life or death, is of no concern to me. Tell us everything you know about Kekten!" Corr demanded with a strict tone in his voice.

The queen nodded in agreement and reached out to grab a papyrus from the table. "As the plague spread through Aranka, King Vihen abandoned the guilds and instead turned to medics and alchemists for help. Thus, the once glorious era of warriors ended. As the guilds were being disbanded, those who once had homes became wandering vagrants, searching every corner of Sankaris for fresh adventures. Others, instead of assisting different communities for shelter and food in change, opted to chase after gold and became mercenaries."

Realizing that it would take longer, Corr poured the brew into a mug and settled into a seat.

"Lady Larissa Eskar had already been aware of those mercenaries," the monarch continued. "In her role as Head, she sent a letter to Kekten, then stationed near the border, and given him an exclusive permit to traverse Casak, a forbidden territory for outsiders, so they could rendezvous in Estolk for a proposal."

"Tell me, Corr. How did you know a vagrant had sold Cassandro Eskar into slavery?" Fabehel asked while the queen took a moment to taste her brew.

"Milady, Cassandro and I endured countless years of enslavement side by side. I learned from him a vagrant had imprisoned and sold him to the foremen in the Mines of Tiunnff."

"Were you aware the vagrant was Kekten?"

"I was not. I was equally appalling when you revealed the name." Corr concluded.

"Indeed, this is how it happened," Queen Shiann asseverated and continued. "Lady Larissa Eskar, disapproving of her son Cassandro's relationship with Princess Natahel, planned to arrest them in Katalk and forever close the Arankan Quarter. However, they had already fled to Ryza, leaving her feeling betrayed."

"I have a vague recollection of when it happened, as I was only five. Tin insisted that, despite my young age, I had to persuade Lady Larissa to allow us to stay in Katalk. Our realm had been impacted by the plague." With a nod, Fabehel continued with what she had said. "Lady Larissa imposed a strict condition on us: we could not leave the Arankan Quarter, we had to stay indoors and avoid mingling with the locals. The only exception was during the Gesha, when those who had lost their families in Aranka could venture outside. Despite the Assembly relaxing the rules, they still confined us to Katalk and prevented us from reaching the continent."

"What was exactly the plan? To catch Cassandro to be sold as a slave?" Corr asked to the queen.

"Lady Larissa had specifically asked Kekten to enslave Cassandro and Princess Natahel, but the princess had already fled to the north."

"Why Kekten said nothing about it?" Fabehel said pensively.

"There is an even major motive," the queen declared with conviction. "What do you know about the name Estherleon?"

"That is Marshall Keleana's surname," Corr replied.

"Estherleon, a name frequently used among the vagrants, holds the symbolic meaning of Warriors of the Future Empire." Queen Shian sighed and continued. "The Empress is in grave danger as a group conspires to depose her and establish their own empire on Sankaris. The chosen ones are those who bear the surname Estherleon."

"Are you certain of it?" Fabehel asked, concerned.

"My sources are credible, my dear." Extending her hand, the monarch boasted a table covered in papyruses.

"To halt Keleana's plans, someone must apprehend Kekten!" Fabehel appealed to Corr. "Please! Hurry! Before it becomes too late!"

"I can not abandon you, milady!" The feline exclaimed.

"The Empress is more important! Go! Save her! Save the Jyistereerk!"

"I. . ." At first, Corr was unsure about her decision, but as he locked eyes with her hazel eyes and pondered in a moment, he nodded in assent and left without even saying farewells.

As Fabehel's Escort disappeared through the door, leaving her with an overwhelming sense that their paths would never cross again. Time seemed to stand still as she remained embedded to the spot, not wishing to move from her position. She turned and saw the queen diligently organizing her papyruses, preparing to take them back to her library while casually taking sips from her brew.

They were both alone.

The sight of the busy monarch caught Fabehel's attention, making her contemplate a thought. Her heart raced as she slowly slid her hand beneath her skirt, as her fingers closed around the hilt of her dagger. This was the perfect timing to make her pay for what she had done to her people. Hesitating, she also considered that she had never taken someone's life before, but there was always a first time.

She had grief, and a burning desire for vengeance.

"I have news for you, my dear," Without interrupting her task, the queen said in a focused tone.

Startled, Fabehel withdrew her hand from the dagger and smoothed down her skirt. "What news?"

"I have sent an emissary to give a message to the leader of the Kiffenn Rebellion offering peace," her response came with a nod and a stare. "Considering that you refused the offer to be my successor, I took it upon myself to ensure a truce in Fenn. As a major threat looms over us. It is imperative that we stand together, not apart."

Fabehel gasped in surprise. She wondered why Aeienn had kept the queen's emissary a secret from her. "Have you received any reply?"

"Aye, my dear. As I can not move because of my illness, I have invited them for a special feast that will take place in my chambers," she answered in her raspy voice. "And I would like to have you with us since you can provide valuable information about those Korbas."

As Fabehel awoke from her recollections, she reached for the papyrus she had written on and rolled it up, joining it with the other six she had written.

Her hand caught her attention as she noticed it trembling because as an anxiety was growing inside her. Seeking solace, she turned to the brew and felt taken aback by how it somewhat intoxicated her fast. Despite her racing heart, she found solace in the medallion, which held memories of Alessandro close.

She usually preferred refreshing juices made from fresh fruits, rice milk, or simply water. However, she had never experienced the taste of fermented beverages before, and even requested a servant to bring some brew to her chamber. Her uneasiness was so bad that it consumed her every thought.

Her soul felt different, as if something had altered within her. The visit to the dead Arankan settlement left her overwhelmed with anguish, hatred, and a burning need for revenge. Despite being alone with the queen, she resisted the compulsion to take her life, which only intensified her frustration.

The queen spoke of Aeienn, although not by name. She invited her to a feast, hoping to restore peace in Fenn after a violent rebellion that Fabehel had only heard about through others, news that was spread around Berrem. The invitation, which was so easy despite the Kiffenn's supposed hatred for the queen, raised suspicions about the upcoming feast. Dienn's ambiguous stance added to the overall sense of doubt.

As fear gripped her, she realized how alone she was, far away from home and the comforting presence of her loved ones.

She held onto her conviction, knowing that once the feast was over, she would confront her own dread and carry out her plan to kill the queen.

With tears streaming down her face, she removed the orchid medallion from her neck and set it on the desk. She affectionately traced her fingers over its surface, lost in a flood of memories shared with her beloved.

"I am sorry, Alessandro," she murmured, her fingers touched the arrows on her wheelchair's arm as she turned herself around.

As Corr took sips from his mug of brew, his intense green eyes remained fixed on Kekten, unblinking.

Branni stood silently behind him, watching both men.

With both hands chained, the vagrant sat across the table with his eyes locked on the feline. He was unsurprised by his arrest, as he was well aware of his past misdeeds.

"Tell me, Kekten. Did you sell Cassandro Eskar to the foremen at the Mines of Tiunnff?" Corr asked with his deep voice.

"Indeed, Corr. I have done it, and the weight of regret has burdened me for countless years."

"Why did you decide to keep this hidden from everyone for so many years?"

"Because of my cowardice, indeed. Da ya know?"

In the feline's observation, he noticed Kekten's serene presence, as he remained calm and showed no hint of resistance or unease. There was a persistent feeling of suspicion, both within himself and surrounding the queen. Besides, he had worked with the Empress with loyalty. "Care to tell me what took place?"

"Lady Larissa's message reached me at the Equatorial Border in Aranka. Indeed, shortly before that, our guild disbanded, and. . . "

"Skip that part and continue until you come across Cassandro Eskar and Princess Natahel." Corr interrupted, moving his hairy and thick index finger.

"Indeed, I found them at the feet of the cathedral," Kekten responded. "I was not alone. Lady Larissa had hired another two vagrants, two mercenaries that I have never seen them and belonged to other guilds. She hired them to keep a watch on me and to assure I could track and apprehend them."

"Did it take long to find them?" After taking a sip of his brew, the feline inquired.

Branni listened attentively by pulling up a chair and sitting on it. She had an intense curiosity.

"It was easy, indeed. If ya da think that if they would get lost in the vast Berrem, then ya are mistaken." Despite his sigh, he maintained the serenity. "In the Berrem before the Gesha, locals did not welcome to outsiders, indeed, they repelled them. Going from burgh to burgh, it was easy to inquire about a Casakan man and an Arankan female wandering together to find them at the cathedral. I mentioned ya."

"Could you specify which cathedral you are talking about?"

"Arrasem."

"Do not hold back. Continue telling me everything."

"We saw them begging outside the cathedral. And, indeed, Princess Natahel's prominent baby bump caught my eyes, intensifying my regret over striking a deal with Lady Larissa. However, my companions showed no emotion as they callously tossed them into a cage in the cart we had purchased, alongside two horses."

"And where did you wander off to after that?"

"We took them and stopped near Siennt, indeed, where we waited as instructed by Lady Larissa and sent a pigeon to inform our buyers of our position. After waiting several nights, we indulged in copious amounts of wine and brew. As a result, my companions fell into a deep, intoxicated slumber, leaving only me awake and alert." He gasped. "Indeed, I opened the cage, select a horse, and grant them their freedom."

"But how did Princess Natahel escape while Cassandro did not?" After taking another sip, Corr continued to move his index finger as he asked.

A suspenseful silence hung in the air, broken only by Kekten's hesitant and difficult-to-utter words. "The empty cage caught my companions' attention, and without hesitation, they set off in pursuit. I had to play the part, sticking close by their side. They could track them, and it was at that moment that Cassandro Eskar surrendered himself to me. Indeed, he was determined to accept a harsh punishment from the mercenaries, even if it meant sacrificing himself by allowing Princess Natahel to escape."

"Did you see the princess again?"

"Those men tried to track her, but it was as if she vanished into air."

Corr turned to look at Branni's eyes, nodding in understanding as he recounted the events that led to the birth of Nehel. It was during Princess Natahel's arrival in Molke that she found Sorcerer Uskam. "What have you done with Cassandro?"

"Indeed, we met with the buyers, displeased by our offer. They expressed disappointment because we did not include a pregnant woman with the man altogether. A newborn held high value for them. They were two nobles from Siennt, a Berremen man and a female Fennen. Despite the situation, their generosity was so immense that they handed each of us a bag of gold coins."

"Do you recall their names?"

"Aye, indeed, I remember them clearly—the guilt of selling Cassandro weighed heavily on my conscience." Kekten replied with a nod. "Lord Doni and Lady Aeienn of Aorr were the two foremen responsible for overseeing the Mines of Tiunnff."

Corr's eyes widened as he abruptly stood up, causing his chair to crash to the floor and startling Branni in the same manner. The feline stood still, lost in deep contemplation, as a whirlwind of thoughts raced through his mind. "Lady Fabehel is in grave danger!"

"What are ya talking about?" Kekten asked, completely clueless.

"Tell me. From where does Estherleon originate?"

"Marshal Keleana takes the surname from Kaiden, our mage and guild leader. Indeed, he adopted that surname from his beloved Arankan novel, *The Grand Conspiracy*."

Trembling uncontrollably, he hurled the mug against the wall, causing a mutual gasp from everyone and releasing a roar. "What is the book about?!"

"I have not read it myself, but Kaiden used to describe it to me," fear coursed through his veins as he replied. "Indeed, the story unfolds as the Estherleon family plots to overthrow monarchs, to establish their own empire."

With a desperate flood of strength, Corr snapped the chain that had held Kekten captive. "Admiral, gather as many guards as you can!" Then turned to Branni. "Lass, gather your comrades and let them know we are launching an attack on Fenn!"

24

TERRA INCOGNITA

The scent of the sweet perfume drifted from the handkerchief as Alessandro held it in his hand. As he stood in awe of the palace's many towers, a bad feeling about his beloved Fabehel crept into his mind.

Frustrated, he leaned on the rail of the *Great Balcony* at the back of the mystical golden building, trying in vain to count the endless towers.

Archmage Missar joined him, taking in the majestic towers with scanning eyes, and spoke. "The palace intrigues me, as its number of towers changes every morning, while the inside remains the same."

"Except the tower over the throne, the tallest, as it stays unchanged." As Alessandro turned around, the sight of a dense forest and a chain of mountains in the distance, shrouded by a thin layer of haze, greeted him. He extended his hand towards the breathtaking panorama to show Missar. "The *Ykarte* reconstructed Aranka, but now we stand before a completely unfamiliar land than the one in the past."

"Aye, those old Arankan maps have become useless. I believe we should send explorers to redraw new ones, Master."

"Did you consider my proposal, Archmage?" as he asked, he recalled their previous conversation.

"I am still the Head, Master. I can not abandon the Assembly and Casak. If I choose to join the Guild, I will have to make sure that the people elect someone to take my place."

"As the election evolves, you can designate someone as your substitute."

With a heavy sigh, Missar lowered his head and rested his hands on the rail. "In this last tikl, Casak has experienced an overwhelming amount of suffering—from relentless wars to crippling poverty and misery. Our realm still bears the harsh consequences of Orssandro's madness, despite the aid of the elves."

Alessandro understood Missar's reply. "The Guild feels empty and different with the absence of Archmage Selee." He turned her gaze once more to the palace's *Great*

Balcony, diverting her attention from the previous topic. "This place is so vast that it could easily accommodate an entire small town, and it would even have enough space for a traveling fair."

"Do you think this new Aranka is ready for a repopulation?"

"The Divine Empress has expressed her desire for an Aranka that is inhabited by a diverse mix of races and half-breeds. Ultimately, it is her decision on how to proceed with the land."

"This feels wrong!" Nehel expressed her frustration as she witnessed her maids' struggles to position the generous circular bed in her vast chamber within the Imperial Apartment. The constant disapproval from Overseer Akhimeni added to the tense atmosphere.

Her juvenile outbursts seemed impossible to evade. Despite her condition, she was still bound by her human nature.

"Keep calm, missy!" Ser Juni reprimanded her. "The maids are working to do their best!"

"I know!" With a sigh of frustration, Nehel replied and shrugged her shoulders. "I have an entire apartment all to myself when I do not need it, and even in the most secluded corners, everything sparkles and shines like gold, hurting my eyes."

"Do you prefer the frigid palace of stone in the Ri?"

"To be honest, I find this one place much more preferable," she replied as she pointed to her new chamber. "In the Ri, I could hear the whispers of the dead and sense their presence, but in here, I am overwhelmed by the energy of pure life."

Despite her last words, Ser Juni could not avoid the feeling of suspicion and turned to Akhimeni. "Madam, I kindly request that you and the maids give us some privacy for our conversation."

Agreeing with a nod, Akhimeni instructed her maids to pause their tasks and proposed everyone to have a meal together. Everyone departed, leaving Nehel and Juni alone in the chamber.

Ser Juni searched through the packed wooden boxes scattered across the gleaming golden floor. He finally found a ripe pear and extended it towards Nehel, along with a small knife.

Nehel, startled, looked at the fruit, then locked into his eyes with a silent inquiry. "Why?"

"I am offering you this favorite fruit of yours to transport you back to the time we met and journeyed through the Black Forest in Berrem, where the memories of your spirit as Lakia remain."

She examined the pear. "Despite my stance as Empress, I was still naïve and lacked the wisdom I thought I possessed."

Missy, it is not just that. "You were a girl with a rare ability to empathize, yet possessed a simplicity and determination in pursuing your purpose. And certainly, you drove Peken to craziness." A gentle smile accompanied his response.

Nehel made a thoughtful reflection, then settled on a nearby chest. "I apologize for my sudden bursts of energy and impulsive actions. Sometimes, my human side takes over and I struggle to maintain control." As she took the knife from Juni, she began slicing her pear, occasionally waving the knife in the air as she spoke. "My sense of identity remains elusive, especially in the wake of the recent losses I have experienced. . ."

"I believe you should continue being Lakia, missy," he cut off her.

"Just like any other girl, I am just a regular person. As I mentioned earlier, I am entrusted with the responsibility of watching over Sankaris, which makes me just an ordinary person with a duty. I also have my necessities and I am not immune to mistakes. And the changes I am experiencing are an essential part of my transition to womanhood."

"If you are going through these changes to womanhood. Why did you request me to join you in matrimony?" As he replied, his words muffled slightly when he took a bite of the pear slice.

"Do not be mistaken, Juni! What you and I share is an undeniable connection, a unique bond that we will cherish and nurture together. My suggestion was not for us to rush into marriage, but for you to handle patience until I am fully prepared. After all, I am only a fourteen-year-old girl."

"Missy, I appreciate your clarification. While it is not uncommon for lads and lasses to wed at a tender age, I am not yet equipped to embrace the responsibilities of a husband. I believe there is still a journey ahead for me to become a man." he accepted another slice. "Becoming a knight is unrelated to my level of maturity."

"With a fond smile, Nehel let out a soft chuckle. And it is said that girls mature faster than boys! The way you express yourself shows a level of maturity that is remarkable."

"The meaning of our conversation was that you should control your outbursts and treat your maids nicely," he replied. "They have already pledged their loyalty to you, sacrificing everything to be at your service."

She stood up and walked over to Juni, planting a swift kiss on his lips. "This is my gratitude," she then rolled her eyes up. "I just remembered that we have our first Guild meeting in this palace!"

"I can not believe how far we have come since that first meeting in Arrasem!" Ser Marissa exclaimed, as her eyes scanned the members of the Guild seated around the golden round table, engraved with the emblem of the Akareen. "All the world is here!"

Besides the usual Pillars by the sides of the Empress, Marshal Keleana and Ser Juni, Captain Kanden and Artifice Jumeni, as well as Akhimeni graced the meeting. Akartaki and Commandant Kartak, accompanied by the

Tinklen Pi-U, received an invitation to join as permanent members. Meanwhile, Archmage Missar and Captain Diesso were the provisional membership until the situation with Casak could be resolved, especially with the presence of a restored Aranka as a neighboring realm.

Lady Fabehel, Corr, and Admiral Kekten were all absent, noticeable as they were currently on the distant continent of Ryza.

Overwhelmed by the greatness of the Guild Room, Dessidere, the indispensable Herald, stuttered at the start of the session. He began the session by naming each member. Then, he acknowledged the current date.

Forty-first day of the Seventh Month in the First Year of the *Tikl the Second of Nehel.*

As witnesses to the event, Lady Tasarissa, Alyssa Taskar, Vasso, and the sisters from the Comforting Wind Sisterhood encircled the Guild. Ti-K, who was standing farther off, also attended.

Elvish soldiers and members of the Imperial Guard filled the room, while tall silvering Artensens stood in every corner and by the windows.

"This is the Jyistereerk I had envisioned, Ser Marissa," Nehel replied with a nod. "An Empire for all, where unity empowers us to stand together and overcome the adversities we encounter."

"When we stand as one, our unified strength knows no limits." Alessandro added. "But despite achieving so much in just one tikl, we still lack the strength to confront the Korbas in this *Deken Karsaker.*"

"While I agree with you, uncle. Do not neglect to consider the current affairs at Fenn." Nehel pointed with a serious expression. "Given the seriousness of the situation in Ryza, I think it is crucial that we find Lady Fabehel and Corr before anything else unfolds." She turned to Pi-U and inquired. "Is it possible to use *The Navigator* to transport us directly to the Port of Finn?"

"As we speak, more vessels are making their way here from Bick, Divine Empress," he responded in his acute voice and paused words. "We believe that *The Navigator* is most suitable for use with large numbers, such as armies. For the purpose you are seeking, I advise using a small-sized vessel."

"If vessels are coming from Bick. Where shall they anchor without a harbor yet?" With his hand resting on his chin, Alessandro inquired. "Can they secure the vessels on the shore, like *The Navigator* did?"

"They may, Master. However, I strongly recommend that my people construct a harbor in the location you deem most suitable."

Leaning forward, Alessandro pressed his hands together as his eyes locked on the Tinklen. "This is a problem that Archmage Missar and I mentioned in a previous conversation. This new Aranka differs from the previous one and requires the creation of new maps to depict its features."

"May I suggest sending explorers to bring us detailed maps of the uncharted land?" Missar spoke. "I would like to propose Captain Diesso, a military officer who possesses a wealth of knowledge in studying, exploring, and creating maps."

"Sir Head!" Diesso exclaimed, dumbfounded.

"Please, be quiet! As your Head, I command you to fall under the authority of the Divine Empress," the Archmage insisted. "And be sure to take the lad Vasso along with you!"

The moment he heard him, Vasso's eyes grew wide with astonishment.

"You have my support, should the Guild agree to it," Nehel spoke to Diesso and Vasso. "Besides aiding in the construction of a harbor, your maps will play a crucial role in the repopulation."

"Now, about the repopulation, Divine Empress," Missar sighed. "I suggest that. . ."

The sudden presence of a ruby pigeon abruptly interrupted the session in the Guild Room, soaring around the tall heights, and captivating the attention of everyone in the room. With a gradual descent, the bird landed directly in front of the Empress.

With surprise, Nehel observed the pigeon, gently took the small paper from its foot and unfolded it. Her face lit up with a smile as she read it.

"My apologies!" she exclaimed, visibly excited. "I must depart to my chambers!"

In a rush, she pushed the chair away and left, leaving an odd atmosphere that was palpable to everyone in the room.

25

SELEE'S RETURN

As the Empress entered her private chambers, she noticed a figure by the window, captivated by the breathtaking view of the Arankan panorama. The man with white hair and azure robes had returned.

Her excitement was obvious, impossible to cover.

He sensed her and turned around with his usual smile and spoke in a gentle, sweet voice. *"Nehel Jyistereerk Mudiuhfaser! Nehel Jyistereerk Friyterkfer!"*

"Archmage Selee!"

She ran towards him, eager to hug him, but he dodged her embrace and asked her to not touch him. Her smile vanished as she noted that behavior. "Is there something wrong?" she asked, concerned. It did not take long for her to recognize him, still dressed the same way as when they first crossed paths at the end of *The Empress' Pass*, following her encounter with Sorceress Dalehel.

"I have fought in Salter and wounds are still in me," breaking away from the subject, he replied as his clear eyes scanned the disordered Imperial Apartment, where he also noticed the noticeable absence of furniture, except for the bed. "Divine Empress, there is still much to be done before your move is complete. Chests and boxes are still everywhere!" However, he also noticed a balcony that caught his attention.

His peculiar response triggered a sense of doubt within her, along with a strange sense of familiarity, as if he had repeated his presence and words from somewhere before. "Tell me, Archmage. I received your private message via pigeon, urging me to keep our meeting secret from others. What is the reason behind your reluctance to reveal yourself to others?"

"I should not expose myself in public at this moment," he roamed through the surroundings, eventually stumbling upon a chest. Intrigued, he opened it and found a small silver candle. He studied it meticulously, making sure not to miss any details. "So this is from Salter. Impressive!"

Nehel's suspicions had finally solidified. There was something about this man that made her realize he was not the Selee she had known. In an instant, the notion crossed her mind that he could be a Korba, using his shapeshifting abilities to take on the appearance of the Archmage. She noticed his obsession with an unfamiliar candle with his unsettling grin. Fear took over her as she sensed a strange void coming from within him, causing her to retreat towards the entrance. As she approached the pair of doors, she pulled them, but they remained shut.

"I wish to see that magnificent new panorama!" The Archmage walked to the small balcony.

Nehel attempted to rely on her mystic abilities to sense him and brace herself for a confrontation, but to her surprise, none of them seemed to function. A strange force seemed to neutralize her.

Nehel could feel the panic seeping into her, causing her teeth to clench in frustration. Being inside with him, she felt trapped, powerless, and affected by a malevolent enchantment. Her eyes remained locked on the balcony, refusing to look away as she contemplated the unknown man.

She cautiously approached her balcony, noticing him leaning on the rail, taking in deep breaths of the crisp forest and mountain air. At the boundary between her chamber and the outside, Nehel hesitated. As she lifted her eyes, she noticed a peculiar sight—a flock of black crows swirling in circles above the palace. "Tell me. Who are you?"

As the mysterious man turned around, his grin became even more sinister. "It is me, Divine Empress." She trembled and turned pale at his vague and cavernous response.

With each step he took closer, her eyes grew wider. "I have a proposal."

"What is it?" Her voice broke as she asked the question.

"Join us to The Aquelarre and serve Lord Ardek. In exchange, Lord Ardek will grant you ultimate authority over Sankaris."

"Who are you?! Reveal yourself!"

The man with the form of the Archmage Selee slowly transformed into a crooked figure, hidden beneath the dark robes, and a sinister grin revealed blackened teeth from his thick-lipped mouth. "Carrasso of Estolk, loyal warlock to The Aquelarre and to Ardek Korba!"

"What Aquelarre? I heard many of them live east of the Karekall."

"It is now The Aquelarre. Ardek has unified us to have a common front." He nodded. "If you and your Jyistereerk join us, the Korbas have pledged to withdraw from the lands they conquered, bringing peace and pre-serving the balance you reestablished a mere tikl ago."

"Never!" she shouted with authority. "My mandate is clear—those demons must be driven away from this world!"

"They will not, Empress. Once they achieve their goal of granting us infinite power through the infections, we will finally liberate ourselves and become capable of transcending to other worlds, leaving behind this dying globe."

"I have heard your words, warlock, but I find it difficult to believe in them. Do you believe they will extend their power to the common people?" She sighed, her breath shivered as she tried to suppress her rising fear. "From the Korbas, I have witnessed nothing but death and suffering."

"Aye, death and suffering dance with their evil music." Carrasso replied with a delirious tone, as he playfully waved his hand in the air. "Come, join us and experience the embrace of the darkness!"

"No! I demand that you immediately leave my palace!"

"In that case, I do not have another choice."

With stunning speed, he seized Nehel's neck, catching her off guard. Using his unusual strength, he snatched her towards him, then pushed her against the balcony's rail. With each tightening grip around her throat, his motive was to send her into a deadly fall.

As she grabbed the rail to avoid her fall, she could feel her heart pounding in her chest, gasping for air, while his sinister hands still tightened around her neck. She desperately tried to fight back, but her abilities seemed to be annulled. In a desperate attempt, she exerted all her strength to reach into the pocket of her leather clothes. She locked eyes with Carrasso and saw his twisted face with madness and with a deadly purpose.

Gasping for air, Nehel fought to stay conscious as she made one last effort and plunged her small knife through his ear, hidden beneath the cowl.

The warlock's screams resounded through the chamber as he entered with frantic movements, trying to remove the knife lodged in his head. With a surprising move, he broke the spell that had seized her, setting her free.

The Empress caught her breath and sprinted towards the doors, eager to swing them open and step into the halls.

"You damn witch!" Once he extracted the knife, Carrasso let out a loud yell, overlooking the bloodstain on his dark clothes. "As I executed the old man Selee, he cried out your name like a child! And you will do the same!"

With the knife inserted in the warlock's head, a surge of power coursed through Nehel as she attempted to open the doors, only to have it extinguished as he quickly regained control.

Nehel sprinted across the palace's aisles, searching for help, but the halls were empty of guards or elvish soldiers. As she kept running everywhere, she noticed the eerie desolation of the palace, making her believe it was a mystical manifestation of Carrasso's power.

As she reached the stairs, her heart raced as she heard the approaching footsteps. By sudden, Carrasso's shadow appeared on the wall, but instead of his familiar silhouette, it took the form of a demoniac dragon.

She understood the warlock had undergone a conversion into a Korbeen, magnifying his power beyond of what he possessed as a human. Distressed with fear, she descended the stairs.

The Guild Room was silent and lacking of any signs of life. Carrasso ensured that the palace remained empty, preventing anyone from interfering with his plans against the Empress.

As she sprinted through the chambers, the feeling of his presence closing in on her only deepened her impotence.

From the very beginning, she realized what it meant to be an ordinary human, and it permeated her with despair. Though she could have dwelled on her current condition, the urgency of staying alive consumed her thoughts.

As she ran across the outside Great Balcony, she glanced back and saw the warlock's determined gaze and confident stride, knowing he would stop at nothing to fulfill his purpose. As she gasped for air and with sweat down her face, she continued running and descended the stairs towards the lush exterior gardens that lay behind the palace.

The feel of the soft petals and the sweet smell of the flowers and pear trees engulfed her as she raced towards the first pines of the newly birthed forest. She left behind a track of long distance. She thought she had lost him. Unfortunately, the clear sky and brilliant sun gave way to darkness as grey clouds engulfed the forest, creating an atmosphere of gloom and unease.

Nehel stopped, choking for breath, and anxiously scanned the frightening trees, hoping to glimpse Carrasso, but he was nowhere to be found. When she believed she was truly alone, she turned her hazel eyes upwards and discovered a sinister flock of crows ominously circling above, revealing her location.

In despair, she collapsed to her knees and her tears streamed down her cheeks as she waited for him, pleading in silence for someone to come to her rescue.

"There you are, Empress!" Carrasso's grin spread across his thick lips as he exclaimed with delight. "You are now at my mercy!"

Seated on the ground in a space between dark trees, Nehel observed the warlock slowly making his way towards her. She felt powerless. Her exhaustion from escaping made it impossible to continue, her legs trembled with weakness. With tear-filled eyes and quivering lips, she saw him standing so close to her.

Carrasso gripped the small knife, the same one Nehel had used to pierce his ear, preparing to deliver a fatal strike. "When I am done with you, they will target your mother's sister!"

As she observed him clutching the knife with both hands, her voice cracked. "What mother's sister?!"

"The Lady of the Red Tides!"

They were both startled by the sound of a horse's quick trotting as the thunderous hooves delivered him with continuous blows, leaving him hurt.

In that instant, Nehel could feel her power surging inside her, empowering her to unleash a forceful gust of wind against the warlock with a swift motion of her hands.

In the end, Carrasso collided against a tree, leaving him dazed and barely conscious. The forest came back alive with vibrant colors and beauty as the sun's rays danced through the branches.

The Empress averted her gaze to examine the horse. It was not your ordinary horse, but a majestic creature with a rainbow of colors adorning its entire body, radiating brilliance and allure.

As the horse approached her, its hooves created a soft thud against the ground, and it lowered its head in a respectful bow.

Nehel observed the black eyes of the animal and could feel its thoughts. She knew it was a mystical creature. Archmage Missar had previously told her he believed the new Arankan forest was bustling with magical beings, waiting to be discovered.

"You have my gratitude!" she said with a light but exhausted smile. "I express my gratitude for saving my life."

The rainbow horse continued to bow with soft neighs, but communicated with her.

"Of course!" Nehel exclaimed with confidence. "I will be your rider!"

"Die you damn scourge!" Alessandro's rage consumed him, causing him to clutch his greatsword tight as he held it menacingly against Carrasso's neck, while tearing at his attire. "You belong to hell!"

The blow against the tree's trunk left Carrasso stunned, his deep and petrifying look fixated on Alessandro as he felt the chilling touch of the blade against his neck.

Ser Marissa repeatedly cautioned him against acting on impulse, but imprisoned. "It is best if we lock him down to interrogate!"

Commandant Kartak stood behind both Pillars as his hand rested on the handle of his sheathed scimitar as a precautionary measure.

As Archmage Missar witnessed, his gaze shifted to Nehel seated on the ground. He observed Akartaki carefully applying a soothing ointment to her bruised neck. Beside him, Ser Juni stood with a fierce expression, glaring at the warlock.

Akhimeni arrived shortly after, accompanied by a few maids who were concerned.

One of the elvish sisters gently stroked the rainbow horse, which remained by the Empress' side.

"That wrecked man used his damn magic to make an exact dimensional replica of our reality!" Missar explained. "That way, only he and the Divine Empress would be by themselves!"

"And even he annulled her in that dimension," Kartak added.

The Imperial Guard members arrived. As they surrounded the warlock, Alessandro's blade still pressed against his neck.

As the warlock regained his consciousness, he uttered a silent spell that echoed unheard by anyone. In an instant, he vanished, leaving only a lingering black smoke that swiftly dispersed.

"Can you track him, Archmage?" Alessandro asked as his eyes widened with surprise after his prisoner disappeared into thin air. "We need to capture him!"

"Forget him!" Nehel said to her uncle with a worrisome tone in her voice. "You shall go to Fenn because Fabehel is in great peril!"

26

PRAIRIE LILY

W ithin days, Lady Fabehel had undergone a profound change, appearing as if she had abandoned
all hope and withdrawn into a solitary life of sorrow and a
thirst for retaliation.

She could not shake off the worry about Empress Nehel's safety, suspecting a presumed conspiracy involving
the vagrants, especially Marshal Keleana.

That is what the queen had told her.

Fabehel's distress grew as she harbored her own suspicions. Fueled by her uneasiness and intense desire to

execute the monarch, she made the tough decision to embrace hate and turn away from Alessandro, whom she once loved.

She picked roses, intentionally letting the thorns prick her bleeding fingers, experiencing physical discomfort and inner conflict.

The realization that the Arankan settlers met their demise while resisting the slavery fueled her rejection of forgiveness.

From her childhood, Fabehel has observed the hardships endured by her Arankan people, from the outbreak of the plague to the forced relocation to Casak. She found herself responsible for the Arankan Quarter in Sarak at a very young age, facing constant threats from the local government, particularly from Guardian Trasso.

The influence and protection from Archmage Yasstro helped the exiled Arankans to settle in the former Head's vacation properties, with years of peace despite the miseries they had endured.

If it were not for Tin, she would not have made it through the difficulties she encountered at an age when she should play with dolls and children.

The Promise's appearance and the subsequent madness of Orssandro, who decreed a siege, altered the lives of many Arankans. Garterrem Isle is now home to a newly established colony. Despite their efforts, they remained vulnerable to the threat posed by the Korbas and were prepared to move once more if the need arose.

Fabehel intended to move the Arankan settlement residents to Garterrem after meeting them.

Sadly, there was not a single living person.

She acknowledged the Arankan race's nearing extinction and worked hard to find every Gesha survivor. She directed her resentment towards those who had inflicted harm, including the Korbas or Queen Shiann, with a strong wish to see them perish.

She had forsaken all hope, love, and the positive qualities associated with Empress Nehel, neglecting the valuable life lessons she had gained during her time with Alessandro over the past few years.

"Milady," the sound of a trembling voice caused her to pause in her task of cutting roses from the palace's garden, prompting her to turn her wheelchair in search of Dienn. "Both the queen and the leader, Aeienn, are all set."

Fabehel nodded in agreement and then followed her. Her expression was one of somberness.

Lady Fabehel's wheelchair was being carried by two robust feline guards as they followed the archivist Dienn through a combination of well-lit and dimly lit corridors that stretched to the farthest reaches of the palace, where she recalled the unpretentious door that bore a striking resemblance to the entrance of a cell.

The suspicious appearance of these corridors and the door caught her attention. Being a foster member of the royal family, she knew monarchs should be visible in palaces or castles.

As she neared her destination, a sudden sense of dread crept into her body. However, she could keep her emotions in control.

After positioning her wheelchair on the floor and opening the door, one guard granted Fabehel entry. She saw Queen Shiann and Aeienn seated at a table with fancy foods and drinks instead of papyruses.

"Welcome back to my chambers, dear," with an invitation, the queen welcomed her to take a seat at the table. "You were the topic of our recent conversation. An appointed to represent the Divine Empress."

Fabehel's gaze shifted between the two female Fennens, observing Aeienn's subtle nod of greeting while holding a mug, and Dienn joining them at the table. By manipulating her wheelchair's arm arrows with her fingers, she intended to get close to the queen to strike fatally.

Instead of succumbing to the urge to use the concealed dagger to harm her on the spot, she inquired further with a sharp tone, showing a desire to gain more information about them. "You both tell me about a civil war in Fenn, but I have seen nothing through my eyes that suggests there is a conflict and everything is in peace. Are you lying to us?"

"Do we have to show a conflict when there is already a war coming from the Karekall Mountains?" Aeienn's uncharacteristic display of egotism in her reply was unexpected. "How come we are required to receive an Ambassador when it was the Divine Empress who specifically banned the extraction of the giefo?"

The words spoken by the Kiffenn leader left Fabehel in a state of disbelief. Uncertain of whether she was the same one she met or her authentic self had a dark side.

"I tried to convince you, dear," with a gesture towards the mysterious book on the table, the queen added her comments. "Despite my offer for you to be crowned as queen of this realm, you turned it down."

Dienn tapped the surface of the table. "We could have benefited from your knowledge and experience, milady."

"What is the meaning of all that nonsense?!" With an increasing rapid heartbeat and a chilling sweat spreading over her face, she demanded answers with eyes widened in anticipation. "Could you tell me the truth?!"

Queen Shiann stood up from her chair with ease, looking slightly younger. In front of Fabehel, she positioned a mug and poured brew from a jar she had picked up. "Please have a drink, dear. We need you to be calm so that we can share all the information with you openly." The queen then sat back down in her seat.

Lady Fabehel wasted no time to grab the mug and drink from it, feeling peace. "I am ready. Tell me what I must know!"

Te queen tossed the book to her. "I am confident that you are aware of the content of this volume."

Fabehel, upon gazing at everyone in the room, took the book and read its title. "Aye, it is *The Grand Conspiracy*, an Arankan classic." With a roll of her eyes and a nod, she recalled. "Estherleon's name is referenced in the book, as

Keleana's surname. . . Have you fabricated all of this? Is this a joke?"

"After finding out that Keleana is the Marshal of the Imperial Guard, I delved into researching more about her and stumbled upon her surname," the queen replied. "We created a story and schemes to have you alone to ourselves, sending Corr away."

"It was our anticipation that Master Alessandro would attend instead of you," Lord Doni emerged from a hidden spot, revealing himself. "Rather, the Empress opted to send you instead."

Fabehel's complexion turned pale. "How is it possible that you are alive?"

The lord continued by stating that it was part of the plan. "The black giant eagle you have sighted in Siennt was none other than Parek, Lord Ardek's right hand, after defeating the brown eagle that protected the burgh."

"In fact, after your arrival in Fenn, all the Siennt locals were infected into Korbeens, and upon my return from the assault on Salter," the queen mentioned with a slight twitch.

"Parek? Are you saying you are not the queen?!" In a state of stupor, Fabehel asked.

"Aye," Aeienn, with a mug of brew in hand, pointed at the queen as he replied. "We took care of the real queen and buried her in the same gardens where you took your roses. Because this one is no other than the same Parek."

"Why are you doing it to us?!" Fabehel asked to the false queen. "Why do you want to bring destruction to this world?"

"Do you believe our sole purpose in coming here was to cause destruction for our own enjoyment?" In his disguised form, Parek responded, using his deep, cavernous voice. "It is the giefo that attracts us, as Sankaris has it plenty in the undergrounds. Hence, we traverse from one world to another in search of valuable resources, yet it is this exceptional metal that makes us gods."

"Let me get this straight—you came up with the plan to enslave the people of our world just to have that metal?!" Fabehel's question had bitterness and resentment. "You are not special, but damn invaders!"

In her serene manner, Parek, resembling the queen, rose from the seat and made his way towards Lord Doni. "The metal we carry with us, the prakstak, originates from our Mother World and possesses mystical abilities that we use and pass on to others, transforming them into Korbeens." With a gentle touch, he revealed a bronze-colored dagger from Doni's sheath, running his fingers lovingly along the blade. "By utilizing a special alloy in the Dominion east of the Karekall, we can create exceptional weapons capable of dominance in both magical and melee. The giefstak."

"By accepting the invitation to join The Aquelarre, you could have a world of incredible opportunities, especially with the powerful Korbas by your side," Aeienn, while drinking her brew, remarked. "Reconsider the option of becoming a queen."

Witnessed by Parek, Lord Doni, Aeienn, and Dienn, Fabehel closed her eyes and lowered her head.

The Lady of the Red Tides exhaled calmly before employing her distinctive technique to throw her dagger at Parek with a look of defiance in her eyes.

The Korba could use his unscathed arm to divert the dagger, sending it off in a different direction.

A cry of agony echoed and the audible thud of a body collapsing resounded. Dienn suffered fatal injuries from the identical dagger.

Apart from the red-haired lady, there was no visible reaction from any of the attendees to the incident.

Parek, with a grin that showcased his terrifying yellow sharp teeth, snapped with his right hand while still embodying the form of the queen.

At that precise time, feelings of dread overwhelmed Fabehel, causing her to clutch at her throat and gasp for air frantically. Her complexion became paler with each passing moment.

The Korba underwent a transformation, shedding his old form to reveal his true self as a large black winged dragon, although he remained smaller than his true form. "That brew that you consumed is identical to the one that the Empress' foster mother once had. The Prairie Lily brew."

As she experienced a moment of intense anguish, she tumbled from the wheelchair in a desperate search for something that she was aware would not prevent her imminent demise. Exhausted and nearly out of breath, she struggled to move forward until her body felt weak, ultimately succumbing just before the abominable feet of Parek. There, on the cold stone floor, she whispered her last word, barely audible. "Alessandro. . ." . Her eyes turned black and lost their sight as she stared up at the cruel Korba, realizing it would be the ultimate image she would see before her breath faded and her heart stopped.

Alone and isolated, Lady Fabehel of the Red Tides succumbed to her death, at the mercy of the monsters she had tried to confront.

"Allegedly, the Prairie Lily acts fast. How you delayed it?" Aeienn, holding a mug in her hand, asked with complete indifference.

Parek, in his natural form as a winged dragon, responded to the question. "I had held it by the time she drank it. If only she had joined us, I might have been able to save her life. She opted for death instead."

Lord Doni walked up to the lifeless body on the ground and delivered a forceful kick to it. "I never liked that damned arrogant witch!"

"We should make our way to the mines and leave Finnerr behind," the Korba mandated. "The Imperial Guard will arrive shortly."

27
THE PILLAGE

W ith an appalling and disgusted look, Branni throttled her horse. Despite hearing about the bustling city of Finnerr from books and felines, she arrived to find a ghost town, with signs of pillage and massacre all around. As she brought her horse to a halt, the ravaging sight of mutilated Fennen bodies, women and children inclusive, on the streets and buildings was unthinkable to ignore.

Dark clouds overhead intensified the somber mood.

The Korbas and their armies showed no mercy towards anyone, regardless of age or gender. They were ruthless creatures devoid of any compassion, not only killing but also pillaging and demolishing everything in the buildings to wipe out all traces of a Fennen culture.

The empty streets were a haunting sight, filled with abandoned steam-engine carts and carriages, bearing witness to the chaos of the pillage.

Branni, the young aspirant to knighthood, could not contain her tears, letting them flow down her cheeks and form wet droplets on her chin.

Her companion, Ommi, rode beside her and addressed his words towards her. "Even with the disturbing view in front of us, can you continue moving forward?"

"Aye," she replied as her voice cracked. "And my concern is Corr."

Ommi, the young sixteen-year-old lad, turned to glance over his shoulder and saw Corr and Admiral Kekten riding into the burgh along with the eighteen Ser Marissa's pupils, hundreds of the Imperial Guard that had departed from Tempest Post were trailing behind them. He was eager to see their reaction.

While riding his horse in his imperial armor, Kekten, ready for any battle, noticed that Corr appeared unfazed by the massacre of his kind, though he understood the pain hidden in his heart at the sight of his city's destruction. "Did ya expect it?"

"I did not," as he tried to regain composure, the feline responded. "We can no longer concern about those who are no longer with us. Our immediate task is to search for Lady Fabehel."

Kekten sensed a hint of regret in his tone, recognizing his unspoken guilt. He came to a halt and turned his horse to have a word with his officials in the Imperial Guard. "I need some of ya to search the city for any survivors!"

Over twenty guards split up and scoured even the most secluded alleys of Finnerr, searching for any survivors.

Her comrades recognized Branni's leadership traits, and in the absence of Ser Marissa or Juni, they entrusted her with leading the group of youngsters because of her firm determination and will. As they began their training for knighthood and had no official name since they were not knights yet, they named themselves *The Unnamed Squires*, inspired by ancient tales of kingdoms long past.

Squire Ommi, riding beside, inquired. "What shall we do?"

Branni struggled with self-doubt as she led her comrades, troubled by the memory of the sneeze she accidentally killed during the *Battle of the Tempest*. The juveniles had their hopes rested on her shoulders, since there was no knight to guide them. "Go to aid any survivors you come across and bring along ten of us."

The youngster nodded in understanding and followed her instructions by riding away.

After riding further on her horse, Branni halted once more.

The girl's eyes landed on the Royal Palace. Its gates were open but with clear indications of a conflict.

Corr and Kekten arrived on horseback to join her.

As the three riders entered, they observed the deplorable condition of the building, noticing the chaos among the

Fennen guards overwhelmed by the mighty force of the Korbas.

The feline remained motionless, his gaze fixed ahead, shrouded in his singular goal. By visually examining the sorrowful surroundings, he felt a deep sense of loss, knowing that Lady Fabehel was no longer with him, yet needing to see her for reassurance. Even as everything seemed hopeless, he could not shake the small glimmer of hope that she could still be alive.

Kekten from the Imperial Guard took charge of securing the palace, designating it as a temporary stronghold for the Jyistereerk while they awaited news on Fenn's status. He knew that the last kingdom on Sankaris had vanished as Fenn fell to the Korbas, mirroring the fate of many regions in Berrem and Salter.

The tenacity of the Korbas made Kekten realize that the completion of the *Deken Karsaker* was a task that would extend beyond his lifetime. He remembered Alessandro's grim prediction about the war lasting eighty years, a prophecy originating from Archmage Selee and the *Frelee Dee*.

Corr disregarded the rest of the group and dismounted his horse and made his way into the palace.

Kekten noticed the feline disappear and spoke to Branni. "All ya squires take charge of the Imperial Guard." He dismounted from his horse and sprinted to catch up with Corr, showing his concern.

Upon entering the palace, indifferent Corr and horrified Kekten encountered a terrifying scene. Wet bloodstains marked every step of the main stairs leading to the upper levels, yet there was no sign of a body. Certain decorative pieces, particularly the ones crafted from gold, were nowhere to be found. The paintings in the room bore the marks of scratches and splashes of the same blood.

"Indeed, the guards defended this estate," Admiral Kekten withdrew his sword cautiously.

"As we crossed through Siennt, it seemed like they had vanished, leaving no proof of their presence." At last, Corr broke his silence and responded.

"Shall we ascend?"

"No, this way," the feline hinted at the time as he gestured towards a small entrance tucked away in the corner. "The queen keeps her chambers shrouded in secrecy, hidden away from prying eyes."

"Indeed, she was insane!"

Corr moved cautiously forward with his senses on high alert, opting to rely on his sharp claws rather than any weapon. Kekten followed behind him.

"The corridors in this system are so convoluted, almost resembling a maze, as one navigates towards the chambers," Corr clarified. "Her illness seemed dubious to me, and I could not help but wonder about the secrets she might be harboring."

"How do ya know? Are ya a medic?"

"The scent of an ill person is very distinctive. I couldn't perceive anything from her."

The corridors grew darker as they ventured deeper, leaving Corr surprised and disoriented as he struggled to recognize his surroundings, even with his intense green eyes.

Upon entering the darkness, the overpowering smell of dampness and an icy breeze immediately greeted them. As they walked closer, the sound of rushing water grew louder, resembling to a waterfall.

With a lack of torches, Kekten's readiness was obvious as he retrieved an object from his waist pouch. With persistent clicking, he produced a small flame using a primitive lighter made of stone and iron, dimly lighting up the area. To his right, he discovered a large opening with bars, and as he brought the lighter closer, he realized it was a square-shaped well where liquid cascaded endlessly from above to an unknown depth. The sight of a cascade inside the palace defied all expectations and seemed ominous. "Do ya recognize this place, Corr?"

"Everything is unknown to me!" the feline widened his eyes as he approached to the well. "I should smell water, but a rusty scent comes from the cascade."

The Admiral listened to him with amazement, as suspicions arose. To get a better look at the falling liquid, he moved closer with the small flame in his hand. "By the goddesses!"

As they looked closer, the men were horrified to find that what they thought was water turned out to be a gory cascade of blood.

"This place is haunted!" Kekten exclaimed in terror.

Despite the eerie atmosphere of the Fennen palace, Corr and Kekten pressed on in their task to find Lady Fabehel. Despite the odds, there was still a slight hope that she would be alive. Yet the sight of the massacre and pillage left them feeling hopeless.

Confused by the corridors, the feline relied on the limited view from the small windows to estimate the direction of the queen's chambers.

After passing the cascade, they proceeded cautiously, alert for any threats in the ominous corridors. While on the way, Kekten spotted a branch among a pile of wood in a room between corridors. He used it to start a fire, aided by the castor oil he carried in a small bottle, transforming it into a torch to light their path further.

It took them a long time to reach the next point. A greenhouse that had crystal tall ceilings with an opaque glass.

On long wooden platforms, hundreds of pots held a variety of flowers and plants. Even in the dimness, the plants appeared to be thriving. While examining the sights, they walked across them.

A long tangerine-colored flower drew Corr in, tempting him to touch it.

"I would not touch it!" Kekten warned. "Do not ya see what plants are here?"

Corr listened and retracted his hand from the flower. "I can smell a powerful, fiery scent coming from them, but I can not identify it."

"All plants and flowers are, indeed, poisonous!" he urged, showing his hand's palm. "That one is the Molkan Prairie Lily!"

Corr withdrew his hand from the flower and scanned the area, nodding in recognition at some plants he spotted. "Aye, you are right. With a deep interest in botany, Queen Shiann has amassed an extensive collection of plants that adorn both the interior and exterior of her palace."

"There are, indeed, the strangest plants no one has seen." Nodding in agreement, Kekten introduced a specimen. "This one will make ya erase your memory forever!"

The feline brushed past the harmful plants, focused on continuing the search for Fabehel. With a sigh of relief, he located an exit. "The corridor seems to have changed a little, but I can still see it as the right path leading to the chambers."

Corr hurried his steps through the corridors he remembered from his previous visit to the queen's chambers, with Kekten chasing behind him. He could feel the turmoil building as they neared their intention.

To ensure safety, the Admiral urged the feline to reduce his speed and instructed to carry his torch to illuminate the path ahead. Despite Corr listening, he refused to let him pass, determined to reach their destination first. His strong eyes could pierce through the darkness, allowing him to observe even the tiniest details.

Unexpectedly, they entered a spacious, circular chamber that Corr could not remember. The first time he went through the corridors with Fabehel, all he cared about was making sure she was comfortable while being carried with the wheelchair by the guards.

He paid little heed to his surroundings then.

Taking in the surroundings, Kekten felt droplets of liquid landing on his head, which prompted him to touch it with his hand, fearing it might be blood, similar to the cascade. As he moved his fingers closer to get a better look, he found it was a sticky, see-through liquid.

The Admiral lit up his surroundings. The first thing he encountered were walls built from solid stone blocks, exuding a dampness that carried the unpleasant scent of fungus. His torch revealed a vast ceiling that appeared to stretch into infinity.

Corr and his companion gazed up to take in the sight above them.

A sleeping black large bat was hanging from the ceilings with its excretions dropping. Corr noticed the sleek, feline features of the creature and understood that it had once been a Fennen now transformed into a Korbeen. "We shall leave now!" he whispered, frightened. "And make no noise!"

With horror, Kekten agreed and followed him slowly to the other side of the chamber.

Both of them walked in silence. As he dawdled away, the Admiral accidentally kicked a stone, causing an echoing cacophony.

They stopped and glanced upward once more.

The Korbeen's red eyes slowly opened before it let out a loud screech. Finally, the creature spread its wings and pursued them.

Corr's heart raced as he ran down the corridor, with the deafening gliding of the monster chasing him.

In a moment of terror and confusion, Kekten fell to the ground as the Korbeen raced past him in pursuit of the feline.

As fast as possible, Corr raced through the corridors. He avoided conflict, knowing the potential threat of being transformed. As the demonic Korbeen chased him at the same speed, he relied on his feline instincts to jump over obstacles in his way. Just as he thought he had reached the end of the corridor, a closed door stood before him, the entrance to the queen's chambers, making him reluctant to open it in case there was someone inside.

Seeing Corr at its mercy, the Korbeen halted and emitted a sharp, ear-splitting screech. As they awaited their own fate, both of them gazed at themselves. The feline believed it was his fate to be one of them, so he extended his claws, prepared to face it.

The creature, hit by a stone, turned around with anger before charging at Kekten, who had distracted it. Saliva from the monster's sharp teeth dripped onto his face as it shoved him to the ground. However, it emitted one last screech before succumbing to gravity and falling onto the Admiral.

Kekten exerted himself to move the lifeless Korbeen's body, standing with rapid, labored breaths. "Go back to hell, ya scourge!" He pulled the sword out from under the creature's neck.

With widened eyes, Corr observed the Admiral as he stood in silence, looking for answers.

"It, indeed, reminded me of the runs I had with the guild," he replied with a smile. "It was like going back to old times!"

Upon opening the door, the strange silence of empty chambers greeted them.

Corr recognized them, but the table showed signs of a feast with fancy foods and many beverages, untouched for a long time, that a swarm of flies flew over them. This made him even more eager to search for her.

Beside the table, he discovered the abandoned wheel-chair positioned next to the seat reserved for the queen. With fear in his eyes, the feline slowly made its way towards the body of Fabehel. Upon closer inspection, he noticed her open eyes, which had turned from hazel to a deep black color, confirming her lifeless state.

He knelt and placed his hand on her neck, confirming the absence of a pulse. With a firm grip, he shook her shoulders, desperate to bring her back.

The scent of Prairie Lily brew in a mug topped Kekten's senses. The truth of her murder unraveled in his mind. With sorrow, he observed the feline's reaction as he drew near. "It is too late, Corr," he interrupted the shaking by touching his right arm, then closed Fabehel's eyes with his hand. "Indeed, there is nothing we can do for her."

The sound of Corr's scream was a heart-wrenching mix of despair, frustration, and guilt. He let her down when she needed him the most.

Kekten stood up, distancing himself from him behind. As he inspected the area, he discovered the unconscious body of a female Fennen, Dienn, next to the wall, with her clothes showing signs of bloodstains. As he got closer, he could hear her shallow breaths, assuring him she was still alive despite her weakened state, and then he spotted Fabehel's dagger sticking out of her chest. The Admiral believed that saving her life was crucial because she held valuable information about the incident.

While Corr sobbed by Fabehel's side, the Admiral got to his feet and surveyed the expansive windows, where he noticed a group of squires exploring the grounds outside. Without hesitation, he picked up a heavy chair and used all his strength to smash the glass, causing the youngsters to turn, surprised. "Go find a ladder and help us!"

The ominous corridors filled Kekten with uneasiness, making him hesitant to go back that way.

28

THE ARRIVAL

U pon arrival at the Port of Finn, *The Navigator* witnessed a scene of chaos as countless Fennens sought refuge from their realm's unexpected crisis.

The disappearance of the last kingdom on Sankaris and the Korba expansion towards different regions of Fenn forced families to escape from the continent, leading them to emigrate to the Island of Aparr on the Gulf of Triem. The sight of the otherworldly colossal Tinklen vessel in the harbor deepened their despair, prompting them to search for a haven far away from the threatening presence of the Korbas on another continent.

Panic, desolation, and despair engraved the faces of the thousands in the crowd.

Inside the vessel, Alessandro observed the panicked multitude and stood with a group of Imperial Guard and elvish soldiers at the end of the inner bridge, ready to exit when the time was right. For the first time in two thousand tikls, the elf Commandant Kartak and his group traveled with him to the continent of Ryza, descendants of the Tannes who departed from Molke after Kasana's execution.

Siblings Marshal Keleana and Captain Kanden, standing alone, watched from behind with wide eyes and furrowed brows.

Through the transformable surface that served as an entrance, they had a view of the outside from the inside, while the crowd outside could only see the immense white vessel.

The Tinklen Pi-U remained in Aranka to supervise the swift construction of a harbor, considering the troubling situation in Fenn and the effect of the *Deken Karsaker*.

Ti-K was not only responsible for the vessel but also stood ready beside Alesandro. "Shall we open the exits, Master?" In his usual tone, he asked with deliberate pauses between each word. "How will we aid all these people?"

Kartak's yellow eyes widened at the pandemonium before him, and he twitched his eyebrow. In a moment of horror, he witnessed the Fennens unleash their feline instincts, injuring and even killing others as they moved towards the vessel, which prompted him to plead in silence for a way to help them.

Alessandro noticed the pleas from the Tinklen and the elf as he placed his hand on his chin, nodding in understanding. "Let us fulfill the command of the Divine Empress. Let them board the vessel and transport to Aranka." Before mounting his stallion, Breeze, he glanced at Kartak and Keleana. "Commandant, Marshal! Take control of your armies and manage this crowd. After you are done, come find me in Finner!" He nodded, signaling the Tinklen, who communicated with others nearby by manipulating the controls within reach.

Upon opening the orifice, Alessandro immediately smelled the handkerchief and urged Breeze to gallop as fast as possible, even through the swarm of people, intending to reach his destination in a swift. He rode on the stallion, Breeze, avoiding any contact with people, until he reached the peripheries of the city where only a few rats scurried around the filthy, littered streets. He led his horse to a halt and grimaced at the putrid smell rising from the black waters of the drainage, taking in the scene of the deserted streets that bore witness to a frenzied exodus.

He also grasped the weight of the situation. As he stumbled upon the dead corpses on the wet surface, he realized that beneath the calm facade of the Fennens, panic unleashed their feline instincts. He had seen it with Corr. The Korbas did not kill the victims, but by their own people to flee.

There was no time to take in the surroundings as he began his journey to Finnerr in the early morning to reunite with his beloved Fabehel. He had studied maps and books detailing the intricate and challenging landscape of Fenn, which is why he decided not to bring Brisel to aid him in speed, instead mentally noting the shortest path to the capital.

He spurred his horse Breeze, heading towards the left side of the sun.

Alessandro rode through a narrow, ancient road instead of going in the newer steam engine carts, as his experience as a Korbeen Slayer taught him to stay hidden and avoid evil creatures.

With his greatsword in hand, he cleared the overgrown plants and bushes that blocked the road while steering his stallion with the other hand. Unlike the tropical forests of his native Casak, this jungle boasted dense, expansive vegetation.

He recalled being close to Gasderfinn, the town renowned in his Academy studies as the birthplace of the steam engine.

The *Tree of a Thousand Branches*, a local natural monument, was visible to him, even from behind the tall palms. He recognized the location he planned to travel through on his journey to Finnerr.

He reined in his horse upon reaching the locally famous tree, only to be met with a horrifying and ominous sight.

Thousands of Gasderfinn locals gruesomely adorned the colossal tree with their corpses hanging from its branches.

He knew the hidden society Carrasso had revealed to Nehel, The Aquelarre, had done it. He remembered historical accounts of kingdoms where warlocks and witches terrorized towns, hanging people to prevent resistance. The method was identical, but on a much larger scale.

Instead of multiple autonomous dark societies, only The Aquelarre existed, serving the Korbas, as the warlock revealed.

A stomach ache struck Alessandro as he viewed the hanging corpses, and he used the handkerchief to detect any scent of Fabehel. Yet, it was to no avail. The only smell reaching him was that of fresh, humid grass, as though the scent had inexplicably disappeared.

To beat the sunset, he bypassed the town and galloped toward Finnerr, suspecting that his unsettling experience with the tree was just a prelude to worse terrors within Fenn. Yet, he resolved that upon completing his affairs in the capital, the victims would receive a proper funeral and burial.

Over the past four years, Corr showed him that felines are just as human as any other race. However, their sometimes animal instincts caused them to be unwelcome in much of Sankaris. In the end, these enduring small, ancient domestic animals trace their lineage directly to cats, surviving many tikls.

With a somber gesture and a silent prayer to the goddesses, he left the tree and continued his journey.

While thunders boomed and dark clouds gathered, Alessandro passed through an unnamed town on his way to a nearby lake, seeking shelter under his black hooded cloak from the downpour.

The town appeared completely deserted, with no evidence of violence or bodies, as if everyone had suddenly left. Even the hanging oil lamps outside each building were mysteriously lit despite the rain, as if they were unreachable.

His stallion's slow pace left a trail of hoofprints in the mud, constantly threatened by the rising water.

As he approached the largest structure in the town, a manor that he presumed belonged to someone of significant wealth or aristocratic lineage, he observed an individual standing watch outside the imposing gates. Alessandro could not discern whether the figure was male or female, or even a Fennen, as a large, rain-soaked gray cloak that concealed the face completely shrouded the person.

Intending to get closer to the enigmatic figure, Alessandro saw it quickly escape, prompting suspicions that, combined with his observation of crows atop the manor's towers, caused him to unsheathe his greatsword cautiously.

He thought the mysterious person could be a warlock, or even a witch, from The Aquelarre.

He rode further, as the crows disappeared completely, leaving behind an unsettling emptiness and silence. It was not unusual for members of that society, skilled in mystical arts and even black magic—taught in their secluded eastern sanctuaries beyond the Karekall mountains—.

His search proved fruitless. He sheathed his blade back and hurried away, only to see smoke rising from Finnerr, a large city on the far side of the lake, nestled amidst rain-soaked tropical grasslands. The downpour was inconsequential to Alessandro, the water merely adding to the wetness of his face and clothes.

As Alessandro and Breeze crossed into Finnerr, the stench of burning flesh reached him, as Imperial Guard tossed corpses onto massive, crackling bonfires amidst the ruins.

As he passed through the streets, the weight of the sentinels' somber gazes made his skin crawl. One of them sprinted towards the palace.

The slow rhythm of his horse's hooves was a steady beat against the confusion Alessandro felt as he tried to understand the reasons behind the strange behaviors.

As he crossed the open gates of the palace, the smell of roasting meat and wood-smoke from a small bonfire where Ser Marissa's squires were having a meal drifted towards him. Their chatter ceased as Alessandro entered.

With a gasp, Branni stood. Her eyes widened and her expression serious as she watched him stride past.

Alessandro saw the Imperial Guard's familiar tents around the palace, dozens of them, just like the ones at Tempest Post.

With wide, blue eyes and a somber expression, Admiral Kekten descended the palace's stairs, dreading the meeting ahead. The heavy stone steps seemed to cry under his burden.

Alessandro noticed his nervous behavior—his rapid pulse, clammy hands, and shallow breaths—and instantly closed his eyes, suspecting something had happened to his beloved. His heart pounded, and a sickening feeling of dread washed over him. Dismounting, he braced himself for bad news.

Kekten stopped before him. His lips shivered, unable to form the words he desperately needed to say. The silence hung heavy between them. "Master. . ."

"Skip the accounts and tell me now!"

The Admiral quivered as he shook his head. "Lady Fabehel is gone," his voice broke. "We were late. I am sorry, Master."

Alessandro closed his eyes. Tears traced paths down his immobile face. " How?!"

"Indeed, it seems she and Corr stumbled into a cleverly concealed snare, no doubt set for ya."

Upon hearing him, a gasp escaped Alessandro's lips as icy paralysis crept up his body. Yet, he was in denial when he made a request. "Take me to her."

Kekten nodded, then gestured towards the largest tent nearby, inviting him to follow. He opened the entrance and let him inside.

A wave of sadness washed over Alessandro as he stared at the unique, gloomy stage. Lady Fabehel lay lifeless on the wooden platform with beams. The scent of beeswax filled the air as he approached her. The four candles cast a soft, inviting light across the tent.

His dark, wet eyes examined her with intensity. Fabehel, with her pale skin and serene expression, held a rose clasped in her hands, which rested peacefully on her chest. She wore her favorite purple dress. "How she was murdered?"

"She drank Prairie Lily brew, Master. Indeed, they offered her during a feast."

He listened to Kekten, nodded, and then sobbed. He wept for a long time over his beloved's lifeless body. Finally, gasping for air, he stopped and wiped his face like a child. With a knot in the throat, he asked. "Where is Corr?"

"He has isolated himself in the gardens, full of guilt. He does not want to eat or sleep, like awaiting a death on himself."

With an angry gesture, Alessandro turned. "Do you know who murdered her?!"

"I am not sure, but we have a survivor who might tell us what happened that day. Indeed, it is Dienn, ya have met her during the Empress' audience."

As per Kekten's instructions, Dienn, the former archivist, received medical attention and was on a makeshift cot of wood and straw, in a room next to the stables and steam-engine depot. While she was recuperating from the dagger wound, a chain from the wall handcuffed her.

Although the Imperial Guard and squires gave her food and water, they mistreated her. Consumed by hatred, they accused her of Lady Fabehel's death and demanded her execution. She only lived because the Admiral ordered it.

Known throughout the Jyistereerk for her kindness, Fabehel of the Red Tides was beloved as a mother figure to the Empress and partner to Alessandro Eskar, who played a pivotal role in helping Nehel, the then-Promise, to build her empire a tikl ago. Her generosity towards the guards, always providing charity, fueled the intense hatred for her killers.

When Alessandro stormed into the room, the clang of his greatsword echoed as its point pressed hard against Dienn's neck, as his fury was palpable.

The greatsword's chill was almost visible as the gray feline glared at him with bitterness. "End with my affliction for once!"

"You despicable scourge!"

Kekten's headshake stopped Alessandro from carrying out the execution.

Turning again to Dienn, the cold steel of the sword still pressed against her throat. "Tell me who in the hell were the murderers!"

Dienn's hand settled on the cold iron of the greatsword. Her touch was surprisingly gentle as she guided the tip to the precise point on his neck. "With nothing left to lose, I will reveal the name of her murderers. After I speak, finish with my life. Could you do it?"

"You have my word if you tell me!"

"It was Parek Korba, Ardek's right hand. With the nasty foremen of the Mines of Tiunnff, Lord Doni and Lady Aeienn, as they joined The Aquelarre." She sighed and readied herself. "Go ahead now! Kill me!"

Alessandro nodded and placed the greatsword on his back as he spared her life. "I lied. Your torment is far worse than death. I will let you rot in it." He then whispered to Kekten. "Question her. Extract every detail, no matter how insignificant it may seem!"

Alessandro's swift mounting of his stallion and departure surprised Kekten. He watched him disappear down the road, fading into the distance.

Corr sat motionless as a stone statue, seemingly oblivious to the world around him. But inside, a crushing guilt overwhelmed him. He had not touched food or water in days. His belief that he deserved to die had engulfed him.

He did not care that the rain restarted and soaked him.

He had sworn to protect Lady Fabehel, a solemn vow broken.

The rhythmic clang of Kekten's metallic armor shattered the silence, announcing his approach. "Leave!"

The Admiral shook his head, cutting off any further discussion before it could begin. "Master Alessandro came, and I could sense the pain emanating from him. But he already departed."

"Leave!"

"Ya are his friend!" Kekten spoke with an unexpected force. "Indeed, I believe he is going to the Mines of Tiunnff to confront the fearsome Korba Parek. And ya know he can not win against him."

"Leave!"

"As ya decide! If ya do not stop him, your damn guilt will be twice!"

A furious Corr stood and turned to Kekten. After a long, suspenseful stare, he shook his head in disapproval. He exited the garden, swung himself onto his horse, Thunder, and departed.

The squire Branni approached Kekten, who had witnessed the earlier discussion with the feline, and inquired. "Is there something we shall do?"

"Get the squires and guards ready," he directed, still giving the back to her. "We are launching an attack against the mines."

29
THE VENGEANCE

After almost two days of relentless riding across the sun-baked Cayderr Range grasslands, Alessandro and his stallion arrived at the Breken border. He reached the edge of Breken territory as the sun beat down on his back as he charted his next course.

The Mines of Tiunnff.

From afar, he saw at least two dozen wisps of smoke rising into the bruised sunset sky that had only just cleared from the dark clouds that had brought days of relentless rain, leaving behind stubbornly muddy ground.

A somber panorama unfolded before him—charred, blackened trees stood stark against the dry, cracked earth. The air was thick with the smell of ash, a proof of the land's deliberate ruin.

He dismounted and tethered Breeze to a large rock before continuing his quiet approach to the mines. As he expected some opposition, he drew his greatsword. He gripped the blade with the engraved Salteran word—*Borsen*—was a gift from his niece, a symbol of their blood bond.

Alessandro took several steps forward, his desperation growing with each stride as he pressed the handkerchief to his nose, but the scent was gone, replaced only by the musty smell of the grass. All evidence of Fabehel's existence had vanished, leaving behind only the faintest whisper of what once was—emptiness.

The closer he got, the more unnerving the sounds became—a chorus of scrapes, hisses, and snaps. He threw himself to the ground and dragged himself to the edge for a better view. He was astonished to find the mines' entrance within a colossal crater with unknown origins.

Alessandro could also discover thousands of people working nonstop.

Torn clothing and chained feet in groups of twenty identified the slaves as they shuffled along in chilling lines. They emerged from the underground and took turns pushing the heavy iron cart under the weight of raw giefo rocks, passing it to another group that disappeared into another entrance of the mysterious dome.

He watched the exhausted, chained slaves fall to the ground. Their meager meal of bread and water offered little comfort against the harsh elements as they lay down on the cold, damp earth, lacking even the simplest of blankets for warmth.

Seeing those emaciated slaves, Alessandro realized the horrific ordeals that Cassandro and Corr had endured.

He kept examining the area, noticing the sentinels' watchful eyes scanning the mines. Though their race was unknown to him, he recognized the scrawny, pale Gray Elves from the Zinte Realm—their black, pointed-eared guards carrying long lances were familiar from his Academy lessons.

Surprisingly, on the crater's edge, Brek soldiers with their bloodstained axes watched the mines, wondering about Chief Senaten's role in the Breken Nation's Giefo Trade.

Mysteriously, Alessandro could not perceive any Berremen or Fennen sentinel but only among the slaves, which were from most races on Sankaris.

But before entering the crater unnoticed, he needed to identify the exact location, studying the terrain for any clues. His goal was to locate Parek and the two foremen before nightfall, as the twin moons, the silvery No Sak and the crimson No Ta, began their ascent. Darkness would not help him.

His next destination was easy to find. He saw a larger dome, easily distinguished among the other structures, with two elegant steam-engine carriages parked outside and knew they were inside. He found the place unattended, a strange discovery that ignited his curiosity. No guards in sight.

As night fell, the desire for vengeance burned into his blind heart. He sat, waiting patiently. He pressed the handkerchief to his nose, desperately trying to detect the faintest trace of the long-vanished Fabehel's scent.

The memory of Fabehel's pale face, immobile, lifeless, weighed on him, a constant reminder of their last meeting. As images of her flooded his mind, his hands clenched tight, tears streamed down his cheeks., he did not stop grinning his teeth.

As the moons hung in the night sky, their glow was a signal to Alessandro. He stood with his greatsword drawn, ready.

With caution, he approached the large rocks, as he descended towards the crater, hiding behind them to avoid the Brek guards. He continued to move until he reached the bottom, cautious and bent low, using any cover he could find to avoid the Gray Elves or slaves.

At long last, he reached the waiting carriages, and then made his way to the dome's entrance.

The effortless way he reached his goal made him suspicious. Yet as he entered wielding his blade, the torchlight lit the rough-hewn walls as the scrape of his boots broke the silence on the harsh ground.

Alessandro halted. Sweat ran down his head as the intense heat hit him. He ventured inside. The place was still empty.

He arrived at an open area where the path crossed a river of molten lava, and the ground trembled somewhat beneath his feet. Despite the oppressive heat, a wave of surprising resilience washed over him. He approached his fingers to the blazing liquid's edge, but the intense heat caused him to snatch his hand away.

Alessandro soon spotted the abandoned tools scattered along the path as he examined his surroundings, wondering why no one was working when someone should be present.

He sweated because of the high temperatures, lifting his head to observe the orifice up high to let the smoke out at the time that the night sky showed the moon No Ta. He returned his sight to the red candent liquid, but still holding the greatsword.

"The giefo, a cold metal like ice, requires constant heating to maintain its molten state."

Startled, Alessandro turned to see a tall, bald Casakan man in black clothing standing across the path. The man's brown skin seemed to absorb the heat of the lava. "Who are you?!"

"Introductions will come later," the mysterious man said. "I felt compelled to reveal the giefo's true essence."

"I am not interested in your damn giefo!" Alessandro screamed with anger. "Who in the hell are you?!"

The man, silent and serene, nodded, unaffected by the oppressive heat. "The shared blood between you and Cassandro Eskar is clear in your impulsive natures."

A gasp escaped Alessandro's lips as his eyes widened in disbelief. "How do you know about my brother?"

"His absurd kindness was legendary amongst the slaves," the man approached with slow steps and halted. "Certainly, it cost him his life. I bet you never knew how he died."

"With Lady Fabehel's lifeless body as a constant reminder, does it matter to speak of him when one of you poisoned her?"

"Ah, that naïve girl," a chilling grin stretched across his face, showcasing teeth so white they seemed unnatural and intimidating. "That pathetic thing fell to my feet and begged for you."

"You damn Parek!" with a roar, he ran after the man with his greatsword.

With a single, dominant slap, the Korba Parek, as a man, sent his opponent sprawling across the path.

Stunned, Alessandro lay on the ground, watching the man as if he was waiting for something before rising and gripped his blade. "I am not afraid of you!"

As he grinned again, he shook his head. "Even that I do not require, but if you insist on an exchange, let the fight begin!" From his dark cape, as if by magic, he drew a stunning light golden blade, as its surface gleamed with the colors of molten gold. "Let us fight and see if you can beat me with my giefstak sword!"

With a cry, Alessandro charged towards the Korba to deliver a mortal blow. In the short time he ran, Parek's transformation was swift. A colossal black dragon emerged. The sword in his hand grew altogether.

Despite its size—three times larger than before—the transformed creature failed to intimidate Alessandro, who pressed his attack, aiming his greatsword for a killing blow just below the creature's throat, aiming for the chest. A vivid memory of Peken's instructions during the *Feast of the Dragoness* rang in Alessandro's mind.

Instead of fighting, the Korba yielded. His movements were deliberate. "Do you really believe that by slaying me, as you did those Korbeens, you can somehow bring back the Lady Fabehel?"

"Why did you end up in this world?!" With a furious yell, Alessandro clutched his greatsword. "What have we done to deserve your misery?!" he screamed and raised his sword, ready to strike.

With a sinister laugh and a flapping of his wings, Parek once again avoided him with a warning, "You can not defeat me!"

"I will do whatever it takes!"

"Very well. . . "

Again, Alessandro ran against him.

Immovable, the Korba let the giefstak blade meet the greatsword in a deafening clash. The latter weapon shattered into fragments.

Startled and terrified, Alessandro's heart hammered in his chest as he stared at the dragon, his hand clutched only the empty hilt of his sword.

Unaffected by the intense heat rising from the molten metal under his feet, Parek stood silent as his stare endured and a strange stillness came. "Did you think that the Empress' magic would harm me?" With a sudden motion, he dipped one wing into the fiery liquid and splashed his opponent.

The intense heat of the molten metal burned Alessandro's left face and neck upon contact, as he screamed and fell in excruciating pain, as his cries echoed through the mine.

As soon as Parek snapped his fingers, he made him to fall asleep. The screams annoyed him.

Aeienn and Lord Doni did not take long to appear, walking along the path before stopping with a pleased expression as they found the unconscious Alessandro at their feet.

"Take him," Parek mandated, with a low growl in his voice, "and do to him what you did to his brother. The Wheel of Broken Bones and make sure his agony can last forever."

A searing pain in his left face, and a blind eye, made Alessandro barely aware of his situation. Rough ropes cut into his skin as he awoke to find himself bound hand and foot to a massive, cold wheel. But instead of focusing on the pain, an irrational fear consumed him himself, as a prisoner himself in some sort of torture chamber.

He discovered several well-known torture instruments.

Aeienn's arrogant attitude was obvious, as she touched him on the chin with a mocking gesture. "Look who is the Master now!" She chuckled maliciously. "This Pillar has how two faces!"

"Enough!" Lord Doni observed with serenity. "Let us not waste time and begin."

With a theatrical sigh and a roll of her eyes, the Fennen Lady Aeienn of Aorr made a mock of his suffering and looked at Alessandro. "You were curious about Cassandro's death, now you know."

With a hushed reverence, a Zinte official leaned close to Lord Doni to transmit the information in an inaudible murmur.

"We must gather our soldiers. The Imperial Guard is on the way here." Doni said.

With a frustrated shake of her head, she placed her hands on her hips. "That damn Korba should have not poisoned her!" Then she turned and spoke to the pair of Gray Elves sentinels standing behind her. "I expect you to follow orders!"

Aeienn and Doni, both hurrying to keep up with the official, departed quickly.

The two elves had their faces engraved with uncertainty, exchanged a hushed conversation in their peculiar dialect before one drew a sharp dagger, moving closer to Alessandro.

The elf's small blade sliced through the ropes, freeing him in a rush. He hit the ground with a thud.

The severe weakness left Alessandro unable to stand, the desperate thirst that threatened to pull him into unconsciousness.

The other Gray Elf placed a worn leather satchel on him, whispering urgent words in a lilting, unfamiliar tongue to him. "You go to Divine Empress."

Both soldiers from the Zinte Realm carried him through a narrow, dimly lit secret tunnel, known only to a select few. The distance was long and took a while before they could reach the outsides, as the sun was emerging for a fresh morning. They carried him another considerable distance before they could drop him on the ground in the middle of the grassland, leaving him alone.

With his one good eye, Alessandro saw the uneven peaks of the Karekall Mountains looming before him. Overwhelmed by constant, searing pain, parched throat, and debilitating weakness, he collapsed, the bitter taste of failure heavy in his mouth as he wished only for death's embrace, to be reunited with Fabehel. Once more, he fell unconscious.

The vultures circled, their cries resounded the anticipation of his death.

Corr had to shoo away circling vultures, as he discovered Alessandro's unconscious body. He dismounted Thunder and approached him, stunned by his lamentable aspect, especially noticing his disfigured left side of his face.

To follow the scent, he galloped from Finnerr with haste to avoid the clash between Admiral Kekten's Imperial Guard and the troops from Tiunff. He encountered the stallion Breeze in his path and was about to enter the crater that sheltered the mines. But the scent attracted him to another direction.

The feline knelt and felt Alessandro's weak, rapid pulse on the neck, and offered him water, but he only took a few sips, showed no improvement. A soft moan of pain was audible as it emanated from him.

Corr hoped to discover something useful, perhaps some medicine, and examined the satchel that he carried. But to his surprise, he only found scattered pieces of his greatsword.

Corr understood it was not time for lamentations and had to act fast to save his life.

He had lost a friend, and can not afford to lose another.

He turned. The uneven peaks of the Karekall mountains soared before him, as a daunting and hard path to the Breken Nation where he hoped to find a healer for Alessandro's deplorable wounds.

With the strength of a feline, he lifted Alessandro, who had fallen unconscious again, onto the horse's saddle. He then tied Alessandro's legs to the saddle to ensure he would not fall off, and leaned him against the stallion's head, assessing his next move.

He mounted Thunder and pulled Breeze towards the Karekall.

30
LADY FABEHEL

S uch utter silence reigned, a grim contrast to the turmoil within Nehel, that the perfect peace could not soothe her into a proper sleep. She felt the anxiety deep inside.

Her encounter with warlock Carrasso instilled a broad and abiding fear within her.

The silken sheets and feather pillows of her round bed offered no solace as a heavy, unsettling thought weighed upon her.

Her concerns for Lady Fabehel and her uncle Alessandro, far away in Fenn, were a heavy weight on her chest. A sudden feeling of unease pierced as premonition whispered their misfortune.

Sleepless and anxious as a torrent of ideas and conclusions swirled in her mind, she stood and walked to the table where the Falte, the Molkan board game, lay. She toyed with it.

But persistent, nagging thoughts never left her mind.

Awake all night, Ser Juni stood outside the door. Ever since the assassination attempt, he had been constantly by her side, always watching over her like a protective friend—or more accurately, a devoted fiancé. Along with him, dozens of Imperial Guard stood watch in the palace's labyrinthine halls.

A sigh escaped Nehel's lips. The Falte was tedious, but a nervous intensity crawled beneath her skin. With trembling hands, she reached for a ripe pear from a woven basket overflowing with fruit from the rear gardens. It was not the same familiar Berrem fruit, a reminder of her journey from Molke to The Lowlands on that tenth birthday. Instead, it was a special pear, golden and plump. The juice was already obvious as she held it.

Juni had given her his dagger to slice the pear. The small knife, a gift from the late Peken, lay untouched in its satchel. It was a grim reminder of her desperate defense against the warlock.

As Nehel walked past her disordered bed, she caught her reflection in the mirror. In her sleeping gown, she rubbed the fading bruises on her neck. Akartaki's elvish ointment sped the healing process.

Her hazel eyes scanned her vanity desk, where scattered papyruses lay in disarray. But one of them caught her attention. Archmage Missar's letter detailed several important announcements and requests.

Missar, shaken by the Empress' assassination attempt, met with Lady Tasarissa to resign as Head of Casak and passed on governmental authority until new elections could be held. Immediately, Alyssa and several sentinels accompanied Tasarissa as they journeyed south, back to her homeland.

Missar accepted Alessandro's offer to lead the Jyistereerk's mystical arm, a position left empty by Selee's mysterious disappearance and suspected death, and become part of the Guild.

The creak of the doors opening, combined with a sudden gust of icy wind, startled her as she noticed the open balcony doors. Initially, the thought of the warlock's return and unfinished business had her reaching for Juni outside the Imperial Apartment, but she sensed a lingering warmth—a recently departed spirit, earthbound before its journey to the Gakia.

As she approached the balcony, bathed in the silvery light of the icy moon No Sak, a gasp escaped her lips as she saw a familiar face.

The Empress' hazel eyes widened tremendously.

A ghostly woman, pale as moonlight, leaned against the rail while the white moon casting an ethereal glow on her. She smiled, captivated by the Arankan forest's ethereal beauty. Even in the dark, the moonlight painted the scene with silver.

She was standing, and she had feet.

The spectral form of Lady Fabehel.

A profound ache swelled Nehel's chest, as tears emerged as the realization of Fabehel's death settled upon her. "No!" She could sense her spiritual aspect in another dimension.

Fabehel turned around and revealed a smile. "Do not trouble for me, Nehel!" She appeared calm. "I can assure you, I'm in a much better place now."

"I. . ." Unable to find the right words, Nehel's lips trembled. "What is wrong with you?!"

"It does not matter now," her face turned serious. "It is your uncle, Nehel. His life is hanging by a thread."

"Where is he?" she asked with great concern. "What happened to him?"

"He battles for his life in the Breken Nation, clinging to hope of joining me in the afterlife." Fabehel shook her head. "I can not bring him, leaving you without him when you need him most. And he needs you!"

Despair and uncertainty washed over Nehel, leaving her paralyzed and unsure of her next step. "I can not leave this palace! But also I can not abandon him!"

"You shall go to him."

"How?! The Navigator just departed for Fenn!"

"No need of Tinklen vessels," Fabehel pointed to the other side of the balcony rail, where a rainbow-colored horse floated in the air. "This horse will carry you to the coast, where Brisel waits for you to cross the sea."

Nehel nodded in agreement.

And I shall depart to the afterlife. This is it, the last time you will witness my presence. Fabehel continued as she inclined her head and closed her eyes. "Farewell." As she faded from view, the balcony became empty as the rainbow horse was still waiting for the Empress.

Ser Juni knocked, then opened the doors, letting a maid enter with a tray of breakfast, and he closed the door behind her. He watched as the maid arranged the food on the large table beside the plush sofas and opened the curtains to let the sunlight stream in before walking to the next chamber to awaken the Empress.

The Second Knight waited, but his patience wore thin as the delay stretched on. A growing sense of unease settled over him as he walked across Imperial Apartment, amplifying his apprehension.

Juni entered the sleeping quarters and found the maid with surprise and fear, frozen in place. Nehel was nowhere to be found.

He spotted the sleeping gown on the bed, then cautiously approached, noticing an open armoire. The missing leather clothes—her usual informal attire for out-doors—confirmed his suspicions.

As he continued his examination, he found a papyrus on the Falte game board. It had his name written on it in Nehel's handwriting. He took the scroll and unrolled it.

Juni scanned the contents of the letter. A sigh escaped his lips as he dropped the papyrus onto the game board, and his head shook. He cleared his throat and spoke to the maid. "Notify Ser Marissa that she will oversee the Jyistereerk temporarily. The Divine Empress has departed for Ryza."

The maid's nod was brief and shaky and left the apart-ment.

Juni's hands, trembling slightly, rested on the small table where the game pieces lay scattered, anxious. "Do not risk it, missy! This is too dangerous!" He murmured to him-self. "My life is meaningless without you!"

31

BREKEN NATION

Alessandro's private geography lessons left a lasting impression on Nehel. The maps inscribed in her mind were a testament to his effective teaching, for which she was grateful to her uncle. Like him, she knew the exact route she needed to take.

Calico, the horse whose coat shimmered like a rainbow—she had not found a better name—carried her to the yet-unknown Arankan shore.

The distant cries of gulls announced Brisel's waiting presence. Nehel knew his runs were always straight, but an impossible task of running across the sea, a feat no mantis could achieve.

But she thought that a burst of wind would propel him forward, preventing him from falling into the squid-infested waters below. If they were fast enough, they would surpass the obstacles of the Beyond Sea.

The risk was immense, but she had to take it.

They chose a straight line southeast from Aranka towards the Port of Finn, feeling the apprehension build as she prepared to use her wind-based abilities as the vast sea stretched before her. Their journey was undisturbed and without incident.

As she left Aranka at dawn, when the sun was just beginning to rise, they arrived in Fenn as the sun sank below the horizon, and the glows of the Moon of Life, No Nunn, and the red No Ta, painted the twilight sky.

As she entered the harbor city, Nehel noted the chaotic destruction—shattered buildings, overturned carts, and the acrid smell of smoke—but the streets were deserted as she rode Brisel. Watching the mantis, she noted its stillness, the way he sensed the air for danger, and the subtle shifts in his posture, urging him to remain visible.

She asked the mantis to proceed at a slow pace, wanting to examine the abandoned city's ruins—its weathered stones, crumbling structures, and the ever-present feeling of rats nearby. The sight of the dead feline bodies in the street, decaying, caused her revulsion. The air floated with the putrid stench of death.

Once they were on the outskirts, she mandated to go northeast.

As the night deepened, they arrived at the burgh of Sinn. To her surprise, she found a scene of devastation and destruction. A recent battle left gaping holes in the buildings and stained the streets with blood.

She saw several Fennen, some limping and bleeding, struggling to reach a cluster of tents erected in the burgh square.

As she neared the group of mostly women and children, a deep sense of pity invaded her.

The locals saw a girl atop a mantis, Nehel, but dismissed her as a curious Casarak girl from Berrem—a place known for its green mantises—never suspecting she was the Empress herself. They eyed her with a mixture of apathy and displeasure.

Fearful of recognition, Nehel muffled her face in her gray cloak. Many Fennens frequently visited the Ri, and she would greet them while strolling through the bustling marketplace or other public areas outside the old palace.

She saw the tents were a makeshift hospital set up by local medics for the injured civilians, guarded by several burgh sentinels. The unaffected slept soundly on the cold, hard pavement.

Nehel dismounted Brisel, and she walked toward the elder. The sleek white feline was eating from a bowl left by volunteers. A whisper made Nehel's question. "What took place here?"

With a deep sigh and a lingering look of mistrust, the elder offered his reply. "Word came that the queen and the Empress' Ambassador had been brutally murdered before the Imperial Guard's enraged response took shape."

The sound of his voice made her gasp, her head shook as a sigh escaped her lips. The last thing she wanted was a war in Fenn, yet here she was, facing that very unwanted outcome. As Empress, she needed to know who started the conflict. She had sent Kartak and Keleana with their armies to maintain order and protect the Fennens, not to provoke a fight.

"Heed in your business and leave now!" the elder requested with harshness. "This is no place for a young outsider like you!"

As Nehel mounted Brisel, the mantis shifted beneath her, and she sensed the hostile glares of the locals, as their silence was heavier than any intimidation. The persisting effects of the outsiders' destructive actions were palpable, fueling the locals' understandable hatred.

She closed her eyes and replayed the geography lessons in her mind. With a decisive nod, she mandated the mantis to continue their eastward journey.

To avoid the Mines of Tiunnff, where a battle was happening, Nehel skirted the Cayderr Range, with her gaze fixed on the distant Karekall Mountains, and beyond that, the border of the Breken Nation.

Brisel halted when the Karekall were at sight and the sun rose from behind.

Nehel contemplated the striking mountainous chain. Its peaks pierced the sky, jagged and imposing. In the almost ten years of her life in Molke, the Karekall was always the first sight she had every morning after a night of sleep, giving a mystery that was both imposing and chilling. From her earliest memories, she sensed a lurking malevolence far to the east, a feeling she could not articulate.

In her present fourteen-year-old reality, she recalled her geography lessons, picturing the Breken Nation across the mountain range—a territory unvisited, a strange culture and remote lands. A realm scarred by the deep divisions between the Jyistereerk and the Korba Dominion, where the tribes faced either choice: side with the Empress and abandon the Giefo Treaty, or join the Korbas and endure. A sharp tension between hope and despair.

"Let us climb it," Nehel said as she dismounted Brisel. Luckily, someone had carved a rough-hewn path—a mixture of uneven stairs and narrow, flat stretches—into the rocky surface. She guessed the stairs were constructed to ease travel between the two realms.

Most green mantises were fast, a unique ability among their kind, and Brisel's speed, combined with Nehel's abilities, was extraordinary. However, he could only run in straight lines, unable to scale mountains or other high places.

The ascent was long and arduous, beginning in the cool morning air, and it took until nearly midday to reach the peak. Even though Nehel could have ridden Brisel by climbing on him, his body structure made it difficult for him to navigate stairs, so she chose not to force him.

Finally at the peak, she and the mantis could take a breather, as the road started the even decline. Those who built the road also created a stone marker defining the exact border between Fenn and the Breken Nation. This pillar is located just before an exterior shrine that was placed precisely at the highest elevation of the southernmost portion of the Karekall region.

Upon discovering the shrine perched atop a small, double staircase, a faint, melancholic smile touched Nehel's lips. She briefly paused her travels to pay a visit and inspect the sacred site, a temporary interruption of her course.

In the shrine, she discovered nine stone figures, each simple and rustic in form, possessing only heads and bodies, devoid of any intricate detailing. Given that the elves' belief in these goddesses was the origin point, and that religion subsequently spread throughout Sankaris, developing a sacred text and many temples, churches, and cathedrals dedicated to their worship—with names varying according to regional cultures and languages—she could easily identify them.

Though the shrine's architectural style was more reminiscent of Brek craftsmanship than of elvish design, Nehel had no difficulty recognizing the figures. The larger one at the center was Askim, the god of the balance, father of the divinities. The smaller figures, positioned to the right, depicted the positive goddesses, and to the left, their negative counterparts. Eight goddesses in total.

The first positive goddess that she recognized was Lakia, a name that was given to Nehel by Venka, her foster mother. In religious theology, she embodied pure love, consistently showing compassion towards others, which brought her many blessings. However, the envy of her sister, Tekia, the malevolent goddess of hatred, resulted in a curse that caused Lakia to be ostracized and left in a constant state of misfortune. Hence, when Nehel was nicknamed *Unfortunate* while being Lakia, it was because of the goddess.

Though burdened by the recent losses of loved ones and the immense weight of her empire, she felt utterly unfortunate.

She dropped to her knees on the ground as a humble offering. She made a fervent plea and prayer to Sakia, the fourth positive statue representing the Goddess of Life.

As she said her appeal, distinct remembrances and memories flooded her mind.

A sudden and vivid memory rushed back to her in that precise moment, a memory of her childhood when, at eleven, she got sick for the very first time in her life, an experience that left an enduring mark on her young mind. A nasty cold, while mild, left her feeling so unwell, with a sense of impending doom, that Archmage Selee ordered her—who, despite lacking formal medical training, had a basic understanding of medicine—to remain bedridden for several days.

Throughout her life, Nehel had never fallen ill, even during the plague in Molke. The relentless humidity in the Ri palace eventually wore down her health.

Despite being a divinity, she was also a human.

She lay there on her bed as her unhappiness grew with each passing moment as she neglected her responsibilities as Empress. For the time being, Alessandro took the reins of the Jyistereerk, pledging to govern wisely in her name until her recovery.

She had beside on the bed some volumes of magic arts and science, a volume of the famed The Grand Conspiracy, and a book of ancient knights, that Selee loaned them to her. She sluggishly flipped through the pages. Her eyelids were always heavy with sleep.

One maid brought a bowl of chicken stew and vegetables, but Nehel only offered tiny sips with a spoon because of persistent nausea.

She longed to be well again.

The sharp creak of a door opening snapped the quiet rustle of paper that she idly flipped through the pages of a book, pulling her from her boredom.

The wheels of Lady Fabehel's wheelchair squeaked on the stone floor as she pushed herself toward the bed, and a worn wooden box clutched on her lap.

Nehel observed her attentively, wondering the reason for her visit. "What brings you to my chamber?"

The red hair girl smiled and nodded. "I wanted to tell you a story."

Pensive, she rubbed her nose from the cold she had.

"I was bedridden, just like you, Nehel, but for a different reason," she sighed, as she gathered her thoughts to begin her tale. "A sudden epidemic devastated the Kingdom of Aranka. Most newborns arrived with deformities."

"Aye, uncle told me that lesson of history," Nehel agreed. "It was the Child's Paralysis. An illness that did not allow them to move properly."

What he did not tell you was that many families, grasped by fear and superstition, believed that their deformed newborns were cursed creatures from the Netherworld, leading to abandonment and even murdered by their own parents. As she recalled the story, Fabehel's face turned somber. "I was left behind to fend for myself outside the walls of Byarte's Royal Estate. That is how your mother, Princess Natahel, found me during one of her morning strolls."

"I recall you mentioning that part. What are you trying to say?"

Fabehel lowered her head, sharing a painful memory. "At four years old, a sudden fever wracked my small body, and the next few days were a blur of worsening symptoms until Sorceress Dalehel, also a medic, diagnosed me with a deadly infection. The grim reality of the Child's Paralysis epidemic became clear as more children with identical symptoms died." She picked up the small wooden box resting in her lap. "She warned Natahel to brace herself for my imminent death. The princess insisted on saving my life, even convinced King Vihen to threaten her. That is when Dalehel suggested that to save my life, the only option was to amputate both of my useless feet."

"This is the reason you do not have them anymore."

"Aye, but I want you to know your mother, Natahel, never left my side during the painful surgery. And she promised me a special prize if I was strong enough and survive," she smiled again. "I was just a child of four who had to go through this suffering."

Nehel glanced at the box she was carrying and gestured towards it. "Is this the prize?"

"Aye, this is," Fabehel opened the box to discover a golden hair comb decorated with shimmering emeralds. For her fifteenth birthday, her father presented her with a gift. "But Natahel insisted that my survival was the greatest gift she could ask for." Tears welled in her eyes, and she sighed. "As a spoiled princess, I was more a toy than a company to her. My infection brought a change. She treated me like the younger sister she always wished for."

"And why do you bring this comb?"

"Seeing you bedridden, I recalled a promise—a gift I meant to give you, a chance I had missed until now." She closed and placed the box in Nehel's hands. "You own nothing from Natahel, therefore, take this. It is yours, a gift from your birth mother."

Knelt on the shrine ground before the goddesses' statues, Nehel broke in cries with sadness and regrets. "Forgive me!" she exclaimed in despair as tears wetted her face, mixed with sweat. "I should not have sent you to Fenn!"

She threw herself to the to the ground as she wept, covering her face. A wave of misery came over her as she remembered the faces of those she had lost—Uskam and the Kannestes, Archmage Selee, and Lady Fabehel, a woman who had grown to be like a mother to her. A dread invaded her as she realized her uncle Alessandro would be next.

She knew the Korbas, and the newly revealed The Aquelarre were the ones behind these demises with one of two purposes—her death or the breaking of her spirits.

The weeping subsided with a pat on her back, prompting her to discover her drenched and grimy face. Brisel's amusing black, round eyes twitched as it offered a sympathetic stare with its moving antennas. The Empress emitted a moving, light smile. "Do not worry about me," she whispered with tears. "I am simply overwhelmed with despair."

With a silent nod and a blink, Brisel requested to mount his steed to resume their travels.

Nehel agreed, wiping her grime-stained face with her leather sleeve before turning to the goddesses. A silent prayer for her uncle's health passed her lips. She mounted the mantis, and they resumed their journey toward the Breken Nation.

The eastern road, less steep than its western counterpart, made the descent from the Karekall Mountains an easy and swift undertaking. Nehel discovered a naturally flat expanse in the desert, unlike the artificial one in Aranka caused by the Gesha. Here, a few cacti dotted the landscape, and small hills rose in the distance.

She spotted a small encampment, a tribe dwelling beside a tiny oasis. A pond ringed by lush vegetation and tall palm trees, where white camels grazed peacefully, the sounds of their chewing and the gentle lapping of water created a serene atmosphere. The scorching desert heat forced locals to stay inside their tents.

As they approached, they expected scattered rubbish, remnants of fires, and discarded food littering in the encampment. The Breks were disgustingly unclean, reeking of sweat and grime, and detested bathing. Their uncleanness, seen as disgusting by other races, was as a longstanding cultural tradition that had spanned thousands of tikls.

A large woman emerged from a tent and waited for Nehel and Brisel. She was the typical Brek with a vast belly and a dry, blood stained axe in her hand. A grim set to her jaw and narrowed eyes hinted at hostility as she planted her ax, bracing for trouble.

It was obvious they were unwelcome in that specific tribe.

"I do not care about you!" Nehel clarified with the authority of an Empress, emphasizing that the Brek woman was completely unaware of her true identity. "Tell me, have you seen a wounded Casakan man?"

A tense silence hung in the air as the Brek observed her sat upon the mantis. "Aye, he was unconscious on a horse, being pulled by a feline. They went that direction." She pointed northeast with her ax.

Nehel offered a grateful nod, then firmly instructed Brisel to follow the designated path. The woman's cautious behavior was expected because she knew not all tribes supported the Jyistereerk.

In a blur of green, the mantis shot forward in a straight line.

Upon arrival, a vastly larger encampment than the first greeted them, next to a massive, inhabited oasis. Palm trees swayed gently in the warm breeze, the sound of running water a welcome contrast to the silence of the desert.

Nehel spotted the familiar Trasken Tribe pennant—a symbol of Chief Senaten's clan within the Breken Nation—raised high on a pole in the encampment.

Dozens of sentinels with raised axes formed a formidable barrier, as their eyes narrowed in warning as she approached with the mantis.

Brisel halted with his rider. The Brek, clearly a person of authority judging by his elaborate axe, drew near. "State your purpose!"

"Let me see Chief Senaten!" she requested with a serious face. "It is an urgent matter I shall deal!"

The official studied her, tugging his long and nasty black beard, pensive for a while with silence. He found it odd to see a girl of mixed race astride a green mantis far from the lands of Berrem. "Who are you?!"

"I am the Empress herself!" she replied with certain despair. "And I am in search of my uncle! Master Alessandro Eskar!"

The official widened his eyes and immediately blew his horn in a special tune to call the chief.

Chief Senaten and his small group of cortege, heads bowed low, immediately knelt before the Empress in reverence, their quiet gasps echoing the awe was felt by everyone else as they followed suit.

Dismounting from Brisel, Nehel called for everyone to rise. "Please, help me look for my uncle!"

A grim expression settled on Senaten's face as the colossal axe thumped heavily to the ground. "He is with us, Divine Empress. He is being treated by our medic."

A shaky breath escaped her lips, a sigh heavy with a mixture of anxiety and apprehension. "Take me to him!"

The Brek's large arm stretched out, signaling his willingness to lead her into the encampment.

A wave of nausea rolled over Nehel as she navigated the narrow passage between huts. The stench of rotting garbage and animal dung, a truly repulsive perfume, roamed the air, along with the sights of excrement from both humans and the ubiquitous white camels. Though she wrinkled her nose at the unfamiliar smells and unkempt appearance, she recognized it as a cultural practice.

"The feline Corr brought Master Alessandro," Chief Senaten informed as he walked her to their destination. "Unsettling events have recently gripped Fenn. First, we have received emissaries Orr and Barr, who escaped a queen—not their own, it seems, though the details remain unclear." He sighed, noticing concerns in his gestures. "But I heard whispers of a wider conflict that could affect us all."

"Aye, word from the Fennens speaks of a fierce battle between Korbas and The Aquelarre against my Imperial Guard, but the rumors are fragmented and unreliable."

The chief and Empress approached the largest hut in the encampment, its thatched was roof visible above the surrounding tents. A multitude followed both.

"I must warn, Divine Empress. That Master Alessandro might not be the same as you knew." As they stopped, he said.

A nervous gasp escaped Nehel's lips as she exhaled, then gave a small, hesitant nod.

As the Brek pushed aside the heavy leather curtain, she stepped into the gloomy interior.

Nehel discovered Alessandro lay on the ground, unclothed except for a coarse woolen mantle. His head rested gently on a small, soft block of stitched leather and wool. Her eyes widened, and a choke escaped her lips as she saw the wet compresses covering the left side of his face and part of his neck.

His breaths were shallow and weak, barely perceptible as he lay unconscious.

A Brek medic, his weathered face etched with concern, approached her with a stick instead of an axe. Beside him, a small wobbly table held various medicines in tarnished containers. "Divine Empress. Master Alessandro's condition is critical. The damage done to him was too extensive. His face has irreversible and unhealable wounds."

Tears streamed down Nehel's hazel eyes as she knelt, taking her uncle's hand. She found the familiar white handkerchief inside, the very one she had given Fabehel at the Berrem villa, sensing he was about to depart to the Gakia. "Please! Do not leave me!" After a few moments of searching, she spotted Corr huddled in a corner, gazing at something. She stood and approached the feline, taking his hands, startling him.

"I have failed, Divine Empress!" the feline said with grief. "I have failed to protect them!"

"It is all my fault!" Nehel replied with sobs. "I should not have sent them!"

Pulling his hands away from Nehel's, Corr buried his face in his arms.

She turned to see her uncle again. Countless lives lost, a war ignited by the Imperial Guard, Alessandro hanging between life and death, and Corr surrendering. The weight of these setbacks was immense.

She felt like the Jyistereerk was shattering. And so the balance, too.

Frustrated, she shook her head between sobs and denials. How she could not see the outcomes with anticipation? Or is that her abilities no longer worked?

In a moment of despair, she left the hut running.

Amidst the grime and litter, surrounded by a multitude of curious onlookers, Nehel searched until she found Thunder, Corr's golden stallion. She raced towards the horse, leaping onto its back before urging it forward with a sharp command.

With the sun directly overhead, she left the encampment, unprepared for the intense heat of the midday desert sun.

Between desperate sobs and cries, she urged the stallion onward, towards the northeast.

The hard fought effort to bring back the balance, four years ago, was futile.

The balance, again, had been destroyed.

And the Jyistereerk about to fall short lived.

At rapid speed, she rode as the rhythmic thuds of hooves beat against the earth as the frantic pulse of her plea she was about to make came to her.

A plea she never expected to do it in the very heart of the Korba Dominion.

32

KORBA DOMINION

A twelve-year-old Nehel asked. "Is the Korba Dominion east of the Karekall? What is in there?"

Seated at a table overflowing with books and scattered papyrus scrolls, the Empress awaited answers. Her gaze settled on Archmage Selee.

He, amidst a chaotic array of alchemical equipment and scattered materials in his cluttered palace chamber, meticulously prepared two cups of black tea, as steam fragrances arose the bubbling liquid. The scent of brewing herbs mixed with the musty smell of old books.

Her curious eyes could not stop looking at him, waiting. "All my life I have seen these mountains, and I have sensed them always."

Turning with his customary amiable smile, he arranged the steaming hot cups of tea upon the cluttered table, setting one aside for Nehel amongst the careless collection of objects that covered most of the surface. "I apologize for the disorder and lack of cleanliness."

"I do not care about this. Please answer to my inquiry."

"Aye, exactly beside Molke across the Karekall." He nodded, puffing out a breath to cool his tea, a puff of cold air that seemed to shimmer with magic. "Though I have never set foot there, whispers from hungry merchants paint a picture of a place where fortunes are made—or lost—in the blink of an eye. Some have perished, while others fell into madness."

"What could you say about Peken?" Nehel asked with a sad sigh. "We are aware of his presence there, and his infection. But he lived on for many years afterward."

Selee nodded, took a sip, and then answered. "We are uncertain about what might have happened to him. But I believe he was one of the few who could brave the treacherous mountains to reach the hidden Korba city of Kerdall, nestled deep within the dominion."

"The Karekall Mountains?"

"Not these," he clarified with his smile. "The nameless mountains, a barrier of rock and shadow, to protect the city."

"Protect?" she asked herself. "If the Korbas are almost invincible. Why do they have to protect themselves? Against who?"

"Those are good questions!" he exclaimed, pointing to Nehel. "Who they have to protect from?"

Even though Thunder was a strong and healthy horse, the lack of water and constant running slowed his gallop to a fatigued pace. Each breath labored, each hoofbeat heavy. Nehel, absent minded, did not care about the stallion's condition although not on purpose.

From the pale dusty sand of the desert, as she rode further north while the sun was descending in its sunset, the ground became from clear to gray.

As the gelid moon of No Sak emerged, the sand turned to be black and dark. Sharp, harrowing monoliths appeared in her way. Nehel observed the panorama was way too different, as if it was another world but Sankaris.

The beginning of the Korba Dominion.

The exhausted stallion collapsed, throwing Nehel to the ground. She landed hard, but only suffered minor scratches. In that sudden moment, the horse's labored breaths and the tremor in its legs made her realize the cruelty of her actions. Its suffering was palpable. Her hand trembled as she petted his head, whispering apologies, pleading for understanding.

It was like her abilities had gone.

But she could not cry either. She was exhausted and had cried all she could. Sadness and frustration overcame her.

She remembered a lesson taught by Ser Marissa. She remembered the First Knight's words on a horse's suffering and its remedy.

Nehel's stomach churned at the idea. The guilt suffocated her. But she had to do it. She had never taken an animal's life before.

She had to sacrifice it.

She unsheathed Juni's dagger and went behind him. Then, with both hands, she slammed against the stallion's head with a swift, brutal blow, the animal collapsing instantly, its lifeblood staining the ground.

Despite her remorse, she felt it was the most compassionate choice for Thunder.

This exact moment marked a significant turning point, a transition into a woman.

Despite not eating or drinking, Nehel experienced weakness but still turned around and sheathed the dagger, which was covered in blood, without bothering to clean it, before resuming her journey on foot.

As she journeyed onward, more monoliths came into view, and No Nunn appeared to join No Sak. Her first impression was of a place that was isolated, desolate, deserted.

But it soon became clear to her it was actually a small town, possessing a bizarre personality, though with lights burning in every building.

Approaching the place hoping to find food or water, the sight of skeletal, naked people, devoid of life, chained to large rocks and digging the ground incessantly with their beaks like automatons startled her, halting her journey. In that instant, she recognized them as individuals who had previously failed to become Korbeen status, yet the infection coursed through their very veins.

Some time ago, Archmage Selee had already instructed her of the existence of these beings.

No longer seeking a meal, she resumed her travels.

Nehel longed to be at her uncle's side, or the familiar quiet of her palace chamber, but the journey was too far advanced and the time for retreat was long gone. She had to make a desperate plea to halt the madness consuming her world. Even as an Empress and a divinity, the over-whelming power of the otherworldly menace, radiating pure evilness, left her feeling utterly powerless.

Despite The Aquelarre's efforts, the unstoppable force aimed to shatter her resolve by destroying her loved ones and throwing the world into disarray, undoing the balance she had restored a tikl ago.

Nehel had not slept all night. Her continuous walking left her weak and swaying. The slow ache in her legs became unbearable, each step a struggle, and she could barely hold herself upright against the impending collapse.

But as sunrise arrived, her hazel eyes finally made out a mountainous range on the horizon. Though the dark gray sky remained unlit by the sun, its muted light barely pierced the gloom. She was aware of the presence lurking behind.

Exhausted, Nehel fell to the ground, with her stomach empty, as she looked at the ominous black mountains looming through the thick, damp mist. She fainted.

When Nehel awoke, she found herself inside a dimly lit tent. Obviously, someone had brought her inside and cared for her. She sat and surveyed her site.

Judging by the sparse furnishings and simple tools, someone made the tent for survival, not comfort. She found a set of knives, some books, a small chest, and a bonfire at the center. Nehel knew it was not any local, but an outsider, possibly a merchant, who found her and bring inside.

Someone placed a bowl of food beside her.

Although the Korba Dominion was infamous for its brutality and disregard for human life, a compassionate soul intervened and saved her. However, she confirmed Juni's dagger was still in her possession, preparing for potential threats.

Driven by hunger, she began slowly sipping the stew, but later devoured it to satisfy her stomach.

But a sudden thud interrupted her meal as a man, shrouded in a dark blue cloak that hid his face, tossed a heavy bag at the ground. He greeted her with a nod and carried on with his task.

"Where am I?" Intrigued, she asked herself why she was not afraid of him, considering how daunting he looked.

In a slow, hoarse voice, he replied, "My tent."

"Who are you?"

He paused in his task of arranging the precious stones and food supplies he had gathered. "Who I am is not important. A girl as you should not be in this evil realm, Divine Empress."

The strange man's recognition surprised Nehel. But she supposed he had seen her during her palace outings in the Ri, where many locals and outsiders greeted her in the bustling streets. "I shall go to Kerdall."

The man placed a small kettle on the bonfire to warm the water. "What is your purpose?"

"I must meet Ardek Korba. I plan to give myself to him, so we can bring the balance and peace that Sankaris deserves. That will be my plea. Because of me, many died," she sighed, agitated. "I will let him take me captive."

The strange man heard her but did not respond. His silence said everything. Instead, he discovered the kettle had made a tootling sound as the water boiled, prompting him to finesse it with the help of a rag. Next, he placed two metallic mugs on the table and carefully measured out ground herbs into each, before pouring a steaming, fragrant liquid over them. He approached Nehel, offering her a mug. "Drink it."

Nehel took the mug and smelled its contains. It had a sweet aroma of imported flowers from somewhere outside. The Dominion was an arid expanse where no plant could survive.

"Do you know the Korbas are creatures whose very essence drips with malevolence and depravity?" He settled onto a small folding stool in front of her. "Their cruelty knows no limits. If you think a simple prison sentence awaits you, you are gravely mistaken."

"I will sacrifice myself!" she insisted.

The mysterious man, with his face still obscured by the hood, took a slow sip of his steaming tea. "These demons, especially Ardek, will steal everything you hold, leaving you with nothing but despair. They will stop at nothing to ensure your suffering is unbearable, even if it means violating your soul. Their depravity knows no bounds, and it is the very essence of terror."

Nehel's gaze remained locked on the man as she placed the mug on the ground, then rose and nodded as the silence tensioned between them. "I am grateful for your kindness and hospitality." She took a few steps toward the exit, then halted. "Can you tell me the direction of the mountains of Kerdall?"

He shook his head in disapproval, then stood to approach a dimly lit corner housing a small pantry. He grabbed a worn satchel, carefully placing a few meager food items inside, and added a canteen filled with water. Later, handing Nehel the items, he gestured north. "Go straight, do not deviate. Once you are in the mountains, you will see an entrance to the Gates' to Hell. As you enter, the air grows hotter. You will know you are in Kerdall when the unbearable heat struck on you."

The man's voice, though unfamiliar, held a strange resonance that made Nehel pause, a glance of recognition before she nodded, appreciating the well-worn satchel slung over her shoulder, and then she departed from the tent.

33
THE GATES

Following the mysterious rescuer's directions, Nehel reached a gate set within a mountain fissure, in an almost complete darkness, illuminated only by the reddish glow emanating from Kerdall.

The first gate marked the entrance to the towering mountains. The path ahead was clearly visible. A flat, rocky track stretching through the solid walls. The crimson glow emanating from beneath the city illuminated the ground, revealing rivers of molten rock surging from the earth. She suspected it was a volcano rather than a mountainous range.

Her uncle, Alessandro, instructed her on the volcanoes that were mostly in the wide eastern parts of the continent of Ryza.

She felt the heat, as the mysterious man described. Looking down, she saw the sheer drop and adjusted her footing to avoid a fall. The river of lava flowed, a horrifying, incandescent stream, forcing her to almost close her eyes. The screams of thousands—men and women indistinguishable in their agony—were silent, yet deafening, as their suffering under lava was unimaginable. Though alive, these people could not perish.

Along with terror, she felt the magic. Once the Korbas discovered the naturally existing power, capable of both good and evil, they twisted it to serve their vicious actions, merging it with their own malevolent intent. The man's words about the harm inflicted on soul recalled in her mind.

These people, victims, proved the Korbas' nightmarish nature.

Nehel sensed Fabehel knew who or what had aided their magical development.

Nehel sensed it, and Fabehel's life was the price she paid for.

As soon as she realized she was approaching the second gate. She stopped at the cave entrance. In the oppressive darkness, she wished desperately for a torch. She was afraid and did not dare to enter.

Nehel searched for anything—a lamp, a torch, even a single burning ember—to light her path. As she turned right, a small lantern with a flickering flame caught her eye, sitting on the ground.

She had not noticed the lantern before and wondered, with a racing heart, if someone was following her. She turned, but saw no one.

Despite her fear, she entered the dark cave, clutching the lantern, and remembering her first encounter with a Korbeen in Laimet, when Lakia was her name.

In the cave's mouth, outside, Lakia stood there, determined, relentless in her resolve. Behind, the captain escorted her.

In the midst of the oak trees, a vast number of intrigued individuals, including children scattered among the branches, silently watched as the girl disguised as a boy awaited her moment, experiencing a mix of emotions and fears.

"How long has he been like that?" she asked, staring into the cave's darkness.

"Six months. The lord had hiked the Karekall, but we found him ill," the captain responded.

She nodded. "Let us enter."

"I have your back." The captain drew his sword.

As Lakia advanced further into the cave, she noticed how the daylight was disappearing around her. She did not need any light or torch since her senses guided her even in total darkness, feeling the tiny rocks under her feet as she took the first steps. Serene though cautious.

In contrast, she heard the captain's rapid breathing of fear yet accompanying her.

As they were in the complete absence of light, in pure blackness, the warmth of the environment turned creepily cold.

In a sudden halt, she pleaded to the captain to remain still.

Evilness in the air.

Horror was also present.

The sound of dragging chains.

A dreadful red light illuminated the cave.

Lakia experienced many startles as a shrieking and speedy grayish-horned demon, with its claws out-stretched, tried to attack her. It was advantageous that the unmovable, large rocks restrained the demon by chains. Constantly moving his mouth of long, dis-arranged, sharp teeth, he stared at her in frustration with his blazing eyes.

The demon, even with his continuous screams and roars, remained unable to lay a hand on her.

With his drawn sword, the captain behind observed the creature shivering in terror.

But Lakia, in total peace, only gazed at it.

Then she pointed her finger at the demon's head with a determined look.

"I order you to leave this body!" she yelled at him with commanding authority.

A burning Akareen star drew on the entity's forehead.

The creature fell, shrieked in pain, and his body changed. The cave returned to darkness as the red light disappeared.

Nehel gasped with humid eyes. Just four years ago, she was a little girl who had lost her elvish mother. However, her determination for her stance and inherent abilities, though immature, presented no challenge to her.

But now, at fourteen, the emotional turmoils left her inconsistent, her usual determination wavered as she navigated the transition to adulthood. Her initial reign as Empress was a crucible of tragedies and adversities.

She gasped again and lifted the lantern to illuminate the cave's mouth. The first steps into the cave revealed thousands of red reflections in the darkness, an awe-inspiring, yet somewhat frightening sight resembling countless eyes peering back at her. Nehel's stomach churned with discomfort and had a growing sense of dread as she walked.

All she could do was to look directly at the path before her, the lantern's beam illuminating the ground. As Nehel walked way inside, she perceived anguish in those red eyes surrounding her.

They were more victims, trapped inside a cave.

As with the people from the lava, they were silent. They screamed, their voices raw with terror, but only silence prevailed.

The Korbas were smart but cruel. They forced their victims to bear the weight of sorrow, guilt, suffering, and anguish, preventing them from unburdening themselves.

It did not take her long to cross the tunnel-like cave. As Nehel left, all eyes disappeared, replaced by utter darkness behind her.

The feeling of the heat was even higher.

As she turned back around, the lantern fell, revealing a third gate. Though near enough to touch, an unsettling distance separated her from it, a nightmarish presence that weighed heavily on her soul.

On the other side of the gate, a reddish haze hung heavy in the air, obscuring the details of a giant, horned creature silhouetted against it, expectant.

His actual form when not in dragon image.

Nehel knew who he was.

Ardek Korba.

The Lord of the Netherworld.

If that outer world of his could be called that way.

The Empress realized it was time to give herself to him.

She made a nod and dropped her satchel.

Nehel gave her first steps.

As Nehel approached Ardek, her heart pounded in her chest. She reached the last gate, ready to surrender herself.

She walked onto the bridge spanning the lava river, heading from the cave towards the gate.

A firm arm clamped around her waist, making her scream in terror before she realized it was Ser Juni who had caught her. With a shuddering movement, she threw herself from his arms, letting out a desperate, tearful scream. "Let me go!"

"I will not, missy!" He replied with a strained voice, trying to hold her close as she struggled against him.

"I have to go!" she pleaded with cries. "Please, let me go!"

"Enough, Divine Empress!" Archmage Missar yelled with authority. "Master Alessandro asked for you!"

As Nehel listened, she halted her resistance, and the hazy silhouette vanished. As she turned, she saw Juni's worried frown and Archmage Missar's serious, almost disapproving gaze. "How did you follow me?"

Ser Juni gestured to his left, and she saw a small, white oval vessel floating nearby—a contrast to the massive *The Navigator*. It was clear the Tinklens had arrived, especially Pi-U, who waited at the entrance with a ramp extending to the bridge. The vessel seemed to hum smoothly.

"Shall we return home, Divine Empress?" Missar insisted.

She responded with a soft nod and a slight murmur. "Aye."

With gentle hands, Ser Juni lifted Nehel and carried her inside the ship. The Tinklen offered his greetings. Missar followed close behind.

Once everyone was inside and the entrance sealed, Pi-U signaled the lone pilot, demanding an immediate departure from the mountains and the Korba Dominion. They made their way home.

As soon as Nehel stepped onto the floor, she saw Alessandro lying on a cot in the center of the vessel. Clean bandages still covered the left side of his face.

He lay unconscious, while a qualified Casakan medic, Ossa, kept a watchful eye.

"How is he?" Nehel asked, concerned, but with hopes.

Ossa made a quick bow to the Empress. "Master Alessandro's face scars will not heal properly and his eye has lost sight. The searing heat from the molten metal had left him scarred and burned, a condition beyond even the finest elvish medicine."

Commandant Kartak and Captain Kanden bowed beside the medic, as a sign of respect for the Empress.

"You may be an Empress, but you are still acting like a spoiled brat, making foolish decisions!" A torrent of angry words poured from Missar's mouth as she screamed at Nehel. "It is equal to taking your own life! By giving yourself, you were also destroying the Jyistereerk!"

"I apologize," she replied, ashamed. "I believed I was sacrificing myself for Sankaris."

"A true monarch stands firm against the looming consequences!" Missar kept scolding her. "Confront the consequences, whether they bring joy or sorrow, success or failure!"

"Archmage. . ." a weak voice interrupted him. Alessandro awoke to find his niece well and, pleased and relieved, requested Nehel come and take his hand. "Leave the reprimands for later. This is my job."

Deeply moved, Nehel reached for her uncle's hand, amplifying the emotion in his single good eye. As the tiny vessel disappeared into the western sunset beyond the Karekall mountains, towards Berrem and the Beyond Sea visible, she spoke to the Archmage. "How did you find me?"

"Messages from the spheres led me to your whereabouts." A relaxed yet serious tone colored Missar's response. "You met Archmage Selee in the tent. He was the one who rescued you after you fainted."

"Why he did not reveal to myself?" she asked, surprised, like most of the passengers. "That is why I felt a sense of familiarity while being with him!"

"He did not want to reveal himself because he got tainted while fighting the Korbeens in Salter, and still could not die because of his immortality."

"We have to go back."

"No, missy," Ser Juni insisted. "The Jyistereerk needs you. Ser Marissa feels overwhelmed as she sits on your throne."

"Besides, Archmage Selee no longer wants to be part of the Guild. Not in this new tainted condition." Missar added. "From now on, he will have the same path that Sorceress Dalehel took."

Alessandro's firm grip sent a comforting warmth through Nehel's palm. A silent vow to remain by his side. "We are going home. Aranka is our home now." With a soft sigh, she gently kissed his hand. They both needed time to heal from Fabehel's passing.

34

IMPERIAL ARMY

With each mighty swing of her sturdy arm, Jumeni's iron mallet, guided by thick long forceps, crashed against the anvil, reshaping the shattered pieces of Alessandro's greatsword. The ringing blows echoed in the forge as the engraved *Borsen* name reappeared. With each turn of the blade, sparks flew from the molten iron as she carefully repaired it as the heat radiated onto her skin. The Artifice laid the sword on the whirring grinding wheels. The sparks flew as the metal shrieked, its surface gleamed, yet the cracks remained a stubborn testament to a brutal defeat.

Dessidere observed her work with crossed arms, as he examined her forge, a structure built specially for her Artifice by the wall, and near the Imperial Balcony. It was a small, two-story building, exactly as requested. Her shop occupied the ground floor, while her private quarters were upstairs.

Although Jumeni did not explicitly say so, her subtle gestures and meaningful glances urged Dessidere to move with her. Though drawn to her, he remained clueless about her motives, her indirect suggestions left him puzzled. Her inability to speak only heightened her despair. From birth, a mysterious impediment stole her voice, leaving her in a world of unspoken words.

Ser Marissa joined him, watching as Jumeni meticulously polished the greatsword. The glint of iron catching the light, and she nodded with a sad smile. "Alessandro could have a gleaming new blade, but he kept his current one."

"Our iron weapons are nothing with those... giefstak blades the Korbas have," Dessidere said. "I question whether it is wise to prohibit the giefo, especially if they overwhelm our defenses."

"But our engineers, through tireless effort and brilliant innovation, built new weapons of superior design and devastating power. Hopefully."

Jumeni submerged the repaired greatsword in a tank of shimmering water, the metal hissed as it cooled. Meanwhile, a serious expression masked her intent as she cast a tempting glance at Dessidere.

As a woman, Marissa understood her intentions. "Are you so damn dull?!" She whispered to Dessidere's ear. "She wants both of you to come together!"

Dessidere got nervous by the Artifice insinuation, and after all that time he finally realized her intention. He had felt an undeniable pull towards her ever since she became a woman, a feeling that left him hesitant about how to approach.

Jumeni nodded before the whispering, then finished to dry the blade with a rag. Once done, she placed the greatsword in the hands of Marissa.

With a grateful reverence, the First Knight left the forge.

Dessidere, alone with Jumeni, watched as her soft gaze, full of unspoken affection, reached him.

The leather apron fell to the ground with a soft thud, revealing a damp, half-open shirt clinging to her body. Sweat beaded on her forehead, trickled down her neck, and clung to her chest as she approached, shaking her tangled hair. At last, she was with him.

His first kiss left him breathless. His heart raced. The scent of wood smoke and sweat clung to her as her robust arms wrapped around him.

With a practiced movement, Ser Marissa took off her black cape, and used it to sheathe the greatsword before hurrying across the Great Balcony towards the golden palace.

The ceremony was about to start.

As she moved from room to room—kitchens, grand dining halls, and comfortable living rooms—she hurried. Reaching the Guild Room, she climbed the stairs. Turning away from the Imperial Apartment's direction, she entered a small, quiet chamber. There, Alessandro stood before a mirror, the black of his attire against the skin of his neck as he finished buttoning his high-collared coat.

Alessandro heard the soft click of the door latch as Marissa closed it, and he turned around. He showed his healed left side of his face, but with deep scars and a blind eye that made the difference with the immaculate right side. Though his appearance was unusual, it was not repulsive. It looked like the aftermath of a hard-fought battle.

His right facial muscles strained in an attempt at a smile, while his left side, paralyzed, remained emotionless and heavy. He approached to the First Knight and received the greatsword, studying it with delicacy as his fingers passed through the blade, feeling the cracks.

"You were warned. The greatsword would not be the same," she noted.

"It does not matter, Marissa," he replied with appreciation. "As my side of the face, these cracks are also scars of a lost fight."

"If you had not. . ."

"Once it is done, it is done," he said while sheathing the blade in his back. "I have learned my lesson. Everyone learned lessons. We can only look to the future to learn from our mistakes and avoid repeating them."

The ringing of bells reached their ears.

"It is time for the reveal," Ser Marissa informed at the time that she noticed the small golden chest he had on the top of his chimney between two candles.

With a silent nod, they turned and walked out of the chamber.

"Is it ready?" Archmage Missar asked to a dozen of volunteers.

The Arankan volunteers, former residents of both the Isle of Garterrem settlement and the Arankan Quarter in Sarak, returned to their ancestral lands, a new realm for them. They had carefully placed a simple white mantle on the statue. Several people nodded.

With a wave of his hand, the Archmage directed them towards the palace kitchens for a quick meal.

After that Missar found himself alone. He studied this special section of the gardens, noticing the way through the trees bordering the forest and the palace. The suggestion to build a memorial honoring the fallen of the Deken Karsaker came from Kartak and the Pillars, intended to capture the solemnity of their loss and the heroism of their sacrifice. With a quick, light step, he went to gaze at the newly carved statues. Squinting against the sun, he studied the newly erected golden sculptures—Peken, the elf, depicted in flowing foreign robes, gazing at the horizon, and Uskam, not as the old man he was, but as a powerful young sorcerer with staff in hand. Missar kept walking, until a colossal golden statue depicting over twenty adults and children of the Kanneste tribe, with Venka seated before the rest, came into view.

As he strolled, turning, the nostalgic image of his former tutor, Archmage Yasstro, appeared before him, standing beside Tin, a fallen from the brutal *Siege of Sarak*. And a line of three large effigies representing the Casakans and elves who perished in *The Assault at the Estos Grasslands*, the ones who died during *The Feast of the Dragoness*, and last, the soldiers who fought in *The Battle of the Tempest*.

Upon the Archmage's return to his post, a sea of faces greeted him—the Guild, the Unnamed Squires, the Court of Maids, a collection of elves, and dozens of Arankans spanning generations.

The unexpected sight of her in an imperial black robe, rather than the customary white, marked Nehel's arrival. The familiar gleam of her golden sandals, same ones from her Salter ascension, that grew with her. She carried her rod. She made her way through the small crowd that was about half a hundred, followed by the Pillars Alessandro and Marissa.

The sight of Alessandro's scarred face and covered eye drew morbid fascination, but people quickly looked away, trying to be polite while still noting his attractive features.

He felt their eyes on him, but he successfully masked his discomfort.

Marissa noticed that not all the Guild was present.

Marshal Keleana still fought in the Fennen conflict. Fabehel's body had to be cremated in Finnerr. The small chest holding the ashes got heavy as Kekten and Kartak, trailed by the solemn squires, carried it to Aranka, presenting it to a heartbroken Alessandro, by Corr. With the war raging, there was no time for traditional funeral rites.

The Empress and the Pillars arrived to the front before the sculpture. No one spoke at that moment.

With a sweeping gesture, Nehel silently signaled two Arankans to remove the mantle, revealing the effigy beneath.

The humid, feline eyes of Corr widened with guilt and revelation as Kekten's hand came to rest on his shoulder.

A stunning statue of Fabehel, seated in her wheelchair with a bouquet of roses resting on her lap. A plaque was on the base had the following engraved words — *Lady Fabehel of the Red Tides, Daughter of Byarte, Ruler of the Arankan Quarter in Sarak and Empress' Ambassador to Fenn who sacrificed her life in the search for her race and the truth, a fallen from the Deken Karsaker.*

Alessandro studied the statue, a perfect mirror of the Fabehel he remembered, a silent gratitude rising in him as he turned to find Jumeni, the Artificer who had also repaired his sword, amidst the murmuring crowd. She replied him with a nod.

Ser Marissa approached him and whispered. "What do you plan to do with the chest containing the remains of Lady Fabehel?"

"I will bury it where Byarte used to be. Once Diesso and Vasso are done with their exploration and the maps drawn, I will take the chest."

As Nehel listened, a faint smile touched her lips as Ser Juni approached, and then, with tears in her eyes, she gazed at the effigy, remembering cherished moments with Fabehel.

Strangely, the presence she had felt on her balcony the last time was gone. Nehel could no longer sense her. She realized she had traveled to Gakia, the afterlife.

A hum of anticipation, a mixture of murmurs and whispers from the fifty representatives, filled the Empress' Throne Room as they waited for the audience to begin. They were the chosen representatives, each embodying their unique race, culture, and quarter within Aranka's glittering new Citadel. The city, a sprawling construction site, vibrated with the sounds of hammers and saws, the movement of thousands of immigrants, refugees, and returning Arankans building their lives around the palace, its foundations stretching towards a new harbor teeming with Tinklen vessels and traditional ships.

Archmage Missar compared the Imperial Assembly and the Casakan Assembly, hence the name, where he recently passed on his powers to Lady Tasarissa. He and Alessandro, with the Empress's blessing, planned a special building within the Citadel, separate from the palace, to house the Assembly's meetings.

Most of the Guild was in the front row.

The Court of Maids and the Sisterhood of the Comforting Wind surrounded the Throne Room and awaited the Empress' entrance. Akhimeni and two maids had readied the throne, while two armchairs, recently added, flanked it.

As Dessidere appeared, everyone went silent.

The Herald slammed his scepter against the cold marble floor in front of the ornate throne. The sound echoed through the vast room before shouting his proclamation. "In the 28th Day of the Sixth Month of the First Year of the *Tikl the Second of Nehel* a special audience between the Guild, the Imperial Assembly, the Pillars Master Alessandro Eskar and Ser Marissa Taskar, with the Divine Empress Nehel of the Jyistereerk!"

From her place in the first row, among the Guild, Overseer Akhimeni of the Court of Maids began the ceremonial hymn, joined by the ethereal voices of the elvish Akartaki and the sisters. "Nehel Jyistereerk Mudiuhfaser! Nehel Jyistereerk Friyterkfer! Laki Lakia Myken Hikis!"

"Nehel Hikis!" the maids responded in a harmonious chorus. Their voices sang through the room as the Empress, in white robes and holding her rod, and the Pillars took their seats.

"Nehel Jyistereerk!" Akhimeni continued.

"Nehel Hikis!"

"Divine Jewel!"

"Nehel Hikis!"

"Divine Empress of Sankaris!"

"Nehel Hikis!"

"Queen of Aranka!"

"Nehel Hikis!"

"Mystical Leader of the Kannestes!"

"Nehel Hikis!"

"High Sorceress of Salter!"

"Nehel Hikis!"

"Queen of Berrem!"

"Nehel Hikis!"

"Sovereigner of Casak!"

"Nehel Hikis!"

"Tinklen Overseer!"

"Nehel Hikis!" the hymn concluded in a soaring tone.

The Empress, with a subtle nod of gratitude, gestured to the Herald, whose descent towards the Guild. She then agreed with her Pillars and spoke. "I demand Admiral Kekten's presence."

The vagrant, separated from the front row and stood before Nehel, making a quick, almost hesitant bow.

"Have you ever wondered why I prohibited you from returning to Fenn?"

"Indeed, I do not know, Divine Empress."

A deep sigh escaped her lips as she squeezed her eyes shut. A mixture of serenity and unease washed over her.

"Let me inquire. Whose idea was to start a war in Fenn? And why?"

Kekten fell silent, his face etched with remorse before he found the words to reply. "It was all my intention, Divine Empress. I thought I had to take actions against those who murdered Lady Fabehel."

"It was an impulse." With a sharp, disapproving tone, Alessandro's intervention silenced the room as he spoke. "When I arrived in Finnerr, I thought you had done well by establishing an encampment there and wait for the others from the Port of Finn." He shook his head as he made a pause. "But you went ahead right after my departure and took all your guards to go against the Korbas and The Aquelarre all the way to the Mines of Tiunnff when Commandant Kartak and Marshal Keleana were on their way to join you with their armies."

"I agree with him," Nehel said. "You could have waited for them to coordinate a strategy, but you did not. Your reckless actions endangered the lives of your guards, with the unfortunate result of some losing their lives."

"If not enough, you took my squires to the battle when they were not ready," Ser Marissa asseverated irritated but with calm.

"Indeed, Corr suggested launching an attack to defend Lady Fabehel, only to find Finnerr devastated by death and misery."

Alessandro lowered his face as he shook, once more, his head. He seemed to have some emotional conflict he tried to hide.

Nehel noticed him, concerned. "Are you all right, uncle?"

Alessandro regained composure. "Lady Fabehel was only doing her job as an Ambassador from the Divine Empress to agree over the Giefo Treaty and to find her people, and she knew the risks while venturing in unknown lands." He gasped. "You, as an Admiral, had a full responsibility of your guards and their actions that only followed your orders. But your impetuous actions caused many deaths, wounded and displaced among the Fennen population. Now, the Jyistereerk is viewed as an evil empire by the Fennen, and we have a long and difficult road ahead to regain their confidence and bring peace to the troubled region."

"And Marshal Keleana has now to fight a war with no end," Nehel stated.

"There is another matter to discuss," Alessandro continued. "The sale of my brother Cassandro into slavery, the father of the Divine Empress, and the escape of Princess Natahel. You kept it a secret, even though you later knew the relation between the Empress and her parents." He sighed with disappointment. "Had Lady Fabehel been aware of that secret and the foremen, she might still be alive. Your silence, your refusal to reveal your secret, condemned her to a needless, avoidable death."

"I. . . have no words to say ya," Kekten replied, ashamed.

"I believe, however, you did not make your mistakes in bad faith, but you also deprived us of the right to know the truth," Nehel said with a nod. "I also have made mistakes which I regret. And one of them was to name you an

Admiral when clearly you were not proper for this rank, even with the experience you gained with your guild." She shrugged. "I strip you of the rank and I forbid you to have any relation with my Imperial Guard. You shall leave this palace and the Citadel. You will join Captain Diesso and Vasso in the exploration of this new Aranka, and help them with the maps. But you can not return nor see any of us in this palace."

"Any other words you want to say before you depart?" Alessandro asked once he made a gesture.

Ashamed, he shook the head, noticing a pair of sentinels beside him. Aware of the eyes on him, he retrieved his pouch of belongings and exited the room.

"Let it be a lesson for all you!" the Empress stated. "If you make any mistake against the Jyistereerk, there will be consequences!"

The room went silent for a while.

"Let us begin with the next matter," she continued. "I call for Ser Marissa and Ser Juni."

A bit surprised, Marissa obeyed as Juni stepped forward, both bowed their heads in a sign of respect before the monarch.

Nehel descended from the throne as Jumeni approached with a simple iron sword she forged to be used in ceremonial acts. The Empress drew a light smile. "I request both of you to kneel before me."

Ser Marissa and Ser Juni, startled by her sudden command, looked at each other, a mixture of confusion and obedience in their eyes, before kneeling on the floor.

Once the Empress had found out the knights' complete submission, she delicately lifted the blade from Jumeni's slack hands, the cool steel a contrast to the warmth of Marissa's shoulders as she brushed them. "With thy sword I name you Grand Knight of the Jyistereerk." She then touched Juni's shoulders. "With thy sword, I name you First Knight of the Jyistereerk."

The people gave a round of applause.

Dessidere, who had been at the edge distancing himself from the throne, opened a papyrus and read loud. "Squires Branni and Ommi! Please present yourselves to bow and kneel before the Divine Empress!"

Unable to suppress their excitement, the two young Unnamed Squires beamed as their comrades showered them with congratulations, as the joyous atmosphere was palpable. With hurried steps, they ascended and knelt, bowing before the monarch.

Ser Marissa and Ser Juni stood beside, witnessing the event.

The Empress spoke to the first squire. "Branni of Carret. Are you willing to dedicate yourself to serve and defend the Jyistereerk?"

As tears emerged, Branni replied. "Aye, Divine Empress."

"With thy sword, I name you Second Knight of the Jyistereerk."

Then Nehel brushed the youngster's shoulders. "Ommi of Doimet. Are you willing to dedicate yourself to serve and defend the Jyistereerk?"

"I do, Divine Empress."

"With thy sword, I name you Third Knight of the Jyistereerk."

A second round of applauses emerged at the time that Ser Marissa and Ser Juni congratulated the new knights.

"I plan to create a new elite force to take on the Korbas and The Aquelarre, bolstering our *Deken Karsaker* with superior strength." The Empress concluded.

"How do you feel, Nehel?" Ser Marissa asked, concerned, noticing her with signs of fatigue.

With a sigh and a shrug of her shoulders, the Empress, seated at the round table of the Guild, surveyed the assembled members. "Sleep offers brief respite, yet I persevere, doing all I am capable of. I long for the days when my abilities flowed freely, but now I struggle."

"I have to admit, I do not understand your dual nature," Medic Ossa, the Guild's newest addition, said. "Demigo ddess... and human... it is quite perplexing. But I believe is it a matter of time before you can regain everything you used to have."

"I trust in the medic's words," Archmage Missar said. "But I assure you, the wounds on your soul will be deep, and the pain will linger, leaving scars that will never fully fade."

Alessandro nodded at his words, a familiar ache settling in his chest. Each word felt like a painful reminder. He then turned to see Corr with fixated eyes to the table, in glum, and with empathy touched his shoulder forever in gratitude by saving his life. "You will be all right."

"No, I am not right, Master," the feline replied with daring eyes, but holding his brew mug. "I no longer have my horse!"

Nehel nodded with certain guilt. "I am sorry that I took Thunder from you and had to sacrifice him. Please, let me compensate for your loss."

"Master Alessandro said that everyone makes mistakes, so I forgive you, Divine Empress. You do not have to compensate me."

"Still, I wish to do so."

A bit annoyed, Ser Marissa intervened. "Could we deal with important matters, please?"

The Empress consented, scrutinizing each Guild member. Some familiar faces were missing, yet newcomers, including the physician Kartak, Akartaki, Pi-U, Fummi—a renowned Berremen engineer—and Missar himself, were present. "We should prioritize the tasks we need to take care of for the Jyistereerk."

"Protecting the remaining population in Fenn and halting the Korba and The Aquelarre advances are paramount."

"Unfortunately, most of the continent of Ryza is now controlled by them," Kartak stated. "Breken Nation might fall too. Even when there are no more obstacles in the Beyond Sea, as I believe the Korbas are now focused on Fenn."

"Can I suggest the use of the Kao Island and all you could assist them as you did with Casak four years ago?" Missar advised. "I think it would be of great help."

"In addition, we could deliver these new weapons to the Imperial Guard on board of that island," Alessandro said. "Engineer Fummi and his team's work allowed us to replicate and produce many of these very useful muskets."

"Yet, there is no assurance that we could recover Ryza," Kartak pointed, twitching his eyebrow. "Despite our magical weapons and muskets, I doubt we can overcome their superior giefstak weaponry, though we might hold them off."

Nehel listened attentively to everyone. After a long sigh, she finally spoke her mind. "I have observed that my imperial forces lack unity and direction. This explains Kekten's reckless action, while Keleana was with us separately, and we still had the elves' army and the knights. We can not fight the Korbas and The Aquelarre like that."

"Got any suggestions?" Ser Marissa asked, taken aback.

"I want all branches to have a single leader." She then pointed at the elf, startling him with another twitch. "Kartak, I appoint you Commandant of the Imperial Army. You will command all guards, soldiers, knights, and a new unit—the musketeers, armed with these new weapons. It would be especially helpful if Archmage Missar could gather a team of mystical fighters. And Captain Kanden could build an Imperial Navy to command the seas."

Kanden and Missar stared in surprise at each other.

"What else do you want us to do, missy?" Juni asked, as a First Knight rather than her beloved.

"Corr, you will deliver a written order to Marshal Keleana, placing her under Commandant Kartak. You are now my Ambassador to Fenn, tasked with bringing peace back to your realm." She forced herself to hold back the tears as the memory of Fabehel surfaced. "Dessidere, announce to the Citadel that the Jyistereerk now has an Imperial Army and we are seeking volunteers to continue with the *Deken Karsaker*."

Jumeni observed, amused by the way Dessidere's quill scratched furiously across the papyrus, his movements jerky and agitated.

By sudden, Nehel excused herself, claiming she was unwell and needed solitude in her apartment. Concerned murmurs rose as everyone stood to show respect. "Please, arrange everything precisely as I have instructed."

As she entered her chamber, Nehel's eyes fell upon the round table, her destination, where Falte board game lay and a wooden chest on top awaited. She opened it to discover the golden comb with emeralds inside.

The appointment of Corr as the new ambassador brought back painful recollections. The memory of Fabehel's fingers gently separating her own lingered a tactile picture in her mind's eye—her own face of assured confidence yet widened with a silent farewell, just before she left Seled Post forever.

Now that Nehel was completely alone, with no one to see her, she could finally release the pain she had been holding inside by weeping as much as she needed.

Despite her best efforts and several weeks since her passing, she found herself still unable to come to terms with her grief.

Sorrow and guilt were heavy burdens.

THE NEHELANTE

A lessandro Eskar finished fixing his dark suit. The crisp fabric whispers against his skin, as a mirror reflects his excitement. Then he gazed at his dual face. After some years, the rough scar on his side, a pale, raised burnt cover against his tanned skin, served as a constant reminder of a lost battle. Yet, though still visible in his haunted eye, he finally healed the deeper wounds to his soul caused by Fabehel's loss and the war that came afterwards.

The conflict in Fenn raged on for three years, showing no signs of ending.

He had transitioned into a young adult, into a mature man.

Ser Marissa entered with her armor gleaming brighter than before. The Akareen star blazed on her chest, and a crimson cape flowed behind her. A playful smile danced on her lips as she moved closer, as she helped him fasten his cloak around his neck. "I could not believe how quickly she had grown."

"Aye," with a one-sided smile. "I confess I had been against their union, but her passionate explanation finally made me understand her reasons. In addition, Juni is perfect for her."

"I remember your fierce opposition, the countless times I had to restrain your temper," she murmured, as her gaze lingered on him as he adjusted his suit. "Is there any possibility that you and I. . . ? You know."

Alessandro sighed and turned to see her in the eye. "I think we spoke about it many times. Just because Fabehel is gone does not mean I must return to you. I have moved on. My heart is not the same as it used to be when we were young."

She shrugged her shoulders with conformity and nodded, changing the matter. "Shall we go? I am sure Nehel is waiting for you."

He approached the chimney and gently kissed the golden chest to leave his quarter next to Marissa.

As the olden world waned, Aranka and Sankaris entered a new era, one defined by the rumble of technological progress, the shifting power dynamics of political reform, and the blossoming of diverse cultural expressions.

The Nehelante Era.

The steam-powered carriage, a gift from the Fennen immigrants, chugged down the road to the Citadel from the palace, its hissing steam and clanking gears had as a counterpoint to the joyous shouts of the crowds hoping to glimpse the Empress heading to her wedding. It took a long and arduous journey, navigating crowded streets and towering buildings, before they arrived at the metropolis' center.

To honor the Empress and her future husband, small, round, white Tinklen vessels glided over the Citadel in a breathtaking formation. Their smooth surfaces reflected the sunlight, leaving the population awestruck as white doves soared alongside them.

The carriage crossed the square as members of the Imperial Army—Elves, Guards, Musketeers, Mages, Sailors, and finally, at the cathedral steps, the Imperial Order of Knights—saluted with a crisp precision.

Aranka's first immigrants finished the Golden Cathedral of the Citadel, a testament to their industriousness, in only two years. It was a temple devoted to Lakia, the Goddess of Love, but also honored all eight goddesses and their father, Askim. Its unique architecture blended Elven, Berremen, and Arankan styles, reflecting the new inhabitants' desire for a structure dedicated to the Empress.

Ser Branni and Ser Ommi, the Second and Third Knights, opened the carriage's door and the first ones to exit were the two Pillars. As a gentleman, Alessandro assisted Nehel to get off from the carriage, at the time that the sounds of the cheering crowds in Citadel Square washed over them as they stepped down.

At seventeen, the Empress, having shed the vestiges of her girlishness, possessed newfound maturity. Akartaki and her sisters crafted her white wedding dress with Elven elements that had golden embroidery. Instead of shoes, she wore the same golden sandals she had worn during her ascension in Salter. In her hair, she secured the golden comb, a gift from Fabehel that had once belonged to her blood mother, Princess Natahel. She could not forgive her foster mother, Venka, either, as Nehel wore a bracelet made of waki bones that used to be a Molkan handcraft.

Gasps of awe loaded the air as the Empress ascended the steps. Her beauty was breathtaking, while two lines of one hundred knights bowed low in reverence.

Waiting until her wedding day, Nehel could enter the newly built cathedral. The cool stone underfoot was a contrast to the warmth of the sunlight streaming through the magnificent stained-glass windows. Gasps escaped her lips as she saw the golden interiors, tall ceilings, colossal windows, and floating Akareen stars that cast a soft, ethereal glow. With a radiant smile, she lowered her head, noticing the deep red carpet beneath her feet and the respectful hush that fell over the crowd. Imperial Assembly members, Guild representatives, engineers, and medics all stood in silent welcome.

Alessandro reunited with his niece and asked for her arm to accompany her to the altar. "I might not be your father, but I wish he could be here."

A rare, radiant smile lit up Nehel's face as she replied. "I truly feel blessed to have a someone as a father always at my side. That you are, uncle!" She nodded with excitement. "Therefore, I asked for your blessing to marry my beloved."

Two small bright Arankan children held the bridal veil as Nehel noticed them, followed by two other girls carrying overflowing baskets of flowers. In the end, Marissa stood ready.

By a gesture, Berremen musicians played the Nuptial March as a signal to start the ceremony.

As Nehel and Alessandro walked past the Court of Maids and the Sisterhood of the Comforting Wind, acknowledging their greetings with a nod, a wave of optimistic whispers and murmurs rippled through the attending crowd. The girls had created a vibrant, overflowing carpet of wildflowers on the floor. behind left an abundant patch of flowers on the floor.

As they passed the Guild section, Commandant Kartak raised an eyebrow, leaning in to whisper to Missar. "Do not you think is it proper to wait until the situation in Ryza calm down and the war in Fenn ends?"

The Archmage turned to see the elf with frowned eyes. "If not now. When? I believe the time has come for the Divine Empress to marry and thus ensure a lineage that will strengthen the Jyistereerk."

"A descendant," Kartak nodded. "I recall when the Divine Empress said these exact words you just mentioned."

Missar nodded, noticing the absence of Marshal Keleana and Ambassador Corr, now a ruler for his land with Orr and Barr as he watched the wedding, remembering their ongoing battle against the Korbas and The Aquelarre. The Guild felt strangely different without them.

When Nehel arrived at the altar, her future husband was already waiting for her with a nervous smile on his face.

Juni, at nineteen, stood before the beautiful bride.

Seven years passed since that fateful day in the Black Forest, and finally they were united.

Alessandro gave his niece to Juni, whispering into his ear. "Please, take good care of her as you always have done!"

"I will, Master. I am grateful for your permission."

With trembling hands clasped together, the couple faced the altar, as Alessandro and Marissa settled into the Guild's reserved seating.

Dessidere struck his rod down hard, and the music ceased abruptly before the altar. He visually caught his spouse Jumeni's eye among the assembled crowd with her child sprouting within her. He opened the papyrus and read. "In the 9th Day of the 24th Month of the Fourth Year of the *Tikl the Second of Nehel*, a nuptial ceremony between the Divine Empress Nehel and the First Knight Juni of Sarrem begins!"

A priest in a tunic opened a book as he approached the soon to be newlyweds, and started with the ceremony.

With Juni's hand in hers, the sound of the preacher's sermon became a distant hum as her hazel eyes drifted to the window, focusing on the comforting image of her home. The living palace atop of the mountain, the *Ykarte*.

The Empress' Palace.

Aranka Ykarte.

As the sun dipped below the horizon, and the moon, No Nunn, rose upon the Arankan forest, Diesso and Vasso sat by the crackling bonfire.

By the crackling fire, the smell of roasting rabbits saturated the air as Vasso shook his head. "The Divine Empress just married, and I am certain she is spending her wedding night with Ser Juni, while we have toiled for years in these forgotten places," he grumbled, gesturing with his thumb toward Kekten, a figure barely visible beneath thick waki furs. "And that old man who caused a war is always drunk and sleeping!"

Diesso, surrounded by the scent of burning candle wax, sketched the coastal map of the vanished Byarte, his quill scratching on parchment spread across a wooden board resting on his lap. "This is our job now. And as far as Kekten, remember that despite his drunk state, he always helped us in these unknown places. He is an excellent tracker." He replied without stopping in his task.

Something attracted Vasso and stood up, interrupting his cooking as he drew his sword.

Diesso watched him disappear into the trees. As he pushed away the maps, he followed him with blade in hand.

Upon arriving at their objective, their eyes widened, as they did not expect to discover it in this far northern place of Aranka.

It was no longer in Salter.

The *Frelee Dee*.

To be continued in The Empress' Reclamation.

SOMETIME IN 1997

The Aranka Ykarte, also known as *The Empress' Palace*, stood as a monumental and millenary golden tower in the middle of the desert, an important and key setting in all my stories. In the earlier versions, as I have mentioned, it was originally a sci-fi story. The planet Aranka served as the palace's site, which was considered the Empire's traditional capital and had witnessed the reign of many emperors prior to Nehel.

The palace was the pride of the Jyistereerk. And the center of everyone's lives, including the empress and her descendants.

The structure was a fascinating blend of palace and city. The original palace had thousands of years since its building,

And to mention the palace was originally gold, but not gold, as we know it. Instead, it was another kind of metal unknown to us. Guess what, made of giefstak, the same one the Korbas had been using for their weapons.

The question arises. Is the palace from this book built with the same metal? I, as an author, can't even answer to it. I will decide and reveal in the third and last installment of this trilogy I intend to complete.

Since is a living palace that emerged from the *Ykarte*, as the deceased Carlissa, it's hard to say if it will have the same material as in my original books.

In a way or other, this certain situation was unavoidable, as it would affect Alessandro in the next book and beyond.

It was a necessary event that I had to write, because he depended on her for his character development and his evolution as the Borsen, a word to be revealed soon. If I had left the way unchanged, Alessandro wouldn't be able to becoming the Borsen, as a primordial figure in the history of the Jyistereerk. To become, perhaps, the most influential personality after Nehel.

Also, it was necessary to illustrate the struggles of everyone. Their sorrows, their regrets, their nostalgias, their frustrations, their reckless actions, their impulses.

As I have mentioned in an interview. That certain character was based on a real person I have met in High School. She was the perfect girl any teenager could dream of. However, I never knew the details of her life other than her problems by the tangent, but one day, in the middle of the school year, she just vanished without a trace. Eventually, I found out she'd moved out the city for a more peaceful countryside life, but silence had been her only communication—until now.

She was never more than a classmate to me, not even a friend, but during breaks between classes, I could chat with her. And I still remember her unique nature that drove me to create her for the drafts in the two books.

Yes, I am averting her name as I give many indirects for those who want to read from the last pages rather than the first ones, avoiding spoilers.

I invented the term Nehelante as I planned a trilogy back in the 1990s —Korbante, Nehelante, Arankante. Despite my efforts, the trilogy featuring the Korbante never came to fruition. Instead, I repeatedly rewrote drafts without an obvious structure.

I then christened Nehelante, ushering in a new cultural, technological, and political era within the book's narrative, a decision that would reshape its entire trajectory. But still not sure when it actually started; perhaps with the Promise, or the establishment of the Citadel. I, as an author, I still have to discover and decide when and how it began.

Perhaps, in the next book, I'll put that answer on top of the question I have mentioned previously.

As you've noticed, this book doesn't celebrate a rising palace, but tells a dark story where battles are not always won, kingdoms fall, and tragedies strike.

It is also, in a way, an homage to Star Wars' second movie, *The Empire Strikes Back,* the darkest and saddest of the trilogy. And I am not even a hardcore fan of these movies.

After the publication of the first book, The Empress's Journey, I made a sketch of what a second book would be. Originally, I planned to tell the tale of Sorceress Dalehel and the secret history of Lady Larissa, the mother of Alessandro, also nicknamed *The Doomed*, as additions to the main narrative. However, too much going to the past and present alongside with the different paths for many characters would be confusing and not according to the purpose of this book.

Over time, I had to redo it and start over every chapter, going from a plotter—a planned story — to a pantser, creating a story as I go writing, in most of the book. Therefore, from six months, it took almost a year since the first book's publication. But the original idea was always still there, but I had to add more elements and create new chapters I didn't plan.

Also, my intention with this book was to ensure Nehel's empire, the Jyistereerk, as it gradually takes a form of the way I had written years ago, giving the world building the original personality I had visualized in the past. But in a more humane and believable way.

From The Empress' Journey, some of my readers asked many questions, but one of them was why I had switched from Space Opera to Fantasy. As I had answered and I say again, most of the characters were flat in a universe that had no deepness, think it was like play and pretend with mini figures—like those Fisher Price toys—in a scenery made of cardboard. I thought that Fantasy genre was a good way to show the colors of a fictional world and the perfect genre for my settings.

And here is where it happened. I didn't think it would happen.

Fantasy meets Sci-Fi.

The Tinklens. There was no other way to reinvent them than keeping them in their original appearance.

To end with this chapter, I wish to announce that my intention is to create a trilogy that comprises the story of Empress Nehel as she grows and solidify her Jyistereerk as she and her people have to confront the obstacles she encounters, named the Korbas and The Aquelarre, which third and last book is to come in 2025.

But it doesn't mean that with the trilogy I stop with the history. There will be other books, not exactly trilogies, that over the years will tell the stories of Nehel's descendants as the *Deken Karsaker* continues.

The current trilogy only covers one eighth of the Deken Karsaker.

This is still the beginning.

ACKNOWLEDGMENTS

Many thanks to the designers at Etheric, my promoters, and my readers for their contributions to my first book. Their feedback and support motivated me to write a second book.

Those near always await my next creation.

Most importantly, I thank my daughter, whose unconditional belief and persistent encouragement pushed me to keep writing.

I encountered many challenges —my Korbas— while writing this book, including time constraints from other activities. Although I had other priorities, these people motivated me to continue pursuing my goals.

Thank you.